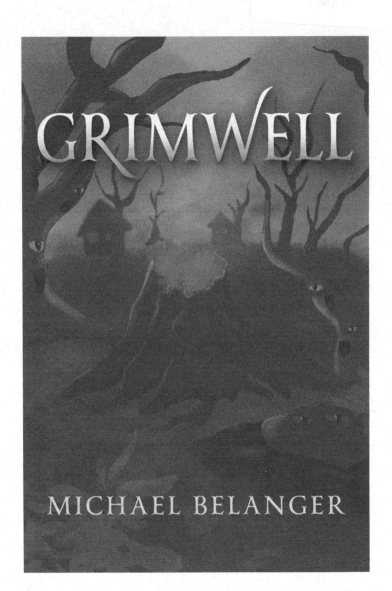

GRIMWELL

MICHAEL BELANGER

GRIMWELL

Michael Belanger

Woodhall Press | Norwalk, CT

woodhall press

Woodhall Press, Norwalk, CT 06855
WoodhallPress.com
Copyright © 2024 Michael Belanger

Cover design: Danny Sancho
Layout artist: LJ Mucci

Library of Congress Cataloging-in-Publication Data available

ISBN 978-1-960456-09-0   (paper: alk paper)
ISBN 978-1-960456-10-6   (electronic)

First Edition
Distributed by Independent Publishers Group
(800) 888-4741

Printed in the United States of America

For Emily, Teddy, and Wesley

Part I

The Tale

Chapter 1

Everyone has a book written just for them—the trick is finding it.

Derek Winnebaker found his book in the back corner of a supply closet, nestled between an ancient coffee pot and a stack of books about the future of US-Soviet relations. He'd been looking for chocolate syrup to make a mocha latte for a customer. He blew a puff of air on the cover and dust cascaded off, revealing a simple graphic: A man with a slight frame, large ears, and a tail, holding what looked to be a glowing red amulet in his hands. Above him, the name of the book and its author were printed in an ornate script: *The Strange Life and Times of Eldrid Babble* by Chester Felten.

Derek ran his fingers across the plastic dust jacket and thumbed through the mildewed pages, long ago damaged by a flood or leaky pipe. On the inside cover, he found a Pemberton Library borrowing card, suspiciously blank. Apparently, the book had never been checked out. He scanned the back cover, growing more and more curious. He felt a pull to read the book, as if he'd been searching and scouring shelves just waiting to find Eldrid's story.

"Everything okay back there?" his boss, Sam, shouted, but for Derek, it felt near and distant at the same time. He fumbled nervously with the book and found himself once again fanning the pages, feeling the cool air on his face. Beneath the glare of the supply closet's lone overhanging bulb, its metal pull chain attached to a coffee cup pendant, he read the back cover:

Dear Reader,

Welcome to Grimwell, a magical land of trolls, sorcerers, and of course, grimkins. Grimkins have managed to keep a low profile in the tales and yore of the past owing to their catlike agility and excellent sense of smell. In fact, only one mention of grimkins can be found in history, a brief sighting in the eighteenth century of a grimkin named Brigglebog Bramble, whose tail was glimpsed at the military encampment of General George Washington.

But it's time for grimkins' long run of obscurity to end, for Mr. Eldrid Babble is about to embark on an adventure. An adventure quite out of character for the unsung grimkin, who prefers to be home building small-scale replicas of famous buildings or playing a solitary game of Fizzle, an even more complicated version of chess.

After being given a magical amulet that spreads darkness all throughout Grimwell, Eldrid Babble leaves the cozy little village of Crimpleton to break Lord Grittlebane's curse. Along the way, he'll meet Chester Felten, the author of this book who accidentally stumbles into the world of Grimwell during a fortuitous walk through the woods.

Located beneath a tree stump in the Ashton Town Forest, Grimwell is easy to trip over but almost impossible to leave. If you follow these pages to the end, you'll encounter giants, a ferocious beast called a brimble, and talking trees (if you cross a talking tree's path, please approach with caution—they're starved for company!). Maybe you'll even see yourself in one

2

of Grimwell's many colorful characters, including Eldrid Babble, his love interest Belinda Grabblebee, the wise and loquacious Grandfather Tree, or perhaps—there is a page for everyone, after all—a goblin or sorcerer.

Chester Felten is a World War II veteran, insurance salesman, and ambassador to the world of Grimwell. After telling Eldrid Babble's story to friends and family at the Ashton Town Picnic, he was encouraged to write the tale down so that others might learn of this remarkable land. This is his first novel.

Sam was knocking at the door, giving Derek just enough time to stash the book behind his back, as if he'd uncovered something illicit.

"Just a second," Derek called out, grabbing the bottle of syrup, and opening the door.

"You've got a customer," Sam said.

"We're almost out of mocha," Derek said, still holding the book behind his back. He'd already started to feel an ownership over the strange title. *My book.*

"She's getting impatient," Sam said.

"Aren't they always?" Derek asked.

"We provide a service," Sam said.

"I'll be right there," Derek said.

Derek followed his manager and stashed the book beneath the till before making the impatient customer's drink.

This job was supposed to have been a brief detour after college until he went to grad school. He'd dreamed of many different lives for himself: a philosopher speculating on the nature of man, an archaeologist traversing the world in search of ancient treasures, a doctor treating and curing some of the world's worst diseases—Derek didn't know if doctors had groupies, though in his daydreams, they did—but in the end, there had simply been too many choices, and Derek had been unable to take that first step in the direction of a career. Career: the word sounded too final, a choice set in stone, a book already written.

Without a clear direction, or simply too many directions, he got a job at the Read and Bean Coffee Shop located right in the Pemberton Town Library. His ex, Janine, had called him "my little barista."

"Did I order decaf?" the customer asked after Derek placed her drink on the bar.

Unfortunately, he couldn't remember. He was usually on autopilot at the coffee shop. The same feeling as driving a car on a desolate stretch of highway only to realize twenty miles have passed without having bothered to take in the scenery.

Derek squinted at the customer. She had her hair pulled back in a bun, not a strand out of place. Lipstick perfectly applied, red and angry against her pale skin. Most likely an executive, making decisions in board rooms, firing people, taking long lunches before returning to the office.

"It should be on the cup," Derek said, pointing at the side where he had written her name (Christina) and checked the decaf box for her triple almond milk one-hundred-eighty-degree no-foam mocha latte.

"I know, but did I *order* decaf?"

"If it's on the cup..."

"No," she said. "I don't care if he's on vacation with his family."

It took Derek a minute to realize she had earbuds in. Dueling conversations.

"I'm sorry, I'm dealing with a situation."

Derek smiled. "No worries."

"The guy at the coffee shop is being dense."

Derek's smile disappeared.

"Could you make me a new one?"

She threw a quarter in the tip jar.

Derek sighed. He was finding it increasingly difficult to be polite to customers.

Still, despite the customer's surly manner, Derek noticed the dark bags under her eyes. That singular look of stress and exhaustion that

4

accompanied the need for caffeine. Maybe she had been up late with a newborn, or fighting with a significant other, or maybe she was just battling insomnia. Or, Derek thought, as he steamed her milk, which Derek always thought sounded like a euphemism, maybe she worked in the FBI and was on the hunt for a serial killer who had left clues in coffee shops all across the country.

Derek often invented backstories for the customers to keep himself busy. And to tamp down the frustration. After all, it was hard to be mad at an FBI agent on the hunt for a serial killer.

In another world—another book, perhaps—Derek and the woman might even team up, traipsing through the pages as an unlikely pair, the barista and the agent, only he wouldn't be called "my little barista" in this version—take that, Janine—he'd be Special Agent Barista.

Too late he realized he'd already read a similar book, only instead of a barista it was a bartender named Jack and a CIA agent with the last name Coke. Located in the Thriller section. Derek couldn't remember the title.

"Hello?"

"Sorry," Derek said, once again coming back from autopilot and finishing her drink.

She grabbed the coffee and raised her eyebrows. Not bothering to say thanks.

"You're welcome," Derek couldn't help but call after her.

The library was located on Pemberton's main strip, and the coffee shop could be found on the ground floor facing the street. Floor-to-ceiling windows had been installed—to lure people away from Starbucks with its grand views of Elm Street—and so Derek often got the feeling that he was in a zoo, an oddity to be ogled at by passersby. From his spot at the till, he had a perfect view of the fiction section on the ground floor and the nonfiction section on the second floor, the shelves lined up like intricately etched dominoes. The ceiling sloped down over the coffee shop and a series of bright globes hung from wooden rafters, as if replicating a solar system in a distant galaxy. The dividing line between art and commerce—or coffee and books—lines which often blurred in the course of a day—was the end of a blue nylon rug and the beginning of checkered red and white tile. The Bean's colors.

Since he first began working at the Bean, both the library and coffee shop had gone through some major renovations, which is why some of the old books had been haphazardly stored in the Bean's coffee closet. All things considered, it wasn't a terrible job, and because the store was part of the library, Derek had access to as many books as he wanted. A perfect excuse to explore the many different lives he wasn't living himself.

At first, he'd stuck to the Philosophy section, reading abstruse Kant and Nietzsche, the English philosophers with their rigid certainty, before finally finishing right in America with freewheeling William James. Still, his learning hadn't gotten him anything beyond a few interesting tidbits to share with customers during the morning rush. Nothing wakes people up like a walk through the history of nihilism. Next, he branched off into fiction, first focusing on the classics, then reading the Book of the Month Club picks, including the previously mentioned *Jack and Coke*. The title had come to him while watching the surly customer walk away. As of late, he'd been in the Home and Garden section, learning all about bulbs and seeds and the best climate to grow echinacea. He didn't think he'd ever actually grow echinacea but he liked knowing he could. He liked knowing things, period. So, when he found the old and tattered book about a strange creature called a grimkin, he happily stashed it in his backpack, looking forward to reading it when he returned home from his shift.

* * *

Derek lived in a studio apartment right above a bar named McDowell's. "Studio" was a generous description for the ten-by-ten box Derek called home. Derek suspected the landlord had gotten away with renting out an old supply closet by making a few haphazard renovations and adding a small window. Still, the apartment was just barely affordable on Derek's hourly wages. It fit a couch that turned into a sleeper, a small flat-screen TV shoved up against the wall, and a coffee table that doubled as his kitchen table. Despite the size, he did have his own bathroom, which was more than Derek could say for some of the other apartments on the market. He also had room for not one, but two hot plates. He had yet to use either.

Derek thought living above a bar would make meeting people easier, as he hadn't really had much of a social life ever since Janine left. Janine had gotten the apartment (which Derek couldn't afford anyway), the dog (a Shi Tzu named Ron), and all of their friends. True, they had been Janine's friends from law school, but he had tricked himself into believing they'd become part of his life too.

As he usually did on Friday nights, Derek tucked a book into his jacket pocket—that night it was *The Strange Life and Times of Eldrid Babble*—and went down to McDowell's for dinner, where he dreamed of being greeted like a regular. "Derek!" they would all shout as he walked in. "Have you met Derek?" someone might say. "He's the lead geneticist on the human genome project." Derek didn't know where that last fantasy came from, most likely from a book (he'd worked through the General Science section about three years ago, just before the breakup, at which point he abruptly switched to Self-Help). Regardless, deep down he still believed he was destined for greatness. That beneath his average exterior lay the thumping heart of a hero.

Instead of shouts and accolades as he entered McDowell's, Derek found himself on the receiving end of a tepid wave from Julius, the bartender, whose day job appeared to be bodybuilder. Derek's sitcom life wasn't materializing.

"You're too in your own head," Janine had told him.

"You have no motivation," she'd added.

"I'm just looking for someone with more of a sense of adventure."

Maybe she was right.

The restaurant was busy, with each shiny lacquer table occupied. Derek spotted a lone stool at the bar, right beneath one of the over-hanging lights—his favorite spot. While an Irish pub in name, McDow-ell's had undergone a fancy makeover, and so the Guinness sign was traded for modernist Rorschach-inspired artwork—is it a dolphin or a physical representation of unresolved issues with my dad? Derek had wondered—the old chalkboards were swapped out for mirrors, and the sticky floor had been replaced with a shiny reflective tile that made you feel like you were walking across thin ice. Luckily, the bar was still dingy and dim, somewhere between a cave and candle-lit.

Derek sat down at the bar and Julius slid a menu toward him, not bothering to say anything. Julius's bulging muscles pressed against his skin-tight black T-shirt, the fabric practically rippling. With a bald head and hoop earring, he seemed to be actively emulating Mr. Clean. At least in appearance. No way was Mr. Clean such a jerk.

"Hi, Julius."

Julius grunted in return.

On Derek's right, there was Boris, a retired "agent" (most likely real estate), and on his left sat Gerald, a semi-retired Town Works employee. They ate at the bar every night—usually on either side of him. For some reason, they needed a buffer seat in between, as if afraid to fully commit to their friendship. Both of their wives had died a few years ago and they'd been thrown unwillingly into bachelorhood again.

"What are you reading?" Boris asked, his mustache wiggling as he spoke. He had a habit of cupping his beer belly as if cradling a baby.

"*The Strange Life and Times of Eldrid Babble*," Derek said nonchalantly, as if announcing the latest bestseller. He looked down at the cover, scrutinizing the strange creature holding a glowing red amulet. Derek had been thinking about the book ever since he left the Bean. Something strange about the cover and the fact that it had been hidden in the back of the supply closet as if forbidden. As he opened the book to the title page, crammed with rudimentary pencil sketches of grimkins and what appeared to be a talking tree, he noticed something he hadn't seen while browsing the book in the Bean's supply closet: A stamp that read *From the Personal Library of Jackson Wilfred.*

Jackson Wilfred had been the director of the library before Derek started working at the Bean. Known for turning Pemberton's small-town library into a world-class institution, he had left his post just as the renovations began.

"Never heard of it," Gerald said. While Boris was short and portly, Gerald was tall and lanky. Similar to an avatar in a video game, he appeared to only have one look: jeans and a tucked-in T-shirt about being a grandpa (today's shirt featured the message *This Is What An Awesome Grandpa Looks Like*). "I'm more of an encyclopedia guy myself."

"I don't read," Julius said, a hint of resignation in his voice.

"You need to read a real novelist," Boris said, turning to Derek. "Dostoevsky. Chekov. Pushkin."

"You're making those names up," Gerald said.

Out of the corner of his eye, Derek saw Kat, one of the waitresses, approach the bar. Kat was a big part of the reason why Derek ate dinner at McDowell's so often, even when a frozen pizza would have been more economical. Whenever he saw her, he couldn't help but think of his foray into the Romance section of the library. Lines describing the sultry sway of hips or the rolling hills of curves (both true in Kat's case). The omnipresent description of hair falling, flowing, or cascading down shoulders (although Kat usually had her curly brown hair tied in a ponytail, Derek imagined it would be a deluge if she let it down). And of course, the eyes: always batting, always shining, always deep as the ocean (McDowell's was dim, but Kat's brown eyes did seem to glow, cliché or not). For Derek, Kat made romance fiction seem realer—or if not realer, at least truer—than any other genre.

"What did we think of the special today?" Kat asked, sliding her tray on the bar. Although Kat was a waitress, the owner let her create a special during each shift she worked, which Derek always made sure to order and *mmm* loudly whenever she was nearby—his approach to flirting.

Boris kissed his fingers in a dramatic gesture.

Gerald showed his clean plate. "One of your best yet," he said.

"I'll take the special," Derek said to Julius. "And a side of fries."

"Already put your order in," Julius said. "Mr. Special and a Side of Fries."

"A bit of a departure for me," Kat said. "Ceviche is an art and Julius didn't think our clientele would go for fish."

"It's not even cooked," Julius said defensively.

"It's the citrus," Kat said.

"Is my orange juice cooked?" Julius said. "Huh? Is it?"

"Ignore this heathen," Boris said. "Any pictures of the little guy?" Kat had a son, around two years old, and from what Derek knew, no husband or boyfriend in the picture. Derek wished there was a formal application process for dating; he could really shine on a piece of paper.

Kat pulled out her phone and scrolled through her photos before showing one of a curly-headed boy going down a slide, smiling wide from ear to ear.

"Look at him," Boris said. "He's going to be an Olympian."

"An athlete if I ever saw one," Gerald said.

Boris and Gerald turned to Derek, awaiting a response.

"Look at those cheekbones," Derek said, spitting out the first thing that came to him.

"Those he gets from his father," Kat said. "His brute strength comes from me." Kat curled her bicep. "Am I right, Julius?"

To which Julius pumped his pectorals. "Not bad," he said.

"Show off," Boris said.

"What are we reading tonight?" Kat asked Derek.

Derek held up *The Strange Life and Times of Eldrid Babble*. Still recovering from his cheekbone comment. Not quite ready to speak. No clever dialogue at the ready.

"Looks interesting," Kat said.

"He needs to read the Russians," Boris said.

"Did you know the Russian alphabet has twice as many vowels as English?" Gerald said.

"Is that true?"

"Yup. Saw it on my grandson's internet."

"And twice as many ways to say fuck you," Boris said, laughing loudly at his own joke.

Kat drummed her fingers on the bar, waiting for her drinks. "And I'm sure you know them all."

Derek got the sense that he was watching the scene from far away. He was tired of feeling like a side character in every facet of his life. Playing a secondary role at the coffee shop, at the bar, even in his own family, where his brother had somehow become the successful one.

He should've listened to his dad and become a lawyer. And not only because Janine had cheated on him with a lawyer in the laundry room of their apartment building (so many books in the Self-Help section, but nothing approaching how to scrub that particular memory). Maybe then he'd have more money. More prestige. More of a life. More Janine.

Silence settled over the bar. Derek didn't know what to say to Kat. She probably had customers hit on her all the time. She was just trying to make a living. But he could imagine a world where he asked her out. He could start with something simple like, "How about after work you let me buy you a drink." Or he could offer to perform some sort of manual labor on her home, like installing a door or re-shingling her roof (he'd finished most of the books in the Home Improvement section just last week). Or maybe he should just go with his application idea and submit a resume detailing the reasons he'd make a good boyfriend.

No, none of those sounded right. He couldn't even get it right in his fantasies. There were just too many possibilities. The world full of blank pages that couldn't be rewritten. So, he didn't say anything. Still waiting for his food to arrive, he cracked open his book and began reading.

* * *

Eldrid Babble was going on a mission to save the world, though he didn't know it yet.

Eldrid lived in a large and rather fine hut in the small village of Crimpleton. Like all the huts in Crimpleton, it was made of stone and crowned with a thatched roof of shabberberry bush, one of the most versatile plants in Grimwell. His front window looked out on Crimpleton Common, a bustling area of town filled with stores, food, and games. Eldrid preferred to keep his window closed. He wasn't very fond of noise. Or other grimkins, for that matter.

What's a grimkin, you ask? Grimkins live just beyond the veil of our world, hidden from the prying eyes of humans in a land called Grimwell. It was a lucky accident that led me to find them myself (of course luck is in the eye of the beholder). But I digress. Because I'm part of this story too. However, I didn't meet Eldrid until later, soon after his journey had begun.

Now, where were we?

Eldrid Babble, the hero of our tale, had large teeth, oversized ears— even by a grimkin's standards—and stringy hair. He had on black trousers, a white linen shirt, and a maroon vest with a gold pocket watch tucked in his breast pocket. He was sitting on a plush purple couch admiring his handiwork on a small-scale replica of the tallest building in Grimwell, a stone monolith that presided over the capital called the Summit. Only one piece remained: the spiral tip. Like most grimkins, Eldrid loved building miniature models—his way of bringing the world to him without all the hassle of venturing to distant lands and sleeping in inns on uncomfortable shabberberry beds.

As he crowned the Summit with the final piece, the doorbell rang.

He quickly got up, walking by the bookcase that featured his mother and father's many books about their adventures around Grimwell (their intrepid spirit had apparently skipped a generation). In his haste to answer the door, his tail clipped the framed photos on the hutch in the entryway, sending one of his grandfather in a soldier's uniform toppling over. Most grimkins are quick and catlike, but not Eldrid. His entire life he'd been called clumsy. Other names too: grumpy, cowardly, antisocial, even brimpled, which is a very common insult in the land of Grimwell that means "unsmiling."

Eldrid liked to stay at home where everything was just how he liked it. If that made him brimpled, so be it. Unlike the other neighboring huts, with their plain stone fronts and black shutters, Eldrid had added a splash of color and painted his door a bright purple, his favorite color, and his shutters a bright blue, his second favorite color. He didn't mind standing out, so long as he could stay in. Last year, after receiving one too many visitors, he'd enlisted Freegle, Crimpleton's blacksmith, to forge a sign that read: Before you knock once, think twice. *The six words made him smile each time he arrived home. In the front of his hut, he planted a garden with squash, tomatoes, and grimplehoot, a bitter herb that Eldrid liked to sprinkle on pretty much everything.*

He opened the door and saw Mayor Frumple waiting on his stoop, hat in hand.

Mayor Frumple was on the larger side of a grimkin and was occasionally mistaken for a growler, a species of troll that inhabits the northern edges of Grimwell. He always wore a suit, which isn't all that different from the type of suit worn by humans, with the exception of a wide tie that looks more like a bib, and, I'm told, fulfills the same function. Grimkins are notorious for their messy eating habits. His large, shifty eyes seemed to never blink, and his mouth only had two expressions: ecstatic and overjoyed. Rumor had it that no one had ever seen Mayor Frumple frown because he suffered from a rare birth defect that gave his lips a permanent curl. Gradually, at least according to gossip, Mayor Frumple had forgotten the difference between smiling and not smiling.

"Mr. Babble," Mayor Frumple said, his voice booming as if giving a speech in Crimpleton Common.

"Mayor Frumple," Eldrid said, peering nervously around his door as sunlight splashed his entryway—much to Eldrid's dismay. Eldrid wasn't all that crazy about sunlight—he sunburned very easily—and he was even less crazy about visitors.

"I'm just going door to door to speak to my constituents," Mayor Frumple said.

Of course, *Eldrid thought,* election season is on the horizon. *"And you want to be assured you have my vote, am I correct?"*

"Well, yes. But I also want to make sure I have your trust." His smile deepened, almost as if someone was turning an unseen fulcrum, stretching Mayor Frumple's skin taut. The election was, as grimkins said, in the hollyhoot (a type of bag worn by grimkins). The only issue to speak of was whether or not Crimpleton should strengthen their ties to the capital, Grim City. Mayor Frumple had outlined all the potential investment opportunities if they chose to align closer to the capital city, while his challenger, the blacksmith Freegle, had advocated for more independence, even sending around a pamphlet claiming Mayor Frumple was a puppet of Lord Grittlebane, who had recently become the mayor of Grim City. However, Mayor Frumple had much flashier buttons. And buttons mattered in Grimwell's elections. Sad, but true.

"I'd like to talk to you a little bit about my plans for the year. If I'm elected, of course."

"I really don't have time," Eldrid said. "I'm in the middle of something quite important."

That wasn't exactly true, then again, it all depended on your definition of "important." After all, he did have to find a place for the Summit and his shelves were already crowded with other builds, including the Golden Pyramid of Frimington, the Shrinking City of Bengaloo, and the Tree House (where the Council of Trees met each fall and embarked on three days of exhausting small talk). The entirety of Grimwell—at least the places worth seeing—all lay right there in Eldrid's hut.

"I'm quite familiar with your platform," Eldrid said, closing the door slightly, a not-so-subtle hint that he was ready to return to the comfort of his home.

Mayor Frumple stuck his foot in the door just as Eldrid was about to slam it shut.

"One last thing." Mayor Frumple leaned down so he was eye level with Eldrid. "I'm also warning everyone that a sorcerer carrying a staff was seen in the forest by a few of the neighborhood grimpledees" (grimkin slang for kids). "Probably just exaggerating or making up stories, but if you see anyone out of the ordinary, please alert me as soon as possible."

Eldrid felt a shiver run up and down his spine. Sorcerer? The word reminded Eldrid of the stories his grandfather used to tell when he was growing up. Tales about the First Grimkins, forced to leave their homes and fight in faraway, unrelenting lands to defeat dark magic. Eldrid was happy right at home. With his small-scale replicas that spoke of civilization. Of order. Of safe adventures of the mind that only cost a few hundred grimkies.

"Thank you, Mayor Frumple," Eldrid said.

As Eldrid closed his door, he made sure to double bolt the lock and place a chair in front of the knob for good measure.

* * *

"Then I say to him, either I plow your street or you shovel your entire neighborhood out," Gerald said as Derek looked up from the book.

"Snow here is like dust. Growing up, it would sometimes be up to here." Boris held his hand over his head. Boris had a way of exaggerating his past. Tall tales that often reached the ceiling. As to whether or not his stories were true, it all depended on your definition of truth.

"To be fair, his wife was pregnant. But it still doesn't give him any right to honk his horn at me."

"How's the book?" Boris asked.

"Interesting," Derek said.

Julius brought over Derek's ceviche and a side of fries.

"Thanks, Julius."

Julius solemnly slid over a napkin and carefully laid out a fork and knife, as if Derek's first bite might be his last. "Good luck."

While Derek wasn't known for his spirit of culinary adventure, he always made a point to order anything Kat put on the menu, which had led him to try escargot (suspiciously labeled from farm to table), beets in a variety of guises, and nachos made with... wait for it... seaweed. All were delicious.

Kat returned for a moment and puffed a few loose strands of hair out of her eyes. Derek took a bite and *mmmed* loudly, pretending to be lost in the book.

"Good, right?"

Derek nodded, trying to think of something else to say besides *mmm*. "Mmm."

Kat smiled, placed a glass of wine on her tray, and once again disappeared.

If he could just ask her out, maybe his life would be different. Maybe then he'd be the hero of his story. But for some reason, whenever he thought about taking that step—taking any step at all—he felt his body tense, and the possibility of speaking became impossible, his voice locked in a cage, only able to rattle bars with a throat-clear or mumble.

He finished the ceviche, dipping the fries in the remaining herbs and spices, and then walked up the flight of steps to his apartment.

Derek was going on a mission to save the world. At least his world. He just didn't know it yet.

* * *

Inside his apartment, he sat down on his couch, which also doubled as his bed. The walls were bare. No time to decorate. At least that's what he told guests. Or guest. That one time Janine had come over to drop off the rest of his stuff. The truth was, he had no reason to decorate. He had reached a point in his life where the need for survival had overtaken any other impulse. Life had been subsumed by an animal instinct, shorn of the usual frills and joys of existence. It was as if the future had receded when Janine left him. Now he was officially on his own. But it wasn't a liberating feeling. It was crushing. Like being lost at sea without a ship in sight.

Luckily, he still had the library. A steady source of ideas to consume on his lunch breaks, during lulls behind the register, while restocking shelves and creating mocha mix, or, if there was truly nothing to do, wiping down surfaces with a rag (he'd gotten very skilled at the one-handed book hold). Books were his escape and ideas were the currency he got paid in—the only problem was those ideas didn't really translate into an interesting life outside the pages.

They were just small-scale replicas of all the places he'd never get the chance to visit. All the lives he'd never get the chance to live.

Chapter 2

Derek had to open the next morning, which meant a five o'clock wake up. Just enough time to roll out of bed, brush his teeth, grumble to the gods of existentialism—that had been a depressing week of reading in the library—and then walk over to the coffee shop.

He didn't mind the early morning walk along the silent streets of Pemberton. The sun hadn't come up yet, but a little light dusted the horizon, looking like a portal to another world ready to open. His breath frosted the air in the early spring chill, and as he heard his steps echo on the sidewalk, he felt a small glow of something warm and bright. If not happiness, then maybe just contentment.

Once at the coffee shop, he prepped for opening. Grinding the beans. Mixing the syrup. Lining up the milk. It was an art to do a job well, and Derek lost himself in the drudgery of preparing for the morning, all the while feeling called to read the book stashed in his bag. Unfortunately, Eldrid Babble's adventure would have to wait. This part was survival. Once the morning rush ended,

Derek could relax and sneak a few pages—depending on when Sam came in.

After Derek finished prepping for the morning rush, he unlocked the door and stood behind the register, his orange apron hanging down to his knees and his nametag askew, which Sam had insisted he wear: "You are not an employee," Sam had said in a tone meant to be inspirational. "You are Derek the Friendly Neighborhood Barista."

"Can that go on my tombstone?"

Sam had also made them choose from an array of kitschy pins connected to coffee, ways to express their personality as a barista, with phrases like "Careful, I haven't had my coffee yet" and "No caffeine, no service." Derek had grabbed a handful without looking and pinned them onto his apron.

When Derek had first started working at the Read and Bean, Sam's dad, Larry, the actual owner of the coffee shop, had a different approach to leading his employees. "Don't do drugs on the job and we won't have a problem," he told Derek on his first day. He treated Derek like a partner, asking his advice about business decisions ranging from where to advertise to whether or not the croissants were too buttery.

When Derek had downtime, Larry encouraged him to read as much as he wanted. "We're in a library for god's sake," Larry had said. "Wish I could get my son to read as much as you."

That same son had become his boss. Back from college on a gap year to prepare for the GMAT, Sam had made it his mission to bring the coffee shop into the 21st century by studying the efficiency of major chains like Starbucks and Dunkin' Donuts. The coffee shop had begun to feel like an impersonal corporation with "rotations," instructional booklets, and acronyms like COFFEE and CREAM (Derek could never remember what the letters stood for).

Derek hated the changes, and lately had grown to hate Sam as well.

The commuters filed in, grunting their orders at Derek, snatching a morning paper, and occasionally ordering a pastry. Derek's mind drifted to the world of Grimwell where Eldrid was building his small-scale replicas, completely unaware that his life was about to change. Looking around the coffee shop with its sodden familiarity, Derek wondered when his life would change. *If* his life would change. Would he notice signs of foreshadowing, cracks and splinters in the façade of comfort and routine? Or would he simply turn a page and find himself in an unfamiliar land?

"Derek? Is that you?"

This happened at least once a week, when someone from his old life saw him behind the counter.

"Steve," Derek said, trying to muster some enthusiasm.

They'd grown up a few houses away from one another and had developed what Derek thought of as a friendship of proximity, ties only held together by simple geography, easily broken by a change in time or space. Now Steve, judging from his appearance, was working in the business world with some fancy job that warranted wearing a suit and tie.

"How've you been?" Steve asked.

Derek always struggled with these conversations. The right balance of backstory and forward momentum. Taking an order as he balanced small talk and catching up.

"Doing well. What are we having?"

"Small vanilla latte," Steve said. "How have things been?"

"Okay," Derek said as he punched the order in the register.

"And your brother. Wow. Who would've thought?"

"Yup." Derek tried to brush off the comment. "Any doughnuts, pastries, or bagels to go along with your coffee?"

"Uh, sure," Steve said. "Maybe one of those apple cheese danishes."

Derek nodded and opened the pastry case.

"I mean, it's funny, seeing his face all over the internet. Last I heard, he's on a billboard in Time's Square."

Derek slipped the pastry in a bag. Took a deep breath. "Yup."

"Could you warm that up?"

"Sure."

Derek tossed the danish in the warming oven.

"I just binged the show last week," Steve said. "Don't know what took me so long. It's all I hear about at work. 'Have you seen *Another Planet?*'"

Through gritted teeth: "That's great."

"It's funny because I always thought you would've been the brother to do something." Steve must've seen the scowl on Derek's face, because he quickly added, "Not that you're not doing something. Just that you're not *doing* something, you know?" Steve sipped his coffee. Grimaced. "Could you put a little more of that vanilla stuff in here?"

Just when he thought he might explode, Derek scanned the shelves of the library. How many frustrated, down-on-their-luck characters had he read about? How many self-help books had told him to get in touch with his anger? Or leave his anger behind? Or that anger didn't even really exist in the first place? This scene had already been written many times before. It calmed him.

"You got it," Derek said, taking on his persona as Derek the Friendly Neighborhood Barista. He took Steve's coffee, squirt a couple of pumps, and passed it back. "Great to see you."

At around ten, Sam strolled into work, peppy as always, holding his GMAT book under his arm, lest anyone forget he was in the process of applying to business school.

"How we doing, D.W.?"

Not only did Sam love acronyms, he also loved initials.

"Good, Sam," Derek said, refusing to yield to Sam's request to be called by his initials. It was the tiny victories that kept Derek going. Not the big adventures.

"You wind 'em up, I knock 'em down, D.W."

"Okay, Sam." *Meaning I come in at 5:30 in the morning and you come five hours later, after the morning rush*, Derek thought.

21

"I noticed you forgot to wipe the steamer wand," Sam said. "You're killing me, D.W." Another one of Sam's annoying habits: make critical observations in a lighthearted tone.

"Guess I was busy."

Sam sighed. "Here's the thing, Derek. We're always busy. I need to know I can count on you, okay?"

Derek thought about all the things he wanted to say. All the different ways to make a scene. Curse words, broken mugs, triumphant monologues ending in stunned silence. But if he said something, he could get fired, and being fired meant he'd have to start over. The thought terrified him. A knock on the door. An abrupt page turn. Derek liked knowing exactly what came next.

"I'm sorry," Derek relented.

"It's okay, D.W. I just really want you to reach your potential."

Derek choked back his anger.

"Rag time," Sam said, as he threw Derek a dry rag. "Let's look busy."

Soon after, Sam went out for lunch, and so Derek was left alone. Which meant he had time to read.

He took out his copy of *The Strange Life and Times of Eldrid Babble*, poured himself a coffee, and heated up one of the remaining croissants. The library was usually quiet after the commuter rush, only attracting a few customers, each of whom remained immersed in their computers, lost in the digital void.

Derek sat down at one of the big center tables, even though they were strictly off limits to employees, and scanned the miniature solar system of lights hanging from the wooden rafters. He let out a deep breath. Finally, a chance to escape. He opened the book to Chapter Two.

Now you're probably wondering how I got myself wrapped up with a grimkin like Eldrid Babble. After all, I'm just a regular guy who grew up in a small town in Connecticut. Suffice it to say that I had just returned from a distant land—in some ways even more distant than Grimwell—and was feeling stuck.

I don't doubt you know the feeling, Dear Reader, just like the hero of our tale, Eldrid Babble, who you've already probably realized wasn't really much of a hero at all. At least not yet. But he was stuck, all right. Just like the two of us.

Derek looked up from the book. *Us?* He wasn't used to books directly addressing the reader, as if he and the writer were on a journey together, the two of them hunched behind a keyboard as they struggled to discover the next plot point. *Must be a weird quirk of the decade he wrote the book in,* Derek thought as he continued reading. The coffee shop remained still. Nothing but the sound of chairs shifting, mugs clinking, and keys tapping. Music to Derek's ears.

The truth is, I was a down-on-his-luck writer who had settled in the small town of Ashton, Connecticut, after returning home from the Second World War, where I did things I had never thought possible. Not even in my worst nightmares. The subconscious can only stretch so thin.

I participated in the D-Day landings, battling my way through a barrage of gunfire, then was stationed in the Bordeaux region of France, where a stray Nazi bullet clipped my ear—not enough to warrant a Purple Heart or a furlough home, but enough to make me realize just how perilously close death was. A constant companion. Some soldiers made peace with it, stolidly walking along as if with a dog on a leash. Some men carried it on their shoulders like a boulder. Some became almost giddy with its nearness, as if holding onto a balloon, waiting for it to pop. Me? I turned death into a sheath of paper, cataloging each day in what I came to call Death's Diary.

So when I say I had returned from a distant land, in some ways even more distant than Grimwell, I don't mean to exaggerate. Distance can

23

mean a lot of things. Time and space, sure, but I'm talking about sense, order, meaning. When something doesn't fit the rules of our normal reality, it might as well be another planet.

That's what it felt like in Europe.

After over a year of intense fighting, Germany finally surrendered and I wrote my final entry in Death's Diary: I am still alive.

When I returned home, I hoped to leave my life as a soldier in Europe in the past, but I couldn't shake that feeling of distance: Still a million miles away right in my hometown.

My dad set me up in the family business selling insurance, but I found myself dreaming of an escape.

Like many others of my generation, I turned to writing as a way to flee the doldrums of the everyday and perhaps capture some of what I had seen in the war. Bring to life the horror and truth of Death's Diary. But for some reason, I found myself unable to write about those experiences. While the words flowed each night during the war, a year later and an ocean away my memories had become heavy and unwieldy, as if distance had waterlogged my mind. Each time I'd try to write about the war, turn my incomprehensible musings into a novel or memoir, the pen would lay limply in my hand, as if on strike, refusing to play a part in documenting such a sordid episode. As if providing a plot or structure to something as senseless as war was sacrosanct. Unable to write the truth about the war, I embellished and exaggerated, writing the hero's tale my fellow countrymen were hungering for: a slim, patriotic volume called Hero's Charge. Maybe I could find myself through fiction, I reasoned. Build a bridge between my two selves, the man before the war and the man after the war.

Now I know what you're thinking, sipping coffee as you read this book. Why am I giving you all this backstory? Get to the grimkin.

But before we get to Eldrid Babble and what happened after Mayor Frumple's visit, you have to understand just what was at stake. And why Eldrid Babble didn't only save Grimwell, but me too.

Derek closed the book, feeling the whisper of a presence in the library. His first thought was to glance behind him, as if Sam might be waiting in ambush. All clear. When he turned back around, he noticed a customer at the register. That must've been it. He gulped the remaining dregs of his coffee and hurried to the counter. Something eerie about the silence as his shoes echoed on the tile, as if he'd expected the pounding of the author's footsteps to follow. It wasn't a stretch for a writer to predict someone would be reading their book while sipping coffee, but the effect was disorienting, as if Chester Felten was telling the story only to him, the distance between writer and reader momentarily abridged.

As Derek approached the counter, he saw Sam wrapping an apron around his waist. He had snuck in after all.

"What can I get you?" Sam asked the woman, who was still reading the menu. Shaking his head at Derek, he mouthed: "We'll talk about this later."

Once again Derek felt rage boil up inside of him, indignation that a pompous prick like Sam would treat him like a misbehaving kindergartener.

"I can't decide," the woman said, tapping her foot. She had on jeans and a red, summery blouse, a look Derek had seen many times before: coffee date-casual. Taken together with her general jumpiness, the fidgeting and indecision with the menu—should she buy her date a drink, too, or just wait for them to arrive?—Derek decided she must be meeting a blind date. Which reminded Derek of the last novel he'd read about blind dates, an overly long Book of the Month pick about two people who start out catfishing one another only to discover true love. *The New York Times* had called it "heartwarming, a love story for the twenty-first century." Derek had hated it, especially the title: *Reel Love.*

"Take your time," Sam said to the woman, smiling widely. His practiced, phony grin. Most likely one of the steps in COFFEE or CREAM.

Derek slipped on his apron, thinking about the masks we all wear. When the woman left the coffee shop, she would remember the friendly man behind the counter while Derek would most likely be the surly, lazy coworker. Unlike books, it was hard to find the main characters in real life: the heroes, villains, and supporting roles all seemed to blend.

After Sam finished making her drink and one for her date too—Derek had been right, and judging from the stilted silence at their table, it may have been closer to the catfishing scenario in *Reel Love*—he called Derek to the back room.

"Do you know why I'm talking to you?"

Derek couldn't help but roll his eyes.

"Don't roll your eyes, Derek."

"I was reading while I should've been working," Derek said.

"Doesn't my dad pay you pretty well?"

Derek nodded. Too well. If it had been a little less, maybe he would've left years ago. Maybe then he would be a philosophy professor or an archaeologist like Indiana Jones.

"This is your last warning, okay?"

Derek remembered Sam coming into the coffee shop when he was still in high school, back when Derek had first taken the job. Never in a million years could Derek have predicted that he'd find himself on the receiving end of a dressing down from Sam.

"Okay," Derek said, as he clutched the book closer to his chest; he hadn't realized he was still holding it.

Sam picked up a dry rag. Smiled. "Just promise me I can count on you, D.W."

Derek nodded again. "I promise, S.H."

"Rag time," Sam said, throwing Derek the rag. "Let your imagination run wild."

Chapter 3

Later that night, Derek stalked Janine on Facebook. Her baby bump was growing. She'd posted a photo of her and her new husband—the same man Derek had caught her cheating on him with, a corporate cutout named Evan with a penchant for wearing argyle—posed in front of their new home, jangling a set of keys in front of them. The house sat in the Upper Crust area of Pemberton, a wealthy neighborhood so named because of the bread factory that used to be located in town. She looked happy. Much happier than when they'd been together. Why had he tried so long to make it work?

The many decisions that brought him to this moment—this place, this time—felt almost too much to bear. The weight of missed opportunities, fear, and complacency. In college, when he'd told his parents he wanted to become an archaeology major, his dad had said to be sensible. Better to move into something practical like accounting. When he had shown interest in applying to grad school to become a school counselor, Janine had laughed and said, "But you give terrible advice."

Instead, he hadn't chosen at all.

He turned on Netflix, only to find his brother's face staring back at him. He and Tom hadn't talked much since their mother passed. In those torturous days before, as they waited for the inevitable ending to their mom's story, they had all gathered in their childhood home, taking turns around her hospital bed.

She had just wanted more time.

His father was there, sure, but he had the nerve to bring his new wife, Shannon, which just felt wrong, as if he was showing off his mom's replacement. Shannon was an elementary school art teacher with the flat affect of an accountant breaking down your taxes, as if two characters had accidentally gotten mixed up. Even though Derek liked her, and didn't understand what a seemingly kind—if not boring—woman saw in his father, her presence had felt like an unwelcome stone wedged between a door.

"I have a big audition," Tom said in the kitchen while they were on break. That's how they had come to think of it. Shifts.

Derek didn't think all that much of Tom's auditions. He'd been auditioning for years, and at that point, the biggest role he'd landed was the lead in an off-off-off-Broadway play about a dentist who dreamed of becoming a candy maker. It was called *Truth Decay*. Coincidentally, his only other credited role had been an orthodontist in a soap opera. He'd said one line: "Open wide."

"Can we talk about this later?" Derek said.

"It's tomorrow. Do you think mom... you know?"

Derek looked angrily at Tom. "You'd leave her?"

"That's why I'm asking you," he said. "My agent says I've gotta strike while the iron is hot. The reviews for *Truth* were really great, but I want to branch off from theater—"

"And playing dentists?"

"I was an orthodontist," Tom said angrily. "You don't understand how typecasting works in the acting world."

"I don't think you should go."

"Don't you think she'd want me to have this opportunity? It'd be four or five hours, tops. Then I'd come right back."

Derek sighed. One of those sighs that just keeps going, like a tire deflating.

"Mom and I always shared a special connection about my acting," Tom said.

But it didn't sound genuine; more like a monologue being rehearsed for his audition. Then it hit Derek: He was already talking about her in the past tense. Backstory to cement the jittery forward momentum of their lives.

Even though somewhere, deep down, Derek knew Tom was right. That to get on with the business of living was not only the right thing to do, but the only thing to do. Still, that didn't mean Derek wanted to make it easy.

Just then, his father walked in from the family room with Shannon. Ready for a break.

"Two brothers conspiring," he said.

"You know us, Dad," Tom said.

"You two were always conspiring. Always with big plans." It sounded accusatory. "Where's Janine?"

"Not here," Derek said, not wanting to further explain.

"Are we ordering pizza? I thought we were ordering pizza. I get cranky if I haven't eaten."

Shannon smiled. "So that's why you're always snacking even though Dr. Felder said to watch your cholesterol?"

"It's a mental health condition," he said. "Right, Tom? Isn't that what the kids are saying these days?"

Shannon poked his father's stomach just as Derek glimpsed his mother in the next room dozing, head lolling to the side. To have these two moments in the same scene was almost too much for Derek to take.

"Fuck this family," Derek had said angrily.

His mother had passed less than three hours later—alone. Derek had gone to the bathroom and Tom, his father, and Shannon had gone on a walk. Tom made it to his audition the next day and earned the part of Sergeant James Wilks on *Another Planet*, which he had called his mom's final gift. As soon as filming started—in Fiji of all places—their father had moved to Arizona with Shannon to retire. Meanwhile, Derek remained stuck in the same place ever since. Unless you counted books. He'd been able to live more than a few lives while working at the library.

And now he was living the life of Eldrid Babble, the grimkin being called to a journey beyond his small-scale replicas.

Derek shut off the TV, feeling the call of the strange title that lay on his coffee table. A world both familiar and strange. He opened the book, ready to once again escape into Grimwell.

* * *

Following his run-in with Mayor Frumple, Eldrid Babble strode through Crimpleton Common, eager to sit down for his evening meal at Crimpleton Tavern. The mist had just begun to settle over the grassland, cloaking the small stone huts in a soft haze, as if a painter had smudged the grays and greens.

He was going to do it this time. No more excuses. It was time he take the first step into his own adventure and ask Belinda, the bar wench—a term of endearment in Grimwell, Eldrid assured me—out on a date.

The same thing he told himself every night.

The truth is, much like you, Dear Reader, Eldrid Babble was afraid.

As he hurried through town, Brittlebee the Baker called out, "Rabble Babble," a nickname from Eldrid's grimpledee years. Grimkins can be just as cruel as humans, a lesson I learned the hard way, when my adventure accidentally intersected with Eldrid's. But that night, mere weeks before I stepped foot in Grimwell, Eldrid ignored Brittlebee and kept going, practically running to see the object of his heart's desire, just hoping for a chance to tell her about his latest build. Maybe there was something in the air that night; the haze had grown thicker, making reality appear blurred, distorted. The fog emboldened Eldrid, as if he could smudge and blur his destiny, too. In that smoky light, he could almost imagine crowning the tip of the Summit with Belinda by his side.

Only steps away from the door of Crimpleton Tavern, he heard a quiet whisper calling him into a darkened alley.

For some reason, Eldrid never could quite say why, he walked toward the voice.

"Hello?"

"Yes, you," the voice whispered.

As Eldrid crept closer to the shadowy figure, spurred on by that latent desire for adventure that lurks within even the most cowardly of grimkins, he saw a cloaked figure, his face darkened in shadow, a glowing red amulet laying in his pale, outstretched hand.

How many darkened alleys have offered the same prospect of mystery and adventure as the one in this tale, Dear Reader?

You see, everyone has a chance to veer into dark corridors, mysteries, blank pages. My chance came during a walk in the woods. Perhaps yours will come while reading this very book. The question is, will you continue on your journey or will you close the book and find a brighter path where the pages are well-worn and dog-eared?

* * *

Derek was growing uncomfortable with the writer's insistence on addressing the reader, almost as if they were involved in a private conversation, and Derek was hearing about Eldrid's tale from a friend over coffee. A sense of danger permeated each page turn, as if he would somehow find their fates inextricably intertwined: Writer, Reader, and Character becoming one.

Derek closed the book and returned to stalking Janine. Much like Eldrid, Derek had lived his life in fear of the unknown. The unpredictable. The unexpected.

He fell asleep with the book on his chest and dreamed of faraway worlds, grimkins, and the near constant steam of the espresso machine.

Chapter 4

The next day, Derek got up and prepared for a marathon day at the coffee shop. Double shift, with only a half an hour in between. Because it was a Saturday, he was working with Sue, who reminded him of an older version of his mom, with long gray hair and a warm smile that often made customers want to stay and chat. She had retired the previous year and taken a part-time job as a barista for "fun."

Sam had taken to studying at the coffee shop on his off days, but Derek suspected it was more to keep an eye on his employees than it was to actually do work. Derek also suspected that Sam would never actually go to business school, that he merely liked collecting reasons to feel superior to others.

"Have I shown you the latest photos of my grandson?" Sue asked during a lull in the morning rush.

"No, I don't think so."

She quickly scrolled through her phone, showing a small child posing behind a toy cash register with the same disgruntled expression

Derek often wore while at the coffee shop—a perfect imitation of reality. "He's a busybody like his grandma," Sue said.

"Very cute," Derek said.

"I don't know what I'd do if I didn't have my routines."

Derek peered at his copy of *Eldrid Babble* hidden beneath the till, and he found himself thinking of the world of Grimwell and the small, quiet life lived by the grimkin.

The truth is, much like you, Dear Reader, Eldrid Babble was afraid.

The words echoed in his mind, but Derek didn't know what he was afraid of. Or maybe just where to begin.

As he steamed milk, ground coffee beans, and cut and shmeared bagels, he thought of the fears that had kept him away from adventure over the past ten years. Was it fear that kept him with Janine even after he suspected her of cheating with a colleague? Was it fear that kept him from becoming an archeology major, remembering his dad's words to find a practical job? Was it fear that prevented him from calling his brother?

Derek didn't know, and to be honest, he didn't have time to figure out such complicated questions with a line out the door.

Just before lunch, Sue called Derek to the back for help. Derek hurried over, only to find the milk from the morning delivery still on the floor.

"Sue? Did you forget to put the milk in the fridge when you opened?"

"I knew I forgot something," Sue said. "These morning shifts really get to me."

"It's happened to me too," Derek said, remembering spoiled milk, unbrewed coffee, and empty pastry cases throughout his decade at the Bean. Just like a book, it was the details that were difficult to get right.

Just then, Sam strode in and saw the crate of milk on the floor, the condensation like evidence of a crime. Sam sniffed the air, as if he'd become a great detective intent on solving a mystery.

"I'm sorry, Sam," Derek said. "Must've slipped my mind."

Derek had no choice but to grovel. Here was the king. And he was but a lowly subject. Did all employees feel that way, just hankering for a revolution? Not with all the beheading stuff, that would make him need to seek help stat, but a peaceful revolution, the kind that only happens in fairy tales. Perhaps a flogging, but only a few light... flogs?

"You mean to tell me that it's not even noon and we have no milk for the rest of the day? Who was responsible for this?"

He had taken on his business executive persona, though Derek knew he was only playing boss. At least until his dad returned from Florida.

"It was my bad, Sam," Derek said.

Sue opened her mouth to speak, but Derek shook his head. No reason for her to be on the receiving end of one of Sam's tirades.

Sam lost it. Derek could see the vein throbbing in the side of his head, and even as he watched Sam's lips move, he felt a disconnect from reality, as if he was reading about this in a book. In one novel Derek had read, the protagonist, Sandy, storms off from her job as an accountant and throws hot coffee in her boss's face (and somehow is never charged with assault). In another book, this one from the Self-Help shelf called *101 Ways to Find Your Inner Peace in the Workplace*, the author suggested tuning out negativity by reciting a mantra. Derek weighed the two options, letting Sam's words ricochet off his consciousness: *Immature. Pathetic. Probation.*

As Sam finished, Derek briefly thought of screaming back. Throwing off his apron and finally starting his own adventure.

"You're on rag time for the rest of the day." Sam ran his fingers through his hair and looked up at the ceiling as if conspiring with the gods of spilt milk. "There goes studying for the day," he said. "Now I'm headed to the grocery store to clean up your mess."

"It's right down the road," Sue said. "And the milk section is—"

"I don't want to hear it, Sue."

"It's not easy being in charge, that's for sure." He grabbed his keys off a newly-installed personalized hook that said *The Boss* (Sam also loved label makers). "I want the surfaces in here to sparkle when I'm back."

Still, Derek had an opportunity to make a scene. Stand up for himself. Storm off. Tell him he was moving on to greener pastures. He didn't need this job. But something froze Derek in place, as if all of the stories and books he'd read had gotten tangled and knotted in his mind. Instead, he found himself hurrying to wipe down tables as Sam frantically ran out of the coffee shop in search of milk, embarking on an adventure to the grocery store.

* * *

During his lunch break, Derek once again opened the book, engrossed in the tale of Eldrid Babble and the darkened alley. No surprise, it had been a sorcerer offering Eldrid a magic amulet that would "make his wildest dreams come true." Eldrid didn't want adventure, but he didn't want things to stay the same either, so almost in a stupor, he took the magic amulet and marched a few paces to Crimpleton Tavern, ready to eat dinner and see Belinda, the grimkin he secretly loved.

With the amulet in hand, Eldrid felt a spark run through his body, no longer blood pumping through his veins, but magic, something electric, practically vibrating. He felt stronger. Taller. Faster.

Now, you must be wondering, Dear Reader, if Eldrid didn't want adventure, why would he take the amulet? I asked Eldrid the same thing when our paths accidentally crossed, and I can't say he was all that sure. Maybe it was somehow in his blood, the same hunger for adventure that had animated his parents and grandparents. Maybe it was the chance to finally ask Belinda on a date. Maybe it was just sheer boredom, the desire to finally see the world beyond his small-scale replicas.

36

However, I have a different theory, a hypothesis borne out by my own descent into Grimwell: We all want adventure. Some prefer adventures of the mind, reading books and taking the ephemeral lump of clay that is an idea and turning it into a beautiful sculpture. Others prefer adventures of the heart, that elusive brand of magic that remains a mystery to humans and grimkins alike. Others prefer adventures of the soul, exploring distant lands, slaying dragons, and battling three-headed monsters. But every adventure, whether of the mind, heart, or soul, begins with a call. Before that, we'll do everything in our power to ignore it. The same way you have, Derek. But when adventure calls—when it whispers, shouts, or screams—you'll answer. Just like Eldrid.

Derek glanced up from the page, his heart hammering against his chest. Had the book really said "Derek"? He reread the line, only to find his name replaced by "Dear Reader." He breathed a sigh of relief and continued reading.

Eldrid didn't walk into Crimpleton Tavern that night. No, with the magic amulet tucked snugly in his vest pocket, he strutted in, shimmying through the doors with a confidence and swagger he'd never known before. The tavern was typical as far as grimkin taverns go, not all that different from the type of places you frequent, Dear Reader. Think shiny lacquered tables, dim lights, and a bar serving up barley cream (Grimwell's version of beer) to its host of regulars. Eldrid sat down at a booth beneath a painting of a horse riding a grimkin, a joke on two levels, as horses are thought to be mythical creatures in Grimwell, much the same way humans view unicorns.

Belinda arrived to take Eldrid's order. It wasn't butterflies beating against his stomach, but dragons. With curly brown hair that fanned out across her shoulders and some of the pointiest ears Eldrid had ever seen—pointy ears are apparently akin to cleavage in Grimwell—Belinda was one of the most beautiful grimkins in all of Crimpleton. As she rifled through her apron pocket looking for her notepad, Eldrid caught a whiff of her perfume, a mix of honeysuckle and grimkinberry. Eldrid thumbed the glowing amulet in his pocket, ready to find out if what the hooded figure said was true. If the glowing amulet really would make his wildest dreams come true.

"You want me to get you the usual?" Belinda asked.

Eldrid looked into her big, brown eyes, and noticed for the first time they were flecked with orange. His entire reality seemed to be more vivid, as if someone had turned an unseen dial, brightening the colors, raising the volume, and sharpening the smells. "Have you ever left Crimpleton?" he asked.

"Why would I ever leave Crimpleton?"

Eldrid didn't have an answer. At least not an answer that made sense. Crimpleton had everything. Still, he felt the walls of Crimpleton Tavern pulse and crackle with possibility, the chance to spark a moment.

"It's just that we've been in the same place, doing the same thing, with the same grimkins all our lives. I work at Templeton's stocking shelves, you work here, and we've never thought about leaving the grasslands? Visiting the capital?"

"Eldrid? What are you talking about? Do you want the usual or not?"

"No, I don't want the usual. I don't want the ordinary anymore. I want the extraordinary."

Belinda seemed momentarily caught off-guard. Her notepad slipped from her hand as she stared at Eldrid. Eldrid reached down with his tail, curled it around the leather notebook, and handed it back to her. A grimkin's tail is like a third arm and leg all in one.

"I'd like to take you out to dinner," Eldrid said, his voice at first shaky, before rebounding and regaining its confidence, a pirouette balanced by the amulet now pulsing in his pocket.

"What?" she asked in disbelief.

"I'd like to take you out to dinner."

Working as a clerk at Templeton's Wares and Wonders, Eldrid had seen a variety of travelers on their journeys through Grimwell. Elves, grumpkins (similar to grimkins, though perpetually in a bad mood), even a few goblins, who often trekked through Crimpleton on their way to the capital (goblins have very sharp legal minds). While it seems silly to say now, especially in light of the next chapter in our tale, going on a date with Belinda was just about as much of an adventure as Eldrid ever wanted. Because isn't that what love is? An adventure?

According to Eldrid, who recounted the story to me over a campfire shortly after our lives—and fates—had crisscrossed, Belinda tilted her head to the side and squinted, as if her world had suddenly become lopsided. "Are you serious?" she asked.

Eldrid reached into his pocket and rolled the magic amulet between his fingers. He felt the same current of electricity, jolting him forward with a certainty he'd never experienced before. As if he were building one of his small-scale replicas and he only had to correctly assemble the pieces.

"I'm as serious as I've ever been," Eldrid assured her. Belinda blushed, her tail wagging back and forth, which turned her cheeks an even brighter shade of red.

"That's a yes?"

Belinda nodded.

Plans were made for the following night, and as Eldrid left Crimpleton Tavern with the remains of his second roast hedgehog packed away in a hollyhoot—a voracious hunger had overtaken him while almost finished with the first—he felt the sudden urge to skip through Crimpleton Common, not even bothering to turn his head when someone shouted "Rabble Babble!" from a window.

Now, I ask you, Dear Reader, would you have taken the same chance as Eldrid?

Derek felt sweat prickle his forehead as he looked up from the book. He still couldn't figure out why Chester Felten insisted on addressing his reader. A strange style that was more unnerving than welcoming, a veiled criticism between the lines of prose, shaming Derek for his similarities to the grimkin named Eldrid Babble.

Derek had read a lot of books while working at the Read and Bean, and none of them had been as... Derek grasped for the right word... Personal. Yes, that was it. None of the books had been as personal as *The Strange Life and Times of Eldrid Babble.*

Derek put the book down and googled "Chester Felten" on his cellphone, hoping for information on the writer. He came up with a long list of search results: Chester Felten the plumber, Chester Felten the doctor, Chester Felten the man who streaked at a football game. And a baseball game. And a wrestling match. A serial streaker, the article called him. After climbing out of that rabbit hole, Derek refined his search: "Chester Felten author and veteran" and found a result about the Chester Felten Memorial Pavilion located in the town of Ashton, Connecticut. Derek paused when he read the dates of his life: *1926–1954.*

1954? The same year *Eldrid Babble* was published.

Below that search result, Derek found information about Chester Felten's service in World War II, including a brief list of the battles he fought in, among them D-Day, Battle of the Bulge, and Torgau. Derek had barely dented the History section of the library, only reaching the Early Middle Ages, but he had read enough to know those were some of the fiercest and bloodiest battles of the war. No wonder Felten was stuck and looking for an escape when he returned home. Even an escape into the fantasy world of Grimwell.

Besides those two webpages, though, Derek couldn't find any trace of Chester Felten on the internet, or information about how or where he died. It seemed especially tragic to survive World War II—Derek remembered his final entry in Death's Diary: "I am still alive"—only to die the same year he published *The Strange Life and Times of Eldrid Babble.*

The mystery of Grimwell continued to grow, both within and outside of the book.

Chapter 5

It was later that night that Derek's life truly crisscrossed with Eldrid Babble's. He had just burnt a frozen pizza. The trailer for his brother's show had popped up on Netflix, and after months of avoiding it, he felt himself get sucked into the autoplay, watching the entire first episode of *Another Planet*.

INT. US MILITARY HEADQUARTERS – UNDIS-
CLOSED LOCATION – NYC – DAY

Sergeant James Wilks sits at a computer crunching numbers. He's in his late
twenties, bespectacled, with the build
of an action-hero. He's a walking con-
tradiction. A bowl of M&Ms sits beside
his monitor.

                    WILKS
        That can't be right.

Wilks shoves a handful of M&Ms in his
mouth. He tears a piece of paper from the
printer and hurries away from his desk.

INT. COLONEL J.W. WETMORE'S OFFICE -
MOMENTS LATER

Wilks stands at attention in the office of
Colonel J.W. Wetmore. Wetmore is your
typical grizzled army commander with a
perfectly creased uniform, chiseled jaw-
line, and arms like steel cables.

                    WETMORE
        Who are you again?

                    WILKS
        Sergeant James Wilks. An
        astronomer, Sir.

                    WETMORE
        I didn't even know we
        had astronomers.

                    WILKS
        Our branch was created as
        part of the SPACE Act. We're

                    42

supposed to be an early
warning system.

                    WETMORE
     For what?

                    WILKS
     Aliens, Sir.

Wetmore begins laughing. A loud guffaw.

                    WILKS
     I wish I was kidding, Sir.
     We've been tracking what we
     thought was a large asteroid
     for the past few weeks. But
     asteroids don't move like this.

He holds up the piece of paper to Wetmore
who quickly brushes him off.

                    WETMORE
     English, please.

                    WILKS
     According to my calculations,
     they'll be here...

Wilks looks down and consults his chart.

                    WILKS
...in three hours.

                   WETMORE
You're telling me they might
as well be driving in from
the Hamptons?

Wilks nods.

                   WETMORE
Get me the Pentagon.

Derek watches from his couch, a feeling
of déjà vu sweeping over him.

                    DEREK
              (from couch)
Wait a second.

    Derek suddenly remembered why the plot felt so familiar. He'd
read the book a while back while making his way through the Sci-Fi
section. He'd cruised through the entire trilogy in less than a week
when he first started working at the Bean. The book had all the trap-
pings of a big Hollywood blockbuster: aliens, Armageddon, and of
course, a love story. Derek didn't dislike it so much as not remember
it: a story told so many times before it had disappeared the second
he closed the book.
    The rest of the episode was your standard sci-fi fare. The spaceships
appear and Tom eventually morphs into an action-adventure hero,
because what scientist studying for fourteen hours a day doesn't have
washboard abs and a black belt in jujitsu?

Derek couldn't help but laugh as the first spaceships hovered over New York Harbor and Tom uttered the line:

```
              WILKS
     I've got a feeling they're not
     just tourists.
```

By the time Derek smelled the burnt crust, the pizza was beyond saving, and so he decided to run down to McDowell's to grab some dinner. He knew he shouldn't, not with his rent set to rise in the fall, but Derek felt himself drawn to the bar, the same way he'd been drawn to *Eldrid Babble*.

A chance to escape *Another Planet* and his poor culinary selection.

Owing to it being trivia night, McDowell's was packed. Derek sat down in his usual spot between Boris and Gerald, wondering if they meant to save him a seat or if they just wanted the extra legroom. Probably the latter.

Julius brought over the specials and Derek scanned Kat's latest creation: "Turniped Bacon." What in god's name was turniped bacon?

Before he could order, the trivia started. They were hemmed in by a group who called themselves the Einsteins and another group who'd taken the moniker The Ken Jennings. Gerald and Boris had signed up with the nickname the Octogenarians, apparently not anticipating a younger member of the group.

The emcee, one of the assistant managers named Greg, drawled through his intro, clearly already a few beers in. He was wearing mesh shorts with a shirt and tie, as if he'd dressed for two separate occasions, neither of them being the one he currently found himself in.

"First question," the emcee said, "What animal would you find on a Porsche logo?"

Boris and Gerald conspired quietly, while Derek readied to take dictation.

"It's a Bengal," Gerald said confidently.

45

"You're sure about this?" Boris asked.

"One hundred percent. I used to know a guy who had a Bengal. Lovely animals."

"You sure you're not just thinking about the football team?" Boris asked.

Gerald seemed uncertain. "Is a Bengal a type of horse?"

Boris shook his head.

"Then yes, I'm sure."

Gerald and Boris hovered close, waiting for Derek to weigh in. Still no sign of Kat. Derek watched as some spittle flew from Gerald's mouth onto the edge of the paper.

"Come on, Derek," Boris said, "you're our secret weapon."

"It's a horse," Derek said sadly. "My brother has one."

"A Porsche or a horse?" Gerald asked.

"Probably both."

Kat stumbled through the crowd, the drinks on her tray sloshing around. Derek made eye contact with her before quickly looking down at his paper, imagining Tom riding around in a Porsche with his latest starlet girlfriend, his co-star Achelia Rose, while he remained boxed in by the Octogenarians.

"Next question," the emcee said, slightly slurring his words. "How many teeth does an adult human have?"

Boris opened his mouth and began counting.

"Boris," Gerald scolded. "We're in a family bar."

Boris closed his mouth. "I count twenty-two, but I can't remember how many teeth I've lost."

"Maybe we should take the average of our two mouths," Gerald said.

"Honestly, I've been saving up for a replacement set," Boris said.

"New or used?"

"I always buy used."

"What should I write?" Derek asked, pencil at the ready.

"Open your mouth, Derek, so we can count," Boris said.

"We only have ten seconds," Gerald added.

"I'm just going to take a guess and write thirty," Derek said.

"Thanks a lot, Derek," Gerald said, "way to take one for the team."

Kat finally made her way to the bar and wedged herself between Derek and Boris, so close Derek could feel her leg on his. "Table twelve is going hard on those g and t's," she said to Julius. "Just a dab of gin. They only live up the block, but if either of them gets run over on their walk home, that's going to be tough on my conscience."

"You got it."

"No food?" she asked, turning to Derek.

"Julius has been busy. Not to mention, he hates me."

"Julius doesn't hate you. He just mildly dislikes everybody. Isn't that right, Julius?"

Julius shrugged as he scooped some ice.

"You want me to get you the usual?" Kat asked.

Derek couldn't help but think of Eldrid Babble. Hadn't Belinda uttered the same line just a few pages ago?

He looked down at his trivia questionnaire. The roar of the bar had swelled, and Derek tried to imagine the scene as it happened in *Eldrid Babble*. Belinda's curly brown hair flowing down her shoulders. Her pointy ears. The scent of her perfume, which Chester Felten had described as a mix of honeysuckle and grimkinberry—whatever that was. Eldrid had been seated beneath a painting of a horse riding a grimkin, some sort of fantasy novelty item dreamt up by the author. That's when Derek realized the same painting was hanging above the bar, only this one featured a horse improbably perched on the shoulders of a man in a suit, because obviously grimkins didn't actually exist. Could it just be a coincidence? Derek steadied his breath and tried to pick up the scene as it happened in the novel.

"I don't want the usual," Derek said. "I don't want the ordinary anymore. I want the extraordinary."

Kat looked at him strangely, as if she'd heard the line before. "Well, the turniped bacon's good, but it's not for everyone."

"I'm not talking about the food," Derek said, finding his footing, as if he'd rebounded on the edge of a cliff. Easy does it.

"Then what are you talking about?"

Before Derek could answer, the emcee interrupted.

"Third question. This country boasts Vilnius as its capital."

"Lithuania," Boris automatically answered. "I did a brief stint there. Very hush hush, of course."

"For the last time," Gerald said. "You worked in real estate."

"My cover," Boris said.

"Lithuania isn't even a real country," Gerald said.

"It's a miracle you have a roof over your head," Boris said.

Derek quickly scrawled Lithuania on the paper. He'd read that in *101 Places to See Before You Die*. The Eastern European edition.

"Ever been, Kat?" Boris asked.

"Is it in the Tri-State area?"

"It's in Lithuania."

"Then no."

"The farthest I've gone is Florida," Derek said.

"There's so much to see," Kat said, "but for some reason, we get stuck doing the same things. With the same people. You know, the usual." She smiled at Derek.

"Feel like that was a shot at us," Gerald said.

"Didn't say there was anything wrong with it."

Julius placed a couple of drinks on Kat's tray.

She thanked him, but didn't rush to leave. With a script, Derek realized, life became much easier to live. Still, he wondered if it wasn't Eldrid's words that mattered, but words in general. To be a character in a book—let alone in your own life—you just had to speak up. Get yourself on the page.

Derek noticed too late that Kat had begun walking away, hurrying to her table. Derek dug deep and mustered the courage to call out: "Would you like to go out to dinner sometime?"

Kat spun around, one hand holding the tray, the other on her hip.

Derek could've sworn he saw her blush, the same rosy red cheeks of Belinda in Crimpleton Tavern.

"As long as it's not here," she said, before placing her tray on an empty table and jotting her phone number on a cocktail napkin.

Derek took the napkin in disbelief and watched her recede into the crowd with the mostly tonic water for her troublesome table twelve. Maybe there was something to the tale of Eldrid Babble after all.

"What the hell just happened?" Boris said.

"Our little boy just grew up," Gerald said.

They both put their arms on each of Derek's shoulders, and despite himself, Derek teared up, as if he'd found two surrogate fathers. In a bar, of all places.

"How long do we have to leave our hands here?" Boris grunted.

"I don't know," Gerald said, "but Derek is very sweaty."

Chapter 6

When Derek returned home, he thought about calling his brother to let him know that he had seen *Another Planet*. Actually, part of him had enjoyed it, the same way he'd enjoy a freezer-burned carton of ice cream. Instead, he stared at his brother's name in his contacts, afraid to call for some reason. He grabbed a relatively fresh carton of ice cream out of his freezer and sat down on the futon with his copy of *Eldrid Babble*.

He opened the book, wondering if the next chapter might contain clues about his upcoming date with Kat, as if he had discovered his own personal self-help book, filled with tips about how to live his life. Advice whispered between the lines of Chester Felten's didactic prose. But he feared if he went too many steps ahead, if he climbed too many plot points, he may lose track of what scene he was living in his own life.

The thought gave him pause. Acting like he'd stumbled upon a fortune teller's book and not a fantasy novel about a grimkin.

This is how people go insane, Derek thought, remembering when he tore through the Psychology section in the library, reading the theories of Freud, Jung, and Skinner in a muddled haze soon after he and Janine had broken up and the well of self-help volumes had run dry. It seems perfectly rational, until one day the people in white coats come take you away.

For a moment, Derek considered getting rid of his copy of *Eldrid Babble*. He'd return it to the library and never speak of it again. But then he remembered the way Kat had blushed when he'd asked her to dinner, copying the same lines and cues—not to mention boldness—Eldrid had used just a few pages ago.

What did it prove? That if he took one measly chance and asked a woman out on a date, she might say yes? Derek didn't need a script to live his life. He'd been doing just fine on his own. He had the coffee shop, he had his books, and most of all, he had his dreams, faint sketches of futures he hoped to one day fill in.

It wouldn't hurt to read a little bit more. Just for inspiration. To add color to those rough sketches. After all, books had been guiding him ever since he took the job at the Read and Bean; the pages like different parts of a map, detours that needed to be traveled before he could find his story, whatever that might be. There was nothing wrong with getting a little help from a book. It wasn't magic. He was nothing like Eldrid Babble. And the world of Grimwell wasn't real.

* * *

Now I should probably tell you a little about Eldrid's life before his great big adventure started. As I'm sure you've already figured out from his love of building small-scale replicas, Eldrid wasn't the bravest of grimkins. Nor was he the brightest, boldest, or best-looking. He was as average and unremarkable as a piece of pillypot pie.

Eldrid worked at Templeton's Wares and Wonders, stocking shelves, doing the inventory, and manning, or should I say grimkinning, the register. As Mr. Templeton would have freely admitted, the store was packed with wares, but short on wonders. Similar to a grocery store that also happens to sell novelty items, Templeton's had a small section devoted to grimkin kitsch: trollywogglers (said to spin when within twenty feet of a troll), juniebees (perfect for supporting a grimkin's tail), and gringleworts (an oversized grimkin bib). Sitting close to a major road, the store attracted both locals and travelers looking to procure supplies or buy a gift or souvenir. Eldrid dreamed of someday having his own store, but to open a rival market would have been too big a risk for the unsung grimkin, who had fallen far from the Babble family tree. His mother and father had been famous explorers, becoming the first grimkins to walk all the way through the Land of Shadow and Mist, and his grandfather, Briggledorf Babble, had fought in the famed Battle of the Trembling Forest.

While these names may sound unfamiliar, I assure you each of these locations and events are real. Just like schoolchildren in America learn about the Civil War or Pearl Harbor, children in Grimwell spend their days reciting names of trolls, three-headed monsters, and of course, the most fearsome of all for grimkins, sorcerers.

In the Battle of the Trembling Forest, which Eldrid first learned about sitting by his grandfather's rocking chair, a colony of trolls threatened to breach the city's walls and take over the village. In Eldrid's grandfather's time, these types of raids were common, and grimkins struggled to find a solution. Trolls are far bigger than grimkins, with some measuring up to fifteen feet tall, and their skin is difficult to pierce with arrows, even the handcrafted stone-tipped arrows that had earned grimkins the admiration of the realm. This particular group of trolls had been wreaking havoc on Crimpleton for years.

Eldrid's grandfather mounted a counteroffensive, hiding out in the Trembling Forest and surprising the trolls with a series of complex traps to stop their advances and lower morale, including riddles (trolls love riddles), challenges of physical strength (trolls can't say no to a thumb war, and luckily for Briggledorf, have very small, stubby thumbs), and the classic rope-hidden-beneath-leaves booby trap that would hoist the trolls far into the air (Briggledorf would usually cut them down as long as they promised to never show their face in Crimpleton again). After months of embarrassment as a result of Briggledorf's cunning, the trolls called a summit to find a peaceful resolution.

Unlike other depictions in fairy tales and books, trolls are not mindless beasts, but quite intelligent and very accomplished in games of strategy. In Grimwell, grimkins and trolls alike play a game similar to chess called Fizzle. Instead of kings and queens, Fizzle uses different types of animals and has over three hundred spaces on a single board. Unfortunately for the trolls, Eldrid's grandfather was a Fizzle Master (the set on Eldrid's coffee table was a hand-me-down), and so in a meeting to establish the terms of the treaty, Briggledorf challenged Cheselwick the Troll to a match that lasted over three nights. After a stunning move where his Brimble took Cheselwick's Hedgehog, Eldrid's grandfather won and extended the boundaries of Crimpleton farther north than ever before.

While I returned home from war to a small parade and my mom's homemade apple pie, Briggledorf came back a hero, eventually settling down with the most beautiful grimkin in Crimpleton and having a child.

Briggledorf's son, Chiselbee, proved to be just as brave and adventurous as his father, collecting model ships, maps, and compasses. On his tenth birthday, he told his father he wanted to become a famous explorer. On his eighteenth birthday, he set off to explore more of Grimwell than any other grimkin before, journeying across its rugged landscape and cataloguing his exploits in a bestselling memoir called Travels and Tribulations, which featured descriptions of his favorite inns, the best places to grab a cup of sweet leaf coffee, and—almost casually interspersed—the time he had to kill a ferocious dragon-like creature called a Boppledoo.

On his next adventure, he passed through the town of Thet, where he met an accountant named Eldrina. Unlike Earth, only the bravest of souls go into accounting, as grimkins have a general distaste bordering on fear of numbers. On the first night, they kissed beneath the moonlight, tails interlocking on the village square. On the second night, Chiselbee proposed, fashioning a ring out of an old juniebee, and on the third night, they set off on an expedition through the Land of Shadow and Mist together, proving once and for all that Grimwell wasn't flat, although the question of whether or not a grimkin could fall off the edge remained in dispute. I tried explaining gravity to Eldrid only to have him summarily dismiss the theory with a terse, "Sounds like magic." On their return to Crimpleton, they penned a follow-up to Travels and Tribulations *called* Shadows and Kisses, *part travelogue, part adventure, part love story.*

Even more popular than the first.

They continued their adventures all throughout Eldrid's childhood, often leaving him with Briggledorf while they traversed the kingdom, and wrote a grand total of twenty-two books, including the award-winning Beneath the Bim Bim Sea, *the gritty* On Foot and Underfoot in Grim City, *and the ambitious, though less-successful* Waxing and Wainscotting, *a journey into various styles of walls across the kingdom. Eldrid had hungrily read each of their books, resenting the spirit of adventure that had confined him to long stretches at home without his mother or father.*

On Eldrid's eighteenth birthday, he blew out his birthday candles alone while his parents attempted to reach the summit of Grim Mountain. They froze to death just a day's journey away from the top. They would've been the first to ever reach the summit.

Unfortunately for our hero, Eldrid had not inherited his parents' sense of adventure, or his grandfather's bravery. At least that's what he thought when his unlikely journey first began. In the course of writing our own story, sometimes we surprise ourselves most of all.

The day after Eldrid received the glowing red amulet, he had an early morning shift at Templeton's Wares and Wonders. It was still dark out as Eldrid walked to work, and while he usually found comfort in the quiet routine, today the path felt claustrophobic, as if Crimpleton Common had begun shrinking, growing smaller and smaller until it would become nothing more than a small-scale replica. A carefully constructed version of reality that would someday sit on another grimkin's shelf.

As usual, Mr. Templeton bossed Eldrid around, treating him like a grimpledee, even though Eldrid was at least ten years his senior. I'm sure you know what that's like, Dear Reader. To be bossed around by someone who's had everything handed to them.

Derek lay the book on his lap, once again disconcerted by the book directly addressing the reader. He scooped the last of the ice cream from the carton. He could've sworn he felt another presence in the room, something sinister, as if a predator was watching him. Then he had another feeling, as if he was looking through the window at himself, becoming both predator and prey. The thought scared him, and although he usually stayed away from the Horror section at the library, he couldn't help but feel that same sense of unease as he continued reading Eldrid's tale.

Because by all metrics, Eldrid should've been the one doing great big things, just like his parents, the explorers, and his grandfather, the war hero, who single-handedly stopped the trolls from invading Crimpleton.

Now that he had the magic amulet—tucked securely in his vest pocket—he felt something inside of him change, which is how he described it to me when we first began our adventure together. Not so much becoming a different grimkin, as a valve opening, a globe turning, a cave being lit from within.

That day, when Mr. Templeton asked him to begin unpacking boxes and taking inventory on the brand-new shipment of trollywogglers,

Eldrid felt his world tilt. A slight wobble that made him question his reality.

It all started with one word: "No."

"What?" Mr. Templeton asked.

"Sir, with all due respect"—even though Eldrid didn't mean it with respect—"I will not unpack the boxes."

"Be careful what you say, Eldrid," Mr. Templeton said. "Your family isn't here to protect you anymore."

"No, Mr. Templeton. You be careful. I'm tired of being treated like the lowest grimkin in the shabberberry bush. I've been working here longer than anyone and yet when you had to pick a manager, you hired Bartle, who can barely count."

Bartle looked stunned from behind the register.

"No offense, Bartle, but it's true. Yesterday I saw you put the decimal in the wrong place and give Mrs. Crabble a hundred grimkies instead of ten."

Bartle shuddered at the thought of doing addition.

"I've had just about enough," Mr. Templeton said.

"Before you go acting like you're better than me, just remember that I started working here long before you. I knew your father." The magic amulet had become warm in Eldrid's pocket. When he looked down, he could see a faint gleam emanating from his vest.

"Eldrid, I think it's better if you—"

"You're probably forgetting something," Eldrid said, feeling the heat of the amulet against his skin. "In the course of my time at Templeton's, I've seen things that the village might find interesting."

Mr. Templeton's mouth hung wide open; Eldrid could see the sharp points of his grimkincisors.

"Don't look so shocked, Mr. Templeton. I've seen you tamper with the scale, for instance. I've seen you water down the milk. I've seen you sell knockoff juniebees as if they were made in the capital. And I know that half the village got sick last year because someone forgot to throw out old

meat." He glared at Bartle, before returning his gaze to Mr. Templeton. "And someone decided to sell it anyway."

"You wouldn't."

"I absolutely would. So until things change around here, I'm putting you on notice."

With great difficulty, Mr. Templeton managed to close his mouth. He gulped as if only now swallowing the mouthful of words spoken by Eldrid. "I'm sure we can work something out."

"Yes, I'm sure we can." Mr. Templeton had a wounded look in his eyes. Eldrid didn't want to admit it, but he liked it, the feeling of power, the look of defeat stamped across Mr. Templeton's face, and, most surprising, the pulsing of the warm amulet in his pocket, almost like a second heartbeat.

Serves him right, Eldrid thought, the way he hovers over me like some finicky king barking orders: Wipe down the counters, Eldrid. Clean up the store room, Eldrid. Greet customers with a smile, Eldrid. No, no, no. Life wasn't supposed to turn out like this. He was supposed to be the adventurer. The explorer. The one in charge.

The amulet grew even warmer, the heat spreading from his chest, to his stomach, to his arms, all the way to his legs, until his body felt on fire.

"Your eyes, Eldrid," Mr. Templeton said, taking a step back. "They're red."

Eldrid caught sight of his reflection in the shiny brass register and noticed that his eyes were, in fact, glowing. A brilliant shade of red, as if a fire roared beneath his skin.

Before Mr. Templeton could say anything else, Eldrid fled the store, feeling both afraid and exhilarated.

* * *

Derek stopped reading, the book spread across his chest like a bird in flight. He could see the outline of a moral forming, the author no doubt influenced by the devastation of World War II: power corrupts. Even a gentle soul like Eldrid Babble, the kindly homely grimkin, couldn't help but crane his ear to its odious melody. But that's where real life and fiction diverged. Because more often than not, the common man, your everyday Average Joe or Mr. Nobody, never got a chance to hear even a snippet of power's intoxicating symphony. Not even muffled through all of those doors that remained closed.

In contrast to his reading at the library, Derek's life didn't conform to neat morals and lessons, a theme to be repeated over and over again. His life had no direction, no conductor, and absolutely no writer. If it did, he wouldn't be alone, watching Janine start a family with the man she had cheated on him with. He wouldn't be going to bed early to try and impress a boss almost ten years his junior. He wouldn't still be working at the Read and Bean, no closer to finding his path.

His story.

The book seemed to pulse on his chest, as if it might suddenly take off and fly out the window.

As he picked it up to continue reading, a thought occurred to him: Maybe he had found his story. It just so happened to be about someone else: a grimkin named Eldrid Babble.

Chapter 7

Derek woke up feeling relieved. He had an actual date, the first one since he'd found Janine sleeping with her colleague (now husband). He'd also come to terms with Eldrid Babble. Not a self-help handbook or supernatural guide, but a novel with some vague similarities to his own life and a narrator who insisted on directly addressing his reader. Maybe that's why the librarian, Jackson Wilfred, had stored the book in the supply closet before anyone had the chance to check it out. It would have angered one too many readers.

The overarching message—how could he not have seen this sooner?—was to simply be a little more confident. Not only in his personal life, but also at work. He had to shake off the feeling of being overshadowed by his brother if he wanted to reach his full potential. And he didn't need a magic amulet—or a magic book—to do that.

Derek showered, brushed his teeth, had some breakfast, and did some pushups. The start of his new life. Sure, he only did ten, but what was that Buddhist aphorism? A journey of a thousand miles begins with a single step? Here was his single step. Ten single steps when you really thought about it.

Not to mention, his life was pretty great anyway. Surrounded by an endless supply of books, free coffee, the occasional stale pastry. Of course, there could always be more, he reminded himself, before tamping down the inner voice of dissatisfaction, the same one that had haunted Eldrid Babble when he met the cloaked figure in the darkened alley.

It was still dark out as he walked to work, and cold, so cold he could see his breath frost in the air. The lights of the Read and Bean blared in the distance, casting an ominous glow in the middle of the dark and deserted street. He thought of Eldrid walking to Templeton's Wares and Wonders, how Chester Felten had described it as claustrophobic. Derek imagined the two sides of Elm Street creeping closer and closer, the road getting narrower until the buildings smashed into one another with Derek in between.

Just like Eldrid, his reality didn't seem big enough for him anymore, as if the world had shrunk overnight. Or maybe it wasn't the size, but the realness of it, as if he was walking through an author's attempt at reality, and that if he looked behind the walls that now seemed to close in on him, he'd find empty husks, a pale imitation of reality.

He arrived at the coffee shop just before 5:30 and stashed *Eldrid Babble* by the till. He didn't remember packing it, but he was glad to have its company anyway. Sue mumbled a gravelly hello as she scrolled through her phone. "Top of the morning to you," she said. "I've been up since three trying to buy tickets to Whipple the Walrus On Ice."

"Who's Whipple the Walrus?"

Sue bellowed loudly: "Whipple, Whipple, Splash, and Ripple!"

Derek looked at her blankly.

"He's every kid's favorite singing and dancing walrus."

"Did you get tickets?"

"Yes," she said, looking disappointed.

"Maybe the morning rush will cheer you up."

"Said no one ever."

In between stacking cups, grinding beans, and taking orders, Derek tried to compose a text message to Kat and solidify plans for their date. Unfortunately, the world of Eldrid Babble didn't have text messages, so the dialogue he'd stolen before wouldn't work now. He riffled the book close to his face, breathing in the sweet scent of its pages, crinkling the cellophane cover, as if its nearness might inspire him. He typed a few words, then deleted them. Typed a few more, then deleted those too. If only grimkins had text messaging. At least he'd have a place to start.

He finally settled on: *Hi, Kat. It's Derek. From the bar.*

The reply came almost instantly: *I meet a lot of guys in bars named Derek.*

Derek felt himself panic.

From McDowell's.

Kidding, Kat replied.

Derek began typing, searching for the right words. Now he was on a timer. If he kept typing without sending anything, she would know that he was painstakingly crafting a message. But if he didn't painstakingly craft a message, he worried he'd say the wrong thing and she'd change her mind.

Look, I can see the three dots moving, but I've got a screaming toddler, so do you want to just get to the part where we make a plan to meet at Que Sera at 8 on Friday?

Derek breathed a sigh of relief. Sometimes the lines of dialogue were written for you after all.

Sounds like a plan, Derek wrote, before adding an exclamation point to properly convey his excitement: *Sounds like a plan!*

He sent the message, immediately regretting the exclamation point, and then stashed his phone in his pocket. Sam had just come in and Derek wasn't supposed to be texting at work, lest it distract from his persona as Derek the Friendly Neighborhood Barista.

The day passed slowly, the familiar rhythm of the coffee shop its own form of time. The steam of the espresso machine. The midmorning mom rush. The constant clicking of keys and shuffling of pages.

During a lull, Sue told her grandchildren the good news about Whipple the Walrus and Derek heard a cacophony of screaming, followed by the unmistakable sound of belching.

"Look," Sue said, "Callie can burp on command."

She turned her phone to Derek to show an angelic little girl belching loudly and giggling. From somewhere off screen, Derek heard another voice: "Is grandma encouraging you to burp again? Mom, I thought we talked about this..."

"I'm sorry, honey, I can't hear you," Sue said, winking AT Derek. "Whoops, gotta go, I've got a meeting with the head of product development."

Sue motioned for Derek to pick up the thread. Create the scene.

"Yes, that's right," Derek said. "I'm hoping to hear your thoughts about a new type of mocha syrup."

"Instead of milk chocolate or dark chocolate, I was thinking we could combine them into one type of chocolate."

"That's brilliant," Derek said

"I know. I also have some ideas about the zucchini and banana bread. Why don't we combine them into one loaf?"

"Wow," Derek said.

"Gotta go," Sue said waving to the screen as she hung up the phone.

"She thinks I'm working my way up to executive and not just using the gig as a way to get away from her father."

Derek laughed.

Derek was nearing the end of his shift, wiping down a table for the fifth time to look busy, when Sam asked him if he wouldn't mind staying late to organize the coffee closet.

Derek looked up and saw Sam standing in front of him, his GMAT book proudly displayed in front of his chest. "I can't," Derek said.

Technically, he could, but to be honest, he was curious to watch the next episode of *Another Planet*. Who knows... maybe call his brother?

"Because I would love to," Sam pressed on, "but I have an important practice test tomorrow and I told my dad it would get done. We have a new shipment of beans coming and honestly, it was a slow day anyway."

"I really can't," Derek said, finding his voice, saying it louder than he meant to.

"It will only be an hour, maybe two max. It would be great if you could also scrub the bathroom. Someone had a little trouble in there and I think it needs a once-over."

"Weren't you just in the bathroom?"

"Hey, this isn't about pointing fingers. It's about banding together as a team. We're a team, right D.W.?"

Derek saw the lights flicker overhead. The library was practically empty, save for a few high school students catching up on homework and a couple of regulars reading books and sipping coffee. He steeled himself. Ready to let loose on Sam.

"No," Derek said, his voice becoming louder.

It all started with a single word.

"What are you talking about?"

"I'm not gonna stay late. And to be honest, I'm tired of doing all the menial tasks while you do nothing. I've been working here the longest and it's about time I got some respect."

Sam held up his hands, still clutching his GMAT book. "Whoa, man I don't know where this is coming from, but if you can't clean the supply closet, I don't think we really have all that much to talk about."

"No, you listen you little pissant." Pissant? Derek had never used the word in his life. But he didn't mind it, either. *Pissant.* It made him feel strong. Powerful. Like Eldrid tearing into his boss, Mr. Templeton. "I'm tired of how things are run around here. Just because your dad left to open up a new shop doesn't mean you can run this place into the ground. Now, here's what's going to happen. You're going to put that little prop away"—Derek pointed angrily at the GMAT book—"and you're going to stay and clean the closet. And when you're done, you're going to scrub the bathroom and finish closing up, because I've been here since the crack of dawn and I'd like to go home now. Sue too. And if you do that, then maybe, just maybe, I won't tell your dad about the way you've been running things."

"You really think my dad will listen to you over his own son?"

"Is that a risk you really want to take?"

Sam stayed quiet and looked down at his shoes. Shiny and completely clear of milk and mocha syrup.

"And when you're here, you should be helping out behind the counter, not just pretending to read that book and looking at your phone." Derek untied his apron and made his way to the door. "Sue, we're done here. And by the way, Sam, would you punch us out before you leave? I think we both earned some paid time off, wouldn't you say?"

"I... Uh..." Sam stood there, still holding his GMAT book, but now it no longer looked like a badge of courage; it looked like a shield. He was afraid of Derek. Derek couldn't help but notice that he liked the feeling of being in control.

Derek picked up a rag and threw it in Sam's direction. "What's that phrase you're so fond of saying? Rag time? Let your imagination run wild."

Derek felt exhilarated as he grabbed his copy of *Eldrid Babble* from beneath the till and rushed out of the coffee shop into the sunny street. He wished he had grabbed some sort of iced drink before the final exit, something foamy and sweet, so he could sip it on the way to his apartment, but oh well, he couldn't have everything.

As he walked back home, he noticed the book felt warm to the touch, as if it had been baking beneath the hot sun. The cellophane cover rustled in his hand and the way the light hit the plastic made it appear to be glowing.

He clutched the book closely to his chest as if hugging an old friend, because in that moment, he truly loved Eldrid Babble and the land of Grimwell.

Chapter 8

The rest of the week passed slowly as Derek readied himself for his first date in over three years. He only looked at Janine's Facebook a couple of times. The baby bump was growing, she looked about ready to burst. She had even posted the obligatory pregnancy picture featuring Evan standing behind her cradling her belly—a must for any couple looking to prove their love to the world. Happily ever after. Derek stared at that one for a while, glaring at the man with a deep abiding hatred, wishing he'd get hit by a car. Nothing too bad, just a minor scrape up, which seemed reasonable considering their history.

His situation at work had improved, and when he came in for his next shift, he found the coffee closet immaculate. He took his time on his breaks, stayed off rag time, and even gave a few orders to Sam, asking him to wash some dishes in the back. Sam grumbled, but the power dynamic had changed between them, as if Derek's one act of courage, if he could even call it that, had rewritten their history, cast them as different characters at the Read and Bean.

Derek decided to take a break from McDowell's, not only because
of his dwindling bank account, but because he thought it best not to
see Kat before their date. Absence makes the heart grow fonder, after
all. He also didn't trust Boris and Gerald not to say or do something
to make it awkward. Actually, he trusted them to do just that. He
loved them, but they no longer had a filter. Old age will do that, Derek
supposed, and to be honest, it's part of what made them so fun to be
around. Anything could happen.

He'd managed to keep *Eldrid Babble* at bay for the past few
days. Not because he didn't want to read it. Quite the opposite. He
thought about reading it constantly. The crinkle of the dust jacket
as he turned a page. The pencil sketch of Grimwell's characters that
Chester Felten had included on the title page, almost like looking at
a photo album of long-lost relatives, both familiar, yet distant. Most
of all, he missed seeing himself between the pages, hidden in the
loops and swirls of Felten's sparse prose.

Despite all that, the almost unbearable call to continue reading
the book, he wanted to be ready for his date with Kat. Even though
he knew he was being superstitious, he thought it best to hold off
on reading about Eldrid's first date with Belinda until his own
date neared. That way it would be fresh in his mind. So instead of
reading, he had binged *Another Planet*, watching up to the fifth
episode where Tom comes face-to-face with an alien for the first
time and says,

                    WILKS
        Am I looking at your butt or
        your face?

And Misha, the army captain turned love interest played by Tom's
real-life girlfriend, Achelia Rose—at least if the news reports were
to be believed—responds,

MISHA
Thought the same thing when I
first met you.

And Derek, sitting on his couch, couldn't help but add,

DEREK
You've gotta be kidding me.

Not that he turned it off. Not a chance. He was hooked, and even
though he vaguely remembered reading the novel, he couldn't wait to
see how Sergeant James Wilks finally brings down the Troglodorfs,
the name for the alien species intent on Earth's destruction.

On Thursday, the night before the date, he surveyed his apartment.
Frozen pizza boxes littered the counter beside his toaster oven. An empty
carton of ice cream lay face down on the coffee table, a small puddle
of melt collecting beneath. Sheets were twisted on his futon, which
he hadn't bothered to make into a couch since Sunday. His apartment
looked like someone had staged a coup at a department store.

Tonight was the night he'd read the date scene. He smiled at the
thought. It had been difficult not to continue his story, and more than
a few times, he'd opened *The Strange Life and Times of Eldrid Babble*
just to fan the pages close to his face and inhale the quintessential old
book scent. Turning to the next chapter, Derek reclined back on his
futon and began reading, cruising through the scene where Eldrid
visits Mayor Frumple's spacious hut for news about the sorcerer seen
in the Trembling Forest—"Nothing to fear when Frumple's here," he'd
said, as if crafting his next campaign pin—before finally landing on the
page where Eldrid begins getting ready for his first date with Belinda.

*He stood in front of the mirror, tossing the magic amulet back and
forth between his hands. He smiled at himself. He was wearing his*

grandfather's old scarlet vest, the one with the shiny gold buttons that had been forged by the trolls in the far reaches of the Trembling Forest, a present following the peace talks. A bold choice, but one Eldrid hoped would pay off. Beneath the vest, he had on his most elegant collared shirt, made of fine silk by his grandmother as a wedding present. The wedding had never materialized, but the shirt, with its long puffy sleeves and embroidered collar, screamed confidence. To complete the outfit, he'd worn his father's black dress slacks and a pair of gold-buckled shoes, cobbled by a group of goblins that passed through Crimpleton every spring (in addition to their legal prowess, goblins also have a passion for feet). He slicked some crushed shabberberry through his hair to give it a shine and then did the same to his tail. Taking one last look in the mirror, he slipped the magic amulet in his vest pocket.

 Eldrid strode through Crimpleton Common ready to finally meet his fate. He'd walked these streets countless times before, but today something felt different. He waved to Brattlebee the Butcher, who was mid-hack on a hedgehog's carcass. Brattlebee held up his knife to wave back, the metal glinting in the sun. He nodded to Brittlebee the Baker, Brattlebee's twin brother, who was loading up a cart with bread and pastries to send to the hinterlands of Crimpleton where the more uncivilized grimkins lived. Next, he saw Rofreena, the Crimpleton tax collector, who squinted as Eldrid passed by, as if she was seeing a mirage. No longer Rabble Babble, the common, cowardly grimkin with the palatine pedigree, he had somehow become the hero of this tale. Although, as you'll come to find out, sometimes the line that separates a hero and a villain is razor-thin, as sharp and narrow as a single leaf of paper.

 They had agreed to meet at Founder's Statue, a monument to the famed grimkin Edelbee Gripplebunk, who had begun Crimpleton as a small trading outpost surrounded by trolls and goblins. A dedication to her heroism was inscribed on the pedestal: In the shadow of the Trembling Forest, let Crimpleton be a fortress and refuge for all grimkins. *When Eldrid arrived, he saw Belinda standing at the base, looking like a miniature replica of the statue. With long curly brown hair, ears with a perfect ninety-degree point, and a spotted tail dusted with auburn, Eldrid immediately gulped. Was he in over his head? He thumbed the magic amulet in his pocket. It steadied him.*

"You're late," Belinda said.

"I was finishing a replica of Cliffhanger's Cliff," Eldrid lied. Actually, he'd been taking his time in the mirror. As I'd come to find out, Cliffhanger's Cliff is a common attraction for daredevil grimkins, where they literally hang off a cliff before dropping into the crashing waves of the Grim Sea. Only for the bravest of grimkins, which is why Eldrid had only enjoyed Cliffhanger's Cliff from the safety of his small-scale replicas.

"I've always wanted to go," Belinda said, surprising Eldrid.

"You have?"

"Why not?"

Eldrid thought of all the reasons not to visit Cliffhanger's Cliff, chief among them the crashing waves and jagged rocks below. Eldrid shuddered at the thought, even though a small part of him, glowing faintly like the magic amulet, craved the danger associated with Cliffhanger's Cliff.

"I guess I don't know," Eldrid said, feeling the magic amulet pulse in his pocket, beckoning him toward adventure. Although in the moment, nothing seemed more exciting than getting to know Belinda.

After a walk around Crimpleton Common and a run-in with Mayor Frumple where he asked if they could count on them for a vote—"As if it even matters," Belinda had said, rolling her eyes—they ended up at Crimpleton Tavern, where Eldrid insisted on a table right by the fireplace, usually reserved for only the most prestigious guests. Until that day, Eldrid had only glimpsed the table from far away, but tonight it happened to be available. Eldrid sensed the magic amulet at work.

The fireplace was truly a grand example of grimkins' skill with a masonry trowel. It featured an arched lintel made of schrimick—similar to clay, but even better, Eldrid told me— below a center stone carved in the style of the first grimkins, hexagonal with a red and blue painted "C." A wooden mantle hung over the top, carved from one of the tree forefathers as a way to honor him. "Which part?" I asked Eldrid later, when he recounted the story to me soon after our adventure had begun, to which he replied, "The head."

They shared a roast hedgehog—bone in, Eldrid had insisted—greens, and a vegetable known in Grimwell as a pillypot. Similar to a potato but with a more bitter finish, pillypots are often cooked in butter and herbs—a grimkin specialty.

"And how about two cups of barley cream," Belinda said.

"My dear me," Eldrid said. He hadn't had a glass of barley cream since the day he learned of his parents' death.

Two glasses of barley cream eventually turned into two more, followed by yet another roast hedghehog and two shabberberry sundaes, both of which Eldrid ate himself. He didn't remember ever feeling so hungry. Or so comfortable in his own skin. By the time he took his last spoonful of the cold cream, they were cozily sitting by the fireplace, having a conversation that Eldrid described to me as the most intimate of his life. No secrets, everything laid bare. Surely the barley cream helped, but Eldrid assured me it was something more than that. As if the amulet had given him the confidence to simply be himself.

"Earlier, you seemed hesitant about visiting Cliffhanger's Cliff," Belinda said. "But your parents and grandparents are known far and wide for their courage and bravery. For taking risks."

Eldrid sipped his barley cream and lifted his eyes to meet Belinda's; suddenly, with the amulet glowing warm in his vest pocket, he realized he'd have no trouble hanging off the edge of Cliffhanger's Cliff.

"I guess I've always been afraid," Eldrid said.

"Of what?"

"Of what I don't know."

"But we don't know lots of things."

"Which is all the more reason to be afraid."

"But if you don't know what to be afraid of then maybe what you're really afraid of is what you don't know."

Eldrid chewed on that; he liked a good turn of phrase as much as the next grimkin, although trolls had left him with a bad taste in his mouth for riddles.

"It's like when my mom and dad returned to Crimpleton from studying in Grim City," Belinda continued. "They said they would never leave the village again. The comfort. The steady and ease. The boredom! They actually said that. They called it the most boring place in all of Grimwell. Just the way they liked it. And later... after... well, after everything..." Belinda grew quiet, and Eldrid got the feeling that she was hiding something, not so much a secret as a message concealed in a bottle, thrown into the ocean, waiting for the right person to open it. "When it came time for me to choose whether to study in the capital or stay in Crimpleton, I didn't really have a choice. Sad to say, but I don't think I've ever had a proper adventure."

The amulet burning in his pocket: "Maybe we're meant to take our next adventure together."

He took Belinda's hands. Her eyes fluttered. Face flushed. Was this how an adventure started? Bathed in the warmth from the fireplace, hands clasped, eyes locked. Suddenly the unknown didn't seem scary, but exciting, full of possibilities.

No sooner had he taken Belinda's hands, did he hear someone yell, "Rabble Babble!"

It was Filly, who had gone to grade school with Eldrid, before becoming a successful businessgrimkin and inventing a brand-new type of juniebee to keep grimkins comfortable, especially now that they spent long periods sitting. The era of Edelbee Gripplebunk was long over, and most grimkins spent their days inside playing games and building small-scale replicas. Similar to the way television has taken over our world, Dear Reader.

"No need to waste your time with Rabble Babble," Filly said, clearly more than a few glasses into his barley cream. "I'm back in town. What do you say we take a walk around Crimpleton Common?"

Belinda didn't bother to look up. "I'm fine, thank you very much."

"*Eldrid, why don't you go fetch us a couple of barley creams, we've got a lot to catch up on. I was just in the capital talking to investors. The Fillybee is going to be big, mark my words.*"

Eldrid suddenly couldn't find his voice.

"*What's that? Are you still working at Templeton's as a stock grimkin?*" *Filly laughed, now unsteady on his feet, his tail drunkenly curling back and forth.*

As I'd later learn, it's easy to spot a drunk grimkin from the motion of their tail, which often flops crazily after a few barley creams.

"*I'd appreciate it if you leave us be,*" *Eldrid said. Quietly, barely a whisper.*

"*What's that?*" *Filly said. "*You always were a mumbler. Or maybe a growler.*" *Filly began laughing even harder.*

The amulet burned white-hot in Eldrid's pocket, and before he could stop himself, he had stood up and taken Filly by the wrist.

"*I said,*" *a voice hissed, "*I'd appreciate it if you leave us be.*"

As to whether that voice was Eldrid or the amulet, I'll let you be the one to decide, Dear Reader.

With great difficulty, as if fighting with his own fingers to loosen their grip, Eldrid let go.

"*How dare you grab me, Rabble Babble.*"

Filly lunged, and even though Eldrid had never been in a fight, never dodged a punch, much less thrown a punch himself, he successfully ducked before landing Filly with a fist to the face. The hit sent Filly tumbling over the nearest table and crashing to the ground in a hail of empty glasses and barley cream.

The entire tavern went silent. All turned to stare at Eldrid, who before standing up to Filly, had blended in with his surroundings, as if cloaked in a perpetual camouflage. Now, his eyes glowed bright, flickering with the same crimson effulgence of the amulet.

"*I think we better get going,*" *Eldrid said, taking some coins out of his wallet and tossing them onto the table. "*After all, we're on a date.*"

Belinda smiled and took Eldrid's hand, both of them carefully stepping over the now crumpled Filly and his bruised face, which had already turned a nasty shade of purple.

* * *

Derek looked up from the book, transported from the land of Grimwell back to his studio apartment. He enjoyed the scene of revenge on Eldrid's childhood bully and the budding romance with Belinda. Glancing around his bare walls, Derek was struck by just how full the world of Grimwell seemed; almost as if the book was borrowing—more like stealing—the color and details of his own life to tell Eldrid's story.

Derek sensed the foreboding of the magic amulet, how it might shine a light on something deep and dark within Eldrid. At the same time, grimkins like Eldrid—and people like Derek, if he was being honest—needed a little bit more backbone, and finally standing up to Filly was the right thing to do. In both fiction and philosophy.

Still, the amulet must spell trouble for Eldrid, and Derek wondered how it would finally lead to the grimkin's undoing. How all this would help him when he met Kat for dinner tomorrow remained a mystery.

Chapter 9

On Friday, Derek trudged through the work day, feeling a little lighter. Standing up to Sam had put him in his place. Evened the scales between hero and villain. Sam hadn't looked at his GMAT book since his morning break and had even voluntarily gone on rag time. Derek was feeling more and more like the manager, the way things were before Larry had gone to Florida to open up his new shop.

Sure, it wasn't filming in Fiji or dating Achelia Rose, but then again, why did he have to compare himself to Tom? Was there really a better? His study of philosophy—he'd scoured that section of the library after a year working at the Bean, when existentialist questions had begun to plague him—taught him that it was difficult, damn near impossible to provide qualitative ratings to fundamentally different things

If you put all the accomplishments on a scale, who's to say his work in the coffee shop didn't have as much of an impact as Tom's work as an international TV star.

Society. That's who, thought Derek.

Later that night, he began to get ready for his date with Kat. He showered, shaved, gelled his hair back, mussed it up, then threw on a hat for just the right amount of hat head, before finally settling on a rough comb to hide his receding hairline. He dabbed on some aftershave, the good stuff Tom had sent him that was apparently irresistible, though Derek suspected Tom's luck with actresses and models had more to do with his fame and million-dollar bank account. Lacking Eldrid's fancy vest and gold-buckled shoes, Derek settled on a faded pair of jeans and his loudest collared shirt, the one crowded with small red flowers. A present from Janine. That would at least make a statement. He wondered if he should take the book, just like Eldrid had tucked the amulet in his vest pocket, but he decided that would make the delusion too real. Standing in front of the mirror, he briefly imagined Eldrid staring back, as if only a thin, vaporous portal separated his world from Grimwell.

Derek left his apartment and walked a few blocks to Que Sera where he and Kat had agreed to meet. Kat was sitting at the bar, long legs crossed, talking to one of the bartenders. Curly brown hair dangled to the small of her back, and something about the gestalt—which book did that word come from?—made him feel like he was in over his head. His hourly wage along with his below average future prospects didn't exactly scream eligible bachelor. Nor did his receding hairline. Hadn't he noticed at least a centimeter more of forehead when he looked in the mirror while getting ready? He was only guesstimating, but it might not be a bad idea to start measuring. Taken together with his doughy center, which made him feel more like a baked good than a man, *his* gestalt left a lot to be desired.

He drew in a deep breath and strode toward the bar, trying to muster his Eldrid Babble confidence.

"Derek!"

He realized too late that he hadn't prepared an opening line, so settled on the basic and not book-worthy, "Nice to see you."

"Nice to see you too. I was just catching up with Todd." Kat motioned to the bartender.

Derek reached across the bar and shook Todd's hand.

"We used to work together at McDowell's," Kat said.

"I recognize you," Todd said. "You'd always have a book. Even on wing night. How the hell you pulled that off, I have no clue. What were you reading?"

"Anything," Derek automatically replied.

"But now we have podcasts," Todd said.

Kat laughed.

"Podcasts are great and all, but nothing draws you in like a book."

"When they took the pictures out of books, they lost me."

"How about a drink?" Kat asked.

"How about some shots?" Todd said, grabbing a bottle featuring a skeleton engulfed in flames before either Derek or Kat had replied. Todd filled three shot glasses to the brim with the dark amber liquid.

Derek threw back a shot, feeling the sting of the alcohol in his throat. "Should we grab a table?" Derek asked.

Kat looked back and forth from Todd to Derek. "If it's okay with you, I figured we'd just eat at the bar."

Derek scanned the restaurant and saw an empty table right beside a glowing hearth. Almost an exact replica of the one in *Eldrid Babble*, as if Chester Felten had been here and painstakingly copied the details. It featured an arched lintel, wooden mantel (most likely made from an oak, rather than a talking tree), and—Derek almost gasped—a letter "Q" carved right in the center in red and blue. Just like Eldrid, that's where Derek had to be.

"Look at that fire," Derek said. "It looks so... warm."

"Are you cold?" Kat asked.

"A little."

"Do you want my jacket?" Todd asked. "It's in my car."

"No, it's just..." *It's just like the fireplace in this quasi-magical fantasy book I'm reading...*

"If the fire really means that much to you, Derek, I guess we can move over there."

"No, the bar's fine," Derek said, trying to sound casual. Relaxed. Cool. But it wasn't fine with Derek. It wasn't how it happened in *Eldrid Babble.* The less variables the better.

Todd brought over a couple of menus.

"You know, I don't think I've been on a date since Mac was born." Kat seemed to be doing the calculations in her head. "I probably shouldn't be telling you that, but it's true."

"I haven't been on a date since..." *I caught my fiancé cheating on me. In the laundry room of our apartment building.* "...Since a long time."

Todd returned with three more shot glasses.

"I'm a mother now," Kat said.

"You're a MILF," Todd said.

"Todd!" Kat said. "Inappropriate."

"Is MILF an offensive term now?" Todd asked. "The rules keep changing on me."

"How would you feel if I said that about your mom?"

"I'd be complimented," Todd said, filling the shot glasses.

Derek smiled. Already a passive participant on his date. Already disappearing off the page.

They threw back another shot. This one went right to Derek's head.

"You know, you look familiar," Todd said.

"Just one of those faces."

"I feel like I've seen you before."

"You have. At McDowell's."

"No, not there. Somewhere else."

A couple had just made their way to the bar, clearly trying to get Todd's attention.

Please go away, Derek thought. He only had enough confidence for a date. Not a throuple.

"Just give me a second," Todd said, walking away to take the couple's order. "Don't worry, I'll be right back."

"Where were we?" Kat asked.

"I think we were talking about our lackluster dating lives."

"Great first date conversation," Kat said, scanning the menu. "It's just that ever since I had Mac, everything in my life became about him. I haven't thought much about myself at all."

Derek had the opposite problem. He thought too much about himself. Even with the many lives he'd lived through fiction. The gardening tips and the inspirational acronyms discovered in the nonfiction section. Stories and ideas collected like old coins or stamps, impossible to know which one would end up being worth something.

He said so. "I'm so stuck in here"—he tapped his head— "sometimes I forget that the world out there is just as important."

"It's funny, I used to be like that. But I just haven't had the time. Either I'm at the restaurant taking orders or at home taking orders—from a toddler. If I didn't live with my mom, I don't know how I'd survive. Now that I'm thirty, I realize I haven't had an adventure..." Kat scrunched up her face, the same way she occasionally would when taking a customer's order at McDowell's. Thinking. "Well, I guess ever."

He heard a faint echo of *Eldrid Babble*. Hadn't Belinda talked about missed adventures? How had Eldrid responded?

"Maybe we're meant to take our next adventure together," Derek said, echoing Eldrid Babble.

Kat looked at him funny. "What are you talking about?"

"I was just—"

"I mean, it's our first date."

"It's a... joke," Derek said, trying to smooth over the moment.

"Oh," Kat said. "Ha ha."

Kat retreated to the menu and Derek followed suit, weighing the pros and cons of each meal: The trout might make him seem classy, but he hated fish. He wanted the burger but he didn't want to get bogged down in balancing bites and conversation. He spotted chicken. The perfect middle ground.

"Now I know where I recognize you," Todd said, returning and stumbling into his scene to take their order. He flashed his phone toward Derek, showing a still of Tom in a shot from *Another Planet*. "You look like the guy from *Another Planet*."

Kat looked from the phone to Derek. "I guess I see a small resemblance, but you're much better looking."

Derek was liking her more and more.

"Are there any specials tonight?" Kat asked.

Todd recited the list as if reading from a script, stumbling over the cooking-related jargon with the grace of a first-grader reading out loud. "Sage and Semi-Dried Po-lenta with a Cherry Cooo-lis," he finished proudly, drawing out the syllables.

Kat smiled. "Bravo. Sounds like the chef's been hitting the cookbook glossary hard."

"New guy," Todd said. "Won't shut up about the time he worked with a Michelin-starred chef. All technique, no heart."

"Are you still writing the specials on your hand?"

Todd nodded sheepishly. "So, what will it be?"

"Que sera, sera," Kat said.

Todd looked at her blankly.

"Forget it. I'll have the honey-glazed salmon with the potato galette."

"Chicken," Derek said, not wanting to try and pronounce "beurre blanc."

"And can we start with the po-lenta? Is that okay with you, Derek? "You're the expert."

"Be right back," Todd said, studying his notepad as if the ink might disappear.

"Take your time," Derek said.

"So why haven't you been on a date in over three years?" Kat asked, turning to him.

Derek drew in a deep breath. Caught off-guard. "Complicated story with the ex?" he said tentatively.

"I love a good story about an ex," Todd said, already back, surprisingly efficient with the computer.

Derek sipped his drink as Kat raised her eyebrows expectantly. "Classic story," Derek said. "Boy falls in love with girl. Girl cheats on boy. Boy wallows in a pit of self-despair before finding a way to climb out of it."

"She broke your heart, eh?"

"Yes, Todd."

Kat's leg brushed against Derek's, which Derek took as a good sign, at least according to a book he'd surreptitiously read in the library called *Dating and Mating in the 20th Century*. A little out of date, but not a bad primer, especially considering the paltry selection in the Self-Help/Love shelf. Of course, a vandal had scratched out "help," so the label simply read "Self-...Love." A cruel—but accurate—defacement describing Derek's three-year stint of celibacy.

"I don't have to worry about that," Todd said. "My heart is made of glass."

"Doesn't that mean it's easily breakable?" Kat asked.

"But once it's broken, it shatters. And that's it. Now I'm officially heartless."

"Good to know," Kat said.

Derek wondered how he should angle the situation. Todd had torpedoed his way into the scene and was now dangerously close to becoming the protagonist: the goofy but lovable bartender who finally gets the girl. Eldrid Babble didn't have to worry about competition over Belinda during his intimate dinner by the fireplace. Not until his altercation with Filly did he really encounter any obstacles. Derek remembered Eldrid had the amulet in his pocket. Maybe the book only exerted power if it was nearby?

The book does not have powers, Derek reminded himself.

"So, what's it like working at the Read and Bean?" Kat asked.

"I hate coffee," Todd said. "I don't think I could work as a barista. Taking advantage of all those people just needing their fix. You know, it's really an addiction."

"You're a bartender," Derek said.

"And?" Todd said.

"Nothing. It's just a temporary gig until I find something else."

"How long have you worked there?" Kat asked.

"Almost ten years," Derek said.

"What's stopping you from leaving?"

Derek saw his opening. His chance to echo Eldrid Babble. "I guess I've always been afraid."

"Of what?" Todd asked.

Derek glared at him, but decided to continue the scene anyway. "Of what I don't know."

"But we don't know lots of things," Todd continued, now truly blowing up the moment.

"Which is all the more reason to be afraid," Derek said, stubbornly adhering to the script.

He looked expectantly to Kat.

"Don't look at me," Kat said. "I don't have the answers."

The fire burned from the far corner of the room, the setting of Crimpleton Tavern come to life. In the table closest to the fire, a couple held hands and stared dreamily at one another, living out the page Derek had originally imagined for himself.

A man in a suit and tie walked in and sat a few seats away at the bar. "Damn," Todd said. "I wish these people could just help themselves, you know?"

"Then you wouldn't have a job," Kat pointed out.

"I don't get paid to make drinks," Todd said. "I'm paid to talk. What I'm doing right now is a service."

"Excuse me," the man said, who Derek imagined as an accountant stopping on his way home from work. *But when he unexpectedly stumbles upon a hidden company account, he's thrust into a web of secrecy, deceit, and lies.* Sometimes Derek didn't see people, so much as book jackets.

"Fine!" Todd said, making his way over to the customer.

While Todd got the man a drink, Derek saw an opportunity to finally take the date in the right direction.

"If you weren't working at McDowell's, what would you be doing?" Derek asked.

"You have to promise not to laugh."

"Okay."

"When I was younger, my dad bought me this play kitchen, and I'd spend hours just pretending to make dishes. When I got older, we'd cook dinner together. It was our thing. Of course, he died of a heart attack, because the world is cruel and ironic and predictable, but I love how food can be comforting."

"Then why aren't you working in the kitchen?"

"Because after a certain point, everything starts to feel like a hobby. It's almost embarrassing to say I'm not on a path yet."

"I know what you mean," Derek said. "Sometimes it feels like my life hasn't been filled in yet. The outline is there, but there's no color. Like I've barely decorated my apartment. And I've lived there for almost three years."

"No, I'm sure of it," Todd said, seemingly popping out of nowhere. "You're related to the guy from *Another Planet*." He turned his phone in Derek's direction. "You're Daryll, right?"

"Derek."

"Wikipedia says Daryll."

"I know my fucking name!"

Kat and Todd both looked taken aback. In the book, Eldrid had dealt with a pestering character by leveling him with a punch. The rules of distant fantasy lands probably didn't conform to the rules—and laws—of Earth, so Derek had little recourse but to back down.

"I'm sorry, it's just..."

"So, you are related to him?"

"Are you, Derek?"

"I guess I am. Brother of the famous TV star Tom Winnebaker. In the flesh."

And just like that, the scene seemed to speed up. Todd asked a few questions about Tom's costar, Achelia Rose, who he had a major crush on—just like most of America—and he mentioned a couple of taglines from the show, but that was it. As for Kat, she hadn't yet watched *Another Planet* and didn't seem familiar with Tom's work, which Derek took as his cue to tell her about Tom's streak of playing roles in the oral hygiene genre.

The polenta came out, along with a complimentary bruschetta from Todd. "Don't worry about it," Todd said after Derek and Kat had thanked him. "That's how I get my jollies."

"It's good," Derek said. "But I like the specials at McDowell's better."

Kat smiled.

"Some people volunteer to help sick kids or whatever. I like to give free food."

"Thanks, Todd," Kat said. But there was something in her tone: Was she shooing him away?

Derek settled in and felt more at ease than he had in a long time.

"I call this part of the date the Blitz," Kat said. "I ask you a question and you have to say the first thing that comes to mind." She took a potato off Derek's plate. Already sharing food.

"Got it."

"Favorite hobby?"

"Reading. That one was easy."

"Favorite food?"

"Cheeseburger."

"You know, they had a burger on the menu. Why'd you get the chicken?"

"I wanted to seem more refined."

"Place you most want to visit?"

"Disney World," Todd shouted, back from refilling a drink. "You know, Epcot has the entire world right there. I've been meaning to go, but it's hard as a single man in his late twenties." Todd looked down at the shiny lacquer bar. "I occasionally look at the app and map out my trip."

Derek found himself empathizing with Todd, the same way cracking open a book seemed to shine a light on detectives, scientists, aliens. A door into another world swinging open.

"You know, I only went once," Derek said, "but I'd love to go back sometime."

It was just before his mom got sick. Derek's dad hated amusement parks and would always find an excuse to steer the vacation somewhere else: the beach, the mountains, the lake. Vacations were about him and his need to relax. "No unnecessary noise," his father would say whenever they embarked on a trip.

But the trip to Disney was just the three of them. With the divorce finalized, his mother seemed lighter than ever before. Tom was moving to the city to make it as an actor, which meant he was going to get a job as a waiter and go on a lot of auditions. Derek was finishing up college and the world seemed bright with possibility. They rode roller coasters, went to character breakfasts, watched movies. As a vacation, it wasn't remarkable, but later, Derek would often revisit those moments, a disconnected chapter in his life protected from the tumultuous plot points of the next act. A perfect escape.

"You and me, Derek," Todd said confidently, "we're going on a trip to Disney World."

"What about me?" Kat asked. "I actually have a kid."

"Which is why you might slow us down," Todd said.

Derek laughed.

"Now who wants dessert?" Todd asked. "Not on the house, just to be clear. I only get one comped meal a night."

They stayed at the restaurant for another hour, the three of them talking and laughing, playing Kat's Blitz game, which yielded an interesting array of responses, including Todd's elbow fetish, the time he ate road kill, and his passion for llamas. "Looking at their pictures just makes me happy."

"Who are you?" Kat asked.

"Todd," Todd said, looking at her confused.

Derek left the restaurant and hugged Kat goodbye, not even bothering to try for a kiss. *Dating and Mating in the 20ᵗʰ Century* had insisted that kissing on a first date was tantamount to blasphemy. If *Eldrid Babble* wasn't going to steer him in the right direction, he had an entire library to consult.

He returned back to his apartment with enough time to watch the next episode of *Another Planet,* where Sergeant Wilks discovers the Troglodorfs aren't there to colonize Earth, but kidnap people to work on their home planet—hence the title. Hidden with the president in a remote bunker in the Rocky Mountains, Wilks and Misha make love for the first time—Derek fast-forwarded through that part—before Wilks realizes they're not alone. Literally.

INT. WILKS'S BUNKER - NIGHT

Wilks and Misha lay in bed, the sheets twisted and tangled.

                    WILKS
Why'd we wait so long to
do that?

                    MISHA
I don't know. Probably the
impending apocalypse.

                    WILKS
I guess that's a good reason.

Something slithers on Wilks's foot.

                    WILKS
You sure you want to go again,
babe? I don't know if I have
the stamina.

                    MISHA
What are you talking about?

Something rises in the shadows. At least
twice the size of a man with large beady
eyes that seem to glow red. The first
sighting of a Troglodorf.

                    DEREK
               (from couch)
Behind you, Tom!

                    87

The scene ended with Tom and the alien in a headlock, with Tom shouting,

                    WILKS
        You got slime on my slippers!

Derek turned the TV off. He loved a good cliffhanger ending. He imagined himself atop Cliffhanger's Cliff with Eldrid Babble, dangling high above the crashing waves of the Grim Sea. For the first time not afraid to let go.

Chapter 10

Derek woke up to a text from Kat:

Had fun last night. Looking forward to our trip to Disney World.

A reference to their date. And she had been the one to initiate. Take that, Universe.

After showering, Derek went down to the Pemberton Diner and set about reading the next chapter of *Eldrid Babble*, where he hoped at least some of the plot threads Chester Felten had introduced would begin to make sense. Who had given Eldrid the magic amulet? Why? Would it lead to the hero's ruin?

As he walked along the sidewalk, he couldn't help but feel relieved that his date had turned out differently than Eldrid's. He'd almost started to believe that real life actually followed a book. But he'd been the one to step inside Eldrid's life, the same way you'd step in footprints on a snowy path. Not an exact match, but close enough. Still, that constant conversation with the reader had been disconcerting, as if Derek wasn't reading the book, but the book was reading him.

Trying to capture his hopes, dreams, fears, and echo his thoughts in the plot. He had seen bits of himself in Eldrid and mistaken the grimkin's story as his own.

When he'd found *Eldrid Babble* in the supply closet, he'd been desperate. He'd been lost. But a piece of him had returned to the surface these past few days, buoyed by the grimkin's encounter with the glowing amulet. It wasn't magic that had shaken up his life, it was a return to reality, a readiness to write his own story by taking chances and making scenes. After reading thousands of books, from meet-cute bestsellers to tomes on medieval property law, he'd finally found his book, a story that seemed to run directly parallel to his own life, as if Eldrid was somehow living in an alternative dimension.

Breathing a sigh of relief as he sat down in a squeaky booth, he ordered an omelet, a cup of coffee, and continued reading about the strange journey of Eldrid Babble, and the book's narrator, Chester Felten.

* * *

By the time I met Eldrid, he was already well within the grip of the magic amulet and had gone too far to simply turn back.

That's when our stories intersected. You see, I was on the verge of my own crossroads, a path hewn from the artillery and bombs of war. And so, I happened to be hiking the forest on my lunch break, desperately searching for quiet, that sense of calm that had eluded me in France and Germany, only to grow even more fleeting when I returned home.

I had a usual loop I'd walk before returning to work, a way to clear my head before filling it with numbers and actuarial analysis, the family business. There was an old donkey watering hole, long ago defunct, that I'd sit beside, watching the still water ripple as I threw rocks and pebbles into its murky center. But for some reason, on that day, I decided to walk deeper into the forest. Deeper than I'd ever gone before.

None of my plans had panned out. I had just received my hundredth rejection and all I could do was keep on walking. By that point, I had given up trying to write my memoir about war, realizing it would be impossible to turn the frantic musings of Death's Diary into a story with a beginning, middle, and end, and had instead begun pitching Hero's Charge, *a novel that turned my service into a simple tale of heroism. A fictional glazing of the truth; I thought it might be what publishers wanted. Apparently, I was wrong.*

Feeling driftless, untethered from my dreams of literary stardom, I escaped into the woods. Past Devil's Rock with its foreboding drawing of two red eyes peering out of the stone, warning hikers to venture back to whence they came. (Rumored to have been a trick by the Pequot to prevent future settlers from walking farther into their territory.) Past Mirror Lake with its almost eerily placid waters reflecting a bright blue sky, as if the world could just as easily be flipped upside down. Past beech trees with eyes and mouths carved into their bark, no doubt a child's prank on some long-ago camping trip.

At least that's what I thought at the time.

After walking for what felt like hours, I saw a strange tree stump, its roots clawing out of the earth. It looked like it had been hastily chopped down, not with an axe or saw, but with a bolt of lightning. I remember staring at the jagged stump, thinking it looked somehow human, a wooden corpse.

I approached the tree stump hesitantly. Near the bottom, I saw a small opening where light seemed to pour through. It had to be an optical illusion, but still, there was something magical about the way the light billowed from below, as if powered by some unseen furnace, the molten core of the Earth churning below.

I knelt down and peered inside, only to discover it was even brighter. Strange, I thought, how a tree could appear to be glowing.

I crept below the tree trunk and continued crawling, following that celestial pool of light, until I came out on the other side. I found myself in a forest that looked almost identical to the one I had just left behind, but at the same time completely different. Let me explain.

After having lived in the town of Ashton for most of my life, I knew the forest like the back of my hand. Knew how to start my own fire, hunt and skin an animal, find my direction by simply looking at the stars—all skills that would come in handy during the war.

Now the topography was the same, but the trees grew higher. The leaves were bigger. And the sky had a cerulean radiance that I had never seen before, as if the sun burned brighter here.

I glanced up and scanned the forest, trying to gain my bearings and plan my route home. Then I heard a voice: "What brings you to Grimwell, Mr. Felten?"

I turned around, searching for the source of the voice, but was unable to locate it. The trees swayed, something almost plaintive about the way the leaves danced in the breeze. I reached for my knapsack to take a sip of water, when I noticed a branch extending toward me like a finger.

"Is it custom where you come from to ignore a question?" The branch tapped against my chest. Once. Twice. Three times.

Still, I found myself searching for the voice, convinced that the wind was playing tricks on me. When I turned around, I could've sworn one of the trees had moved closer and was now only inches away. As I studied the tree, I noticed large round eyes carved into its rough exterior and a mouth curled into a smile, the bark thicker to outline the lips, teeth like shingles on a house. As the smile grew, the bark seemed to ripple.

I assumed I must be dreaming. I pinched my arm, hoping to wake up. It wasn't my usual dream about the war: marching in the French countryside, green grassy hills littered with burnt tanks and blackened bodies. All true to life, except sometimes, in the terror of sleep, those dead soldiers would grab my leg and begin pulling me down to the underworld.

But this wasn't like one of my nightmares. This was fantasy.

The tree laughed, the bark sloughing off as the trunk shook and rumbled. An avalanche of noise.

"I regret to inform you that this is no dream, Mr. Felten," the tree said. "Pinching yourself will do no good. You've entered Grimwell. And I am Grandfather Tree, one of the citadels of the forest, Guardian of the Realm, and leader of the Council of Trees."

"Okay," I said uncertainly, fearing I was caught in a hallucination. Back in Europe, I saw more than a few soldiers slowly lose touch with reality, until they were seeing things that weren't there. Hearing voices that came from ghosts.

Now I could've turned around; I could've crawled back through the trunk into the small sliver of light below. Back to my world. Back to safety.

But as you probably suspect, that's not what happened. Instead of running away from my adventure, I ran toward it.

Just like you, Derek. You've decided to keep reading about Grimwell. You've decided to shake up your life with the tale of Eldrid Babble and the glowing red amulet.

And now it's too late to turn back.

* * *

Derek peered up from the pages, glancing around the diner.

He reread the last line, assuring himself that he had dreamed his name being there. It was simply his imagination acting up.

Just like you, Dear Reader.

He breathed a sigh of relief, but still, it didn't change the way the chapter ended. Ominous. Threatening. Foreboding.

Sweat prickled his forehead. It didn't make sense. Why would Chester Felten choose to write his book that way? Sentences sharpened to a point and aimed directly at the reader.

Derek could see where the book was headed. After having read hundreds of books in the library, he could practically write the book himself. No doubt Eldrid would become corrupted by the power gained from the magic amulet. There'd be a dramatic scene where

93

Eldrid throws the magic amulet away, preferably while standing on a mountain. And then of course, Eldrid and the fictionalized version of Chester Felten would team up to fight against the unnamed sorcerer, whose intentions and goals remained some shade of world domination.

That was that. Derek had enough of the world of Grimwell and the mysterious hobbit-esque creature who haunted its pages.

He sipped his coffee and slammed the book shut. Time to move on to his next read.

Just as he slid the book to the edge of the table, he felt a pain in his abdomen. He clutched the table with both hands and noticed his knuckles had grown hairier. Even stranger, his skin looked wrinkled, fingers gnarled, as if he'd spent a lifetime working with his hands.

He caught a glimpse of his reflection in the metallic napkin dispenser. The surface was smudged with grease and ketchup, but even so, he could tell he looked tired. Straggly was the word that came to mind.

The noises of the diner grew louder, and he swore he could hear every sound on speaker: Cups clinking. Coffee sloshing. Teeth grinding and chewing.

A discordant din that grated on Derek's ears.

He felt that pain again, moving down from his abdomen into his lower back. A crunching and grinding unlike anything he'd ever felt.

He held up his hand to the waitress, hoping to get the check. And that he'd have time to make it to the bathroom, because whatever was happening wasn't normal.

"Excuse me…"

The waitress nodded.

The pain grew stronger, a pressure needing to escape, rising along with the racket of the diner: his senses seemed to be blurring, sounds connected to sensation, the world gone electric. He heard the sound of glass shattering, and in that very same moment, felt a sharp pain at the base of his spine. He reached down and was surprised to discover

94

a small bump. A vibration shot up and down his back, nerve endings like little feet stitching together a path right to his brain. Suddenly, the small fold of skin wiggled against his fingers.

What the hell was happening?

The nub continued to grow, until it was pressing up against his pants, desperate to break free.

He laid out some cash, not bothering to ask for change, and rushed out of the diner. He sprinted up the stairs to his apartment, imagining his bones rearranging. That's how it felt. Like the entire Earth was moving inside of him. By the time he opened the door to his apartment—the book tucked snugly beneath his arm—he didn't remember snatching it off the table, and in that moment, he desperately wished to be free of it—he dropped trow and turned to crane his neck, just in time to see a tail creeping behind him, wagging excitedly, rising up to his shoulders before shooting back down on Derek's command.

He looked at the picture of Eldrid Babble on the cover of the book, his tail swinging behind him as he held the glowing red amulet.

Part II
The Tail

Chapter 11

Okay, so he had a tail. So what? Not exactly a medical emergency. More like a neat bar trick. Standing in front of the mirror, where the tip of the tail floated just over his shoulder, Derek took a deep breath. Now he was rationalizing, instead of prioritizing. He should be searching for doctors. Or maybe a veterinarian?

Unless of course this was just a delusional episode. He closed his eyes, hoping that when he opened them, he'd wake up in a cold sweat, relieved to be free of his new appendage, happy to once again be plain old Derek, not some sort of hybrid human-grimkin. Already nostalgic for his recent and unremarkable past. When he opened his eyes, though, he found himself still standing in front of the mirror, his tail swaying with abandon behind him.

As far as tails go, it wasn't remarkable, except for the fact that it happened to be attached to a human. In proportion to the rest of his body, it was a little longer than a cat's tail and covered in a light brown fur, the same color as his hair.

He clenched muscles he didn't have a few hours previously and the tail stopped moving. Tucked behind him like an obedient pet. That's better.

His phone rang just as he was experimenting with different tricks (he couldn't figure out what else to call them): swinging the tail from side to side, retrieving a bottle of water from his coffee table, and opening his closet door, the end of the tail curlicuing around the brass knob, struggling to take hold.

He fished his phone out of his pocket and saw *Tom* on the caller ID. Calling from Fiji where he was filming the second season of *Another Planet*. Derek accepted the call, hoping it might ground him back in reality.

"Hey."

"There you are," Tom said.

"Hi, Tom."

"Feels like we haven't talked in forever. How's my favorite big brother doing?"

You know, trouble with the boss, rent's due, I have a tail. "Great."

"You sound flustered."

"No, not at all, just distracted." Derek sat down on his couch, momentarily forgetting about the tail. He grimaced in pain. Readjusted so his tail had some breathing room.

"Were you, you know, jacking off?"

"No, I wasn't jacking off."

"Because if you were, it's completely normal. Especially if you're lonely."

"I'm not lonely."

"Even if you're not lonely..."

"I wasn't jacking off," Derek yelled.

"Okay, take it easy, man."

"Come back to bed, Tommy."

Derek recognized the voice. Tom's costar, Achelia Rose. It was jarring to hear the beautiful actress's silvery croon intrude in such a mundane conversation, as if his life had collided with a TV show. Here his brother was living a Hollywood fantasy while he had somehow entered a dark comedy about a man who wakes up with a tail. Some sort of twisted take on a Tolkien novel.

"Anyway, I'm calling to let you know that we've wrapped up filming and Achelia and I were talking about coming back to the States for, you know, Mom's anniversary. Maybe go out to a nice dinner and reminisce."

Derek remained silent.

"Don't worry, I'll pay for everything."

That made Derek even more annoyed. "I'm not poor," Derek said, even though the truth was, according to his latest bank statement, he was in fact poor. Not to mention, now he'd need to save money to pay for the tail surgery he'd inevitably need. No way insurance would cover that.

As if in protest at the thought, his tail curled angrily up in the air. "Relax," Derek whispered to his tail, which made him even more uneasy, as if his tail had become sentient.

"Look, man, I know things haven't been easy for you these past few years. I really don't know how you do it."

"Do what?"

"Go to work every day as a barista. Or is it bear-ista?"

Derek heard Achelia laugh. "I'm imagining a bear in a barista outfit," she said.

"Write that down," Tom said. "Let's pitch it to the studio."

Derek rolled his eyes. Somehow, even with a tail, even with a potentially cursed fantasy novel on his hands, his brother could somehow still become his primary source of angst.

"Anyway, when it comes down to it, you're the real hero. I just play one on TV."

"Come on, Tommy," Achelia Rose said, "I'm drawing a bath."

Derek felt a pang of jealousy at the thought of Achelia Rose undressing to take a bath. He remembered the intimacy he'd shared with Janine. He'd wished they'd taken more baths together.

101

"It sounds like you have your hands full."

"You have no idea."

Looking around his studio apartment, the walls still bare, the stock couple from the department store photo staring at him from his only picture frame, he had to agree with his brother. He could only imagine the life of a TV star dating a famous actress.

"If I come back next week you'll make some time for your little bro?"

"Absolutely."

"Love you, bro."

"You too," Derek mumbled.

Derek hung up. Got up off his couch and began pacing the apartment. The call had brought him back to reality. His life was complicated enough without adding a tail to the mix. He was not a grimkin from a mysterious land named Grimwell. He was Derek the Friendly Neighborhood Barista, as Sam liked to remind him.

And friendly neighborhood baristas didn't suddenly develop tails.

He reached his hand behind him to touch his back. Nothing but skin. So far so good. Slipped a little farther down. Still no tail. He could feel the phantom appendage, wagging in excitement or fear, he wasn't sure which. But that was only in his mind's eye. He was tricking himself. The many books he'd read at the library had taught him that the mind could conjure up anything, from distant fantasy lands to planets filled with little green men. His wires had gotten crossed, that was all, the world of Eldrid Babble accidentally intruding on his reality.

His hand crawled farther down his back.

Still no tail. He continued on, edging closer to his waist. Growing more and more relieved with each flat patch of skin.

Until finally, he stumbled upon the tail, now swinging wildly, as if reminding Derek that it was here to stay. Permanently.

He glanced at the copy of *The Strange Life and Times of Eldrid Babble* on his kitchen counter. The way the plastic jacket caught the light made it appear to be glowing, practically pulsating in the midmorning sun.

* * *

The rest of the weekend passed in a blur as Derek tried to convince himself that having a tail wasn't so bad. Meanwhile, he exhaustively searched the internet for information about tails, which only yielded results about people with vestigial bones in their body. Nothing about suddenly waking up with a fluffy, long, and—if Derek was being honest with himself—luxurious tail.

He did his best to ignore *Eldrid Babble*, as well as the impending notion that things would only get worse. Ever since the tail appeared, his life had started to feel less real—maybe even fictional.

On Monday, he went to work, wearing extra baggy pants to give his tail room to breathe during a long shift. In order to hide his new vestigial companion, he duct-taped it to the side of his leg, so as to prevent an accidental ripple in the fabric. At first it twitched angrily, straining against the duct tape, until Derek shushed it, and it quieted down.

For the first hour, he was afraid someone might notice something wiggling in the seat of his pants. When Sam asked him to retrieve some milk, he walked backwards just in case there was an accidental twitch or flutter. After the first few hours with no questions, Derek figured the tail was safely hidden.

Despite his newfound appendage, he still couldn't stop himself from placing *Eldrid Babble* in his bag. An almost existential hunger to be with the book. To live inside its pages. He wondered if his current debacle might somehow connect with Jackson Wilfred's mysterious exit from the library after thirty long years as the head librarian. Could it be that he too had seen himself in the pages of *Eldrid Babble*?

During a lull, he googled Jackson Wilfred on his phone but didn't find anything, at least anything recent. The image results showed what looked like a typical librarian, a thin reedy man who wore glasses and had an enthusiastic smile. After scrolling through a barrage of articles

103

about Wilfred's contributions to the town—"Librarian Wins State Grant"; "Librarian Petitions State Lawmakers for Funds"; "Librarian Spreads Love of Reading to Local Children and Parents"; "Librarian Saves Child From Drowning" (that one caught Derek off-guard)— he found one commenting on the search for a new librarian to fill Jackson Wilfred's post after he had taken a "sudden leave of absence."

When Boris and Gerald came in for a coffee, Derek asked them if they remembered Mr. Wilfred, but they didn't have any information, except for Boris to say he'd have his contacts look into it, and Gerald telling a long story about the time he tried lobster only to realize it was actually crawfish and the hilarity that had ensued as a result.

Not exactly helpful.

Dale, the current head librarian, who'd taken the library more in the direction of audiobooks and e-books, didn't have much to offer except to say that Jackson Wilfred was old school. And to remind Derek, as he did most mornings when he ordered his triple shot mocha latte, that he was a member of the new guard trying to bring libraries into the twenty-first century.

"By getting rid of books?" Derek asked, taking advantage of the midmorning lull.

"By redefining what a book is."

Derek's tail twitched angrily beneath his baggy pants. "Then why even have a library in the first place?"

"It's the twenty-first century public square. The only problem is we're still stocking it with twentieth-century artifacts."

"But isn't that part of the magic?" Derek asked. Even as he said it, he thought about *Eldrid Babble*, currently hidden away in his backpack. *Magic*. He felt a desperate pang to continue reading Eldrid's story but stifled the desire, or more accurately, buried it, only to have it emerge again and again, the proverbial hand reaching up from a grave.

He needed to know what happened to the unsung grimkin.

Or maybe *needed* wasn't the right word. It was as if the book *demanded* he find out how Eldrid's tale ended.

Could magic be so... insistent?

"In any case," Dale continued, "he used to be friends with an old science teacher. They would grab coffee together all the time. Even during the school day sometimes. I think his last name is Wise. You should probably start there."

"How would I go about finding him?"

"You could look up his email address on this new thing called the internet."

"Thanks," Derek said. "Your sarcasm is noted. And not appreciated."

"Anytime."

Taking Dale's advice, he sat down at a computer during his ten and looked up Wise in the Pemberton High School directory. After browsing the site for a few minutes, lost in the endless scroll of photos from his old alma mater, he clicked to the Biology Department and found Rich Wise's profile.

Rich Wise looked almost hobbit-like, staring at him from across the digital void, a pocket protector on his breast pocket like a badge. If this were a book, Derek knew he'd email the aging biology teacher and find clues connected to the disappearance of Jackson Wilfred. But in real life, answers didn't come so easily. Mostly, life was a plateau, and people wandered from one end to the other, aimless and dazed, until one day they fell off.

Derek made a note to keep away from the Existentialist section of the library. It was affecting his mood by simple proximity.

Without much hope of finding a lead, Derek sent him an email:

Dear Mr. Wise,

My name is Derek Winnebaker and I graduated from Pemberton High School in 2008. I was hoping to speak briefly with you about your friend Jackson Wilfred. Please let me know if you have any time to meet and discuss in the coming weeks.

Derek erased the last sentence. That was the old Derek. Weak and timid. Plus, the situation with the tail had become urgent. Instead, he added, *I'm going to be in the area and I was hoping to meet for lunch.*

That was more like it. Main characters chiseled their own plot points. He hit send.

Meanwhile, he continued texting with Kat throughout the day. Tail or no tail, he hadn't been out with a woman he liked since Janine, and he wanted to keep the momentum going. Such was the fundamental drive to connect. Or maybe procreate. Derek wasn't sure which, even though he knew which one sounded creepier and to never utter aloud. Besides, the tail might be permanent, in which case he would have to learn to live with it. And maybe someone could learn to love it. Not likely, but a grimkin—Derek shook his head—a person, could hope.

While he waited for a response to his last text message—*How are preparations going for wing night?*—he cracked open *Eldrid Babble*, hoping to find a clue about how to solve his current predicament.

* * *

There was a strange feeling in the air the morning after Eldrid's date with Belinda. He awoke with a start, grasping for the glowing red amulet. His source of power. Confidence. Ambition. He had grown to depend on the amulet over the past week, and only now did he notice that parts of Crimpleton had changed.

If the amulet had taught him one thing, it was that wanting more wasn't a character flaw, but the only way to live. He had grown complacent with his work, his life, his position as the grimkin with the famous parents and grandparents.

Now was his chance to take what was rightfully his.

He stared at the amulet, now shining even brighter than before. The color seemed to pulsate, scattering the air around it, a hazy red cloud that defied category—not quite solid, not quite steam, beautiful and dangerous all at the same time.

When evil finds a foothold in a village, it spreads like a virus. The best magic—and the most dangerous—is the subtle kind, not a magician's wand, but a sorcerer's staff.

Eldrid didn't know it at the time, but that chance encounter in the back alley of Crimpleton Tavern had introduced him to the oldest, most fearsome, kind of evil: A bright red stone forged in the blood of corrupted heroes. Without heroes, stories flounder. Life is much the same, because when it comes down to it, what is life but the collective stories of heroes and villains? As you probably know, Dear Reader, after reading so many tales yourself, a story can't survive without a hero. Especially an unsung hero who never got the chance to live out his adventure. In another world—another book, perhaps—Eldrid would have had to overcome his flaws and embark on a journey before finding his true worth. Unfortunately for the little village of Crimpleton, the amulet provided Eldrid with a detour around his adventure instead of through it.

Which is exactly what Lord Grittlebane hoped for when he scattered bits of the Hero's Stone all over Grimwell. As heroes waned, villains grew stronger.

That day, Crimpleton Common seemed empty. The purple magnolias that bloomed each year in front of Eldrid's hut seemed less vibrant. Worse, Eldrid's small-scale replicas now seemed painfully small. It was as if the glowing red amulet had muted his world, made everything appear dull and lackluster in comparison to the sheen of the mysterious stone...

Derek became aware of two distinct selves while reading the book. One, the discerning reader, dismissing Eldrid's tale as a story he'd read thousands of times before. Similar to Eve eating the forbidden fruit in the Garden of Eden, Eldrid had tasted power and, in the process, unleashed pain and suffering on the idyllic land of Grimwell: *Without the trials and tribulations that curve a character's arc,* the book continued, *the world has no choice but to bend. Warped and twisted.* Derek had rolled his eyes at the line. Playing around with the conventions of the hero's journey to build a mythology around the Hero's Stone. All those embattled protagonists who never reached their potential. Clearly, Chester Felten had drawn on his own life experience.

In the pages that followed, Eldrid realizes the risk the amulet poses to Crimpleton, including a memorable scene where Brittlebee the Baker pummels his brother, Brattlebee the Butcher: *Brattlebee's head cracked, a violent echo in an otherwise still day, and a small pool of blood formed beneath, spreading across the cobbled stones. Brattlebee quickly picked his head up and dusted himself off, more embarrassed than broken, before tackling Brittlebee and pummeling him in a sea of fists.*

As Derek predicted, Eldrid tries to get rid of the amulet—throwing it not from a mountain top, but a bridge, only to dive in after it. Crimpleton is soon taken over by Lord Grittlebane's henchmen and a new flag, an ominous stitching of two red eyes in a sea of black, is raised over Crimpleton Common.

A clear—and cliché—sign Act Two had begun.

And so, as Eldrid escaped to the Trembling Forest—as a result of cowardice or bravery, Chester Felten wasn't quite clear—part of Derek knew he was reading hackneyed drivel.

The other part of him—the part with the tail, Derek supposed—relished the tale as if reading his own biography.

Chapter 12

A little while later, Derek received an email from Rich Wise, saying he'd be happy to meet about his old friend over his lunch hour, and so Derek told Sam he'd need some extra time for his break.

"But Sue can't come in today," Sam said. "Something about a walrus." He sprayed the pastry case and wiped it down, the rag squeaking on the glass.

Derek shot him a sharp look. "And?"

Sam opened his mouth to speak, then apparently thought better of it. "Nothing."

"By the way," Derek said, "I noticed some of the inventory needs restocking. I was hoping you'd be able to take care of that before your lunch today."

"But I still have to clean the bathroom, mop the floors, and place the order..."

"Might want to make it a working lunch then, huh?"

Derek knew he was relishing his power too much, showing the same level of enjoyment as Eldrid in the scene with Mr. Templeton, but he didn't have time to worry about that. One problem at a time.

"Yes, Sir," Sam said, trying to sound sarcastic, while still hurrying to the back room to begin stocking shelves. Derek was amazed at how quickly characters could change. Watching Sam's frenetic buzzing around the shop, Derek almost felt bad for him. Almost.

Derek walked a little way down the avenue, passing shops, restaurants, and Jerry's Party Supplies—somehow still in business, despite Derek never having seen a customer there—before arriving at an imposing brick building with tall Greek columns and gargoyles at the top. Whoever designed the building clearly was making an argument; though as a high schooler, Derek couldn't figure out whether that argument was to stay away or to come in.

Derek had often glimpsed the neoclassical building in the distance on his walk to work, the flagpole shining like a needle-point in the predawn light, but he hadn't stepped foot on school grounds since graduation. Derek remembered the day well. His parents were still together—meaning they still slept under the same roof—while Tom had found theater and become something of a local celebrity for his rendition of King Lear in the school play. Derek, on the other hand, had met his graduation milestone as undistinguished as possible: middle-of-the-road grades, no extracurriculars or sports, and a conditional acceptance to a small liberal arts college with a hefty price tag. After the ceremony, his family went out to dinner at the old McDowell's—before his father abruptly stormed off after a fight.

His father was in the middle of telling a story that Derek had heard many times before, all about how he and a few friends had skipped their own graduation—"Even though I was the valedictorian for Chrissake!"—to drive cross-country and visit Yosemite, a place he called the Last Great Unknown.

"So we're in the car when I realize... I forgot my suitcase!"

"We know, honey," Derek's mother had said.

"I'm going to be camping for an entire month with only one outfit. So I tell Frankie to—"

Derek's mother turned to face her son: "So what are you most excited about for college, Derek?"

"Can I finish?" he'd said, glaring across the table.

"I was just—"

"You always interrupt me."

"Let's not do this now."

"Let's not do this now," his father imitated.

Derek and Tom exchanged glances. Derek had long chosen his mother's side in his parents' daily spats, while Tom seemed to be still unsure of his allegiance.

"I'm sorry. Finish your story."

"I don't want to finish my story now."

"Today's a day for celebration," his mother said, gently placing her hand on Derek's arm. "We're so proud of you."

"Practically everyone graduates from high school now," his father said, still stewing.

"Kevin."

"What? It's true. And if Derek wants to make it—if he wants to make anything—he better realize that now. At least Tom puts himself out there with his acting. Sure, it's not a career, but it's something. Derek just goes through the motions."

Derek looked down at his empty plate. It wasn't that he didn't agree with his father. He *had* just been going through the motions, half-heartedly following a script handed to him from his parents and guidance counselors. Unfortunately, he'd never learned how to break character.

"That's no way to talk to your son," his mother said.

"Don't tell me how to talk to my son."

Derek saw a deep rage stir in his father as his eyes narrowed. A storm creeping at the edge of the horizon. No way to know which way it would blow.

"Let's just order," his mother said.

Derek and Tom remained still, carefully watching the radar on their father's face.

"Now I'm the bad guy, right?" his father said. He hit his fist against the table. Heads turned. Derek's classmates were gathered around, each table in the midst of their own graduation celebration. "Isn't that how it always ends up?"

"You're the bad guy because you're acting like an asshole."

Derek had never heard his mother come right out and say it. Always a delicate dance, stepping around the cracks and crevices of the relationship, until tonight she'd finally fallen through. It was almost a relief.

Derek's dad stood up, the table shaking with the force of his knees. He threw his credit card on the table and disappeared. He didn't come home for three days.

* * *

After signing in at the front of the school, Derek hurried down the hallway to the science wing. The school hadn't changed much since Derek graduated. The tile remained the same linoleum, designed with a pattern that looked like spilled coffee. The bulletin boards had been updated to include recent accomplishments, but many of the pictures remained the same, including one of Tom's portrayal of King Lear in the "Recent Happenings and Goings-On" section. Derek could've sworn one of the empty bulletin boards, clad with bright blue poster paper, had been the same when he was a student, a perpetual blank space the school couldn't figure out how to fill in. The lockers were the same metallic scarlet, and Derek remembered, without any hint of nostalgia, carting his textbooks from one side of the school to the other because he could never quite get his locker combination to work. His past felt distant, the type of unremarkable backstory he might read about in a book. Derek gulped, realizing that unremarkable backstories usually turned into unremarkable novels—and lives.

Rich Wise had a large cavernous classroom in the basement, almost like a cave, replete with a taxidermy groundhog, poster featuring Bill Nye from the early nineties, and of course, the obligatory skeleton wearing sunglasses. To Derek, he didn't look all that different from a skeleton himself. With yawning cheeks that seemed to wax into a hollow, and eyes that sank into his head like deep and unexpected puddles, Rich Wise was another era of teacher. Although Derek had never been in his class, he remembered him as old—and old school—even when he attended high school almost fifteen years ago. The type of teacher who still wore a pocket protector filled with markers for the projector. The type of teacher who still used a projector. Rich Wise was a dying breed who seemed to be minutes away from retirement. Maybe even death.

Mr. Wise sat behind his large desk eating lunch, which smelled strongly of tuna fish. Derek strode past the desks lined up in neat rows and sat down at the one nearest Mr. Wise's, lowering himself carefully to avoid accidentally sitting on his tail—a lesson he'd learned the hard way. Derek found his eyes drawn toward the skeleton and its lower spine, trying to imagine how his bones had rearranged to accommodate his new body part, before Mr. Wise brought him out of his trance.

"I call her Darla."

"What?"

"The skeleton. It's for my Human Biology class. I call her Darla."

"Oh."

He peered up from his tuna sandwich and scarfed a bite. He chewed loudly with his mouth open, and Derek couldn't help but wonder about the lines that separated flesh and bone, life and death, reality and fiction. Maybe they weren't as fixed as Derek had once thought.

"So," Derek said, still with his eyes on Darla. "I was hoping you could answer a few questions for me about Jackson Wilfred."

"No one's talked about my old pal for years." He spoke in a gruff voice, a low rumble that made Derek imagine a train skidding into a station. Mr. Wise bit into his sandwich, smacking his lips together as he chewed. "You know, I've been having the same lunch for the past forty years. A tuna sandwich with apple slices. Isn't that right, Darla?" He patted the skeleton on the tail bone—which for some reason made Derek's tail curl in his pants, straining against the duct tape. "It was better when Mrs. Wise used to make it... She would cut the crusts off, peel the apples, even sometimes leave me little notes in the lunch box."

"Did she pass away?"

"Hell no. Ran off with her tennis instructor."

The proverbial tennis instructor. The proverbial run off. Derek wondered if every relationship was so fragile, at the precipice of a chance encounter with a particularly charming tennis instructor or young and upcoming attorney.

"Jackson Wilfred," Mr. Wise said, once again grabbing hold of his sandwich and choking back another bite. "From another era of my life. Back when things were still good in this school. Hell, I was Teacher of the Year when he disappeared. Before all this...technology." He motioned to the computer angrily. "Isn't that right, Darla?"

Derek glanced at Darla as if she might reply, already drawn into Mr. Wise's illusion.

"What happened to him?"

"Had a nervous breakdown. Couldn't take the pressure."

"Of what?" Derek asked.

"The accolades. It was the same year he saved a kid from drowning in Crystal Lake."

Derek remembered seeing the headlines on the internet.

"It's funny," Mr. Wise continued. "We were friends most of our lives. I always thought he had it all figured out. Your classic overachiever. He was the director of the library, National Librarian of the Year, saved a kid from drowning, for god's sake. He was on a roll. But I think it was all just a little too much for him. He stopped taking my calls. Stopped meeting me for lunch. Stopped going into work. You know, everyone says they want to be top dog, but what they really want is comfort. Complacency. The same reason I've been teaching for forty years. It's comfortable. Anyway, one day he calls me and says he's down in Florida on break. Get some R and R and all that. I thought he'd be there for a few weeks but that was over ten years ago. I still get a call from him once in a while."

"You mean he's still alive?"

"Unless he's calling from the other side." Mr. Wise glanced at the clock. "We've got about five minutes until the kids come. I'm doing a lesson on photosynthesis."

"Interesting."

"It was. The first twenty years I taught it."

"What does he call about?"

"Asks me questions about his wife. Makes sure everything's okay with his boy."

"Why would he need you to check on his son?"

"That's the million-dollar question, now isn't it?"

Mr. Wise folded up the saran wrap, along with the remaining scraps of his tuna sandwich, and shot the empty wrapper into the garbage can. Slowly and sloth-like, each movement calculated and measured, he propped himself up. Holding onto Darla for support, he reached for the marker at the edge of the whiteboard.

"They wouldn't let me keep my chalk board," he said sadly, before turning around and writing on the board: PHOTOSYNTHESIS.

"Was it something to do with Mrs. Wilfred?" Derek asked. He stood up, afraid that he might get stuck in a lesson about photosynthesis with Mr. Wise as his guide.

"There was some big falling out and all I know is that Mrs. Wilfred didn't want him in their lives anymore. She made that abundantly clear."

"There was a fight?"

"Not so much a fight, more like a blowout. The details are thin, but it never made sense to me. My ex-wife and I, we were like cats and dogs. I guess that's what drew us together in the first place. We could scrap with the best of them. But Jackson and Cynthia? They were high school sweethearts. Best friends. Whatever it was that broke them up, it must've been bad. Like screwing your tennis instructor bad. Right, Darla?"

"And then he left?"

Mr. Wise nodded. "Drove down to Florida and called me the next day. I helped him get his affairs in order. Got him a lawyer for the divorce. But his time in Connecticut was done. Fin. Finito."

"Did he say anything about a book called *The Strange Life and Times of Eldrid Babble*?"

"Not that I recall."

"You never tried to visit?"

"Oh, I tried all right. Even flew down there once. He wouldn't see me."

"Do you have any way to reach him?"

"Sure, I do. But would Jackson want me to give it to you? No."

"Please." Derek heard the pleading in his voice. The desperation.

Mr. Wise ran his tongue over his teeth, making a loud, squeaking noise. "You know, I still think about her. Isn't that right, Darla?"

"Who?"

"My ex-wife. Darla. After all these years. I still sometimes wake up, roll over, and expect to find her there. There's basic science. Biology. Anatomy." He motioned to the board. "Photosynthesis. But then there's something else."

"You mean like magic?"

Mr. Wise scowled. "Hell no. I mean..." He glanced at Darla, momentarily studying the bespectacled skeleton as if she might have the answers. "There's basic science and then there's *complicated* science. And most of us are too dumb to understand it. Myself included."

Derek couldn't help but agree. He understood the complicated nature of heartbreak. A break implied two pieces that could someday be put back together, however tenuously. But the reality was more like something shattering, just like Todd had described: thousands of tiny pieces scattered without any hope of ever being found yet alone repaired. That's how it felt when he caught Janine in the laundry room with Evan. Now that he had a second chance with Kat, he wondered if he could understand the complicated science currently messing with his life. In the form of his tail.

"Now I take it you've got a reason for trying to track down my old pal, and I've got a feeling your reason has got something to do with why he left all those years ago."

Derek remained looking straight ahead at *PHOTOSYNTHESIS* scrawled across the white board.

"You can nod, or you can keep looking at the board, it's all the same to me. The student that sits in that desk in my next block—girl by the name of Rebecca—has got that same look most days. I call it the 'Biology Blues.' But if I'm going to give you his email address, I'd like to get something in return."

Derek nodded.

"If you do manage to find what you're looking for, I just want you to share the same courtesy—and curiosity—with me."

"I can manage that," Derek said.

Mr. Wise snatched a Post-it off his desk and scribbled something down. "His email," he said, handing it to Derek. "I don't know what you already know, but I want to know what you find out. Is that clear? Not to mention, a little connection to his hometown might do him some good."

"Thanks," Derek said. "You've been very helpful."

"Haven't heard that in a while. You know, as a teacher, people constantly make demands on you. Kids, administrators, parents.

And you start thinking you're only useful if you can teach things. If people listen to you. If people *need* you. I don't know if that's a healthy way to live, but it's the only way I know how. But at a certain point, people just stop listening to you. No matter who you are or what you do. They just stop listening." He looked out into the rows of empty desks, his stadium, his coliseum. "Sure, you keep talking, but do they really hear you? I don't know anymore."

Derek knew what he meant. He hadn't felt listened to in a long time. More like talked at. Not until he'd taken a stand against Sam had he felt his voice come back. *The Strange Life and Times of Eldrid Babble* had given him that. Along with his tail.

But luckily, Derek now had a lead. And an email address. Someone else who knew about the strange tale of Eldrid Babble.

* * *

He spent the rest of his lunch break—and, if he was being honest, part of Sam's lunch break, too—composing an email to Jackson Wilfred. He couldn't come right out and ask about the tail; after all, that would put his worst fears into writing, and potentially, end up read at a court hearing to have him committed. Instead, he tread lightly, delicately inquiring about the book.

Dear Mr. Wilfred,
I work at the Read and Bean in the Pemberton Library. It's come to my attention that you're familiar with the tale of Eldrid Babble by Chester Felten. I picked it up during a break and was immediately pulled into the young grimkin's story. I'm trying to figure out a few things about the book and was hoping you could help me. Please write me back as soon as possible.
Sincerely,
Derek Winnebaker

He sent the email and then remained staring at his inbox, eagerly awaiting a reply. Meanwhile, Kat had responded to Derek's last text about wing night: *I've made sauce using ghost peppers. Do you dare try it?*

He had to keep a hold on reality. Especially the good parts.

I'm feeling bold, he wrote back.

Chapter 13

Derek got back to his apartment a little past six o'clock. He immediately pulled down his pants and ripped the duct tape off his leg. His tail shook and stretched before resting comfortably behind him. The relief was instant; there was something almost cruel about keeping his tail tied up all day. Something unnatural about hiding such a glorious appendage.

Dressed only in his boxers, into which he had ripped a strategically placed hole to allow his tail to breathe and move freely, Derek paced the kitchen. *The Strange Life and Times of Eldrid Babble* lay on the counter, taunting him to continue reading.

He began breathing heavier and heavier, until he was practically hyperventilating. The shock had worn off, and now he was confronted with the startling reality that he would have to live life with a tail. It was just his luck to develop a malady that he couldn't even post about on Facebook. Not to mention, it wasn't exactly life threatening—if anything, it was an evolutionary advantage.

But still. It was a tail. And he was a human. And humans weren't supposed to have tails.

He picked the book up from the counter, once again looking for clues to his current predicament. Studying the front cover, he could now see the similarities between himself and Eldrid. The mottled hands. The tail curling behind him in a letter S. The straggly hair. There was no denying it now. He was becoming the hapless grimkin who had unknowingly unleashed the magic of Lord Grittlebane on the entire world of Grimwell.

He thought about throwing the book away, but his fingers trembled at the thought of never learning what happened to Eldrid.

Feeling stuck, afraid to consult the book that seemed to be ensnaring him in fiction, he lay face down on his futon and threw on the next episode of *Another Planet*. If he wasn't going to find answers, at least he could be distracted. The dramatic opening music began, timpani thundering through the speakers, before fading into a wide-angle shot of Wilks and Misha on a deserted road passing a sign that said *Welcome to Washington, D.C.: Our Nation's Capital.*

EXT. WASHINGTON, D.C.– NIGHT

Wilks and Misha stare at the rubble of
the White House.

                    WILKS
        There's nothing left.

                    MISHA
        We're still here. And how many
        others are hiding out?

                    WILKS
      And how many have they
      already taken back to their
      home planet?

Misha kicks a pile of rubble only
to reveal a human hand. She backs
away, afraid.

                    WILKS
      Still think the Troglodorfs can
      be reasoned with?

Misha shakes her head. Wilks looks around
at the darkened landscape. A single light
blinks in the distance.

                    WILKS
      Wait a second. I just realized
      something. What was the first
      thing the aliens did?

                    MISHA
      Cut the power. Why?

                    WILKS
      Think about it. We take elec-
      tricity for granted, but the
      only way we can harness it is
      through electromagnetism.

                    122

MISHA
Maxwell's Equation. I've taken
freshman science.

DEREK
(from couch)
Tom knows about electromag-
netism? Not a chance.

Derek flipped the TV off. Tom rattling off scientific theory was too much for Derek to believe in the moment. His newfound tail had already stretched his ability to suspend disbelief.

Derek scrambled off the couch, his tail helping him keep balance as he slipped on the rug, and began to get ready. Instead of moping around his apartment, he might as well head to McDowell's. His version of an adventure. First, he taped his tail to his leg, remembering to add two layers to keep it pinned down. The tail protested, darting away from Derek's hands, until he was able to catch it and wrestle it to his outer thigh.

"You know the drill," Derek said in the same tone you'd use on a misbehaving dog or cat.

Next, he threw on a collared shirt and a pair of sweatpants—business on top, gym class on the bottom—and went to the bathroom to splash some water on his face.

He stared at himself in the mirror, cataloguing each of the changes that had accompanied his tail. His hair had grown thin and stringy, his hands were mottled and hairy, and a few of his fingers now curved in unnatural directions. Even though he had shaved that morning, he noticed a thick layer of fuzz sprouting on his cheeks, as if he had specifically carved out eighteenth-century muttonchops. In an attempt to look presentable for Kat, he shaved, found a hat from his closet with the Pemberton Library logo, and put on a pair of leather

123

gloves his brother had sent him last year as a Christmas present. He packed the book in his jacket pocket just for safekeeping and walked downstairs to the bar.

McDowell's was packed. Derek found his usual seat at the bar, right between Boris and Gerald. He struggled to find a comfortable position on the stool, adjusting so his tail had room to breathe, although it strained against the tape, struggling to break free. He made a mental note to buy some baby powder.

"You look a little green," Boris said, sloshing around his whiskey. "Julius, get this man a beer."

"I'm busy," Julius barked.

"But you're the bartender," Boris said. "Aren't you bound by a code?"

"On wing night, it's every man for himself," Julius said, before retrieving a long line of tickets from the printer.

"Are we allowed to ask about the date?" Gerald asked.

"Young love," Boris said, sounding almost wistful.

"It was just a date," Derek said.

"I hate young love," Boris finished. "Stupid. Wasteful. Immature."

"Is there a second date planned?" Gerald asked.

"I guess. Right now."

"Never visit a woman at work," Boris said.

Gerald lowered his head to peek at Derek beneath the brim of his hat. "I like the new look. Going for that rugged vibe I keep hearing about on the dating blogs."

Boris seemed taken aback, as if Gerald had just admitted to cheating on him. "You're dating?"

"Just putting my toe in the water, that's all," Gerald said guiltily. "My sister-in-law has got a little chippy who wants to meet me. I'm thinking she's too young for me, but then again, beggars can't be choosers."

"How old?"

"Seventy-three."

Kat waved to Derek from the crowd and he waved back. Surrounded by a sea of sloshing beer and cheap metal buckets stuffed with buffalo wings, she shrugged shyly. It was enough to make him momentarily forget about his tail. After all, if he figured out a way to stop the process now, she would never have to know about it: he could hide it with artfully placed underwear for the rest of their lives.

A thought which the tail apparently didn't like, as it thumped against the bar stool, still yearning to swing freely.

"Cool it," Derek said.

Julius returned. "Going incognito?" he asked, motioning to Derek's hat.

Derek nodded.

"Wouldn't want people mistaking you for your brother," Julius said, practically snorting.

"Kat told you?"

Julius nodded. Now laughing even harder.

"You can be a real asshole, Julius," Derek said sharply. The words had left his mouth before he'd had a chance to evaluate whether insulting Julius, who could probably bench press two Dereks, was a good idea.

Julius's eyes widened. He leaned across the bar until he was only a few inches from Derek's face. Derek could've sworn he saw his pectoral muscles ripple beneath his shirt. A challenge.

Derek held his gaze.

"Don't forget," Julius said. "I control the alcohol supply."

"Take it easy, you two," Boris said.

"I haven't been in a bar brawl since '74," Gerald said.

"Who won?" Boris asked.

"It depends on your definition of 'won'. Also, the meaning of the word 'in.'"

"Are you going to let your grandpas fight your battles for you?" Julius asked.

125

"They're not my grandpas," Derek said, trying to make it sound threatening, also realizing it was probably one of the least cool lines in the history of bar fights. "I'll take that beer," Derek added, still looking Julius directly in the eye. "And a bucket of wings."

Julius backed away. "Mild, medium, or shit-your-pants-hot?"

Derek squinted, attempting to burn a hole through Julius with his stare. Smoldering. That's the type of stare he was going for. "Shit-your-pants," he said fiercely. "Or my pants. Shit *my* pants."

"You got it, buddy."

Derek's phone vibrated in his pocket. It was a text from his dad: *Close to the anniversary. Can we talk?*

"No thanks, Dad," Derek said, placing the phone face down on the bar.

"Trouble with your father?" Boris asked.

"You could say that."

"Blood runs thick," Boris said.

"Not anymore."

"No, literally. It's a very disturbing sight to see." He winked at Derek.

"That's the one thing I always regretted," Gerald said. "Not having a better relationship with my father." He looked off in the distance as if browsing a catalogue of his life's regrets. "And not going on tour with that nice group of Englishmen in the 1960s. And not buying that stock when I gave a ride to that surly man in the turtleneck and glasses. And not eating more meatloaf."

"In that order?" Boris asked.

Julius slid a beer toward Derek. "On the house."

That was more like it. Maybe his fear had been the problem all along. Always being afraid to take action had confined him to a world of background noise, a passive set piece in other people's lives: Derek the Friendly Neighborhood Barista.

It was time he started acting like a hero.

Derek's eyes fluttered past the dart board and he almost jumped out of his stool. Janine stood there, holding a dart, poised in mid-shot.

Not the Janine he stalked on Facebook, but the real Janine. Her pregnant belly strained against the fabric of a long flowing dress, too elegant for wing night at McDowell's. She had that look of carefree nonchalance worn by people who've undertaken a journey with no forks or splinters in their path: a direct line right to the horizon. Tanned and glowing, she had an undeniable effervescence.

To her left stood Evan, the man Derek had caught her cheating on him with.

Evan wore wingtip shoes that sharpened to a narrow point, what could only be described as elf-like, which Derek knew was rich coming from a future grimkin. Everything about him seemed severe. His angular glasses pushed up against his eyes, his aquiline nose, and his pursed and puckered lips, almost as if he were sucking a sour candy.

Derek hid his face. The last thing he wanted right now was a run-in with Janine. He felt something vibrate in his jacket pocket, but that was strange, because his cellphone was still face down on the bar. Still, he could've sworn he felt a buzz. And wasn't his jacket growing warmer by the second? He unconsciously reached for the book, realizing it had grown hot to the touch. By the time he looked up, Janine and Evan were walking toward him.

Derek lowered the brim of his hat and placed his hands on his knees just as Julius brought over his bucket of wings.

"Derek," Janine said. "Great to see you. You remember Evan, don't you?"

Derek swiveled on his stool, leaving the comfort of the bar for the chaos of the dining room: only one-hundred-and-eighty degrees away, but Derek could've sworn he felt a dramatic shift in tone and mood. The lights were lower. The rumble of voices louder. The smell of barbeque sauce stronger.

Evan extended his hand. Derek looked down at his own hands, concealed in leather gloves, hiding his mottled skin beneath.

"What's with the gloves?" Janine asked.

Derek folded his hands under his arms. "It's a long story," was all he could muster. And that much was true.

"How are you going to eat those?" Evan asked, pointing to the wings.

"With a fork and knife," Derek said, as if the answer was obvious. Even though he knew he shouldn't say anything else, he was now a hero, and heroes didn't take slights. "Got a problem with that?"

Boris cleared his throat and looked over his shoulder: his signature half-turn. "Are you going to introduce us?"

"No," Derek said, his tone sharp and cutting.

"Oh," Boris said, his eyes widening, wrinkles on his face creasing, almost as if he were disappearing into himself: "It's *her*." The way he said "her," you would've thought he was talking about an evil sorcerer in Grimwell.

A moment of awkward silence followed as Janine looked from Boris to Derek. The book seemed to pulsate in Derek's jacket pocket, and his tail fluttered, straining to break free of the duct tape. "This is Janine," Derek said. "And her friend Evan."

"Husband," Janine said.

"Husband," Derek said through gritted teeth.

By now, Gerald had glanced over his shoulder. He shot Derek a look, eyebrows slightly raised, mouth askew, revealing the ruins of a smile. "We're Derek's friends," Gerald said.

"More like a long-lost son," Boris said.

"And we know all about you," Gerald said, now staring directly at Janine. Over countless beers, wing nights, chili nights, and a smorgasbord of Kat's specials that pushed his palette to the limit, Derek had left no stone unturned in his stories about Janine. Reliving the saga over and over again, Derek had told them about the laundry room, the breakup, and the death of his mother, which cast the entire sordid tale in a cloak of grief, as if a romance had accidentally gotten mixed up with a drama. But that was life: completely genreless.

"Maybe not son," Boris said, "but a nephew."

"I'm actually glad we ran into you," Janine said, lowering her voice, as if attempting to shield it from the ears of Boris and Gerald. Which was a distinct possibility considering their hearing loss and Boris's refusal to wear a hearing aid.

"You are?" Derek couldn't keep the surprise out of his voice.

Janine rubbed her belly and offered a sad smile. "When everything happened, I think we both got so caught up in the moving on part that we forgot to remember what we were moving on from."

Evan shuffled back and forth uncomfortably, hands in his pockets, and Derek could see a look of irritation on his face.

"You were such an important part of my life," Janine continued. *Were.*

"And little Phillip's given me perspective."

"Phillip?"

"We're having a boy," Evan beamed.

The book thumped in his pocket, a phantom heartbeat. Derek was sure that if he took the book out it would glow with the same mysterious effulgence of the magic amulet. Guiding him. Urging him on. Toward what, Derek didn't know, and he felt that same sense of suspense when preparing to turn the page of a book.

"Are you feeling okay?" Janine asked as Derek stared off into the distance at Kat taking an order. She was gesturing wildly with her hands, as if engaged in a game of charades. He smiled, remembering the scene when Belinda takes Eldrid's order at Crimpleton Tavern. Didn't Chester Felten describe it not as butterflies, but dragons flying around Eldrid's stomach?

"No," Derek said, returning his attention to Janine.

"You're not okay?"

Just then, someone crashed into Evan, and he toppled into Janine as his drink went flying. Janine shielded her belly, and just as it looked like she would fall, Derek sprang off his stool and extended his arms to catch her.

Derek pulled her up and felt her body press against his. A man twice Derek's size stood by laughing. He had spiky black hair, a chin strap beard, and skin so tanned he looked as if he'd set the tanning booth to extra crispy. Derek couldn't ignore the word that came roaring to mind with neon brightness: *Villain.*

"Apologize to her," Derek said, before he knew what he was saying. And why. This wasn't his fight.

"What?" The man stepped forward, blotting out the light, casting an ominous shadow on Derek.

"Apologize to her." Derek heard his voice, but it felt like he was on autopilot, wound up by some unseen hand and set in motion. "And him too," he added, pointing at Evan.

"We don't want any trouble," Evan said. Evan looked like a deer caught in headlights, which Derek always thought was a stupid phrase. Really it was the driver caught by surprise. The driver who had to stop short or swerve. The driver caught *with* a deer in headlights.

"Who the fuck do you think you are?" the man said, stepping so close that Derek could see the sweat glisten on his forehead.

"I'm Eldrid Babble," Derek found himself saying.

"What?" Janine said.

Boris clambered out of his stool, taking his place beside Derek. "I've got your back, Derek."

"Me too," Gerald said, though he was holding a chicken wing at the time, so it sounded slightly less convincing.

"I've got this," Derek said, calling them off.

"Okay, Eldrid Babble, let's rumble."

The man attempted to shove Derek, but Derek easily dodged him. With more agility than he thought he possessed, he twirled in the opposite direction and swept his leg under the man, sending him toppling to the ground.

Derek hovered over the giant, remembering the way Eldrid pummeled Filly in Crimpleton Tavern. "I'm going to say it again. Apologize."

He raised his fist. Ready to unleash hell. All of the pent-up anger and rage of the past few years. Now it was no longer droplets of sweat, but entire rivers running down the man's face. He flinched and turned his head toward the floor.

"What's going on here?"

It was Kat. And just like that, the spell broke. Derek looked around the room, realizing that people were staring. He wrung out his fist, looking down at his gloved hand as if it belonged to someone else.

The man scrambled up, dusting off his pants. No longer Goliath, he didn't even look like a David. He was a Filly.

Derek looked at him fiercely. He imagined his eyes glowing red, just like Eldrid Babble's.

"I was just apologizing," the man said, looking down at his feet.

"What the hell happened?" Kat asked, trying to piece together the scene. A still life that didn't seem to have any logical explanation.

"Sorry," Derek said, coming back to himself as if he'd momentarily lost the thread of the story. "I guess I..." But Derek didn't know how to explain it. His foray into heroism defied heroics. Common sense.

"He bumped into me," Janine said. "Derek was protecting me."

"I thought I told you you'd had enough," Kat said, taking the man by the arm and guiding him away from the bar. "Let's get you out of here."

Kat escorted the towering giant to the door, leaving Janine staring dumbfounded at Derek.

"I think this is yours," Derek said, crouching down and handing Janine her purse. "Now, if you don't mind, I'd like to get back to my dinner." Derek sat down, grabbed a fork and knife and began poking at his wings. After an awkward attempt to dip a piece in blue cheese, he threw down his fork and knife and began eating with his hands. Actually, eating wasn't the right word. More like chomping. He began sweating profusely, the spice making his eyes water. But it didn't bother him; on the contrary, he only wanted to devour the wings more, as if he was readying to swallow a burning sword. A rite of passage on his journey to becoming a hero.

"I'll go get our jackets," Evan said. Footsteps retreating. The mumble of voices grew quieter. The lights grew dimmer. Until it was just Derek and his bucket of wings, a voracious hunger that had suddenly pounced on him, trapping his senses in an instinctual haze.

"Take it easy," Boris said.

"You're scaring the children," Gerald added.

"I'm starving," Derek said.

Within that soporific cloud, Derek felt a hand on his shoulder. He turned around and found Janine standing there, her head tilted in a look of bewilderment. Wonder. With grease-covered gloves, he continued devouring the chicken, the sauce staining his face in a red aurora. He gulped down his beer, feeling himself growing fainter and more powerful at the same time.

"What?" he said through a mouth full of food.

"Maybe we made a mistake."

"We made a lot of mistakes," Derek said. "And I still love you, Janine. Think I always will. But that doesn't mean I want to be anything other than what we are: Characters from another story."

Derek couldn't believe it. It sounded like the lines of dialogue had been written for him by Chester Felten himself.

Staring for a beat too long, Derek got a funny feeling that Janine was lost in the past. Gazing at him from another time. "Love you Bumble Dee," she said.

Derek turned around and banged his glass on the bar for a refill. "You better get going, Janine," Derek said. He motioned to Evan waiting at the door with their coats.

Looking over his shoulder one last time, he saw the confused look on Janine's face, as if she had momentarily fallen under a spell herself. Slowly, as if straining against the boundaries of story, those predictable plot points every protagonist hopes to follow, she turned around and walked to the door, where Evan helped her into her coat.

Evan placed his hand on the small of her back, guiding her through the open door, which slammed shut as soon as they had left. A chapter closed on Derek's old life and he'd scarcely realized he'd been turning the pages.

Chapter 14

After the bucket of wings, three beers, and an ice cream sundae, Derek was stuffed. At a certain point he'd thrown the gloves off and stopped worrying about his hands. After all, he was in a dark bar, and if someone did see his mottled skin and gnarled fingers, he could just claim a skin condition. Which in a way is exactly what Derek was suffering from.

As the bar thinned out, and Boris and Gerald turned in for the night, Derek had more time to talk to Kat, who was either so distracted by the customers or hampered by the dingy light that she didn't seem to notice anything amiss in Derek's appearance. If Derek didn't know any better, he might even say she was flirting with him.

Like when she ran her fingers over the buttons of his shirt and said, "Have you been working out?"

Or when she raised her eyebrows, bit her lip, and told Derek she had her mom watching Mac. "Grandma's babysitting, if you know what I mean."

Or when she blatantly came right out and said, "You do know I'm flirting with you, right?"

It had been so long since someone had flirted with Derek that he wasn't quite able to decode the signals.

His bravery with the ghost chili sauce, even more than his exploits with the giant, had also gone a long way in securing Derek's status as a hero.

"I can't believe you ate the entire bucket," she said. "Are you sure you're okay?"

"To be honest, I wanted them spicier," Derek said, which he didn't mean to be a euphemism, but Kat's cheeks flushed, as if he'd just smoothly cinched his seduction.

He did have the tail to contend with, which seemed to beat in wild excitement at each of Kat's overtures. If he did get lucky enough to bring Kat back to his apartment, would he be able to hide it? Could it be an asset in his skills as a lover? He struck the thought from his mind. Now was not the time to be considering tail play. Still, weighing the pros and cons of bringing Kat back to his apartment, he decided it would be better to try and fail, then not try because of a tail. A worthy motto to follow.

So instead of going home alone and ending the night with a solitary bowl of ice cream and an episode of *Another Planet*, Derek decided to take a chance. Maybe it was because he had Eldrid's blood running through his veins. Or maybe it was the wings and booze colliding in a miasmic cloud that blurred his inhibitions. Or maybe it was just that Derek had finally found closure with Janine and now felt ready to start a new chapter in his life. In any case, Derek found himself asking if Kat would like to come upstairs to his apartment for some dessert.

"Didn't you just have an ice cream sundae?"

"It's been a long week."

Then Derek, or maybe Eldrid—he couldn't tell who was who— took Kat's hand and they walked out of the bar together.

On the way into his apartment building, Derek felt a piece of his old self returning, nervous that he might somehow mess up this opportunity. He realized that he now thought of himself as two distinct personas: Eldrid had become the risk taker, the protagonist of his story, while Derek remained an anchor of doom and gloom in even the most promising situations. He wondered if these two selves could somehow find a way to coexist, or if Eldrid would gradually extinguish the flame of the old Derek.

Derek opened the door, and instead of turning on the bright overhead lights, he quickly moved to the lamp beside his futon and switched it on. But that was still too bright, so Derek fit a T-shirt from the laundry basket over the lampshade.

"Mood lighting," Kat said.

Derek smiled, still unsure how he could conceal his tail. Eldrid had an equal playing field by pursuing a fellow grimkin. Derek was in uncharted territory.

Derek took off his jacket and draped it over the side of the futon. He sighed with relief, happy to be free from the book's warmth.

"Are those your parents?" Kat asked, pointing to the framed photo on the TV stand.

Derek shook his head. "Not exactly. They came with the frame. But they're *someone's* parents. And I have plans to put *my* parents—at least my mom—in the frame as soon as I have time."

"This is the least personal apartment I've ever seen. It's almost like you're hiding something. Are you hiding something, Derek?"

Derek felt his cheeks grow flush. *Just the fact that I'm turning into a fantasy character from a book written in the 1950s.* "What you see is what you get," he said.

"Good, because after what I went through with Zeke, I only want the truth."

"I assume Zeke was a pet?"

Kat laughed. "He was a dog, all right."

136

Kat sat down and Derek went to the kitchen to get two bowls of ice cream. He hadn't felt this hungry in years. Insatiable was the word that came to mind. Like he just wanted to consume the world.

"While I was pregnant with Mac, he had a Tinder profile going."

"What an ass."

"Get this. One of the pictures on the profile was a sonogram of Mac. He was using my pregnant belly and Mac to get laid."

Derek brought the overflowing bowls of ice cream to the living room. He handed one to Kat.

"How does that even make sense?"

"The world is a fucked-up place," Kat said.

"I had a similar experience."

"The pregnant woman at the bar?"

"My ex."

"Her husband had very shiny shoes," Kat said, taking a bite of her ice cream.

"Thanks for saying that. Anyway, I caught them in the laundry room of our apartment building."

"That's so ironic."

"How so?"

"Doing the dirty in the laundry room."

"Never thought about it like that before."

"I didn't take you for the knight in shining armor."

"What do you mean?"

"Standing up to that troll."

"Troll?" Derek's heart started racing.

"The guy from the bar."

"Oh." He sighed with relief, glad that his fictional life wasn't further creeping into the real world.

"You must really care about her."

"I just don't like bullies."

Kat's phone pinged. "Sorry, give me a sec."

She grabbed her phone out of her purse and said, "Awww." She tilted her phone to Derek to show Mac sleeping peacefully in his crib, tucked in with a small teddy bear.

Derek greedily shoveled a few scoops of ice cream into his mouth. "Very cute."

"By the way, I have something for you."

"You do?"

"Well technically it's from Mac." Kat rifled through her purse and pulled out a small, four by four canvas covered in blue paint. "He's in his blue period," Kat said. "Meaning he'll only paint in blue. The other day you mentioned you needed some help decorating. I've got about a hundred of these and I figured you could use it to splash some color—at least a color—on the wall."

"Thanks," Derek said, smiling as he took the painting and stared at the thick clumps of blue caked on the canvas. "I love it."

"Anyway, what do you say we start making out?"

That sounded like a good idea to Derek, so they did.

At first, it felt strange to be kissing someone new. Kat's lips felt foreign, different from Janine's. But after a moment, he lost himself in the kiss, only briefly wondering whether or not he should open or close his eyes before deciding it was best not to stare in a moment like this. The kissing became more intense. A spark of electricity flew back and forth from Derek to Kat.

Kat tugged at Derek's shirt, but he tried to distract by focusing on her. After all, he had a tail to contend with, and if there was anything that could ruin the moment, it was a discussion about why he had a tail, future prospects of a man with a tail, and whether or not he was going mad or if the book in his jacket was actually magic. No need to derail the lovemaking with all that.

Their breathing intensified, the two of them pulsing as one, as Derek unbuttoned her shirt, unzipped the fly of her pants, and tugged her jeans down to her knees, sliding them off one leg after the other.

She fluttered her legs as Derek inched closer to her underwear, feeling that same voracious hunger he'd felt for the wings and the ice cream.

Just as he was about to peel back her underwear, she tensed. "Oh my god," she said. "What's that?"

"What's what?" Too late, Derek realized the duct tape had come undone.

"Something just moved under the blanket."

"Probably a mouse." Which was the exact wrong thing to say. But not as wrong as disclosing his tail.

Kat sprang out of bed in her bra and underwear.

"It's friendly," he said, standing up alongside Kat, still fully clothed. Careful to keep his back facing the wall. "His name's... Filly."

"You have a pet mouse named Filly?"

Derek shrugged. "He's not exactly a pet. But we have..." Derek grasped for the right words. "An understanding."

Kat had a look on her face like she'd just stuck her hand in a bowl of cold spaghetti. "Is Filly gone now?"

Derek drew in a deep breath, wishing he'd created a different lie. A different fiction. "He knows he's not allowed in the bed."

Kat shook her head as if trying to scrub the memory of Derek's pretend pet mouse from her mind. She reached for his belt. He delicately moved her hand away, but she kept her fingers curled around the leather, until they were caught in a game of tug-of-war.

"Can I?"

"Just a second."

Derek ran to the bathroom, realizing too late he'd left the duct tape on the kitchen counter. Rifling through the cabinet beneath the sink, he found the plush purple robe Tom had mailed him a couple of years ago, *Another Planet* emblazoned across the back.

Derek cloaked himself in the robe and emerged from the bathroom feeling like a billionaire playboy.

139

"Wearing a robe? You're a classy man, Derek..." Kat placed her finger to her chin. "What's your last name?"

"Winnebaker."

"Sounds made up."

"Aren't all last names made up?"

"Touché."

Derek raced under the covers. He could feel the tail swooshing wildly, ignoring Derek's commands to remain still. Trying his best to keep Kat from noticing his tail thumping beneath the blanket, Derek kissed his way to the smooth fabric of her underwear.

She ran her hands through his stringy hair but didn't seem to mind as she cried out. Once again, Derek felt part of his old self disappearing as he moved his tongue in ways he didn't even know possible. Kat responded to each of his overtures with a quiet scream, letting Derek know that his new hunger was satisfying her.

After Kat finished—not once, but twice—grabbing hold of Derek's hair and moaning with delight, she began to make her way under the covers.

"That's okay," Derek said, quickly sealing the robe around his body.

"It's only fair," Kat said.

"It's really fine," Derek said as Kat continued her journey below.

"I want to," Kat said.

"I cut myself shaving," Derek blurted out.

"Down there?" Kat's head reappeared above the covers.

Derek nodded sheepishly. "The doctor said to keep it dry."

"Jeez. You had to go to the doctor?"

"For the stiches."

"Stitches? Did you... you know... nick a part of it off?"

"No," Derek said. "It's just... tender."

Kat furrowed her brow. "No secrets, remember?"

"No secrets," Derek said, reaching for her hand and interlocking pinky fingers. "I pinky promise. You'll be a welcome visitor next time." Derek kept his eyes on Kat. "If there is a next time."

"I hope so."

They lay awake with the shades open, moonlight pouring through the window creating a checkered pattern on the floor, as if a dungeon existed below.

"When I became a mom... I kind of lost interest in all this for a while. Dating, guys, sex. It's just that Mac takes so much of my energy. I didn't realize until now just how much I've missed it." She rolled over and nestled into Derek's neck. "It's like life is always waiting for you to come back to it. But you have to be ready."

Derek breathed in, inhaling Kat's scent, which prickled his nostrils as he detected floral and citrus notes. He'd never smelled anything like it before. "I feel like I've been running away from life. At least *my* life."

"How so?"

Derek thought about Tom's call. How he'd soon be coming back to visit after not having seen each other for close to three years. "I've just been hiding."

Derek looked out the window. Kat nuzzled in closer. A perfect contentment flooded over him, so much so that even his tail quieted down. His eyes drooped as he heard mumbled voices from downstairs. Crickets from the nearby park. The whoosh of a car passing by. The everyday sounds of reality were far more perfect than anything a book could capture, because even the best scene would always be incomplete. Unfathomable to distill life into mere words.

At a certain point, he must've fallen asleep, because when he woke up, he found Kat still beside him.

Awake.

Entranced in *The Strange Life and Times of Eldrid Babble*.

Chapter 15

Derek sprang up and swatted the book out of her hand.

"What the hell?" Kat yelled.

The book slid across the floor with alarming speed. Was it just him or was it moving as if with a mind of its own, slithering across his faux hardwood in search of a new reader?

"How much did you read?"

"Just a few chapters." Kat stared longingly down at her hands, as if seeing phantom images of the words in the air. "I don't know, I lost track of time. Maybe half."

"It's my book," Derek said, sounding harsher than he meant to. After all, the book was dangerous. Not to mention, the book was *his*.

Kat looked more fearful than anything else. Still in only her bra and underwear, she tightened the blanket around her, a look of stunned disbelief on her face.

Derek ran toward the book, which lay splayed by the front door, its pages fanning open, as if moving of its own accord.

142

He closed the book and clutched it against his chest, worried it might suddenly jump out of his arms and land back with Kat.

"What's going on?"

Derek sat down on the edge of the futon beside Kat and slipped the book beneath his robe. "It's a long story." Having uttered the phrase for the second time that night, it only seemed to be getting longer.

"I was really enjoying it," Kat said. "Never read anything like it before. Weird fantasy world but it felt very..." Kat's voice trailed off as she glanced at the book peeking from beneath Derek's robe.

"Personal?"

Kat snapped her fingers. "That's it. Like the author was talking to me. Or maybe at me. I'm not sure which."

"Something about Eldrid draws you in," Derek said.

Kat shook her head. "No. Eldrid's fine and all. A bit wimpy for a protagonist. But I really connected to the other main character... Belinda."

"Belinda?"

"And I was surprised so much of it was written from her perspective. Like way to go, Chester Felten, giving us this kick-ass female grimkin. I'm no expert in American literature, but it does seem pretty innovative for him to focus on the girl grimkin. I mean, how many strong female leads do you remember from *The Hobbit*?"

Derek pulled the book from his robe and flipped through the pages, carefully looking for a chapter from Belinda's perspective. There it was, on page twelve, just after Eldrid sees her at the restaurant. The text abruptly broke off and switched into her point-of-view. Derek hadn't missed it. It hadn't been there before.

Belinda's heart fluttered as she spotted Eldrid walking toward her. She had known Eldrid ever since he was a grimpledee in primary school. Somehow, they had both ended up staying in Crimpleton. Not that it was necessarily her choice. She had dreamed of moving to Grim City and living the life of an actress. As a girl, she'd watched with delight as a traveling theater troupe performed a play about Edelbee Gripplebunk. With passion and fury, the lead actress brought to life Edelbee's heroic battles against trolls, her romance with an elf named Frankenmore Rickledrum, and her tragic death at the hands of a giant. Through it all, Belinda sat mesmerized, losing herself in the illusion; somehow that hour on the stage felt realer than anything she'd ever seen in her life.

But before she could begin her journey, her father was struck ill with grimkin fever, and she had no choice but to place her dreams on hold and help her distraught mother.

Her adventure was over before it had even begun.

"You want me to get you the usual?" Belinda asked Eldrid as he sat down. One thing she could count on was Eldrid's order. Eldrid was a grimkin of routine.

Eldrid looked up from the table and met her gaze. Something seemed different about him tonight. Something almost dangerous.

"Have you ever left Crimpleton?" he suddenly asked.

"Why would I ever leave Crimpleton?" Belinda immediately replied. Sure, she had read of distant lands and adventures, but the day she gave up acting was the day she left all those other lives behind.

"It's just that we've been in the same place, doing the same thing, with the same grimkins all our lives. I work at Templeton's stocking shelves, you work here, and we've never thought about leaving the grasslands? Visiting the capital?"

Belinda grew nervous. Strange the way Eldrid was talking and fidgeting. He seemed almost jumpy. Much different than the grimkin who'd come in almost every day, order his dinner, and mumble polite pleasantries.

"Eldrid? What are you talking about? Do you want the usual or not?"

"No, I don't want the usual. I don't want the ordinary anymore. I want the extraordinary."

Belinda dropped her pad, staring at Eldrid as if seeing him for the first time. And somehow, seeing herself too, the little girl who'd dreamed of playing Edelbee Gripplebunk, only to end up stuck in the same place, doing the same thing, with the same grimkins. Isn't that what Eldrid had said?

"I'd like to take you out to dinner," Eldrid said

Derek glanced up from the book, the horrible truth dawning on him. "The book changes based on the reader."

"What?" Kat said. "Don't all books?"

"Not like this," Derek said.

"Holy crap," Kat said, looking at her phone. "I didn't mean to stay so late... But you looked so peaceful and then that book fell out of your jacket and I just couldn't put it down. My mom is going to be pissed. Whatever. Everyone deserves a night out once in a while. Anyway, this was fun." Draping the covers around her shoulders, she got up and began collecting her clothes around the room. Had Derek really thrown them that far? She slipped on her pants, and despite the fact that he was holding an eighty-year-old magical book—why even lie about it now?—he couldn't help but marvel at the casualness that had developed between them. Then he remembered that Kat had read the book, and just as he had seen himself in Eldrid Babble, she had connected with Belinda Grabblebee. Did that mean she would start changing too?

"Do you mind if I borrow that?" Kat asked, reaching toward the book once she had her jacket on.

"It's due back at the library," Derek said, unsure if he was lying for her or himself. He couldn't let Eldrid's tale go.

"Tonight was fun," Derek offered weakly.

Kat looked at Derek, to the book, then into her purse, where her phone had begun vibrating. She answered: "Yes, I'm on my way."

She leaned forward, kissed Derek on the cheek, grazed the book with one hand as if caressing an old flame, and then pried herself away and marched to the stairs. "When you say projectile, are we talking the Exorcist or was it more of a spit up?"

145

Derek closed the door and found himself once again alone with *The Strange Life and Times of Eldrid Babble*. The book had mysteriously changed to accommodate its latest reader, and Derek wondered if other readers had encountered different characters in the land of Grimwell.

"It just doesn't make sense," Derek muttered out loud. Even though his tale had stopped making sense long ago. Just like books conform to their own rules, Derek had to allow Grimwell to declare its terms. Only then could he understand how to fight back.

If he even wanted to fight back. He could get used to living in Grimwell.

Despite the risks associated with continued reading—what other attributes of Eldrid Babble would Derek take on?—he found himself opening the book to where he had left off, when Eldrid Babble and Chester Felten meet for the first time.

Chapter 16

By the time I made my accidental journey into Grimwell, Eldrid had already fled Crimpleton in pursuit of the capital, looking for answers from the newest leader to take charge, Lord Grittlebane.

While still in conversation with Grandfather Tree, I heard the sound of leaves crunching underfoot. My attention drawn to the edge of the tree line, I caught my first glimpse of a grimkin. I'll try to describe my first impressions of Eldrid as vividly as possible, because I can't overstate the strain his appearance had on my psyche. Sure, I'd just had a brief conversation with a tree, but part of my brain still hoped to wake up from this strange dream. I'd open my eyes and feel a crick in my neck from sleeping at my desk, happy to return to the minutiae of drafting and approving insurance policies.

But that day, as I squinted into the distance, and Grandfather Tree appeared to swivel on his stump, the bark shedding once again, leaves swaying and crackling in the light breeze, I saw someone sprinting through the forest.

Or if not someone, some thing—at least that's what I thought at the time, before I'd become a true initiate into the world of Grimwell. Before our worlds had become one.

The creature—again, that's what I thought at the time, not what I think now—had long shaggy hair that sprouted from its head in thick curls. As he sprinted faster, just barely tripping over a stump and recovering gracefully, almost graciously, as if admitting fault to the trees of the forest, I saw a tail trailing behind him, sweeping across the tall grass and low branches as if fanning the foliage. As he got closer, I saw his feet were hairy and padded, with thick soles and long toes, almost finger-like. When he got close enough for me to see his face, I saw a visage both familiar and distant, as if I was looking at a different model of human; someone with a rounder head, sharper nose, and larger ears.

He saw me as well, and I imagined him having a similar feeling of dissonance, the gears of his world suddenly losing tread, and he stopped dead in his tracks, right in front of Grandfather Tree. For his part, Grandfather Tree seemed to be enjoying the spectacle, laughing heartily as his bark continued to slough off and his branches swayed noisily in the wind.

"Eldrid Babble finds a stone, Eldrid Babble leaves the known," Grandfather Tree said, his laughter hollow and menacing.

Eldrid looked at Grandfather Tree guiltily. "What do you know about the amulet?"

"Trees talk," Grandfather Tree said. "We have nothing to do but talk. Stuck in place all day. News travels fast."

A look of recognition dawned on Eldrid. "The river."

"The river," Grandfather Tree confirmed.

"And who is this?"

"Why don't you ask him yourself?" Grandfather Tree said.

Eldrid looked at me and I did my best to hold his gaze. The army had hardened me, given me the fierce look of a soldier, but it was only a façade. Similar to the skin on a fruit, peel and find the squishy center.

I imagined Eldrid scrutinizing me with a preternatural judgment, as if he'd read Death's Diary from start to finish.

"Who are you?" Eldrid asked.

"Chester Felten," I said.

"But what are you?"

"A human."

"A human," Grandfather Tree repeated giddily, thrilled beyond explanation. "Oh yes, yes, I've heard of your kind, though I've only seen one."

"A few years back," Eldrid said. "Brattlebee made the claim. Everyone in Crimpleton laughed at him."

"Must've wandered through the stump. Summarily removed," Grandfather Tree said solemnly. Some of the humor was gone, his smile now tinged with fear. My experience in France and Germany had taught me the danger of euphemism. Words can be a shield, but they can also be a cloak.

"A bit of a coincidence, wouldn't you say?" Grandfather Tree said.

Eldrid shrugged.

"An amulet thrown in the river and returned. A human thrown into Grimwell. Stuck."

I looked back at the tree stump. The opening remained. I could see a faint sliver of sky on the other side.

"I'm not stuck," I insisted.

"I'm the tree and yet you're the one rooted in place."

I had to give him that one.

"It reminds me of the time I encountered my first troll."

As you'll learn, trees are talkers. Imagine being stuck in the same place for hundreds of years. It's only natural that when someone finally wanders into your shade, you'd do anything to keep them there. And so Grandfather Tree told a long story about meeting his first troll when he was just a sproutling, and how he had saved his bark by arguing he wouldn't make a good fire. "But of course, I would've made an excellent fire," he assured us, as if defending his honor. "Especially in my younger

*years. Ever since I turned two hundred, everything's started to fall apart.
I've got arthritis like you wouldn't believe in my taproot. I've lost almost
all my root hairs. And my leaves are dry and brittle. Which reminds
me of the time..."*

Eldrid began walking away.

"Where are you going?" I called out.

"I guess I'm going on an adventure."

"Can I join you?"

*To this day I don't know why I said it. Maybe it was an excuse to
duck away from Grandfather Tree before he began another soliloquy.
Maybe it was the hungry writer in me searching for a story. Or maybe
I just wanted an adventure, the chance to live a tale fit for a book.*

*Grandfather Tree looked back and forth from Eldrid to me. His
branches slumped and the canopy of green that had been providing
cover parted, revealing a sun like I'd never seen before, closer, hotter,
redder, somehow fuzzier, as if brought to life in a child's crayon drawing.*

*Eldrid hesitated. Reached for something in his knapsack before
withdrawing his hand in haste.*

"As long as you don't slow me down," Eldrid said.

*"The journey for one has become a journey for two," Grandfather
Tree said. "Why don't you stay a little longer? I've accumulated a great
list of jokes over the years. Do you know what the oak said to the beech?"*

But we were thankfully already on our way.

*"I promise it's a good one," he shouted at our backs. "Don't you want
to hear the punchline?"*

* * *

*I struggled to keep up with Eldrid as he hurried through the forest.
While grimkins aren't necessarily known for their athletic or warrior
prowess, they are quick and agile; Eldrid was no exception, dodging
trees, ducking under branches, and jumping over rocks with a speed I*

couldn't come close to matching. The army had toughened me up, but it had been years since those long days and nights of cold and dark in Europe. Sitting at my desk had made me softer than a stick of butter left out on the counter, melted my stamina into a soupy indolence.

It must've been hours before Eldrid finally slowed down, at which point my feet were sorer than they'd ever been, and that's including the long march after D-Day through the French countryside. We'd wandered through forest, across shallow streams, past hillsides with small picturesque villages, before once again losing ourselves beneath a canopy of tall trees, Eldrid guided by some unseen compass. As night fell, Eldrid finally dropped his knapsack in a small clearing.

He gathered a pile of kindling and began rubbing two sticks together. Right away I could tell his technique was all wrong.

"Do you mind?" I asked.

Eldrid sighed but dropped the sticks.

Within a few minutes, I'd started a respectable fire, flames crackling in a steady nonchalance.

We sat on either side of the fire, and as the smoke rose between us, I got the strangest feeling that the veil separating us had undertaken a similar process of transformation, becoming as thin and permeable as fog.

"I was always more of an indoor grimkin," Eldrid admitted.

I stayed silent, staring at Eldrid through the smoke.

"It's a funny thing," Eldrid said. "Adventure. I've spent my whole life shying away from it. Trying to control my reality. Until I realized I was being controlled by it."

I could relate. My experience overseas had been like a relentless shadow, always trailing me; at a certain point I stopped trying to escape. Stopped trying to find light.

Eldrid fiddled with his pack. There was something inside. Something drawing Eldrid toward it. A faint light seemed to emanate from beneath its closed latches, and for the briefest moment I fantasized about opening the pack and looking inside, drawn toward its warmth.

151

"What are you running from?" I asked.

Eldrid appeared scared. His tail fluttered behind him and grabbed another stick to throw on the kindling.

"I'm looking for answers," he said. "I've never been brave. But I think I was chosen for some reason. There's an evil spreading in Grimwell. A darkness. And I think I'm the only one who can stop it."

"Evil? What are you talking about?"

"You wouldn't understand."

"I assure you, I've seen more evil than most see in ten lifetimes." But I couldn't elaborate. I couldn't tell him about Death's Diary. The bodies lying charred and ruined on the battlefield. The shambling march through time, unhinged from good and evil, cause and effect, sense and story.

Just then, I noticed two eyes staring at me from the darkened foliage. Almost as soon as I registered the glowing eyes, something pounced toward Eldrid.

He ducked just in time. The creature stopped just short of the fire, sending sparks and flames everywhere, and in that brief flash, I caught a glimpse of one of the scariest sights I'd ever seen. Picture a wolf, but at least twice the size, with a short pig-like nose and bat-like wings that allowed it to stay airborne as it pounced on its prey.

That was my first sight of what grimkins call a brimble.

Eldrid reached for his pack and grabbed something out of it. In his hand, I could see a small stone glowing red, and in that moment, Eldrid looked downright menacing.

The animal regrouped, crouching low, readying for another pounce.

Eldrid found his footing and stood up straight. The forest became darker as the stone grew brighter. I felt my mood change as well, as if the strings holding the world together had been strummed. Suddenly, I was in Alsace once again, machine-gun fire whirling around me as I stood frozen, helpless, afraid.

The beast charged and Eldrid grabbed one of the logs in the fire, beating the brimble back, which only seemed to make it angrier. It clamped down on Eldrid's arm, and as he shrieked in pain, the stone fell from his hand. Still crowded by thoughts of war, stranded on the eternal battlefield of my memories, the moment seemed to unfurl until it became unwieldy. Downright heavy. I grew dizzy. The brimble kicked up dirt, let go of Eldrid's arm, and began hurtling forward. Right toward me.

Just in time, I shook off the flashback, crouched low, and threw a small rock I'd found on the ground at the brimble. It bounced harmlessly off its coat, which is when I realized the creature had a shield of spiky horns on its back, Grimwell's own version of natural selection.

The trees shook violently but I didn't feel any wind.

A second brimble emerged from the woods and pounced on Eldrid's tail. Eldrid howled as he attempted to pry himself free from the brimble's mouth, frantically wiggling his tail from beneath its locked snout. Blood dripped on the dirt and clumps of fur scattered in the still air, hanging like filament in the night sky. Eldrid dug his fingers into the ground, crawling toward the small red puddle of light, desperately trying to reach the stone. I swear I could sense the trees scattering, distancing themselves from the fight.

Just as it appeared our journey would be over before it had truly begun, a story not of heroes but of two background characters killed on a distant page, Eldrid finally grabbed hold of the red stone. His eyes glowed with the same effulgent light; the brimble spit out his tail almost immediately. I once again felt a change in mood, the air weighed down by Eldrid's fury.

Just as quickly as the assault began, the two brimbles retreated into the shadows, leaving Eldrid and me panting in the clearing.

The red light beamed even brighter as Eldrid held the stone in the basin of his palms as if cradling a baby bird. Eldrid and I made eye contact. I could see him struggling to put the amulet down.

"You asked me what I was running from," he said.

I nodded.

"It changes things," he said.

"It helped you," I said. Eldrid had just somehow faced down a ferocious beast. Actually, two ferocious beasts.

"But at what cost?"

I looked around and saw that the trees had withered, stripped bare of their leaves.

"It takes in order to give," he said. "The more I use it, the better it gets at taking. I didn't see it before but I see it now. There's a cost to becoming a hero. And in this case, the price is becoming a villain."

"We'll find a way to make this right," I assured Eldrid as we stood in the dark clearing.

"I hope you're right." He placed the amulet in his knapsack and the night seemed to sigh with relief, escaping from the amulet's clutch. The trees straightened, branches already rustling with new leaves. The sound of crickets, strangely absent during our fight with the brimbles, returned with a crescendo. I breathed in something pungent and sweet, felt my head momentarily spin. Only later would I learn about the healing properties of the shabberberry bush. A moon hung solemn and low in the sky, a strange red hue staining its pockmarked surface. And then a hand—hairy, mottled, gnarled—curled around my shoulder.

"Ready for an adventure?"

"You're looking at it all wrong," I replied. "I hope the adventure is ready for me."

That was the end of the chapter, but as Derek readied to turn the page, more text appeared, as if being added by some phantom keyboard.

Of course, in the book, that's how I ended the chapter, the perfect combination of sentimental and sweet. Two buddies embarking on an adventure to save Grimwell.

As you know, Dear Reader, real life's more complicated than books make it out to be. And while I didn't run away from my adventure, I can't say I uttered that exact line.

But what matters is that I didn't turn back. Even though the world of Grimwell proved more dangerous than I could've ever imagined.

Just like you, Derek. When adventure called, you decided to keep on turning the pages.

And you'll keep on turning the pages until you reach the end, no matter the cost.

Don't roll your eyes at me.

Derek looked up from the book, startled and confused. He had in fact rolled his eyes. Chester Felten had known and scolded him. Derek watched as letters continued crawling across the page, the author now in conversation with the reader. A primitive version of the internet.

Because I know you, Derek, better than you know yourself. You're just like Eldrid. He was tired of being weak and powerless, and the second he cast aside convention and norms, he became the hero of his book. Nothing's sadder than being a supporting character in your own story, but that's exactly what you've been. Playing a minor role to your brother the TV star. Losing the part of leading man to Janine's colleague. Too weak and timid to speak the lines you've dreamed of shouting to your father. Allowing that little prick Sam to set the scene each day at the Read and Bean.

It's time you saw yourself on the page.

It's time you became Eldrid Babble.

"No," Derek uttered aloud, questioning his hold on reality. First the tail and now the book had begun talking to him? He closed his eyes, jamming his fingers into his eyelids to erase the lingering impression of those menacing letters, as if they'd been burned into his retinas. When he opened his eyes once again, he saw the letters had disappeared, leaving the neat and tidy chapter ending:

"Ready for an adventure?"
"You're looking at it all wrong," I replied. "I hope the adventure is ready for me."

Despite his growing hesitancy, Derek continued reading. And reading. And reading. Just like the book said he would. He read about Eldrid and the mysterious Shrinking City of Bengaloo, whose inhabitants and buildings grew or shrunk depending on the placement of the moon. Probably not the best place to invest in real estate, but Derek could almost feel the change in gravity as Eldrid and Chester tried to locate a childhood friend of Lord Grittlebane. He read about Eldrid and Chester meeting a mysterious wizened elf in the forest who tells them the story of the amulet and the prophecy about a hero who would redeem the realm. More like a memory than a scene in a book; he could even taste the elf's homebrewed sweet leaf coffee as Eldrid and Chester sipped from their wooden mugs and heard about the dangers that awaited them in Grim City. He read about a giant ant that almost eats Eldrid in his sleep, clearly a riff on the giant spider in *The Hobbit*, before Chester befriends the ant and they ride on its back toward the capital using a series of underground tunnels. Derek had never even ridden on the back of a horse, but he could've sworn he had the muscle memory of riding an ant, how to grasp their antennae and properly mount the thorax. Derek kept reading until he came upon Eldrid and Chester just a few miles outside of Grim City, their journey ready for its final leg, no more than fifty pages left. He could feel the fear and anticipation of finally meeting Lord Grittlebane, who'd spread pieces of the amulet all throughout the land, ready to corrupt Grimwell and turn it into a colorless landscape conducive to his mind control.

Derek read so much, that at a certain point, he couldn't tell what was dream or reality, where he ended and Eldrid began.

Chapter 17

Derek woke up to a text message from Tom: *Just boarded. The prodigal son returns!*

Along with the message, there was a selfie of him with Achelia Rose, who looked just as much a movie star as any person Derek had ever seen. With long black hair dotted with artfully placed beads, a green scarf slung loosely around her shoulders, and a smile as bright and shiny as Rich Wise's companion, Darla's, she looked ready for a photo shoot. Their faces were smooshed together, and they looked to be sharing a small apartment on the airplane. Ahh, the joys of first class.

Staring at the photo of Tom and Achelia, Derek was surprised to find nostalgia nipping at his heels, like a small dog trying to assert its dominance. He couldn't help but remember the two of them running through the backyard playing Indiana Jones. Derek had been the leader back then. He'd actually been the one to don the cowboy hat and play the professor of archeology, while Tom had played a Nazi, information that surely wouldn't please his publicist. Something about his German accent.

Now they barely talked.

But that had been Derek's choice. Or maybe a need. To distance himself from his famous brother in order to find his own path. His own life.

Some good that had done.

He liked the text message, careful not to hit the "love" button. While Tom probably wouldn't notice the distinction, he needed a way to express his sulky ambivalence. Based on when Tom had sent the text, he and Achelia would be landing in New York later that night. They could figure out a plan then. Now, Derek had other, more pressing concerns, including what to do about *The Strange Life and Times of Eldrid Babble.*

He took stock of the situation, trying to figure out if maybe he'd been overreacting about his "transformation."

His hair had become a little stringier, but that was just a natural part of the aging process.

His skin had become mottled, but it was really only noticeable in the light, and it could always be allergies.

His fingers had become gnarled, knobby even, and his pinky finger resembled a claw curled in striking position. Despite their strange appearance, his hands and fingers had also become stronger, and if he had a phone book, he might try ripping it in half just to see if he could.

His teeth had become sharper. Not so noticeable that he looked like a vampire, but sharp enough that Derek had accidentally cut his tongue while smoothing it over his incisors—or grimkincisors, according to the book.

His eyes had a reddish tinge, but instead of making him appear tired or withdrawn, he looked to be glowing from inside, as if he was on the verge of spontaneous combustion. To be honest, Derek didn't mind the eyes.

And then there was the tail to contend with. A curlicue appendage that Derek discovered had the ability to bend and twist on command—at least when it wanted to cooperate. He experimented with retrieving a drink and was surprised to find the tail sturdy enough to hold a twelve-ounce can of soda, although it couldn't quite reach his mouth. From a purely functional standpoint, the tail was undoubtedly an asset. Maybe even a superpower.

The only unknown variable was how much more of the transformation would occur. Jackson Wilfred had yet to reply to his email, but Derek reasoned he must've had a similar experience with the book to move all the way to Florida and cut off contact with his wife and son, only remaining in touch with Rich Wise to keep his affairs in order.

But beyond the physical transformations that had occurred, Derek also knew there was another, even more troubling change afoot: His two selves. On the one hand, he remained Derek, the same man who had voraciously read volumes in the library and dreamed of being someone else. The same Derek who fantasized about finding love, embarking on an adventure, and occasionally, during his weeks in the General Science section, solving the climate change crisis or curing a particularly vicious disease, like ebola or leprosy.

On the other hand, he had recently begun hearing a different voice, an angrier, jealous Derek, who wouldn't let anything stand in his way. The Derek who gleefully barked orders at Sam and leveled a giant in a bar all because of a spilled drink. It was that voice that had been leading the charge lately. Could he control it or would he end up living by the rules of some outside narrator?

He felt the walls of his apartment closing in on him. It was his day off, and he normally would have looked forward to spending the day on his futon reading, watching TV, stalking Janine on Facebook. But now he felt an unbearable claustrophobia, as if his life was no longer big enough for him. The routines and rituals that had previously sustained him now laid bare as steps for living a small life. A simple life. A secondary life.

He dressed, brushed his teeth, paying particular attention to his newly sharpened grimkincisors, and put on gloves, a hat, and sunglasses, just in case his new appearance attracted unwanted attention. He walked toward Pemberton Park on the other side of Elm Street, drawn toward the fresh-cut grass and tall trees, a small-scale replica of Grimwell's lush greenery. He longed to be home.

It might have been in Derek's head, but he could've sworn his sense of smell had grown even more vivid, and when he breathed in the outside air, he experienced an intense rush, as if reality had been put on steroids, some unseen hand turning up the volume on his previously muted senses: He detected hints of different flowers—he didn't have the vocabulary to name them, but they were there all the same, as clear as different notes in a song. He smelled food from the nearby diner, the various menu items as distinct and varied as fine wine. Most surprising, he discovered scents he'd never experienced before, including something that could only be described as orangehoneyexhaust.

Could the world really be this vibrant?

However, he also noticed something else: People stopping to look as he passed. One child, a little girl with bangs and rosy cheeks, even paused and pointed, exclaiming, "Look at his ears!"

Derek immediately pressed his hands to the side of his face, discovering that his ears had practically doubled in size, a detail he had missed when looking in the mirror before. Although they didn't have as sharp of a point as Belinda Grabblebee's ears—apparently that was only a female grimkin trait—they still felt wrong, as if he was having an allergic reaction. A severe allergic reaction.

The book beat in his jacket pocket like a heart. *Buh Bum. Buh Bum. Buh Bum.* Even now, after the havoc the book had brought to his life, Derek felt helplessly drawn to it, as if the answers to his predicament might be found in its changing pages—even as it continued to create his predicaments.

No longer able to wait, he found a park bench, sat down, and opened the book.

You're still reading, even though you know what the book's doing to you. Just like Eldrid couldn't stop himself from rolling the magic amulet between his fingers, you can't ignore the power contained between these pages.

Derek looked up, got the strangest feeling that someone was watching him.

The trick to capture a world is to see it through the eyes of your character. Collect the sights and sounds of your protagonist's life and distill it down to the essentials. The smell of freshly cut grass.

Derek inhaled.

The sound of laughter from the children playing nearby.

Derek heard the laughter.

The bustle of traffic grinding up and down the street. Its own symphony of the everyday. A facsimile of a world. Your world.

Derek pried his eyes away from the page. It was as if the book was narrating his life. The immediacy of the story became apparent, the book now updated for the twenty-first century, a catalogue of its reader's life and times. Part of Derek was frightened to keep turning the pages, afraid he could live his entire life inside the book all the while sitting on the park bench. It was dangerous and exhilarating to know that answers to life's most vexing questions—to be specific, his life's most vexing questions—could all be found through simply reading. No need for adventures, quests, or journeys. The key to the next few moments, next few days, next few years perhaps, lay right within his hands.

The thought scared him. Just like Eldrid's story would soon end, did that mean his days—his pages, so to speak—were numbered? The finite mortality of his existence shook him to the core, and he abruptly closed the book, leaving the scene off at exactly the moment he had just lived.

He was startled by the appearance of another man on the bench beside him. Despite the onset of spring, the man wore a thick winter coat, gloves, turtleneck, hood, sunglasses, and a hat, so practically no portion of his face or body was visible. He was at least twice Derek's size, and despite his attempt to conceal his appearance, Derek noticed a small bit of flesh creeping out from the sleeve of his shirt; it looked rough, piled on in thick and scaly sheets, more like the bark of a tree than skin. Derek fought back the urge to open the book and see what lay in store for him, but it was becoming difficult to discern between protagonist and reader, so he forced himself to keep the book shut, an almost existential pang as he kept the covers closed.

"Hello?" Derek said, the stranger's gaze now becoming uncomfortable.

Although the man didn't reply, Derek had no doubt who now sat beside him.

"Mr. Wilfred?"

The man on the bench nodded, though he stayed looking straight ahead. "Do you have the book?" he grumbled.

Derek held it up to the light, but it must've been so jarring to see the cover that Mr. Wilfred turned away, his sunglasses slipping to the edge of his nose, revealing the same texture of skin Derek had seen poke out of his sleeve, as well as eyes that looked cartoonishly big, like the kind you'd see on a children's character. Glassy and vacant.

"Put it away," he hissed. Something about his voice sounded strange, almost subterranean, a deep growl churning and grinding from within.

"I shouldn't be here," he said, "but I wanted to do everything I could to once and for all destroy that book." He remained rooted to the bench, a strange stillness in his demeanor, not a placid calm, but as if invisible chains held him in place. Even though he scarcely resembled the bespectacled twig that used to preside over the Pemberton Library, some small piece of him remained, a vestige of a past character still glowering from behind the eyes. "I did my best to destroy it, but no matter how hard I tried, I just couldn't."

A phosphorene glow emanated from the book, as if the mere presence of Jackson Wilfred had stirred something inside of it, the proximity of an old friend who had once lost himself between its pages.

"I guess it wouldn't hurt to take one more peek," Jackson Wilfred said, reaching toward the book. Derek abruptly stood up, clutching the book to his chest. The cover, sheathed in cellophane, seemed to glow brighter, and Derek's hands burned through his gloves. Mr. Wilfred attempted to follow, but he struggled to get up, his body slow and rickety, as if he was planted to the ground. That's when the terrible truth came to Derek.

Jackson Wilfred hadn't identified with Eldrid Babble or Belinda Grabblebee. No, his transformation had been of the arboreal variety. For some reason, he'd identified with Grandfather Tree, the wise—and loquacious—Guardian of the Realm Chester Felten first encounters in the Trembling Forest.

"How much have you read?" Mr. Wilfred asked, finally pushing himself off the bench. Standing up, he towered over Derek, probably close to eight feet tall. A fantasy creature from Grimwell come to life.

Just like Derek.

"Almost all of it," Derek replied.

"Eldrid Babble, huh?"

"What?"

"The character you identified with."

"How'd you know?"

"For god's sake, look at you."

Derek nodded. "You've figured it out too?"

Wilfred responded with a loud bark of a laugh. "Don't you think I've thought about this? The truth is, the book is everybody's story."

"Like magic," Derek said, the word no longer conjuring magicians and tricks, but sorcerers and spells.

"Like a magic amulet," Wilfred said. "Where'd you find it?"

"It was in the back of the Read and Bean's supply closet."

"I buried it," Wilfred said, swaying slightly in the breeze as if standing on stilts. "I swear I did. But the book finds a way out. Always does."

"What are you talking about?"

"When we started the renovation, I found it in the basement. It must've been there since the library was first built in the 1950s. We're talking back in the days when Mr. Dewey Decimal reigned supreme. It had a borrowing card and everything. But for some reason, it had never joined the collection. Nothing sadder than a book without a shelf. Seemed like a strange story so I figured it'd be fun to read a few pages. Probably not for circulation, but who knows, maybe part of me thought I'd be discovering an unsung literary talent. And I'd be the one to bring him to the masses. Every librarian's dream. I stamped it right away for my personal collection, which was weird because I never did that with any of the books in the library, especially an old volume like *Eldrid Babble*. Even back then the book had its hold on me, I was just too dumb to realize. Then I started reading... and you know the rest of the story, don't you, Eldrid?"

"It's Derek."

"Sure, it is."

"You saw yourself in Grandfather Tree?"

"My entire self," Wilfred replied. "But not only that. Little clues and challenges. Like the author was talking to me. I thought I had everything when I started reading *Eldrid Babble*. I thought I was happy. But the book thought different. *Knew* different. By the time I was able to pry myself free of the story, I was already too far gone." He sighed deeply. Derek noticed him shuffling his feet, as if afraid he might accidentally lay down roots. "It almost killed me."

"How do you stop it?"

He laughed again, a deep throaty gurgle. "You can't stop it. At least I haven't figured out a way yet. But you can slow it."

"How?"

"You have to stop reading."

Derek felt a sudden sense of relief. "Is that it?"

"Easier said than done," he said. "Easier said than done."

Derek imagined the way the scene might appear in a novel: Jackson Wilfred cracks open a book, previewing it for the library's Local section. Only it's not easy to shake off the similarities between him and Grimwell's own talkative timber, so he keeps reading, only to find their stories meshing and melding, Chester Felten lulling him into a deep and resonant understanding, until it's difficult to discern real life from the book, the book from real life, and the two become one. That was the book's magic after all, to make reality disappear into the world of fiction: that glorious reader's high Derek had grown used to chasing at the library, often ignoring the demands of the real world in favor of fictional worlds. That same reader's high that had become a delusion when reading the tale of Eldrid Babble.

Derek tucked the book back into his jacket pocket, feeling it ready to rewrite its pages to accommodate another reader, a rubber band stretched by magic and imagination, only to snap back to its original form as soon as the book closed.

"It's a paradox," Wilfred said, presiding over Pemberton Park, its very own walking, talking, deciduous denizen.

"How so?"

"Each person reads their own story and yet the book tricks you into believing it's universal."

Derek thought about his escape into the labyrinthine shelves at the Pemberton Library. How many times had he encountered a book and believed it was written just for him? The novels, philosophical tomes, gardening guides—there was something magical about the way a book could reach out and grab hold: A gentle hand coaxing you forward. But Eldrid Babble had sunk his teeth into Derek. His sharp and pointy grimincisors.

Jackson Wilfred reached down and picked up a small brown accordion file folder that he'd placed beside the bench. Worn and weathered, it had the look and feel of a much-loved book, as if it had become a substitute in the wake of fleeing *The Strange Life and Times of Eldrid Babble*. With his documents in tow, he began trudging across the park lawn, slow and steady, as if walking on quicksand, his shoes slightly sinking with each step.

"Where are you going?"

"You want my help, don't you?"

Derek nodded.

"Then come on. There's something I haven't told you yet."

Chapter 18

Jackson Wilfred and Derek sat on the futon in his apartment. Mr. Wilfred opened the accordion file folder and tilted it toward Derek. "All the information I've been able to compile about the book," he said.

Derek leaned forward to inspect the folder, brimming with paper. Neatly organized sections with labels like "Biography," "Book," "Possible Others?" Wilfred had kept his hat, hood and sunglasses on, still so covered that Derek had trouble seeing his face. He sat in shadow careful to conceal his appearance. *How bad could it be?* Derek thought.

"You're staring," Wilfred said, as he thumbed through the files, looking for some key piece of information from his research.

Derek looked away. "I'm sorry. I'm just—"

"Trying to take a peek at the sideshow?"

"Trying to figure things out."

Derek's tail struggled against the duct tape. No reason to continue hiding it in front of a fellow citizen of Grimwell. While Mr. Wilfred scanned his files, Derek reached down and freed his tail, letting it plume out behind him. The dappled fur seemed to ripple with relief as it rested comfortably in between him and Mr. Wilfred.

Mr. Wilfred looked at the tail and then at Derek.

"I'm sorry," Wilfred said. "It's just that I'm not used to seeing people. Or having people see me."

Wilfred took off his glasses, revealing his large circular eyes and small ink-spot pupils, more like something you'd see on a theme park ride than on a human being. Clumps of bark crowded around his eyelids.

Derek couldn't help but scoot away on the futon. A few weeks ago, he was just Derek, the Friendly-ish Neighborhood Barista, and now he was playing a twisted game of strip poker with a tree. He caught a whiff of Kat's perfume, infused into one of the pillows. A mix of honeysuckle and grimkinberry. He shook his head. Wrong world.

"You've got to understand," Wilfred said. "That book ruined my life."

He glared at the book, which peeked out from Derek's jacket. Hungry was the word that came to mind, as if Wilfred wanted nothing more than to devour the book whole.

"I was the director of the Pemberton Library," Wilfred began. "At the top of my game. I'd turned that library from a Podunk small-town book repository to a real cultural institution. I had it all. The career. The wife. The..." He stumbled over the last word as if slipping on a sheet of ice, struggling to find his footing. "Family."

"That's when you found *Eldrid Babble*?" Derek asked.

"That's when I found *Eldrid Babble*," Wilfred repeated, his voice deep and gravelly, as if buried inside of him, yearning to break free. A small twig crowned with a green leaf extended from his left ear, a tree in the process of blossoming. Derek wondered, only with a slight hint of humor, mostly horror, as to whether or not he had to prune himself.

"And?"

"I started reading. That's it. I spent my whole life trying to spread the magic of reading. The joy of finding yourself in a story. And that's what I thought when Grandfather Tree makes his first appearance in the Trembling Forest. I just got him, you know? And then I guess he got me. What better host than a librarian."

Host. Derek hadn't thought about it like that before. As if the book was a virus intent on spreading.

"That's when I noticed the first piece of bark. First just a small patch on my knee. And I could've sworn my legs had grown thicker, muscular, like I'd been hitting the gym. Which was impossible. I was a bookworm, for god's sake. As sedentary as a sloth." He pulled out a yellowed piece of paper from the folder and then tied it shut, patting it as gently as you'd pat a dog or cat.

Wilfred described how he had retreated further into the pages of *Eldrid Babble* even as he descended deeper into what he came to believe was a minor psychosis spurred on by stress from work and family, an overachiever who'd finally burnt the candle, set ablaze the wick and accidentally torched his life. "All I ever wanted to do was read. To share books with people," he said sadly.

He discovered the next piece of bark while in the shower, peeling it off in painful clumps, even as he washed the dirt down the drain.

"I kept it all a secret from my wife. She actually thought I was having an affair. Can you believe that?" Wilfred asked, now holding the yellowed paper pressed against his chest, the accordion folder on the couch beside him. "I guess it's more plausible than the other scenario. That I was turning into a fucking tree."

Anger in his voice. Desperation in his cartoonish eyes. A broken man—or felled tree?—Derek thought as he watched Wilfred and peered at his gloves, hiding long, spindly fingers, which Derek assumed had become more wood than bone.

"The bastard threw every trope in the book. I mean, as a piece of literature, it's garbage, but that's not why it's impossible to stop reading, is it? There's something magical. But not in the good way. There's a darkness to the book. It ensnares you. And when you see yourself in one of the characters, it's damn near impossible to stop reading."

"Why Grandfather Tree?"

"Being Guardian of the Realm means he's also in charge of Grimwell's history. Knowledge and stories passed down from generation to generation. Kind of like a librarian, I guess. But not only that. What do librarians love to do more than anything? *Talk.* God, I miss that. Talking about books. The weather. Mr. Gardner's hip replacement. The subject didn't matter. A library isn't just a place to find books. It's a place to find people." He paused, as if waiting for Derek to applaud. A vestige of the man who'd deliver speeches at library conventions, celebrating the joy of reading. "Do you know what drew you to Eldrid?"

"No," Derek lied. "Not a clue."

Jackson Wilfred took a deep breath and shuddered, the leaf on his ear shaking and rattling from the force, the same way trees sway in the wind.

"I retreated further into myself, until I stopped going to work, stopped going to lunch with my old pal Rich Wise, stopped leaving the house period. I became obsessed with finding an answer to my predicament. How to turn back the clock—or pages, so to speak— back to the beginning. Before I found that damn book.

"It was late on a Sunday when my wife noticed the bark creeping out of my shirt. I told her the whole thing, about Eldrid, about Grandfather Tree, the magic of the book. That's when she took the kids and moved in with her parents. She didn't think I was safe to be around anymore. And to be honest, I think she was right."

"But there's one part of the story I'm missing," Derek said. "She left. And you left. But if she really thought you were crazy, why not try to get you help?"

"She may have thought I was crazy, but then again, I think part of her believed in the book. Believed I was turning into a tree. Because one night..." His breathing slowed, as if his insides were hardening and turning to bark, the battle between becoming real and fictional always raging inside of him. As Wilfred told him the painful truth in excruciating detail, Derek found himself once again imagining the scene as if reading a novel:

Wilfred carries the book in his hand. It's late. Moonlight pours through his living room window. His wife and son are asleep. He can feel himself becoming more tree and less man, but still the book wants more. Needs more.

He tiptoes down the hallway, the book pressed against his chest. He's not thinking, only operating under commands, dictums and shouts from between the covers. He sees his cat, Hemingway, who quickly bolts away, hissing as he escapes to the kitchen. He keeps walking, his footsteps creaking in the hallway, wood on wood, as he gets closer to Jason's room. His door has a UCONN Basketball banner on the outside along with a hastily scrawled note with different types of knocks, privacy starting to become not a request, but a demand: Knock once for dinner, twice to come in, three times to discuss chores.

He'd been proud of his son when he came up with the system. Back when he could still wholly feel the bonds of fatherhood, now just a faint whisper of familial remembrance, thanks to Grandfather Tree's tale of redemption in the strange land of Grimwell.

Wilfred slowly turns the door knob, the room dim and humid. He sees little gold figurines emerging from the dark in a perpetual state of diving. Other figures stand in a batter's swing. Others in a runner's start. He pads across the carpet and sits down beside his son, that little perfect boy with the curly brown hair, in the chair he used to read bedtime stories: *Where the Wild Things Are. The Lorax.* All the way back to *Goodnight Moon*, which they'd read every night before bed, pointing out the bears, the chairs, the bowl full of mush, the red balloon. Haunting that red balloon, Wilfred always thought, just hanging limply beside that sleeping bunny. Books had always been in his blood, but not in the way *The Strange Life and Times of Eldrid Babble* had wormed its way under his skin. Instead of a spark of inspiration, this book seemed to be sending a current of electricity through him: Relentless. Merciless. As dangerous as touching a live wire after a storm. He shivers, cracks open the book, even as Jason remains sleeping. He wants Jason to join. Feels it deep in his bones. Needs to share it with his son. He opens the book to the beginning and starts reading. The book has changed once again, greedily sensing its victim, a story not about Eldrid or Grandfather Tree, but a small goblin named Creteor. Jason stirs groggily, but before long, he's sitting up, riveted by the story, or maybe just the strange presence of his father in his room in the dim light, his long spindly fingers creeping over the edge of the book. It's about an hour into reading that the book loses hold and Wilfred begins to question what he's doing. Why he's doing it. But it's only a momentary pause, a faint stirring of morality, the same way a child might feel guilty after stealing a cookie from the cookie jar, enough to pause but not enough to alter course. His wife discovers him just as the sun crests the horizon, screaming for him to stay away from Jason.

"And that's when I knew I had to get away."

"Did your son... turn?"

"Not that I know of. Maybe because it was only the one night. Or maybe the changes were too slight to discover. Or maybe it works differently on kids. Or maybe he just never told me."

"And then you left town?" Derek asked.

"Not quite. You've gotta understand, I wasn't thinking clearly. Really, the book was doing the thinking for me. Because I couldn't stop reading, and at a certain point, I couldn't tell whether the book was about me or the damn tree, about my life or about Grimwell. It all kind of blended together. You've heard of a writer's voice?"

Derek nodded. While he generally preferred fiction, he'd once in a while sneak into the How-To section, and so had learned how to write a book, how to bake a cake, how to start a coin collection, a useless theoretical assortment of knowledge without any practical experience. Unless he wanted to write *How To Accumulate Useless Knowledge* by Derek Winnebaker.

"It's a writer's essence," Wilfred said. "After a while, Chester Felten, or whoever the narrator really is, extends his essence beyond the world of Grimwell. Beyond the story. Until the book becomes about *you*."

Wilfred sighed. He took his gloves off, revealing fingers that looked more like branches. His hat followed, and Derek saw a lush canopy-in-miniature crowned with vibrant green leaves. A human Chia Pet.

"I have to cut it every day, otherwise it gets out of hand," Wilfred said. "Especially in the spring."

"What'd the book say?" Derek had grown alarmed. If the book extended beyond Grimwell, did that mean Derek's earlier fears about living his entire life through its pages could come true?

"I read a scene. Where I saved a drowning child." Wilfred said it guiltily, staring down at the ground.

Derek remembered the article from the newspaper that described him as a hero.

"I thought if I did something good, maybe I could get my family back. So, after I read the chapter, I went down to Crystal Lake on my lunch break. I saw a little boy playing at the edge of the water. The same way it happened in the book. Soon, the little boy would fall in, I would jump in after him, and I'd be a hero. Maybe that would also reverse the curse. A test of my mettle or something like that. I didn't understand the rules of Grimwell. Not yet. Well, after about thirty minutes, he still hadn't fallen in. I stayed, watching like a hawk, waiting for my opportunity. His friends had moved on to the playground, but he remained at the edge of the water tossing pebbles, almost as if he were waiting for me. I decided to just speed up the story." He flashed defensive eyes toward Derek. "It was going to happen, I just moved ahead a few pages."

"You pushed him in?"

173

"And wouldn't you know it, the little guy couldn't swim." Leaves hung over his forehead in a perpetual shade. He brushed a few over-hanging branches out of his eyes, the foliage rustling as he bent the thin twigs back. "I jumped in, got him out, gave him CPR. Someone from the town newspaper happened to be passing by—I swear it read the exact same way in the book—and the next day, it was front page news. But even though the scene played in the right way, I knew I was no hero. Quite the opposite. I'd become a villain."

He shifted in his seat and Derek heard a cracking sound, as if a branch had just snapped under the weight of heavy snow. "If I don't move every few minutes, I get stuck. I guess planted is the word for it." He laughed in a deep resonant boom, almost as if the sound was struggling to break free of his wooden innards. "After the chapter at the lake, I knew I had to do the right thing. What was left of me, anyway. I needed to know my wife and Jason were going to be safe, so I tried getting rid of the book. I threw it in a fire, but it wouldn't burn. I swear I could feel the flames on my skin. I tried to rip the pages out, but they're indestructible. Might as well try to tear a sheet of steel. So I buried it. I needed to get rid of it, even if it meant never figuring out the ending. The resolution. A way to reverse the..." He scrunched up his forehead, and Derek watched as the branches on his head seemed to grow bushier. "Curse, if that's what it is. Somehow, it must've ended up back at the library. The book calls to be read." His big round eyes darted to the book. "Screams."

Derek took a deep breath. He'd known the hunger Wilfred was talking about. The desire to become the hero of his own story.

"Is it a... happy ending? Does Eldrid defeat Lord Grittlebane?"

Wilfred laughed again. "I never got that far. Otherwise, I don't think I'd still be here. I knew if I kept reading, I'd somehow end with the book. At least the part of me known as Jackson Wilfred."

Wilfred passed Derek the wrinkled paper he'd taken out of the accordion folder. "I tracked down this map to Chester Felten's papers.

174

All through intermediaries on the internet. I've had a lot of time on my hands." He glanced down at the gnarled twigs that had become his fingers. "It's drawn by Chester Felten and his family has been holding on to it, thinking it was just a map of the Ashton Town Forest."

Derek peered down at the map. He recognized a few of the places Chester Felten mentioned on his walk through the woods, including the donkey watering hole, Devil's Rock, and Mirror Lake. He almost gasped when he saw a drawing of a tree stump on the Northeast edge with an X on it. A reader's treasure map.

"They thought it was just a book, but I know better. Here it is," he said excitedly. "The way to get to Grimwell."

"You mean you think it's real?"

Wilfred nodded. "The world of Eldrid Babble isn't really fiction after all. At least according to this map. And because he wrote the book, we know Chester Felten was able to leave Grimwell. Which is one reason I think he and Eldrid defeated Lord Grittlebane in the end."

"Then why the curse?"

"That's where you come in. What do you say, Eldrid... I mean, Derek. Ready to be a hero?"

Derek leaned back on the futon. His phone pinged. Probably his brother letting him know he'd landed and that he'd soon be on his way for a reunion in their hometown. Where Derek had stayed.

"I don't have the will or the way to travel in the woods. Call me crazy, but I think you might be able to go there and finish this thing once and for all."

"Go to Grimwell?"

"No, fucking Disney World," Wilfred said angrily. "Of course, I'm talking about Grimwell."

Wilfred erupted into a coughing fit, flecks of dirt spraying onto Derek's futon. "Can you water me?" he asked, lowering his head.

"Uh, sure," Derek said. What other choice did he have? He retrieved a glass of water from the sink and poured it onto Wilfred's scalp, watching the shrubs greedily drink. Nothing to see here, Derek thought. Just two guys watering each other.

"And would you mind opening the blinds a little bit more? Photosynthesis is a bitch."

His old pal Rich Wise might agree. Derek opened the blinds and Wilfred's mood seemed to improve immediately, a smile creasing in his bark-like skin. "What do you say?"

Derek weighed his options. He had a job. Access to as many books as he wanted. Maybe a girlfriend. The beginnings of a life. The book seemed to grow warm and vibrate in his jacket, beckoning to be read. Needing a break from its relentless prodding, he placed it on the couch beside him. Derek knew that if he opened it, he might see the outline of his journey in between its pages, his world colliding with Eldrid's. Becoming Eldrid's.

But he also knew that to open the book and read it would somehow permanently make his journey fictional. If that made any sense. Confine him to a world in which he only barely existed. Like all great heroes, he knew exactly what he had to do.

Take a break.

"I'll be right back."

Derek hurried to the bathroom, hoping for some clarity as he splashed his face and looked in the mirror. His ears had grown larger and even more of his hair had disappeared. His tail fluttered behind him, straining against the waist of his pants. He couldn't reverse the process but he could freeze it in place by never opening the book again. Or he could try to put an end to the curse once and for all by visiting the land depicted on the map.

Stuck between a rock and a tree stump.

By the time he left the bathroom, Wilfred was gone, and the pages of the book were splayed open. Derek peered down at the book, realizing that the story had once again changed to accommodate its latest reader.

Ever since hearing about Eldrid Babble's journey to Grim City, Grandfather Tree had mobilized his fellow trees into motion. Or if not motion in the usual sense of the word, action.

After all, trees are not known for their ability to perambulate easily, and indeed, as Grandfather Tree often remarked, "A tree in motion isn't a tree at all."

While trees are careful to stay out of politics, and often have their heads buried in the sand—or dirt, so to speak—the trees had a vested interest in Eldrid reaching the capital and destroying the spell that bound Eldrid's magic amulet—and indeed all the other pieces of the Hero's Stone—to Lord Grittlebane's staff.

But I digress, a common habit of trees as you've surely learned, because as Grandfather Tree rallied the troops, there was a lot of catching up to do, which trees refer to as "barking it up," or "laying roots down"—there is no greater joy for a tree than a well-placed pun.

Grandfather Tree first began with the sycamore trees, who are known for their stubbornness in getting involved in grimkin disputes. Similar to the way telegraph wires work, Grandfather Tree sent a message through the vast underground root system to Siddlebee Sycamore, the sycamore representative to the Council of Trees.

"It reminds me of the time Briggledorf Babble requested our involvement in his war against the trolls," Siddelbee responded, following it up with a quick, "By the way, how's your mother?"

To which Grandfather Tree replied that his mother had been struck by lightning, which is actually one of the most common forms of death for trees, while heart attacks are unheard of (trees don't have a heart, and coincidentally, are not known for their compassion).

What followed was an hour-long detour into Grandfather Tree's mother's funeral, and the current state of Sidelbee Sycamore's own parents, who he hoped to move to a quieter part of the forest for their retirement, a difficult, though not unheard of, process for trees in particularly unfavorable environs.

"And your brother?" Siddelbee asked. "How's your brother?"

What followed was a story told in excruciating detail about Grand-father Tree's brother, Oakenmore, who had been invaded by a vicious band of squirrels.

Derek looked up, unsure how anyone had connected with this part of Grimwell's history, as if a trumpet solo in a jazz quartet had veered off the rails and lost the thread of the melody. This was not his book. He could scarcely believe it was anyone's book.

He slammed the covers shut, hoping that when he opened it, the words would once again rearrange themselves into Eldrid's story. His story.

He shook his head. Already dreaming of losing himself between Eldrid's pages. "Easier said than done," Jackson Wilfred had said.

How cruel that he'd found his book and couldn't read it.

He tucked it in his dresser drawer beneath a pile of socks and was now faced with what to do without the book. Not only for the next few hours, but the next few days and months and years.

Luckily, it was Tuesday, and every Tuesday night Kat added an unlikely ingredient in McDowell's chili that somehow made it both more delicious and chili-like than ever before. Turning into a grimkin had made him perpetually hungry.

In the past, he may have played it cool, not daring to visit Kat until she texted him or they arranged another date. But he was no longer the same passive Derek with his nose in a book waiting for someone to turn the page.

He might as well have been a different character entirely.

Even as his stomach rumbled, he felt his eyelids droop, and he lay down on his futon trying—and failing—to imagine an eternity free of Eldrid Babble.

Chapter 19

He dreamed of Grimwell, running through the grasslands, drinking a barley cream at Crimpleton Tavern, even riding on a friendly giant ant, holding fast to its antennae as the wind rushed through his hair. A strangely pleasant fantasy, which is why he took so long to register the knocking on his door.

"Who is it?" Derek shouted from the futon.

The knocks came louder, more aggressive.

Fading sunlight slanted through the window, meaning Derek must've been asleep for a few hours.

He scrambled off the futon and zombie-walked to the door, assuming it was Wilfred. Perhaps he'd gone to reunite with his family and had returned a new man, having found that the key to breaking Eldrid Babble's curse was to make amends with those he'd hurt. A twisted take on a twelve-step program in the form of chapters.

But when he opened the door, he found his brother, Tom, standing in front of him with a large duffel bag slung around his shoulder. Tom looked older, but in the way Hollywood stars often do, his features now more defined, sculpture-like. His eyebrows were shaped in an aggressive arch and a five o'clock shadow dusted his cheeks and chin, signaling a curated ruggedness. But, for the first time, Derek could also see dark bags shadowing beneath his eyes, a sign of his demanding shooting schedule.

"Surprise!" he shouted. "We were going to stop at the hotel, but I thought, why wait to see my big bro?"

Derek heard footsteps on the stairs.

"Come on, Achelia," Tom said, turning around, his duffel bag awkwardly swinging over his shoulder.

From behind Tom, Derek saw the woman he'd watched in countless movies casually walking up the stairs. Thanks to his landlord's lackadaisical approach to changing lightbulbs, the light was patchy—one bulb on, one bulb off, one bulb blinking—giving a surreal quality to her ascent, as if she'd just wandered off a movie screen. She had dark skin and long black hair that haphazardly swooped across her shoulders, the type of messiness you'd see in a movie: a deliberate disorder. She was wearing a red hoodie with matching sweatpants, but with the green scarf wrapped loosely around her neck, she appeared casually elegant, something the press might call a fashion statement. As she smiled, Derek noticed a small gap between her front teeth, the iconic imperfection that made her seem almost obtainable to the average viewer. There was something bright and glittering in her eyes, and Derek felt the urge to look away, as if he were staring at an eclipse without sunglasses. The light continued to pulse, punctuating her movements in a silvery mosaic. The way she walked—glided was more like it—only added to the impression that she was posing for a camera. As she reached the top of the stairs and drew closer, Derek noticed she was at least a few inches taller than Tom. Goddess was the word that came to mind as Derek stood there speechless.

"Derek, this is Achelia, Achelia, this is Derek," Tom said, peering over Derek's shoulder into the apartment.

"So wonderful to finally meet you," Achelia said, surprising Derek with a hug.

In that moment, pressed against one of the most beautiful women in the world, Derek felt more like a creature than ever before.

"Mind if we come in?" Tom asked.

"Sure," Derek said, stepping aside, careful to keep his back against the wall. He hadn't had time to tape his tail, nor was it properly trained.

Tom walked in and dropped his duffel bag on the ground. Achelia Rose followed with a small leather satchel, less than half the size of Tom's bag.

"I'm trying to lower my carbon footprint to net zero," she said proudly.

"How about some lights, bro?"

"Bulbs are out," Derek said. He wondered if Tom had noticed his change in appearance or if the darkness had concealed the worst of it.

"This is bleak," Tom said, sweeping his eyes across the room. "I mean the light. I'm not talking about the apartment."

Which Derek knew only had to be clarified because Tom *was* talking about the apartment.

After receiving few visitors for the better part of three years, Derek's living room was suddenly heavily trafficked. But his guests only made the apartment feel smaller, more impersonal. More like a display at a department store than an actual life he inhabited. The absence of pictures on the walls only added to the impression.

"Cozy. I'd call it cozy. Wouldn't you say, Achelia?"

"Like a warm hug," she said.

"Did you just move in?" Tom asked.

Derek shook his head. "A little while ago."

"Come on, man, you've gotta splash some color on the walls. It looks like you're getting ready to sell."

181

"I like the simplicity," Derek said.

"One lesson I've learned is to always put a few roots down no matter how long you're going to be staying somewhere. When I first started shooting *Another Planet*, I was living in a hotel. But on the first night I put a picture of Mom and Dad right on the desk. It made the place feel like home."

"I'm working on it," Derek said, unable to keep the edge out of his voice. His interior decorations were currently the least of his concerns. "Actually, I just bought a piece of art from an up-and-coming artist," Derek added, remembering Mac's four by four canvas. He pointed to the splash of blue now lying on his TV stand.

"Oh my god, I love that," Achelia said. "Who's the artist?"

"His name's Mac," Derek said.

"Is he local?"

"You could say that," Derek said.

"I haven't seen his work before."

"Well, he's going to be big someday," Derek said. Which was technically true. From a purely physical standpoint.

Opening the fridge, Tom looked over his shoulder and said, "You don't mind, right?"

"Go for it."

But apparently the selection wasn't what he'd hoped—a jar of olives and an expired carton of eggs—because he abruptly closed the fridge and paced back to the futon.

"What's that?" Tom asked, pointing to the map left by Jackson Wilfred lying face-up on the coffee table.

"Nothing," Derek said. He quickly scooped up the brittle paper and folded it inside his copy of *Eldrid Babble*.

"What are you reading?"

"Just a book," Derek said, his voice dropping an octave. He might as well have growled as the part of him becoming entangled with the book asserted its ownership. *My book.* He shimmied backwards

182

to the kitchen and stashed the book in a drawer. He could feel the book protest against being shut away, as if Derek himself was being thrown into a dungeon.

"I know it's a book," Tom said. "What's it about? You know, I'm always looking for my next project."

"Just something from the library," Derek said. Derek had already accidentally brought the story of Eldrid Babble to life; he didn't need Hollywood tampering with Grimwell's brand of dark magic.

A moment of awkward silence passed between them as Tom surveyed the apartment and Achelia stood by Derek's lone window, framed by the fading evening light.

"I don't know how you do it," Tom finally said.

"Do what?"

"This." He motioned around the apartment as if gearing up for a monologue. "Make all those drinks. Deal with all those asshole customers. Earning just enough to get by. There's a story here." He must've seen the look of anger on Derek's face, because he quickly added, "No offense," which Derek had learned usually meant even more offensive comments were on the way. "You played a barista, didn't you, Achelia?"

She nodded, her eyes fixated on the scene outside the window. "Early in my career. Arthouse flick about a down-on-her-luck barista who's struggling to make ends meet."

"Sounds about right," Derek said.

"Before finding a hidden backroom where she can travel back in time."

"Didn't see that coming," Derek said.

"But only five minutes into the past. Consequently, she never learns anything all that useful."

"I'll have to check it out," Derek said.

Tom parachuted onto Derek's futon and put his feet up on the coffee table. "I thought we'd go to the city, grab some dinner at Daniel, and then maybe check out this club on the Lower East Side called Fishbowl. It's supposed to simulate the feel of being underwater."

"I kind of had plans tonight."

Tom tilted his head. He clearly hadn't expected that.

"Look, Derek. I understand you're angry. I'm angry too. What happened to Mom..." He abruptly broke off, as if waiting for someone to feed him a line. "...What happened to Mom just wasn't right. And Dad would be the first to admit he didn't handle it correctly. But that's grief, man. No one has an app to tell them where to go. How to get there. We're all just... lost."

Derek looked at Tom, unsettled by his words, something approaching wisdom.

"Did you get any of that, Achelia? I think it'd be perfect for next season when Wilks and Misha find that encampment of rebels."

And just like that, Derek's anger returned. Impossible to untangle the actor from the person.

"I'm sorry, I missed it, honey," Achelia said. She walked away from the window and looked at the three closed doors of Derek's apartment: a closet, a bathroom, and the front door. The sum total of Derek's daily decisions. "Which one is the restroom?" Achelia asked.

Derek pointed straight ahead and Achelia marched past the futon. Derek couldn't help but stare at her as she passed, once again feeling fiction invading his life, as if a rom-com had joined the list of genres currently upsetting Derek's reality.

As soon as the door closed, Derek turned his attention to Tom. "Are you even going to visit her?"

Tom sighed. "It's a stone, Derek. Mom's not there. I talk to her all the time. From Fiji. You know, life isn't meant to be lived staring down at the ground. It's meant to be lived looking up at the sky."

Derek almost nodded in agreement at his brother's sagely advice before realizing the line sounded familiar. "Wait a second? Isn't that from *Another Planet*?"

184

Tom smiled. "You've been watching, huh?"

Something about the accidental admission cracked the ice that had begun to freeze over the reunion.

"I like it," Derek said. "Even better than the book. When you put that alien in a headlock and yell—"

"You got slime on my slippers!" Tom shouted, disappearing behind the façade of Sergeant James Wilks.

Derek laughed. "Classic."

And for just a moment, it was like old times. The silence expanded. The unsaid. The impossible to say.

"Have you seen the last episode?" Tom finally asked. His tone had turned serious.

Derek shook his head. "I just started and I've been"—in the process of turning into a grimkin, but Tom didn't need to know that—"busy," Derek said instead.

"You've gotta watch. Promise me you'll watch the whole season." An urgency to his tone, as if his life depended on it. Was he really just that proud of his performance?

"Of course, I'll watch," Derek said.

Derek joined Tom on the futon, the square of light on the floor from the window slowly retreating as if being consumed by shadows. He thought of Wilfred's request to open the curtains. "Photosynthesis is a bitch," he'd said.

"Hey man, don't take this the wrong way, but I have to ask. What's going on with your ears?"

Derek self-consciously ran a hand over his ear. "Oh, you know, aging."

"Really?"

"And..." But Tom stopped himself. Maybe he'd picked up some tact after all, because there was no way he hadn't noticed Derek's thinning hair, his mottled and gnarled hands, or his gruff and shaggy appearance, the sum total of changes turning him into a grimkin.

185

"Nothing. It's probably just dark in here. Look, I haven't seen you in what, three years? And you have plans tonight. A date?"

"Sort of."

"There's no such thing as *sort of* having a date."

"I was going to visit her at work."

"Ah, Derek. Come on. First rule of women is to never visit them at work."

"Thanks for the advice."

"That's their domain."

"Still, I said I was going to see her. We're just... starting to figure things out."

"What's she do?"

"Waitress."

"Oh no! Chasing the waitress. Rookie mistake. Unless..."

Derek felt his cheeks grow flush. He looked away.

"You dog. My big bro. Banging the waitress."

"We're not *banging*."

"Sorry, sorry. Making love. Come on, let's go grab a bite so I can scope this chica out."

Derek suspected that *chica* was the only Spanish word Tom knew.

Achelia emerged from the bathroom, bringing with her a cloud of perfume that smelled like the ocean, as if she'd somehow bottled the beaches of Fiji. "Ready?"

"What do you say, bro?"

Derek reluctantly agreed, something in his intuition telling him that this was somehow important to his journey, or to use the language of story, which had begun to animate his life with a daring bravado, his plot points. After a brief detour to the bathroom for some tape, Derek and his brother, along with the Hollywood starlet Achelia Rose, climbed down the stairs in the flickering, hazy light to grab a bite at McDowell's.

Chapter 20

McDowell's was already busy with its geriatric dinner crowd: aging pensioners, widowers looking to grab a bite on chili night, overflow from the nearby town-subsidized nursing home, and of course, local celebrities Boris and Gerald in their usual stools at the bar. Derek hadn't been out in public with his brother since before the success of *Another Planet*, and now he could definitely feel a few heads turn as they made their way to a booth near the bar. Julius gave Derek a look, a head tilt that signaled surprise. Kat must've been in the kitchen, because by the time they sat down, Derek still hadn't seen her.

"Is this your hangout?" Tom said.

"I guess."

"Very quaint," Achelia said. "Kind of like a sitcom, eh?"

"Sure." *A dark, twisted sitcom where the main character suddenly wakes up with a tail*, Derek thought.

"What's good here?" Tom asked.

"Well, it's chili night."

"I'm currently on a keto diet," Tom said.

"Keto?"

"It basically means you can't eat anything."

"That's a pretty good description," Achelia said.

"Sounds healthy."

After Julius came over and took their order, scarcely looking down as if to show he didn't give a damn about celebrity—a beer for Derek, cucumber water for Tom and Achelia—a woman and her young daughter approached the table uncertainly, cellphone held aloft. "Sorry to bother you. Do you think we could have a picture?" the mother asked.

"Of course," Tom said.

Derek could see the pride in his brother's eyes. The feeling Tom had been chasing his whole life, from school plays, sports games, and academic spelling bees: The overachiever who could never quite achieve enough. And now he was soaking up the limelight, like a flower craning its neck toward the sun. Derek had never seen him so happy.

"Do you mind?" the woman asked Derek, handing him her cellphone.

"No problem," Derek said. He gritted his teeth and smiled. While he hated the idea of taking a fan photo of his brother, he also didn't want to make a scene. At least not for such a petty reason. Every hero had to learn when to take a stand and when to turn the page.

Achelia and Tom got up and posed for a picture with the mother and daughter, recreating one of the now iconic scenes of *Another Planet*: Sergeant Wilks and Misha looking up and pointing at the sky while spaceships hover over New York.

"Say cheese," Derek said, immediately hating himself for uttering the cliché phrase.

He snapped the photo, handed the phone back, then Tom and Achelia returned to their side of the booth. Tom shrugged his shoulders as he slid in, as if to say, "Just part of the job."

"That's the most surprising part of fame," Tom said. "Living in so many people's minds as someone else. More of a character than a person. Some people expect me to start shouting lines at them. Here's the thing: I've never even read the books." He pressed his finger to his lips and looked down guiltily at the shiny lacquer table, as if scrutinizing his reflection. "Don't tell anyone, but it's true. With all the scripts and..." He paused, delicately considering how to phrase his litany of distractions—Achelia? Drugs? Booze? Tea tree-infused facials? "...Stuff that goes along with fame," he finally said, "I haven't really had the time. Plus, while I was getting ready to audition, Mom was... you know..." He ran his fingers through his hair and lifted his eyes to meet Derek's. "That was tough. Really tough. But I channeled it, you know? I put it into the character. I put my whole damn self into it."

Achelia gently took his hand. "You really did. It's what makes the show so special."

Derek's beer arrived, along with Tom and Achelia's cucumber water. "Thanks, Julius," Derek said, but Julius had already walked away.

"Cucumbers are really making a comeback," Tom said.

"From what?" Derek asked.

Either Tom hadn't heard or didn't want to dignify Derek's question with an answer. Instead, he took out his phone. "Have I shown you pictures from the set?"

Derek shook his head.

"You've got to go to Fiji." Tom now seemed shaky. A little nervous. Jumpy almost. His hand trembled as he swung the phone around and showed Derek a zoomed-out photo of a palm tree, and for just a moment, Derek could've sworn he saw a flicker of doubt in Tom's eyes.

Achelia steadied his hand. "Take a breath, honey."

"It's a different way of life. Drinking kava. Walking on hot stones."

Eating people, Derek thought, remembering a sordid library book he'd read called *A History of Cannibalism*. "No offense to the

Fijians," Derek quickly added, wondering how this might play in a book about his life. Which, in a way, is exactly what *Eldrid Babble* had become.

"We're thinking about moving there full time," Tom said.

Achelia, mid-sip, practically choked on her cucumber water. "If you mean thinking about it for retirement, or another dimension where we both don't have careers and families in the US, then yes, we're thinking about it."

"My Rosey just needs a little convincing."

"Sure, Tom," she said, rolling her eyes as she rubbed his back, and Derek was struck by the mundanity of their relationship. Cues shared between millions of couples all around the world. For some reason, Derek had thought their lives might be more exciting. But when you stripped away the movie sets, the paparazzi lights, the immense wealth and glamor, what were you left with?

Boris and Gerald soon wandered over, pushing into the booth beside Derek, pressing him against the wall.

"I'm Boris," Boris said. "And this is Gerald."

Gerald waved.

"If you want your picture taken with us, we'd be happy to do it," Tom said. "But just coming here and sitting down..."

Tom's voice trailed off, caught off-guard by Boris's confused expression.

"What's he talking about?" Boris said.

"Why would we want our picture taken with you?" Gerald asked.

"Boris and Gerald are my friends," Derek said.

"We're his *best* friends," Boris added.

He was right. Sure, they were at least fifty years older than Derek, but for all intents and purposes, they really were Derek's best friends. Pretty much his only friends.

Tom and Achelia looked from Derek to the two octogenarians on his left, as if waiting for someone to jump out and prank them on a hidden camera reality TV show. Which, given their celebrity status, was a distinct possibility.

"What do you guys do?" Achelia asked. "I love learning about people's stories."

Boris motioned to the bar. "This."

"But we're not drunks," Gerald said, "if that's what you're thinking. We started coming here a few years ago after our wives passed away. It turns out we were right across the hall from each other in the hospital, and well, I guess we've been keeping each other company ever since."

"What a story," Tom said, reaching for his phone to jot down a note. "And it must've been around the same time Janine broke up with Derek?"

Derek hadn't thought about it like that before, but Tom was right. "Pretty much," Derek said.

"A real buddy comedy. Maybe a dramedy, depending on who we get to write the script. Three characters from different walks of life brought together by heartbreak."

"And there's a love interest too," Achelia pointed out, just as Kat entered the dining room from the kitchen.

She had a thick headband covering her ears. Could she be hiding her transformation into Belinda? Derek quickly brushed the thought away. She'd only read for one night. No way the magic worked that fast. Still, Derek noticed she looked more tired than usual: her eyes were bloodshot and there was a sluggish quality to her movements, like she was dragging her feet through seaweed. But wasn't that just parenthood?

She spied Derek from across the room and gave a quick wave. Then she saw Tom and Achelia, world-famous movie stars. Her eyes widened, but only for a moment. Her attention was pulled to one of her tables, where a man with bushy eyebrows and a caveman-like jaw had called to her, holding up an empty glass of wine. She held up an index finger to Derek and hurried to the bar.

"Not bad, bro," Tom said.

"What?"

"She's a..." He glanced at Achelia. "...a very beautiful woman."

"She's a saint," Boris said.

"We're just feeling things out."

"Is that what the kids are calling it these days?" Gerald said.

Julius placed two bowls in front of Gerald and Boris's spots at the bar.

"Anyway, that's our cue," Gerald said, clearly eager to get to his food.

"We'll be in touch," Tom said.

"That's okay," Boris said. "We're not for sale." At which point, they both got up and retreated to their steaming bowls of chili.

"Such a cool place," Tom said. "I love it here. Being among the people. The real America. What was that word Thomas Jefferson used? Yeoman?"

"Now you're quoting Jefferson?" Derek asked.

"They want me to play him," Tom said, lowering his voice, as if a reporter might be hiding beneath the table. "A story told from the perspective of Sally Hemmings. Let's just say it's a side of your Founding Fathers that's never been shown before."

"There's already Oscar buzz," Achelia said.

"But it hasn't even been made."

"That's how the industry works," Tom said.

Derek sighed. Sipped his beer.

"You sure you're feeling okay?" Tom asked.

"Yeah, why?"

"It's just you look... Don't take this the wrong way, but you look kind of haggard."

"Tom!" Achelia said, surprised.

"Gee, thanks."

"Hey, that's not what I meant. It's just that you look..."

"Older?"

192

"Yeah. But, *a lot* older. And *a lot* different."

"It's been three years."

"But you don't look three years older. It's almost like you're someone else. Look at your hands, for Chrissake."

Derek quickly stuffed his hands into his pockets. "Well in the working world, we don't get everything handed to us or have time for massages or fucking keto, whatever that is. Worrying about money, rent, all that stuff. It takes years off your life. There's a study on it. Somewhere."

"Okay, okay."

"I'm serious. You're off shooting a show on the beach. I'm waking up at five a.m. to open the Read and Bean. It's just not fair."

He realized he was yelling, the anger of Eldrid and the amulet somehow worming its way beneath his skin.

"Where's this coming from?"

"I don't know," Derek said, gulping down his beer. His story felt fragmented; plot points thrown to the wind. He wished he had *Eldrid Babble* to consult: a playbook to offer him insight into how he should act and what his next steps should be. A clear narrative arc, a sense of purpose when living moment to moment, not a scattered and chaotic mishmash of unresolved emotions and issues.

He'd grown dependent on Chester Felten's asides, offering him counsel and wisdom in the form of Eldrid's tale.

"Look man," Tom said, his voice strained, as if struggling through poor reception, "I know things have been tough between us. The truth is..." He took a deep breath and sipped his cucumber water.

Just before he was about to speak, Julius came over. "What can I get you guys?" he asked gruffly, as if forcing himself to take the order.

"What'd Kat put in the chili tonight?" Derek asked.

"Apricot," Julius said. He pretended to gag.

"Sounds interesting. I'll take the usual."

"Bowl of chili and a side of fries, you got it," Julius said.

"My big bro has a usual!"

Derek's tail twitched in hunger. That was new.

"House salad for me," Tom said. "Hold the dressing. Please no onions. Tomatoes are fine but can you make sure they're crisp and not slimy?"

"And for the lady?" Julius asked. Derek couldn't tell whether he was being sarcastic or fawning.

"The burger," Achelia said. "Medium. This place looks like it would have a hell of a burger."

"Okay," Tom said, "I guess we're living it up. Add some chicken to my salad, please. But no seasoning. Grilled, not fried. Just a little salt and pepper."

"Got it."

"Is the lettuce organic?"

"It isn't not organic," Julius said, taking the company line.

"Ahh, forget it. Let's live dangerously."

Julius rolled his eyes and disappeared into the kitchen.

"Now tell him," Achelia said.

Derek looked to Tom for explanation. "Tell me what?"

Achelia slid closer to Tom, and the faux leather made a farting noise, completely the wrong tone and mood—but that was real life without the careful curation of a book.

Tom sighed, his body leaning against Achelia's. "Remember when we both got tested for mom's disease?"

Derek nodded. They'd gone to the doctor's office together in a brief moment of brotherly solidarity. Derek didn't know if he wanted to find out if he carried the gene. To have a countdown clock appear over his head. But their mother had encouraged—more like demanded—they do it, even as she was fighting her own battle against the illness. Derek had been relieved and guilty to receive the news. The results came back negative. The genetic misfortune had skipped him and Tom. They had even celebrated with a glass of champagne.

Tom poured some water onto his hand and dabbed his neck. *Cue the dramatic scene*, Derek thought. *Lights, camera, action.*

"I don't know why I didn't tell you... I guess I thought... To be honest, I don't have a clue. I just didn't want to add to the shit. Does that make any sense? Like I thought if I kept it to myself, maybe me and you could have this one win. Maybe Mom would be okay. And then after Mom died, it seemed like a lie I had to live with."

"Wait. What are you talking about?"

"The test. Mine came back positive. It's been like this ticking time bomb in my head. And then a few months ago, I started to get dizzy, so I went to the doctor... And it's the same symptoms Mom had. There's no timeline or anything. Nothing like that. It just feels like I'm in my third act."

Derek's beer continued to set, little foam bubbles bursting.

"I'm much better with a script."

He saw Kat out of the corner of his eye, carrying a tray filled with food—wings, burgers, fries—and he felt desperately hungry. All he wanted to do was eat. Some people lose their appetite when hearing bad news, but Derek had the opposite reaction: a desperate desire to bury his feelings in a bowl of chili.

"You there, bro?"

Derek forced himself to meet Tom's gaze. "I just didn't see it coming." One of the unfortunate consequences of not being able to flip to the end.

"Look man, it's all good. I'm sure I'll be fine. But if not... I just wanted to get a chance to figure things out with you."

"Figure what out?" Derek had assumed Tom didn't think of him at all beyond the occasional lavish gift: the bathrobe, cologne, leather gloves, all of which had come in handy recently. Definitely not in a mathematical sense where they'd have to figure something out. They were two independent variables who happened to come from the same formula.

"Just all of this," Tom said, circling his hands around an imaginary cloud.

"You two are brothers," Achelia said sagely, and even though she was only stating fact, it seemed to resonate with a deeper truth. It could've been how beautiful she looked while saying it, too.

"We are," Derek said. Not exactly words worthy of a script, but that's all he could think to say in the moment.

"Brothers," Tom said.

Maybe that was enough. Maybe being brothers was enough. Before either of them could add to the moment, spoil the simple understanding with an attempt to elaborate or explain, Kat approached their table holding an empty tray. Derek looked closer at the headband, still covering the tips of her ears.

"Chili night is my least favorite night of the week. All-you-can-eat and people think it's a competition. All this extra work and no extra tip. But wait until you try the apricot. I'm very proud of that combination. I was giving Mac some apricot the other day and the idea suddenly came to me."

"The artist?" Achelia asked.

Kat hugged her tray close, tapping along the edges in a frenetic rhythm. "Maybe. But he also really loves blocks and music and letting milk dribble down his chin."

Achelia nodded, as if Mac's behavior was just another embodiment of an artist's bohemian lifestyle.

"You must be her," Tom said.

"Her who?" Kat asked.

"Her." Tom paused. "Just her."

"I guess I'll take that." She turned her attention toward Achelia. "I have to say I really loved you in *Just a Minute of Your Time.*"

"Thank you," Achelia said.

"I swear I can recite almost every line."

"It was a bit of a departure for me, but clearly it connected with my demographic. You know, I can't play high school or college anymore, so they were like, what do we do? Let's make her a single mom with a kid, trying to make ends meet as a telemarketer. The hard-luck story. Everyone can relate to that."

"You have no idea," Kat said. "Haven't seen *Another Planet* yet, but the preview looks amazing."

"My agent just told me there's a Tagalog version," Tom said. "I thought he was making it up. But it's real. I couldn't even tell you where Tagalog is on a map. Guess it just goes to show that a good story is a good story. No matter where you live."

Derek couldn't help but agree. He'd become fluent in story thanks to the shelves of the Pemberton Library, his own Rosetta Stone helping him translate the complex vowels and consonants of life.

"Anyway, I better get going," Kat said. "My table twelve is very demanding."

"Why is it always table twelve?" Derek asked.

"One of the great mysteries of the Twilight Zone. Nice meeting you two."

Kat walked away as she hummed the theme song.

"She seems nice," Tom said.

Derek nodded, unable to contain his smile. "We've just been on a couple of dates."

"But this is your place?"

"I guess so."

"That's nice. I've always wanted a place."

"Everywhere you go is your place."

"But it's artificial. That's why I want to move to Fiji. Put down roots, you know? With my Rosey. The second *Another Planet* dips in the ratings or audiences stop liking my character—it's all over. But this." He banged on the lacquered table. "This is stable."

Maybe it was. And the whole time Derek had been waiting for a change—dreaming of a change—it hadn't been about his work or life or love, but about him. He'd been wanting a change of character.

"Cheers to Mom," Tom said, holding up his cucumber water. In the chaos of all the latest revelations and twists, Derek had forgotten it was his mom's birthday. She would've been sixty-four.

"Cheers," Derek said.

The three of them clinked glasses.

Chapter 21

After dinner, Tom and Achelia took an Uber to their hotel in the city. "Wish we could stay longer, but we have an early morning TV appearance," Tom said. "Fucking Good Morning America."

"Fucking Good Morning America," Derek agreed.

Despite the last three years thinking of his brother as some Hollywood star, a strange and distant species of human, Derek was surprised to find that he was still the same little brother. Pushing jealousy to the side—after all, Derek could see himself moving to Grimwell before Fiji—he wished Tom good luck and told him not to wait three years to visit again.

"You're always welcome to visit us in Fiji," Tom said.

"Or Los Angeles," Achelia said pointedly.

Derek settled in at home, still puzzling over the map drawn by Chester Felten. If he drove up to Ashton, wouldn't that make the book more real than it already was? For all Derek knew, it might even speed up his transformation into a grimkin. Not to mention, a journey to

199

Grimwell ran the risk of angering whatever evil had placed a curse on the book in the first place. And on the off chance that this was all just some big misunderstanding, a shared delusion between writer and reader—the fictional dream, one of the books in the library had called it—a trip to Ashton would hasten his descent into madness until he became Pemberton's eccentric bench-sitter, a novelty to be ogled at by neighborhood kids. In any case, he had work tomorrow, so he had no choice but to delay his journey into Grimwell's dark and twisted pages. His literal journey, at least.

Needing a mental break, he threw on the next episode of *Another Planet*. Sergeant Wilks and Misha had figured out the Troglodorfs' plans to ferry workers to their home planet and discovered the aliens' one and only weakness: electricity. Then Sergeant Wilks and Misha had a cringeworthy sex scene in a power plant replete with over-the-top puns:

```
              WILKS
    Now do you feel the spark?
```

And Wilks and Misha eventually traced the alien headquarters to the subway tunnels of New York City, where Wilks had uttered the show's tagline:

```
              MISHA
    This doesn't look like
    New York.


              WILKS
    It may as well be
    another planet.
```

When the credits played, Derek closed his eyes and almost immediately fell asleep, as if desperate to escape the world of fantasy for the driftless soft-edges of dream. In the hazy realm of his subconscious, he found himself sitting at the table by the fireplace in Crimpleton Tavern, and when he looked up, he saw Kat, part grimkin, part human, waiting to take his order.

* * *

The next morning, Derek dressed, combed his hair, and then brushed his teeth, once again marveling at his grimkincisors in the mirror. He made sure the edges of his ears were hidden and then powdered his tail to prevent chafing. He concealed his mottled skin with some makeup he'd bought online—not too greasy, he wouldn't want the errant handshake to slough off the cover and ruin the illusion—and then put on his shoes. Barely. His toes scraped against the edges and he wondered if it was time to order the next size up. Instead of dreaming of adventure, he found his mind focused on the task at hand. He wasn't becoming Eldrid, he was becoming Derek, and that felt right to him, to be finally settling into his life in all of its strangeness.

Still, it didn't stop him from tucking *The Strange Life and Times of Eldrid Babble* into his jacket pocket for safekeeping. Just in case. He didn't know what might necessitate an escape into its pages, but that was all the more reason to be prepared.

He still hadn't heard from Wilfred, but he wanted nothing more than to believe that Pemberton's missing librarian had finally had a moment of reconciliation with his family. Sure, he couldn't exactly explain the whole situation, but he could certainly own up to his mistakes and promise to do better—if they'd have him back. Everyone ages and Wilfred's aging had just so happened to turn him into somewhat of a tree. There was probably a disease for that.

After watching the penultimate episode of *Another Planet*—god, the show was addicting, he had to give his brother that—Derek made his way to the Bean, gulping in the crisp morning air. He felt alive, emboldened, ready to take on the world as it came, with or without a plot point to follow.

Especially the ever-changing plot of *Eldrid Babble*.

As Derek approached the library, his phone buzzed in his pocket. He fished it out and saw that his brother had sent him a selfie from the set of Good Morning America. They had cleared the air and had a moment of resolution—at least according to the language of story. Derek loved the text and wished him good luck in the interview. He said he'd be sure to watch, and who knows, maybe he could even relinquish some of the hatred and resentment he had for his father too. He didn't text that last part, but he hoped Tom would catch the subtext. Some of the sting of his mother's final days were gone, like a bite that had been properly taken care of, just a faint scar and the lingering memory of pain.

The morning passed quickly. In between customers, Sue showed photos of a large and lumbering walrus perched on ice skates—she'd taken *a lot* of photos—and Sam stayed on rag time, wiping down tables with a ferocious dedication that both pleased and saddened Derek. After the morning rush, they ate lunch together, each of them grabbing an item from the fridge and gathering around the center table.

"And then Whipple—that's the walrus's name—did a backflip," Sue said excitedly, still high off the thrill of watching a walrus ice-skate. "Right on the ice! My little Robbie pretty much lost his mind. And all I could think about was the person inside the Whipple costume. Probably trained their whole life thinking they might go to the Olympics only to one day wake up as a walrus. Not exactly known in the animal kingdom for its grace and elegance."

"At least they're doing what they love," Derek said.

"I love playing gin rummy, but I don't think I'd want to do it in a walrus costume," Sue said.

Derek looked across the table and realized Sam was staring at him. "Everything okay, Sam?"

Sam narrowed his eyes. "It's just you look... tired."

"When I turned thirty-five, everything just went to hell," Sue said. "Don't worry, Sam. You'll get there."

Derek didn't take Sue's reassurance as a compliment. He took a bite of his turkey sandwich, lifted his gaze to meet Sam's across the table. "Everything's fine. Everything okay with you?"

"Sure, why do you ask?"

"Just haven't seen you with your GMAT book lately."

"Oh, that. I've thought about it and I don't think I'll be applying to grad school. Not sure if the business world is right for me."

The table stayed quiet. At first, Derek had been happy to see Sam get his comeuppance, but now something worried him. He liked the pained look on Sam's face. He liked knowing that he'd been at least partially responsible for his defeat. He remembered something Eldrid Babble had said soon after his journey began: "There's a cost to becoming a hero. And in this case, the price is becoming a villain."

A little while later, Derek looked up from the register to see aging science teacher Rich Wise walking toward him. Actually, walking wasn't the right word. More like shambling. He seemed lost without his marker and whiteboard, somehow smaller. Pathetic was the word that came to Derek's mind as he reached the register. As if without an objective on the board and a room full of desks, Mr. Wise didn't really exist as a character at all.

"What can I get you, Mr. Wise?" Derek asked.

"Have you seen our mutual friend?" he growled.

"Why?"

"Because something happened last night," he said hesitantly. Mr. Wise leaned against the counter and Derek recoiled; he didn't think Mr. Wise would suddenly lunge at him but there was something in his eyes: not so much a crazed-look as a malignant malevolence. "I was home last night and I'm almost certain my old pal came to visit," Mr. Wise finally wheezed.

"What do you mean?"

"I guess I left a part out when I first told you the story." Mr. Wise clutched the counter for support, his hands white-knuckled as his belly drooped in between. A pale lump of flesh peeked out of his shirt, as if his belly was squinting at Derek through a slitted eye. "There's a biological imperative," Mr. Wise said. "It's what I've been teaching for over forty years. At least trying to teach. It's why people get together and sometimes why people leave. Basic biology." He said it with a hint of disgust. "I guess the loneliness just got to me after Darla left. And Cynthia was lonely too. That's Mr. Wilfred's wife in case you can't read between the lines. Living in that big house. Jason asking all those questions about where his dad ran off to. And I was sad too, I suppose. Because I missed my old friend. And Darla. Always Darla. I guess you could say Cynthia and I leaned on each other for support." He kept his eyes focused on the counter, as if he had just been reprimanded for using his cellphone in class—a look Derek was certain Mr. Wise knew well. "And we're still leaning on each other for support."

Sam had taken notice of Mr. Wise and retreated even farther away, now wiping down the table closest to the stack of library shelves in the fiction section. Most likely Sam didn't have fond memories of Mr. Wise's lectures. The lights hung bright and low from the wooden rafters, and in that moment, one began to flicker, a dying star.

"Did Wilfred know?"

"I tried telling him but I worried it would hurt him too much," Mr. Wise said, his voice now practically a whisper. "And last night"—Mr. Wise breathed heavily, as if straining to finish the sentence—"Last night we heard something scrabbling at the window. Like a branch scraping against the glass."

"And?"

"The nearest tree is about a hundred feet away."

A customer had come in, craning their neck to study the menu.

"Listen Mr. Wise, I—"

"You've gotta understand. We were devastated and absence has a way of making the heart grow fonder. But it works in more ways than one. His absence made us grow fonder for each other. Now, I don't believe in coincidences, and I've also dealt with more than a few mendacious students in my day. Don't forget we had ourselves a little deal. I can always see the truth in the eyes."

Now Derek was the one who leaned forward. "I saw him. Briefly."

"Did he say anything about..." His voice trailed off, unable to verbalize his deceit.

Derek shook his head. "He must've visited me before."

"How'd he look?"

Such a mundane turn of phrase, but how could Derek explain the strange new body Wilfred inhabited? "Not like himself."

"I've got a feeling you're not telling me the whole truth," Mr. Wise said, his belly still resting on the counter.

"It's like that complicated science you were talking about," Derek said. "There's an explanation, I just don't fully understand it. At least not yet."

The customer glanced impatiently at her watch, one of those fitness trackers that measured steps, heart rate, sleep. Why read when you could learn more about yourself from a watch? "You should get going."

Mr. Wise nodded. "You look different, David."

"It's Derek."

He waved him off, as if such trivial matters weren't important. "You know what the Buddha says about secrets. 'Three things cannot stay hidden. The sun, the moon, and the truth.'"

"Now you're quoting Buddha?" Maybe Darwin or Bill Nye, but Mr. Wise didn't strike Derek as the religious type.

"Saw it on a fortune cookie. Right around the time Cynthia and I started seeing each other. And I've been waiting for Jackson to find out the truth ever since. After a few years, I started hoping he'd find out. Secrets don't nag or gnaw or needle. They devour."

Something about Mr. Wise's declaration struck a chord, and Derek wanted nothing more than for him to be gone.

"Say hi to Darla for me, Mr. Wise," Derek said as he motioned the next customer forward.

"Will do." He backed away, shuffling past the customer. When he reached the door, he glanced over his shoulder. His face looked tired and withdrawn. Skeletal. Derek almost felt guilty about breaking his end of the bargain. But the alternative wasn't possible. Especially to a science teacher. While Mr. Wise may have believed in complicated science, Derek had a feeling the magic of Grimwell would be an unwelcome page in his textbook understanding. And lead to a lot of questions. Questions Derek still couldn't answer.

The rest of the day droned on. Derek couldn't shake the image of those branches scraping against Mr. Wilfred's old house. Like a scene from a horror movie. How easy it was for fantasies to become nightmares. It made Derek wonder what he'd find if he actually journeyed to Grimwell. Would Crimpleton Common be packed with grimkins hurrying on cobblestones to drink their sweet leaf coffee and eat their shabberberry scones? Or would he find something more sinister?

He didn't see Kat's text message until the last few minutes of his shift, fishing his phone out of his pocket as he undid his apron and threw it in the laundry basket.

Need to talk.

Derek puzzled over the message. It could be about anything. Their newly budding relationship. Her burning desire to see him again. His thoughts on the subtle hint of apricot in the chili. Okay, who was he kidding? He knew exactly what this was about. The book. The story that had become both his captor and his chance for redemption.

At work, Derek wrote back. *Call you later.*

He wasn't ready to answer questions about *Eldrid Babble* yet. For one, he didn't think he had any answers. While Jackson Wilfred had taken copious notes, none of his scribblings shed light on why the book turned its reader into one of Grimwell's characters. Most of Wilfred's hope had been pinned on visiting the world of Grimwell. A prospect that didn't seem quite so appealing. Derek didn't know what he'd find in Grimwell—he hadn't even finished the book, and so had no idea how Eldrid's journey ended—but all the same, worlds with magic amulets and ferocious wolf-like creatures generally weren't the most inviting to outsiders. Would Mayor Frumple, if he was even still alive, roll out the red carpet when Derek strolled into Crimpleton Common? Not likely. What if Lord Grittlebane was still in power? It made Derek feel ridiculous to even think of Lord Grittlebane as anything other than a rip-off of Sauron from *The Lord of the Rings*, but still, something about the dark magic of the amulet and shining spire of the Summit in Grim City gave Derek pause. Sure, the name sounded ridiculous, more like a character from a Disney movie than an actual dictator, but Grimwell wasn't Earth, and names could be misleading.

After work, Derek walked to the park and sat on the bench where he and Wilfred had met yesterday. Derek realized the spot seemed shadier, more covered than before. When he turned around, he saw something that startled him. One tree stood out of line, as if it had taken a timid step forward. Standing tall and resolute, this tree seemed to blot out the other trees. It looked eerily similar to Wilfred, at least as much as a tree could resemble a person. With a large round trunk, two indentations on the front that resembled eyes, and a small upside-down crescent that crisscrossed the bark, the tree appeared to be shouting in pain.

Looking around, careful to make sure no one was near, Derek got up off the bench and walked toward the tree. *My descent into insanity is complete*, Derek thought as he placed a single hand on the bark, before abruptly moving it: something too intimate about touching this particular tree, as if he'd accidentally caressed a cheek or ran his fingers through chest hair. Its branches looked like arms and Derek couldn't help but think of Ancient Greek myths and their twisted punishments.

"What happened?" Derek whispered.

No response.

Even though he knew he looked insane, he didn't care. What was the difference between magic and insanity, anyway? Both required a leap—whether by choice or circumstance—away from the rational into the gaping chasm of the irrational. As Derek stared at the rugged bark, he knew that Wilfred must have finally worked up the courage to face his family, looking to make amends for his long years of absence. Derek imagined his long spindly fingers curling around the corner of the house, peering into a large picture window in the family room only to find Mr. Wise and Cynthia curled up on the couch, Jason sitting in his old rocking chair, a boy now on the cusp of adulthood. Did he think about doing something more violent to his philandering friend? A final step away from heroism into the abyss of Lord Grittlebane's evil?

More likely, Mr. Wilfred had known he'd run out of pages. After all, he'd been a librarian—he knew when a story was over. Without the hope of reconciliation, Derek assumed he meandered through back roads, standing still in the headlights of cars, his feet clawing at the pavement, desperate to finally put roots down. By then, the bark would've practically encased him, his head sprouting a thick canopy of leaves, his arms held out straight on either side of his body, until he could barely move. Sometime before dawn, he must've finally reached Pemberton Park and let his feet sink into the dirt. Deeper and deeper, the soil lapping at what had once been his ankles. While Derek liked to believe he felt relief, he knew it must've been short-lived: a momentary respite before the realization of his wooden prison finally dawned on him and the sun cast its first muted rays.

Derek moved closer to the tree, until he was only inches away, look-ing right at the indentations where eyes might've been, had Mr. Wil-fred lived in Grimwell in the copse community with Grandfather Tree.

"Hello?" Still looking over his shoulder to make sure no one could hear him.

A light breeze crawled through the air. Derek buttoned up his coat. Soon, the flowers would start to bloom and the rainy and dreary winter would officially end. At least the part that wasn't a state of mind. The winter became colder—and longer—when you didn't have something to keep you warm. Or someone.

Just as Derek was about to turn around, he heard something clear its throat. A deep and guttural growl. As if it was coming from beneath a thicket of wood. Very faint, almost a whisper from another time. Maybe another world:

"Destroy the book."

He'd heard the three words unmistakably. As he stepped away, startled by the wrecked voice, as well as the prospect of Wilfred now having become a tree, he felt the book pulse in his jacket pocket, once again demanding to be read. The sensible thing to do would be to bury the book, just like Wilfred had done all those years ago. Or, better yet, throw it overboard in the Atlantic Ocean with a heavy anchor. Sure, he'd have to go on a cruise, but what hero wouldn't take one for the team?

No.

This time, the word came from his own conscience, the part of him that had waded into heroism over the last week before being caught in the undertow of *Eldrid Babble*. The memory of getting the girl, telling off his boss, and fighting a literal giant had stayed with him. He liked the feeling. Actually, he loved the feeling. Maybe a little too much, the same way Eldrid had loved the magic amulet, but that didn't mean it was all bad.

Derek had to keep reading. He knew he shouldn't, but he needed to see how Eldrid's journey—maybe even his—ended. Jackson Wilfred said the book had captured the writer's voice, but Derek knew it was more complicated than that, because it wasn't simply a book, but a conversation between writer and reader. As Derek opened to the next chapter, he felt himself dissolving into Eldrid Babble. Becoming Eldrid Babble.

* * *

We were in the heart of the Trembling Forest, about ten miles away from Grim City. Eldrid and I had set up camp in a small clearing, calculating our next move. After all, we couldn't simply stroll through the city's gates and ask to see Lord Grittlebane. We'd be target practice for the Lord's Guard. Slipping in under the cover of night didn't seem possible, either. The wizened elf's warning made it seem as if the city was alive, pulsing with the dark magic that had transformed the small village of Crimpleton.

The trees were greener than I'd ever seen them before and seemed to hum in the afternoon sunlight, singing a merry song of spring. Whatever had taken over Grim City and the surrounding villages and hamlets clearly hadn't yet reached the lush wood of the Trembling Forest, though I did notice these trees seemed more reserved. Tight-lipped—at least at first—compared to the loquacious ramblings of Grandfather Tree.

Nothing much of importance happened in that week we hunkered down in the forest surrounded by the whispering oaks, trying to find a way to slip into the capital undetected. After a couple of nights, the trees loosened up, grateful for the company and eager to share family histories, gripes about the beeches, and, during one interminable soliloquy, the oft-misunderstood question of how trees reproduce.

Eldrid would stay up late into the night and look up at the strange constellations of the Grimwell sky, reminiscing about the land he'd left behind, the comfortable little village of Crimpleton with its small-scale replicas and plentiful glasses of barley cream. Eldrid also spoke often of Belinda and their date in Crimpleton Tavern. In a book, the author could add chapters from other perspectives, zigzagging characters through the complex web of plot. But in real life, we were left to guess at the fates of others, and I knew Eldrid longed for news about his beloved and his fellow grimkins. I didn't want to tell him about the dark premonition creeping in the back of my mind.

As for me, I had resurrected Death's Diary, filling my actuarial analysis notebook with musings on the peculiar land of Grimwell. Whereas before my fount of inspiration had felt like a dry well, Grimwell had opened a gushing faucet, and I couldn't stop cataloguing the world around me. I guess part of me knew that someday I'd be drawn to tell the story of Grimwell.

The trees seemed to enjoy conversation and told many tales of the Trembling Forest. Sometimes it was hard to find the line between truth and lie, as oaks are known to exaggerate and turn an acorn of truth into an oak-sized story. A common turn of phrase in the world of trees, I'm told.

We learned of the blight that almost wiped out the oaks in the time before grimkins, and how they'd enlisted the help of trolls to cut down diseased branches and even move some of the trees to greener forests. We learned of the internecine war between the oaks and beeches, before the Council of Trees had been formed to mediate disputes. We learned of family histories, filled with many saplings and acorns far too numerous (and boring) to recount, even one stand of trees that somehow intersected with Grandfather Tree's plentiful branches.

On the fifth night, after much chitchat and winding detours through thickets of story, one of the trees, a small oak named Ogbar, revealed a rumored entrance into Grim City through a sewer.

"Why didn't you mention that earlier?" Eldrid asked, clearly annoyed.

"We had a lot of catching up to do," Ogbar said plainly.

We debated and ultimately decided it was our only chance. On the one hand, it might be a trap; on the other, it was the only way to keep turning the pages of our story.

211

On the day we finally set off on our journey to the capital, a chill had settled in the air, not so much biting, as devouring, ready to eat us alive. The Summit loomed in the distance, a stone spire crowned with Lord Grittlebane's flag: the ominous red eyes floating in a sea of black, all thanks to a dark magic that had brought the surrounding villages to their knees and consolidated Lord Grittlebane's power.

Eldrid could scarcely believe he'd built a small-scale replica of the Summit mere weeks ago.

As we tramped through the forest, I noticed the bright green leaves began to fade. The deep cerulean blue sky muted into a dull gray. While the curse of the Hero's Stone hadn't yet ravaged the interior of the Trembling Forest, the trees on the outskirts slumped uncomfortably, quiet and withdrawn, their leaves withered, some turned black. One tree had fallen over and snapped in two. It looked to be in pain, and when I walked by, I could've sworn I heard a haunting moan.

A twig snapped, jarring me out of my mournful trance.

Eldrid reacted first, turning around to meet the noise, while I was only a hair behind. I couldn't believe my eyes. A giant towered over us, its single cycloptic eye blinking in confusion. It wore tattered clothes, more like a potato sack than an outfit (giants are terrible tailors, given their clumsy and fat fingers). Lopsided ears bulged from either side of its misshapen head, making its face resemble a piece of modernist art. Large red boils erupted out of its cheeks and a sheen of pus ran toward its chin. Lizard-like, a large tongue lumbered over puffy red lips to slurp the gooey liquid.

We might have been able to escape the glare of the giant's lone eyeball, but no sooner had we turned around than another giant had clambered up behind us, this one even uglier. It must have recently been in a fight because its eyelid was partially closed, oozed over with a green film.

"What do we have here?" the giant with the injured eye gurgled. It sounded as if his vocal cords were slicked in molasses.

"Smells like a grimkin to me," the other giant said, his voice less phlegmy, but by no means pleasant. Grating was the word that came to mind. "Wouldn't you say, Frem?"

Frem nodded his bulbous head. He momentarily lost his balance before slamming against a tree. Now I was sure of it. Frem's last meal had given him hell before sliding down his gullet.

"Tasty, but their screams give me heartburn," the other giant replied. I never learned its name, but for the sake of story, I'll call him Brem.

"How many times do I have to tell you to make sure they're dead before you start eating them?"

"That's rich coming from you," Brem said. "And what's this?"

I felt a grubby finger grab my leg and pick me up. My world tilted as gravity lost its hold on me. The giant dangled me in front of its face and began speaking, its sharp, dagger-like teeth filled with rotting flesh. The smell was so strong I had to choke back vomit.

"What are you?" Brem asked.

"A human," I responded shakily, by this point accustomed to answering the question.

"Get your hands off of me," Eldrid screamed. When I glanced over my shoulder, the blood still rushing to my head, I saw that Eldrid now hung upside down in Frem's clutch.

"A human?" Frem asked, his attention momentarily pulled away from what I assumed he hoped would be his lunch.

"I've heard they're delicious," said Brem, which is really the last thing you want to hear when a giant is dangling you two feet away from their mouth.

Eldrid had gone catatonic, clutched in Frem's meaty hand. I'm ashamed to admit it, but I thought Eldrid had given up, resigned to a murky tomb within the giant's belly. But a true adventure never brings you back to where you started. Amulet or not, Eldrid was not the same grimkin that began this tale.

213

*"We could split them halfsies," said Frem. "Right down the middle."
As he spoke, I saw a piece of bone caught between his molars. His gums
were swollen and blood oozed from the place a tooth had once been.*

*"Grimkins are also very helpful," Eldrid said, suddenly coming to
life. "Especially to giants with bones stuck between their teeth."*

*Frem wiggled his fat fingers. A look passed between Frem and
Brem. Blood dribbled down Frem's chin; clearly, his injuries hadn't
properly healed.*

*"You see, grimkins are small and dexterous," Eldrid continued.
"Probably delicious too, but meals are plentiful in the forest." I realized
he must've been holding the amulet. His source of power. Bravery. Maybe
even recklessness.*

"He was playing dead," Frem said sadly. "Nasty little creature."

"Nasty indeed," Eldrid said.

*Even as I hung upside down in Brem's clutch, I longed to reach for
Death's Diary and scribble down these lines of dialogue. I didn't want to
jinx it, but somehow I knew this was Eldrid's chance to become a hero.*

*Eldrid then offered to climb inside Frem's mouth and remove the
bone caught between his teeth, which was almost certain suicide.*

"But first," Eldrid said, "you have to let my friend go."

*Frem and Brem considered this, blinking their heavy lids in unison,
as if lost in thought.*

"My tooth does hurt," Frem said.

"My stomach is rumbling," Brem countered.

*"Maybe we should bring them back to the cave and think on it,"
Frem said.*

*"You idiot," Brem said. "Then the others will want some. And I never
get the leg. I want the leg!"*

"But I want the leg too," Frem said.

"Settle down," Brem said. "There are at least four legs to choose from."

*To which Frem smiled and licked his lips. Something almost childlike
about the look of wonder on his face.*

"I guess we could let the grimkin remove the bone and then eat them anyway," Brem said, who was apparently the brains behind the operation. Although giants are quick, they are apparently also dumb.

It's always unfortunate for a writer when a stereotype proves to be true. I would've loved giants to be smart and cunning, so as not to fit the archetype of the giant oaf. A writer's job is to surprise, not merely capture.

"Now they've heard you," Frem said.

"What difference does it make?" said Brem.

Frem shrugged; Eldrid jittered up and down.

"You may remove the bone," Frem announced, as if Eldrid had just won the lottery. "And if you do a good job, we will let you live."

Giants aren't good liars, and I could see the truth in his infected eyeball: he had every intention of eating Eldrid.

Eldrid cleared his throat, his face now a garish shade of maroon as the blood rushed to his head. "First, let my friend go."

Frem rolled his large eye beneath its half-closed lid. Amazing that some gestures transcended dimensions. Still, Brem set me down. I brushed myself off and retreated to the tree line. After all, I was no protagonist. This was Eldrid's tale; if he was going to die, the least I could do is catalogue his adventures, and I wouldn't be able to do that in a giant's belly.

Frem brought Eldrid up to his razor-sharp teeth, and I'll never forget the look Eldrid gave me: Brave. Determined. Frightened. When people tell you bravery requires having no fear, they're lying.

I remember a moment on Omaha Beach when, through my haunted perch on a hillside, I saw a soldier charge across the pale strip of beach through a volley of gunfire, making it to cover without even a scratch. Looking over the carnage, he suddenly bolted back into the fray and knelt beside a wounded comrade. As he attempted to carry the poor soldier, whose right leg had been blown off, a stray bullet caught him in the neck and he collapsed just a few feet away from safety. That's when I learned that bravery is about controlling your fear just enough to do what's right—or foolish. Sometimes there's no difference.

Eldrid clambered into Frem's mouth, stepping carefully among his teeth as if jumping on stones in a creek of water. I can only imagine what the stench must have been like for Eldrid, who'd always been so fastidious with his own hygiene, only to now be bathed in Frem's putrid breath.

Eldrid tugged at the bone, trying to yank it free of the molar. He heaved and sighed, but the bone didn't budge. The raw patch of gum missing a tooth oozed blood. The giant must've pulled it himself as a failed attempt to dislodge the bone; instead, the wound had become infected.

Frem gurgled something incomprehensible, his large tongue bobbing Eldrid up and down.

"Hold still," Eldrid hissed, his hand still clutched on the bone.

Finally, Eldrid sounded a note of triumph, holding the bone aloft in his hand. Frem let out a deep sigh and immediately shut his mouth. A devilish gleam spread across his face. I heard Eldrid's muffled voice screaming for help. One chew and our hero's journey would've been over once and for all.

And then, miraculously, Frem's lips parted, thin strands of spit and pus crisscrossing that gaping yaw in a horrific web. Eldrid stood there triumphant, holding a dagger up to Frem's red-gabled roof of a mouth, ready to pierce his brain.

"We had a deal," Eldrid said, the point of the blade pressing into Frem's squishy flesh. "Don't try to talk, as this dagger, belonging to your last victim I assume, will almost undoubtedly pierce your brain and kill you."

Frem remained still.

"Now, I'm going to climb out of your mouth and my friend and I will be on our way."

Still holding the blade aloft, Eldrid stepped carefully across the giant's gums, leapt to his tongue, and paused at the precipice of his sharp teeth. His tail swung wildly, grazing the cavernous roof of Frem's mouth. Stepping over those crooked calcified blades, he finally jumped to the ground, landing in a swirl of dust. He walked backwards, keeping the dagger in front of him, slashing it wildly between the two giants. While I knew Frem and Brem might still eat us given the opportunity, I also assumed Frem didn't want to risk another dagger to the eye.

Taking one last look at Frem and Brem, we turned and sprinted in the direction of the capital. After about a mile, we slowed, panting and out of breath. The forest had become a barren wasteland. Leafless branches reached toward the sky like angry arms cursing the heavens. I wondered if Eldrid's use of the amulet had unleashed even more darkness in Grimwell.

"Did you use the amulet?" I asked.

Eldrid shook his head and tapped his pocket, where I could see a faint red glow, the amulet still beckoning Eldrid to unleash its power. "I supposed I've changed more than I thought," he said. He then revealed that an errant ray of sunlight through the gray cloud cover had illuminated the dagger's blade; only then, when all seemed lost, had he concocted his plan.

"Brilliant," I said, slapping him on the back in a show of affection, which seemed to catch him off-guard. Eyerolls crisscrossed dimensions, but backslapping was apparently forbidden. Regardless, I was so overcome by emotion that I couldn't help but do it again.

If Grimwell had taught me one thing it was that a journey would never bring you back to the beginning no matter which loop you took. You'd always come out different on the other side. I'd later come to realize that it's not only the character that changes in a book, but the reader as well.

That's the true mark of a good story. Wouldn't you say, Dear Reader?

Chapter 22

Derek slammed the book shut, regretting his descent into Grimwell. Reading the book had become an immersive experience, as if the pages had hijacked Derek's imagination. But this was no flight of fancy across the Reading Rainbow; the latest chapter had violently pulled Derek inside its mildewed pages, dragging him kicking and screaming through the Trembling Forest. Derek could feel Eldrid's fear as Frem held him upside down; he could smell Frem's breath as Eldrid clutched the dagger inside that gaping yaw; and he could feel himself becoming braver as Eldrid skipped over the giant's teeth and sprinted to safety.

With each page, he became less Derek and more Eldrid, and he knew if he kept reading, he'd end up just like Jackson Wilfred who now stood mere feet away, a wooden monument to a man who'd lost himself inside the pages of *The Strange Life and Times of Eldrid Babble*.

When he looked up from the faded cover, he saw Kat peering at him from the other side of the park. Remembering the pull of the

book, Derek quickly stashed it in his jacket and held up his hand
to wave.

Kat hurried across the grass with purpose. Sunlight stroked her
hair and created a patina of light around her head, making her face
momentarily appear featureless, blurred. She was dressed in her
McDowell's uniform: dark slacks, white collared shirt, and those
geriatric black sneakers that somehow only added to her sex appeal.
As she got closer, her crisp visage was filled in with the details of the
day, a story told in food and drink: A glob of ketchup stained one of
her sleeves and light brown droplets—most likely coffee—spattered
her shirt. She wore a ponytail, but one of her curls had escaped, giving
the appearance of suspended motion. Much to Derek's dismay, she
still wore a headband over the tips of her ears.

"I thought you said you had to return the book to the library."
There was anger in her voice. Sharp and scolding.

"It's complicated."

"What are you talking about, Derek? No secrets, remember?"

Derek saw the pleading. The desperation in her eyes. And that's
when he knew he had to tell the truth. Honesty was the only way out
of the web of lies fiction had forced him to create.

But he knew he couldn't just tell her. He had to show her.

* * *

It was one of the more humiliating moments of his life, inviting
a woman up to his apartment only to drop trow and show her
his tail.

"What the..." Kat whispered, covering her mouth with both hands.

"Let's not make it worse," Derek said.

"It's just that I've never seen a tail before. I mean, a tail on a human."

"Are you done yet?"

"Can I touch it?" Kat asked, her eyes growing wide.

219

Despite himself, Derek's tail extended toward Kat in excitement. Derek clenched his tail muscles to stop it—because apparently now he had tail muscles—but the tail had its own agenda and curlicued in an arc toward Kat, brushing her hand. She ran her fingers across Derek's fur, and he felt an odd sensation, a tickle that ran from his tail, up to his spine, and through his entire body. It wasn't sexual, thank god—he didn't want to walk down the tail fetish path—but it was pleasant, and he realized he wouldn't mind if she pet him again. Which she did.

"Can I put it away now?" Derek asked impatiently.

"I'm sorry," Kat said. "It's just that when I asked if you had any secrets, you said no. We pinky promised." Her eyes flashed accusingly toward Derek in a withering stare. Mac's blue canvas remained on the TV stand. Was it just him or did the canvas now contain hints of cobalt and gray, as if a sky from another world was darkening? "I'd say this counts as a pretty big secret. Is it a birth defect?"

The tail slumped. *Defect.* Harsh.

Derek shook his head. "It's not a birth defect. And it's not really a defect at all," he added, feeling the need to defend his new appendage. He stopped short of thinking *companion*, but only just. "If anything, it's an advantage."

"So how does this relate to the book?"

Derek tucked his tail back in his boxers, buttoned up his pants, and pulled the book out of his jacket pocket. "The book gave me the tail." Derek then told Kat about finding Eldrid's story in the back of the Read and Bean's supply closet, his research into Chester Felten, and the surprise meeting with Jackson Wilfred, who now stood sentinel in Pemberton Park. As he spoke, fully aware of how crazy his story sounded, he knew the conversation could go one of two ways. Either Kat would run screaming out of the apartment or she'd politely find an excuse to leave—and then run screaming.

But neither scenario happened. Instead, she remained still, staring at Mac's canvas as if watching a storm roll in. After Derek finished, recognition flickered in her eyes. Maybe fear too. Like she could see a car speeding toward her. She just couldn't jump out of the way.

"What's wrong?" Derek asked.

Kat pulled back her headband showing off pointy, elf-like ears. No, Derek thought. Not elf-like. Grimkin-like.

"I thought maybe the pregnancy did it and I just hadn't noticed until now. But I couldn't find anything about pregnancy and pointy ears online, and when I looked back at old pictures—even from just a few weeks ago—they were round. Normal, I mean. No offense," she added, which made Derek take offense because of the implication: Derek the Friendly Neighborhood Barista had become the antithesis of normal.

"The book changes you into the character you identify with most," Derek said, reaching out and running a finger over the sharp point of Kat's ear in a gesture meant to be comforting. Maybe even romantic. Thanks to *Dating and Mating in the 20th Century*, Derek knew the theory, but was still fuzzy on the application.

Kat flinched and turned her head. As usual, Derek's timing was all wrong. Never a good idea to sidle into romance after having just broken the news about a curse.

"So that's why I couldn't stop reading," Kat said. "Why I can't stop thinking about Grimwell. The book changed to lure me in."

"Exactly. Think of it like a jazz song. Everyone has the basic formula. The basic notes. But there's a lot of improvisation in the book depending on who the reader is."

"And now I'm changing too."

"I think so. I don't know how fast or how much... Wilfred thought you could pause the curse by getting rid of the book. But I think he was tortured by never knowing what happened to Grandfather Tree. By the time I saw him he was—"

"A tree himself?"

"Pretty much." Derek opened the book to Felten's drawing of Grandfather Tree on the title page: a rough pencil sketch of a wide,

221

rough-barked trunk with a thin-lipped mouth, crooked nose, and two owl-like eyes. Similar to the tree that was now rooted in the park. A wooden corpse of the retired librarian.

Derek couldn't help but notice Kat's eyes linger on the drawing of Belinda Grabblebee with her long flowing locks and pointy ears.

"It's magic or something," Derek said. "And Wilfred thinks—or thought—I don't know if he can still think—I kind of hope he can't—that the only way to stop the curse is to journey into Grimwell."

Kat ran a hand over the small of her back and glanced over her shoulder as if checking for any unknown protrusions. "Do lady grim-kins have tails?"

Derek nodded. "As far as I know."

Kat plopped down on the futon, springs squealing from her weight. "When are you going"—she gulped, eyes once again drawn to Mac's darkening canvas— "on your adventure?"

The line sounded forced. As if some outside narrator had inserted it to drive home the theme. Hit the reader over the head.

"Day after next. I need some time to prepare. And then I was hoping to head to Ashton early in the morning. Wilfred gave me a map that shows the way to Grimwell."

Derek liked how he sounded. Confident. Resolute. Brave. A proper protagonist. Emboldened by his speech, he joined Kat on the futon.

Kat slid her headband off and undid her ponytail, letting her curly hair tumble down her shoulders, obscuring her ears. "I'll go," she said.

"No," Derek said. If this was a fantasy novel, Kat was either a princess in need of rescue or a damsel in distress, and Derek couldn't hope to become a hero if he put her in harm's way.

"It's not up to you," she said, bursting the bubble of Derek's chauvinistic fairy tale. "I'm changing too. Mac's with his dad for a couple of days and you could probably use the help."

Derek didn't disagree. He barely liked traveling across state lines, let alone to other worlds. "You sure about this?"

Kat nodded gravely.

"It'll be dangerous."

"What other choice do I have?"

Derek knew what she meant. For a time, Derek felt as though he had too many choices. The sheer unfathomable depth of the world had paralyzed him and prevented him from ever truly finding a path. Instead, he'd become an observer, sitting on shore with a book as the world flowed by. But now he saw the truth: much like a character in a story, he could trace a direct line from his mother's illness, to the coffee shop, to Janine's betrayal, to finding his story in the back of the Read and Bean's supply closet. Now, the only way out was to find a way to reach the end.

"It seems like a nice world—at least the first part of the book seems nice—but clearly there's a dark side." Derek almost mentioned Lord Grittlebane, but couldn't bring himself to utter the name. It sounded too much like a caricature of an evil sorcerer.

"I need to fix this," Kat said with a calm determination. Derek knew she was talking about much more than pointy ears. Books have a way of grabbing hold of you, gently taking your hand and walking you down bright corridors and darkened alleys. But *The Strange Life and Times of Eldrid Babble* wasn't gentle; it was violent, unrelenting, and cruel. It didn't take your hand so much as shove you from behind.

Pressed together on Derek's small futon, their legs touched. Derek placed his arm around Kat and pulled her closer. Now wasn't the time for romance, but then again, Derek was tired of life always dictating the circumstance. The plot. The genre. They kissed—sloppily, greedily, no careful choreography or rehearsal. It was messy and real and all-consuming. For a moment, the world—both worlds—fell away. Kat reclined back on the futon and Derek felt his insatiable appetite return as he undid the buttons on her collared shirt, suddenly overcome by an unbridled hunger. Kat reached down toward his pants and he instinctively pushed her hand away. Undeterred, she slid her hand back toward his waist, her eyes glowing with a brilliant red sheen. Or was that just his imagination?

"You don't mind the tail?" Derek asked breathlessly.

"I think it's kind of growing on me," she said.

Derek's tail broke free of his boxers, coiling around his waist as if beckoned by Kat's voice.

Chapter 23

After they made love, Derek reclined on the now-converted futon and stared at the ceiling. Kat nestled into the crook of his neck, and Derek was surprised by how well they fit together. Literally. Like two puzzle pieces. As they spoke, Derek's tail thumped on the bed, rippling the sheets; clearly, he was anxious.

"I think we have to get a gist for how the story ends without actually reading it," Derek said. "So we know what to expect when we reach Grimwell."

"How do we do that?"

Derek had an idea. "Maybe it's the book that's magic and not the words. If I take pictures of the last chapter with my phone, maybe it will capture it. Make it static or something?"

Derek knew it sounded flimsy, but he'd seen many other books resolve their plots on a lot less. And it did make a certain amount of sense. After all, what was technology other than a type of magic that hadn't been discovered yet?

"It's worth a try," Kat said, not sounding convinced.

Derek sat up, took out his phone, and pried the book open. It seemed to struggle against his hands, not wanting to lay its pages bare to the digital age. But when he snapped a few photos in quick succession of the page where he'd left off, as Eldrid and Chester hunkered down just outside of Grim City, The Summit looming over them like a minacious obelisk, he discovered the images were blank. As if the words had been erased. Apparently, whatever evil had cursed the book had planned for the invention of the iPhone.

"Wait a second," Kat said, sitting up and holding the sheet over her chest. "What if we go backwards? What does a story hate more than revealing its secrets?"

"What do you mean?"

"I say we start at the ending and then go back, one page at a time. That way the book can't adjust. Because the journey's already over. Maybe that will make it less dangerous."

"Maybe." Now Derek was the one who didn't sound convinced. He opened to the last page. Once again, he felt the book protest as he riffled to the end, fighting the urge to continue reading and once again dissolve into Eldrid. Life was meant to be lived forwards and books were meant to be read from beginning to end. Blasphemy for a book lover to read the last line before fully immersing yourself in a story. Like having dessert for breakfast or putting your shoes on your hands. It just felt wrong.

Derek paused once he reached the last page, staring at the white space and the two bittersweet words every reader must eventually face after climbing Freytag's pyramid and sliding down: *The End.*

Reluctantly, Derek read the last line out loud:

Eldrid and I said goodbye at the tree stump where my journey first began, and while the next part of our tale would bring us to other worlds, we had found a magic more powerful than distance, more enduring than an amulet, and more determined than any sorcerer:

Friendship.

"It's a happy ending," Kat said. "A story can't change if it's already over, right?"

"You're a genius," Derek said.

"I know," Kat said. "There's only one thing missing."

"What's that?"

"Some shots. I really need a drink."

* * *

Flanked on either side by Gerald and Boris, squished together in a space that usually only accommodated one, Kat and Derek prepared to finish the tale of Eldrid Babble, unspooling the ending by reading it backwards.

With two shots in front of them, along with an ice cream sundae, Derek once again read the last line.

Eldrid and I said goodbye at the tree stump where my journey first began, and while the next part of our tale would bring us to other worlds, we had found a magic more powerful than distance, more enduring than an amulet, and more determined than any sorcerer:

Friendship.

Shot.

"So it all turns out well for Eldrid," Kat said, gulping down a glass of water.

"Still reading that book?" Gerald said.

"You sure you guys don't just want to sit next to each other?" Kat asked.

"We need a buffer," Boris said. "Too much human contact makes me squeamish."

Kat read the next line. Derek could smell the alcohol on her breath as she said:

"The forest smelled alive; Grandfather Tree stood upright, his branches bare save for a tiny sproutling that had already emerged, bright green against the dusty gray sky. A journey of one had become a journey for two and now a journey for all of Grimwell. 'You always have a home here,' Grandfather Tree thundered in his rumbling voice."

"They both became heroes," Derek said as Kat looked up from the book, shielding her eyes as if the pages burned too bright.

Scoop of ice cream.

Boris and Gerald had begun eating their meatloaf; it wasn't on the menu, but being a regular had its advantages. Kat had perfected the recipe herself. Julius brought over two more shots but didn't linger; maybe he could sense the dark magic of the book; that or he just wanted to play Minesweeper unbothered by the whims of his customers.

Kat and Derek continued trading paragraphs and then pages, summarizing the story in bits and pieces, the journey now sealed in reverse.

Eldrid and Chester returned to Lord Grittlebane's castle, where they stood over his lifeless body after having broken the curse.

Shot.

Lord Grittlebane, who had bright green skin and a serpentine tongue, was resurrected and gave the speech that every villain must give, where he unveiled his plan for total domination of Grimwell, revealing the prophecy of the magic amulet that had been foretold in the time before grimkins about a stone unleashing darkness on the entire realm by corrupting the hearts of untested heroes.

Scoop of ice cream.

Derek and Kat read line by line, as Eldrid and Chester's plan untwisted in front of their eyes, no longer surprised by the story: Because as they read backwards, they'd already watched Eldrid smash the amulet on the floor in order to break Lord Grittlebane's hold on Grimwell. They'd already known that Eldrid and Chester had dressed up as guards to enter the castle. They'd already watched Chester defeat one of Lord Grittlebane's henchman after having been ambushed in the sewer beneath Grim City, betrayed by Ogbar the Oak. Reading backwards had dissolved—not resolved—the narrative tension, making the story feel like a deflated balloon. Finally, Eldrid and Chester crawled backwards through the sewer until they were once again in the Trembling Forest, fleeing from Frem and Brem.

Three shots and two sundaes later, they'd finally learned the last of Grimwell's secrets.

"Nothing about Belinda," Kat said, clearly disappointed. "I thought maybe they'd end up together."

"Maybe they did. Just because it's not in the story, doesn't mean it didn't happen after."

"If I read just a little bit more—"

"No," Derek said. "It's too much of a risk."

Kat sighed, abruptly turning away from the book, clearly still tempted by its pages. "These bad guys are always the same."

"What do you mean?"

"They want control but you never know why."

"Isn't that just it?" Derek said. "They want it for the sake of wanting it. It's a cycle. All villains lack real motivation. That's how you know a real hero. The motive makes sense. Not just logically, but ethically."

"A hero is someone who does the right thing even when it's easier to do the wrong thing," Boris said, sounding sagely, even with grease from the meatloaf dripping down his chin.

"Then is a villain someone who does the wrong thing even when it's easier to do the right thing?" Gerald asked.

"Maybe," Boris said. "But life is usually a lot more complicated than sayings make it out to be."

Derek thought back to Rich Wise's description of love. There was basic science and there was complicated science. The same was true for heroes. There were basic heroes and complicated heroes, and the only way to test your mettle, to find out exactly where you fell on the hero-villain continuum, was to go on a journey of your own.

"Cheers to us," Derek said, holding up his water glass, now slightly dizzy from the shots and woozy from the ice cream.

The four clinked glasses.

Chapter 24

Before going to bed, Derek wrapped the book in duct tape and secured it in a box, adding additional layers of tape over the top and then stashing it away beneath the kitchen sink. He tied string around the cabinet knobs and placed a chair in front of it. It wasn't foolproof, but it would have to do. The pull to read the book had grown stronger throughout the day, turning from a whisper into a shout and then a deafening roar. In a moment of desperation, Kat had asked if she could read just one page, still searching for Belinda in its tendrilled plot.

Shutting it away had quieted the worst of it, but still, Derek knew they'd only be able to bury the urge for so long. Maybe a day. The stakes had grown even higher, which Derek knew could only mean one thing: he was about to enter the third act of his journey.

He'd started the book as a hapless barista who couldn't even stand up to his boss. Now, he was about to become the hero of his own tale—if his foray into the land of Grimwell went well. If it didn't, he'd

Grimwell

probably dic a terrible death and never be heard from again. But he
didn't want to think about all that. He wanted to focus on the accolades of returning to reality after having broken the curse haunting
Eldrid Babble's pages. Sure, Tom had fought to save the world on TV
in *Another Planet*, but now Derek was going to save an entire realm
in a real fictional world. Somehow, that sounded more important.

He listened to the still night air as Kat snored gently beside him.
He didn't like the idea of Kat going with him, but he knew it wasn't
his call. The truth was, after she'd read the first page, she'd become
ensnared in her own tale of heroism, and until they broke the curse,
there would always be part of her searching for the novel, desperately
seeking resolution in Belinda's story. Somehow, the book would find
her, just like it had found Jackson Wilfred, whether by magic or by
chance. Maybe the two weren't all that different.

Complicated science, as Rich Wise would say.

Derek's eyes grew heavy, and before he knew it, he'd drifted off
to sleep. When Derek stirred in the middle of the night, he found
his arm strung over Kat, the two awkwardly pressed together like an
unmatched pair of socks.

The next morning, after Derek had said goodbye to Kat, lingering
at the door for a hero's kiss, he found that his feet had grown a thick
layer of hair, which he promptly covered with an even thicker pair
of socks.

Maybe the book was accelerating its process, fearing Derek's
eventual journey into its pages. Needing distance from the book, he
happily went to work, mixing the chocolate syrup, filling the pastry
case, and taking order after order with his friendliest greeting.

"Everything okay?" Sam had asked after the morning rush. Derek
couldn't believe how much Sam had changed since his journey first
began. The pompous, baby-faced manager had become meek and
humble, barely a shadow of his former self. Yet something about
it felt off, as if the price of a character changing so quickly was a

232

fictional glazing of the world replete with a superficial and dull cast. As Derek scanned the coffee shop, the overhanging bulbs dim, now resembling harvest moons, he couldn't escape the feeling that he'd already stepped inside the pages of a book.

At the whims of a cruel author.

"I'm doing great," Derek said gruffly, wearing a Read and Bean hat low to shield his face. "By the way, I noticed the milk bar needs a quick cleaning," he added, feeling the vestiges of power the book had provided him: that intoxicating elixir that he'd gladly drunk, hastening his transformation into Eldrid Babble.

"I'll get right to it."

But Derek knew he was triumphing over the book, bending his own character arc against Eldrid Babble's ironclad plot points, because he quickly added, "You know what, forget it. I'll take care of it."

"You sure?" Sam asked.

Derek nodded magnanimously. "And if you really want to go to business school you should keep studying for the GMAT."

"Really?"

"Yes. You just have to promise me one thing?"

"What's that?"

"You won't be such an asshole."

Sam winced, caught off-guard, something in his eyes betraying a newly discovered humility. "Okay, D.W. I mean, Derek."

During his lunch break, Derek realized he'd shrunk by at least two inches. Shelves that were once in arm's reach now hung just a little too high. The Read and Bean looked different from his new vantage point, and he found himself clumsily walking through a world that no longer felt right. Actually, a world that just felt plain wrong.

By the time he clocked out, he scarcely recognized the person staring back at him. He had comically large ears that extended from his shaggy hair. While he'd started the day with a dusting of stubble, his muttonchops had returned. His forehead had developed a small ridge over his bushy, caterpillar-like eyebrows, giving him the appearance of a caveman. The pages were turning faster now, and he no longer had the option to put the book down, say "so long," and start a new story. His only choice was to rewrite the ending.

On his way to the store for some supplies, he texted Kat to let her know she could still back out. Her reply came a few seconds later: *There's no going back now.*

With the weight of the adventure pressed squarely on his shoulders, Derek began preparing. Wearing a hat and sunglasses, he embarked on a much shorter adventure to his neighborhood CVS. How does one go shopping for a sojourn into a world that you thought only existed in your imagination? Derek didn't know, and because time was limited, he had to make some executive decisions. It felt wrong bringing a gun to a fantasy world, not to mention, Derek had no idea how he'd even go about procuring one, so he decided to buy a Swiss army knife. As he walked the aisles of the CVS, he saw his reflection in the overhead mirror and was frightened by the person staring back at him. Next, he went to the toiletry aisle and found a travel toothbrush, just in case he needed to spend a night in Grimwell. Oral hygiene was important no matter which dimension you happened to be in. He threw in another for Kat, hoping to get brownie points for being so thoughtful. With his basket growing fuller, he went to the snack aisle and procured two boxes of granola bars; while his palette had been stretched by Kat's culinary creations, hedgehog wasn't at the top of Derek's favorite foods. Dubious about Grimwell's sweet leaf coffee, he also grabbed a few bottles of iced coffee for his caffeine fix. Working at the Read and Bean had spoiled him, and he didn't want to risk a terrible headache. He thought about buying condoms, but ultimately decided against it. Would Bilbo or Frodo worry about having sex on their journey? Not a chance.

Just before checkout, he realized he needed a few more outdoorsy items, considering he and Kat would most likely be camping out, which made him double back to the condom aisle and throw in a three-pack just to be safe. He then grabbed a small tent, portable grill—maybe Kat knew how to hunt—and an umbrella. Feeling sufficiently prepared, he went to the self-checkout machine, his eyes on the ground, lest someone grow alarmed by his appearance. He was right on the edge of human, and while he assumed people would simply think he was ugly, he didn't want to risk questions—or hear the gasps that accompanied sorrowful and pitiful looks. After all, this could be his forever.

Now that he had procured the necessary materials, he had to make one more stop. In the tumult of planning for his trip to Grimwell, he hadn't forgotten that it was the anniversary of his mom's death. A morbid milestone to mark, but Derek had been adamant not to forget the date. If he did, he worried that her memory would some-how start to recede.

He parked his car—his mom had left the old sedan to him in her will—and walked over to the gravestone. Tom must've rethought his views on cemeteries, because someone had dropped off a bouquet of flowers along with a colorful bracelet, most likely a token from Achelia.

Derek kneeled down and touched the stone. It was cold. A puny marker for a life that loomed so large in Derek's memories. Based on the many novels he'd read, he knew this would be the perfect moment for resolution and reconciliation, a chance for the author to tie up loose ends in preparation for the final step of the hero's journey. A surprise appearance by his father perhaps, stumbling into the scene and saying something cheesy like, "You know, our first kiss was in a cemetery." (It wasn't).

And Derek would tersely reply, "Where's Shannon?" (A nice woman who Derek couldn't help but hate beyond any rational mea-sure. Sometimes plot trumps character).

And his father would say she was back at the hotel, before making a joke about the old ball-and-chain or some other sexist cliché. (His father made a perfect villain).

Derek would ask how things were in Arizona, and his father would say something like, "It's hot as balls" or "Imagine Satan's ass crack on fire." Derek would laugh, but it would be one of those obligatory chuckles, the sound without the smile. And then his father would offer a tepid apology for the mistakes he'd made as a parent. About how he thought if he pushed Derek, he'd someday thank him for it. There's no handbook for raising a child and he did the best he could—all the clichés that are true enough, yet don't seem to heal rifts, like spackling plaster over cracks in a foundation.

After trading barbs and teetering on the edge of a fight, they'd come to an understanding, not as hero and villain, but as father and son, where those labels don't quite make sense. It would have to end on a bittersweet note, perhaps an awkward hug, then add a tinge of humor with the realization that no one had bothered to bring a flashlight and dark was fast approaching. Whoops! Though now he was mixing media and veering off into sitcom. But what did it matter, anyway? Because it was all fantasy, not even as real as Eldrid Babble and Grimwell.

Instead, as Derek hunkered down at his mother's gravestone, staring at an unusually vibrant sunset melting into the Earth like a candle almost burned to the wick, its wax crooked and slumped, Derek took out his phone and scrolled through his text messages. *Can we talk?* his father had written. And even though Derek wouldn't write back, at least not today, he thought maybe someday he would. Maybe his mom would even want him to. Heroes had to act, but Derek knew heroes had to be ready to act. No magic amulet was going to change that. He slipped his phone in his pocket and sat there in silence, watching the sun dip below the horizon until it was dark out, the moon had blinked on, and the hum of the cicadas had risen to a crescendo.

When he arrived home, he packed up his mom's old car with plans to set out at first light. He retrieved the box containing the book from the kitchen cabinet and added additional layers of tape. Still feeling the urge to open it and find out what lay in store for him and Kat—now that he knew the ending of Eldrid's story, what would the book have to say to him?— he stashed it in the trunk and returned to his apartment. Like a man on death row eating his last meal, Derek greedily gobbled up a carton of ice cream, numbing himself to the call of the book, which he could somehow still hear like a faint heartbeat, a scraping against the window, a low buzzing just beneath the surface of sound. Remembering Tom's insistence that he finish *Another Planet*, and truthfully not knowing if he'd ever have another chance, he threw on the season finale of his brother's hit show.

EXT. NEW YORK CITY - NIGHT

Sergeant Wilks stands below the darkened lights of Times Square and looks at the bruised and beaten landscape. Crumbling buildings. Shattered glass. Small fires still burning.

                    WILKS
        Come out, come out, wherever
        you are!

                    DEREK
                (from couch)
        Get 'em, Tom!

                    WILKS
        You made a big mistake. Wrong
        stop on the interstellar gravy

train. Whatever you want to
call it.

A faint clicking can be heard in the
background. Their enemy's on the move.
They take cover behind a flipped car.

                    MISHA
You think we have a shot?

                    WILKS
Normally, I'd say no,
but today...

                    DEREK
               (from couch)
I like my odds.

                    WILKS
...I like my odds.

An eerie silence settles over the battered city street. A true wasteland. Burning rubble. A pair of shoes
lies discarded on top of sheaths of
twisted metal. A blanket of darkness beyond Wilks's flashlight. This is
the APOCALYPSE.

                    WILKS
When I was younger, I remember my brother giving me some
advice. My parents were fighting. They were always fighting. And my brother got me
through it.

                    DEREK
              (from couch)
Wait a second…

                    MISHA
Now's not the time for a stroll
down memory lane, Sergeant.
This is do or die.

                    WILKS
Hear me out. I might not have
another chance to get this off
my chest, so you're my only
shot. A captive audience.

The clicking grows louder and faster.
Derek, sitting on his couch, leans closer
to the TV.

FLASHBACK

A seven-year-old Sergeant James Wilks
sits on a bed with his big brother, ERIC.

A stack of books lies on the bed. Eric picks one from the pile and opens it, angling it toward Wilks. Faint yells can be heard in the background.

> WILKS
> Why are they fighting?

> ERIC
> That's what adults do.

> DEREK
> (from couch)
> That's really what I thought.

> WILKS
> Should we fight?

Eric shakes his head and places the book on his lap.

> ERIC
> Only if we have something worth fighting for.

> WILKS
> How do you know?

Eric holds up the book.

ERIC

Books.

WILKS

What do you mean?

ERIC

That's why there're so many
books. So many stories. Pretty
much every situation you can
find in a book.

WILKS

What if I can't find the
right story?

ERIC
(thinking)
You write your own, I guess.

END FLASHBACK

MISHA

Cute story.

WILKS

Well, I think it's up to us
to write our own story. And
there's no room for Troglodorfs
in my book!

```
                DEREK
            (from couch)
        You included a real memory.
```

Derek doubted he said those exact lines, but he couldn't help but feel moved, as if he'd watched a dramatization of a home movie. A moment never captured in film or written in a book, plucked like a glittering pearl buried beneath an ocean of memories. Even though it was cliché for the hero to tear up, he couldn't help himself. Through misty eyes, Derek returned his attention to the screen.

```
The clicking gets louder. And louder. The
alien is closing in.

                WILKS
        Here goes nothing.

Wilks jumps out from behind the car and
runs toward the sound of the clicking. He
dives just in time to avoid a laser beam.

Misha approaches from the right and kicks
the laser out of the alien's tentacle.

Finally, a fair fight.

Wilks and Misha charge toward the alien
and begin pummeling it with their fists.
There's a ferocity to their fighting. An
apocalyptic anger flowing into their fists.
```

The alien is a bloody pulp. Misha drags
Wilks off the alien.

          MISHA
    Take it easy.

          WILKS
      (breathing heavily)
   They killed… everyone.

Misha grabs the laser and stashes it in
her pack. Just then, a light appears
over them. Overpowering. They shield
their eyes.

Suddenly, they're sucked into the portal
of light. The screen goes black.

CREDITS

          DEREK
      (from couch)
   That's it?

The theme song begins playing, timpani
and horns straining against the speaker.

          DEREK
      (from couch)
   No resolution?

CREDITS continue to play, bathing Derek's apartment in a faint glow.

                    DEREK
                 (from couch)
I can't wait for Season Two.

Part III
The Tail End

Chapter 25

Derek picked up Kat the next day, just as the sun was cresting the horizon. The idea was to get to Ashton around eight o'clock and then do some poking around to see if they could follow Chester Felten's hand-drawn map. Kat had texted him her address, and as he drove in the hazy dawn light, he realized he didn't know that much about her, not just where she lived, but about her past, her backstory. What had led Kat to take the job at McDowell's? Why had Kat returned home to live with her mother? But as Derek's foray into fantasy had taught him, it wasn't the backstory that mattered, but what happened next that fueled their narrative arc. That's what made the pages keep turning.

Derek pulled into her driveway, wondering whether or not he should go to the door, and what he would say if her mother answered—*Hi, I'm turning into a grimkin and I'm here to pick up your daughter to join me as we search for a fantasy world called Grimwell*—no that wouldn't do. It would be impolite to just honk the horn, but getting out of the car in his current—"condition" was the only word that came to mind—probably wouldn't give the best first impression.

Turns out, he didn't have to worry either way, because Kat was waiting on the porch, sitting on a step with her arms folded over her knees. The glare from Derek's headlights illuminated her eyes, and Derek was once again reminded of the expression "A deer caught in headlights." Light had the ability to surprise and capture, to peel back night's black velvet curtain with nimble fingers and reveal the truth beneath.

The house was a modest ranch, located about a quarter-mile away from the highway. Derek could hear cars and trucks whooshing by as he parked. The house's paint—a patchy, faded yellow—was peeling and there were no railings on either side of the porch stairs, hinting of home improvement projects begun and then abandoned. At the end of the driveway, a small shed lay past an overgrown path. Still farther back, a swing set without any swings slumped ominously in the dark.

Kat made her way to the passenger side door and opened it. The book seemed to bang against the trunk as if it had become sentient. At first, Derek thought it was only his imagination, until Kat also turned her head in the direction of the noise. He tried to ignore it by focusing on Kat, who somehow looked even more beautiful, elf ears and all, which made Derek worry he had a grimkin fetish. Then again, considering he was turning into a grimkin himself, he supposed it was only natural that his taste in women would start to change as well.

As far as Derek knew, elf ears were the major characteristic Kat had taken on of Belinda Grabblebee, while he'd developed more severe markers of difference, like the tail, the gnarled fingers, and the miracle-grow facial hair. Still, compared to Wilfred's transformation, he'd gotten lucky: If he'd identified with a tree or even Lord Grittlebane, with his green skin and serpentine tongue, the stakes would be even higher.

Kat buckled her seatbelt and stared straight ahead.

"You're sure you want to do this?"

Kat nodded. Still not turning toward Derek.

"You know, when this is all over, I'd like to meet Mac."

Kat let her head fall against the passenger side window. The street-lights created an eerie doubling effect, as if Kat was coming face-to-face with Belinda Grabblebee, her alter ego from another dimension.

"I know this isn't the right time to be saying it. But then again, I don't know if there ever is a right time."

Sure, there were wrong times, like proposing at a funeral or some-how having to pee when embarking on a two-hour drive—Derek shouldn't have had that second cup of coffee—but right times were in the eye of the beholder. Only after a story had been written would the right time become apparent.

Derek backed out of the driveway, the gravel crunching under the tires, making the journey seem even more arduous: just a popped tire away from failure, a very anticlimactic end to a heroic journey.

"I don't know if Mac will even recognize me when this is all over," Kat said, her voice breaking, as if her words had grown heavy, unwieldy.

As she turned to face Derek, he saw that she had changed even more overnight: Her teeth had grown more pronounced, almost rabbit-like, and similar to Belinda, and just like Derek, she now had thick bushy eyebrows.

"I've been hiding my face from my mom, but she knows some-thing's up. Are we doing the right thing? I mean, so what if I have elf ears and you have a tail. We could still be happy, right?"

The book had destroyed Wilfred, one page at a time. Derek knew that if they didn't break the curse, they'd forever be chasing their stories in the book's pages.

Derek remained quiet.

"Why is this happening?" Kat asked.

"I don't know," Derek said honestly. "But we're going to find out. I promise."

* * *

By the time they reached Ashton, a few more cars were buzzing on the highway. They pulled off I-84 and found themselves on a long and winding road, flanked on either side by dense forest. Instead of a sign welcoming them to Ashton, there was a cemetery filled with crooked headstones and a rickety black iron fence that spelled out *Ashton* in a swooping cursive. The ground was covered in leaves and branches; green moss blanketed the stones.

"That's a cheery omen," Derek said, looking in the rearview mirror to watch it pass safely out of sight. He didn't hold his breath, but he definitely considered it. He caught a glimpse of his reflection. His face looked wrinkled and his eyes were aflame; a deep, glowing red.

They drove on, passing a small town green, gas station, and church that advertised "Bingo Mass." Kat looked at the map trying to make sense of the compass. "We should soon be passing a rock called"—Kat scrutinized the map— "Grim Rock."

"Is that the actual name?" Derek asked.

"Think so. I guess *The Strange Life and Times of Eldrid Babble* was a hit up here."

Derek remembered how his early research had uncovered the Chester Felten Memorial Pavilion. "He must've been a town hero. But if that's the case, why is there no information about his disappearance?"

"There it is," Kat said, pointing toward a large boulder, perched precariously on the edge of a sloping bluff.

An eerie feeling settled over Derek as they drove by a rock painted with a set of blood-red eyes in a sea of black, the same eyes that appeared on Lord Grittlebane's flag. Was this a warning from Chester Felten or celebration of the world of Grimwell?

After a few more miles, Derek pulled to the side of the road onto a small patch of gravel, where the forest was enclosed by a chain-link fence featuring signs announcing "Private Property," "Beware," and most troubling, "Active Bear Area." It would be just Derek's luck to be eaten by a bear so close to the end of his journey.

"According to Wilfred's notes, this used to be all town land until the University took it over," Derek said. "Now it's used mostly for research."

"Time to do some 'research,'" Kat said, putting the word in air quotes.

Derek got out of the car and opened the trunk. He couldn't believe what he saw; the box was battered with large chunks of the cardboard peeled away, as if a ferocious beast had taken bites. Derek hesitantly picked up the book, now freed from its confinement, and stashed it in his backpack, ignoring the urge to peel off the tape and read about the end of his journey. He'd stuffed his pack with as much of the supplies as it could hold, but decided to leave the tent and portable grill behind, thinking—or maybe reminiscing—about cozy stone huts and local delicacies at Crimpleton Tavern.

The air was cold and the early morning sky dim. A flock of birds scattered in the trees, letting out a haunting screech. Kat joined Derek at the edge of the tree line, and together, ignoring the signs which clearly foreshadowed danger, they began climbing the chain-link fence, which was a lot more difficult than books and TV make it out to be; Derek had more than a few false starts. Kat remained stuck at the top for close to five minutes, as she ungracefully attempted to lift her leg over the bar. Finally, after she had ripped a hole in her jeans and Derek had cut himself on a rusted piece of metal, they began the search for Felten's mythical land of make-believe.

Kat held the yellowed and brittle map in front of her, trying to orient herself in the forest. Derek remembered Wilfred's hesitancy at taking the journey himself and now understood why: surrounded by trees, Wilfred would've been too tempted to let his feet slide into the dirt, becoming one with the forest. Grandfather Tree's story had found him in the end, but at least he'd put up a good fight.

"Felten painted his initials on trees and rocks to mark the path," Kat said. She pointed at the paper, showing Derek the various symbols drawn by the author.

Derek, who'd never been one for maps or compasses or finding places without his phone navigation, took her word for it. However, before they began, he had to pee, which was not the ideal way to start a heroic journey, but Derek had no choice.

"Do what you've gotta do," Kat said, as Derek slipped behind a tree and unzipped his fly.

Once he finished—hopefully trees on Earth weren't too sentient—it was time for the journey to begin.

After about thirty minutes, they stopped at the donkey watering hole for a water break and granola bar—*Good call on the granola bars, Derek,* Derek told himself—and continued their trek through rough terrain. As the path grew faint and the hills grew steeper, they passed Mirror Lake, which made Derek feel oddly disoriented, as if his world had turned upside down—*Damn you, symbolism,* Derek had thought. Hiking deeper into the woods, they'd found *CF* on a boulder called Devil's Rock, featuring those same red eyes in a sea of black, on a beech tree carved with a set of eyes and a mouth, and, ominously, on an old hunting stand with its roof caved in. More than once, Derek's shoe slipped on a protruding root and he had to use his tail to steady himself. He'd ripped a seam in his sweatpants to allow the tail to move freely. Why hide it around a fellow grimkin? Not to mention, Kat seemed to like it.

Finally, after following the last of Felten's initials through a winding path deep in the Ashton Town Forest, and more than once having to double back in pursuit of the faded letters, they found the spot labeled The Door, which wasn't a door at all, but a decaying tree stump. Derek searched for a mouth or eyes, but found no signs of life on the scarred bark. Beheaded was the word that came to mind. Beneath the tree stump, in between roots that clung stubbornly to the ground, a hole just big enough for a person wound its way into the earth.

"It's almost like he left a secret key, just in case anyone needed to visit," Kat said, folding up the map and slipping it in her pocket.

"Lucky us," Derek said, now with his hands and knees buried in dirt. He began crawling beneath the tree stump. Derek looked back and saw Kat standing with her arms crossed, and suddenly felt extremely stupid. The shared delusion of Grimwell now clicking into place: the world was only as real as its readers made it. Still, he kept crawling. Somehow, the lines between fiction and nonfiction had been blurred and words like illusion, delusion, and fantasy had intersected, like an unfortunate game of Scrabble, becoming one mega-word with an indeterminate meaning. Fiction or not, Derek knew this might be the only chance to change the trajectory of his plot and break the curse.

He kept crawling until he couldn't see a dark and dingy hole anymore; he saw a forest coming into view. He called back, but all he could hear was his voice echo and reverberate, straining against the two dimensions. His stomach dropped out from under him and the strangest feeling of dizziness overtook him, as if he and the world were spinning in opposite directions. He closed his eyes to prevent himself from throwing up and only opened them again when he felt cool air on his face.

The world had gone still. At first, he thought he'd just crawled beneath the ground and come out on the other side of the tree stump. But the more he scanned his surroundings, the more differences he noticed. The trees were just a little taller here. A crow, at least double the size of any crow he'd ever seen, flew high above. An owl watched him from a nearby branch, and as it opened its wings, Derek was surprised to see two additional eyes blink to life, unlike anything he'd encountered in the volumes on ornithology he'd browsed in Pemberton Library's cozy corners.

He was officially in Grimwell.

But it wasn't alive with abundance as Chester Felten had originally described. It was... gasping. Like it was just struggling to breathe. The trees were missing their leaves. The sky was a dark gray. Leaf litter and moss blanketed the floor, making the path barely noticeable. That's when Derek heard a tree speak, its voice loud and resonant in the forest. Kat joined Derek just in time to face the ancient oak.

"We don't get many visitors," Grandfather Tree said.

"We're looking for Eldrid Babble," Derek said.

Grandfather Tree narrowed his eyes, his bark flaking off in thick clumps. "What is it you seek with Eldrid Babble?"

Derek and Kat exchanged nervous glances.

"Many years ago, an author by the name of Chester Felten accidentally found this world. He wrote a book about his adventures. It was published in my world. And for some reason, the book is cursed." Derek reached into his backpack to show Grandfather Tree the book, still covered in tape to prevent an accidental peek into their journey. "I'm here to break the curse."

Grandfather Tree smiled at this, revealing large woodchip-like teeth. Hearing about a talking tree in a book is all well and good, but to actually see a talking tree in person was disturbing. Something about the teeth, cavernous mouth, and tongue with its grayish-brown appearance made Derek slightly queasy—unfortunate for a protagonist to be perpetually on the edge of vomiting. Derek was reminded about the thin gauzy line between fantasy and horror.

Just then, Derek felt a branch graze his shoulder, and the book was snatched away.

The tree in the book was friendly. Avuncular even. This tree seemed beaten down. Withered. Dying.

"I remember when they first met," Grandfather Tree said, bringing the book closer to his trunk to get a better view. "I had such hope for their journey."

"What happened?"

"What do you mean?" Grandfather Tree asked, still inspecting the book.

"This is nothing like the world Chester Felten wrote about."

"Don't tell me you believe in happy endings."

"I thought Chester and Eldrid vanquished Lord Grittlebane. We read the book. Backwards."

Grandfather Tree shook his trunk. His bare branches crisscrossed the gray sky, and Derek couldn't help but imagine the dense canopy of leaves that used to blanket the Trembling Forest.

"That's not the way the story ended?" Kat asked.

Grandfather Tree shook his trunk again.

"What really happened?"

The old, gnarled tree told them.

"By the time Mr. Felten and Mr. Babble reached the castle, Lord Grittlebane was ready and waiting for them. The guards seized your *heroes*"—he said the word with disdain—"and threw them in the castle tower. Lord Grittlebane is a dark wizard, but I think even he didn't know if it was safe to imprison a being from another dimension. So he let Mr. Felten go. On the condition that he never speak or write about the land of Grimwell as long as he lived. After Mr. Felten left the capital, Mr. Babble was later executed—I think he was beheaded, but then again, they're always thinking of new and innovative ways to kill people in the capital—and the light that had glimmered in Grimwell flickered out. Mr. Felten fled Grimwell through that very tree stump in the dead of night, which, by the way, has been the only portal between this world and yours since I was but a sapling. Rather grisly when you think about it, considering that that tree stump used to be none other than Brendel Beechington, a fine tree who I had the pleasure of knowing in his old age. When Brendel was a sapling himself he made a deal with a sorcerer—"

"I'm sorry, but we don't have much time. Can you—"

"Get to the point?" His voice rose slightly. "You humans are so focused on getting to the point that you often forget how sharp a point can be. Us trees prefer the soft edges of a good story."

Grandfather Tree seemed proud of his witticism. He smiled—if that's what you could call the jagged crescent crisscrossing his bark—and resumed his story.

"As I was saying, Mr. Felten crawled back inside Brendel, but before he left, he told me all about his journey and Eldrid's imprisonment—he hadn't been executed yet—which, come to think of it, somehow consisted of a three-headed beast, a trollywoggler, and a pack of brimbles, but don't quote me on it"—he flashed a devilish, dilapidated grin—"and Mr. Felten bid me good luck and that was the last I heard from him. The next part of Mr. Felten's journey I know only through the whispering of trees. You see, we trees like to talk, and our network of roots is quite extensive, which makes information travel fast. When Mr. Felten returned to your world, he was called to speak about his experiences fighting in something called World War II—we trees are very impressed with humans' attention to peace. Only two wars in all of your history! Amazing. Try as he might, Mr. Felten couldn't bring himself to dredge up all those painful memories and so instead he decided to tell a story about Grimwell. Of course, he changed the ending for the children. What is it you humans like to say? Happily ever after? Yes, everyone lived happily ever after in the story he told. And his fellow townsfolk loved it. He was asked to speak at the next picnic, and then the picnic after that, until someone asked if he would be interested in writing his story down. And so he did. Snatched his glowing amulet by stealing another man's story. Mr. Babble's story. Grimwell's story. Of course, Lord Grittlebane heard about his transgression, and so cursed the book the moment it was published."

"And you never saw Chester Felten again?"

"I never said that. I said it was the last I *heard* from him. We trees are very precise. We have to be. Nowhere to run." He laughed heartily, bark sloughing off in rough clumps. "Have I ever told you about my cousin..."

Derek remembered Chester Felten's description of trees. He'd really gotten that part right. Trees loved to talk.

"Can we stay on topic?"

Grandfather Tree harumphed angrily. "As you wish. Soon after, I saw Mr. Felten crawl from beneath Brendel's stump and set off in the direction of the capital. I wondered if he was trying to rescue Mr. Babble. Clearly it didn't work"—he laughed again, but this time his laughter was subdued, solemn—"and that was the last time I saw him."

"Might he still be here?" The possibility that Felten had ended up becoming a hero—even a failed hero who was killed or captured in his pursuit to save Eldrid—seemed to strengthen Derek's resolve.

Grandfather Tree shrugged, scattering a few of his remaining leaves to the forest floor. "Anything's possible."

Chapter 26

After Grandfather Tree had finished telling them the true ending of *Eldrid Babble*, Derek and Kat huddled even closer together, realizing what was at stake in their journey into fiction: A chance to give Grimwell a sequel.

Grandfather Tree proceeded to give a long and detailed history about the Council of Trees, the governing body of trees which he presided over. Derek nodded along as best he could, not wanting to be rude, but also not able to focus on the minutiae of tree government when his and Kat's fate hung in the balance. Finally, pretending to take a call on his cellphone, which of course had no service, Derek excused himself from the conversation and bid goodbye to Grandfather Tree.

"You do know he has no idea what a cellphone is," Kat said. "Right?"

"It worked, didn't it?"

"But why pretend it was a telemarketer?"

"I wanted it to be believable."

"That just might be the saddest thing I've heard all day."

They continued walking through the forest, which remained dark and dim, sunlight barely escaping the dull, gray sky. It was as if the light couldn't reach the land of Grimwell, cursed by Lord Grittlebane to remain in the shadows, a land of villains.

Leaves crunched underfoot as they carved a path toward Crimpleton, guided by some preternatural call home. Derek heard whispering as they passed and more than once saw branches move unexpectedly along their path. Derek couldn't help but feel a tingling in his stomach as he marched beside Kat, the same butterflies he'd first experienced when he met Janine, but this was somehow amplified, as if an author were writing his feelings, taking a vague word or phrase and turning it into a paragraph of description. Sure, he'd known he liked Kat, but the dizzying pace of the last week had made him realize something else. Before, he'd infused her with the seductive qualities of a romance novel: hair tumbling down her shoulders, the sway of her hips, her heart-shaped face and pouty lips. But now it had deepened into something realer, something literary—that's the only word Derek could think of to describe it. He now saw a quiet determination in her eyes and the triumph of the human spirit in the stern look of resolve on her face; in other words, he saw a proper hero, no longer just a love interest or romantic diversion, but a protagonist following the hills and valleys of her own character arc.

That's the moment he realized he loved her.

He never believed love could happen so quickly in the real world, but Derek knew it to be true, as if an outside author had made it so with a scribble of his pen or stroke of his keyboard.

Maybe even Chester Felten himself.

They finally left the forest and stood on a hill looking down at the small village of Crimpleton. Smoke from chimneys rose from small stone huts.

"It's beautiful," Kat said.

"It's like another time," Derek said.

"Another planet," Kat said, and Derek couldn't help but think of his brother's starring role in the hit Netflix show.

Excitement rushed through him. Derek the Friendly Neighborhood Barista had somehow become a main character in a novel that had already been written. The odds! He also got the impression that he was somehow on display for posterity, as if an author was waiting to challenge him, put him through the wringer to earn his title: hero. He caught a brief glimpse of a writer slumped on a couch, cloaked in a hooded sweatshirt, struggling to get in his 5:00 a.m. writing session. Maybe he was a teacher who had just discovered a dead mouse on his kitchen floor, and had gotten a late start thanks to the unpleasant task of disposing of its body. Maybe that was too specific of an image, but Derek saw it clearly in his mind as he and Kat raced down the hill toward the small village where Eldrid had first begun his journey.

Hard to describe the feeling of running down a hill toward a fantasy village that had previously only existed in the pages of a book. No, not difficult, impossible: part surreal, part excitement, part nostalgia, part dream.

At the bottom of the hill, a sign welcomed them, just like in one of the early pages of the book: *Welcome to Crimpleton, Population 134 ¼*, the fraction representing the magic head that lay on the hutch of Susina, the town witch.

As they strolled through the wide thoroughfare toward Crimpleton Common, there was one key difference between the world depicted in *Eldrid Babble* and the world in which they found themselves. There was no hustle and bustle. No ruckus and racket. No evidence that anyone lived in the town.

Kat must've been having a similar thought, because she turned to look at Derek, and for some reason—Derek couldn't help but feel a flutter of excitement that his fantasy quest was turning into a romance—took hold of his hand.

"This is fucking eerie," she said.

"Fucking eerie," Derek repeated, not caring that the dialogue would feel off in the world of Grimwell.

Although there was no one on the cobblestoned streets, the town had a sheen of newness not mentioned in the book.

Shops looked pristine, polished, practically gleaming. New construction dotted the town, including two-story huts and a stone fountain in the middle of Crimpleton Common. Founder's Statue, with its homage to Edelbee Gripplebunk and the First Grimkins, had been removed and, in its place, stood a life-size replica of Lord Grittlebane—at least a version of Lord Grittlebane, posed with his staff and looking somewhat like a grimkin-action hero. Derek assumed the reality of his green skin would be less appealing. Judging by appearances alone, Grimwell looked like a thriving center of commerce—minus the familiar faces of Brattlebee the Butcher, Brittlebee the Baker, and Mr. Templeton, Crimpleton's very own asshole-boss.

They continued walking down the deserted street, and Derek got the peculiar feeling that grimkins were peering at them through curtained windows. Eyes shut to the world, only momentarily blinking.

Still, he continued walking, Kat's hand inside his, which felt rather clammy if he was going to be honest. Maybe not suitable for fiction, but Derek was happy for the reminder of reality's imperfections.

* * *

In the distance, Derek saw the sign for Crimpleton Tavern, the place where Eldrid first asked Belinda on a date. Strangely, Derek felt called to it, the same way he'd be called to a place of his own personal history, like McDowell's, where he'd first laid eyes on Kat, or the Pemberton Library, his refuge of books and beverages. How was it possible to feel nostalgia for a place he'd never been?

"Should we—"

"I'm starving," Kat said, speeding up toward the tavern. "And let's face it, it's probably our best chance to actually talk to some grimkins." That settled it.

Practically running, they passed the alley where the hooded figure had called to Eldrid from the shadows to take the magic amulet. It looked ominous, infused with its sordid history and consequences, like a gun that had been fired.

Pausing beneath the Crimpleton Tavern sign, still holding hands, Derek's mood changed. The nostalgia had taken a turn toward grief. Grief for a love story that had been unfinished, blank pages splayed open for posterity. What had happened to Belinda Grabblebee?

Shaking off the thought, Derek led the way into Crimpleton Tavern and—no surprise—found it completely empty, save for a bartender polishing a glass, like an extra playing a part, feigning normalcy.

The bartender seemed surprised by their sudden entrance, as if someone had breathed life into him unexpectedly. "Hello?" He said it as a question.

After a brief recoil of horror at the fictional creature, Derek collected himself and took in the sight of his first bona fide grimkin. He was short and mouse-like, with a small button nose and thin lips, puckered in a perpetual frown. His cheeks were red and rosy, and just slightly puffier than an average human, as if he'd just had his wisdom teeth removed. He wore a green vest with a bright red tie—well it wasn't exactly a tie, more like a triangle-shaped bib that took up half of his shirt. A bushy white tail with orange spots peeked over his shoulder, swinging with abandon.

"Hello," Derek said, still stunned. With great difficulty, he forced himself to take in the surroundings. Usually, in these types of books, the setting would provide some essential piece of information for the protagonist: a clue, a weapon, a back door?

Just like most of Crimpleton, the bar had clearly been recently renovated. A board announcing the drink specials, including the town favorite barley cream, which Derek had always thought sounded delicious, hung above a mirror. A flag had been posted on the opposite side of the bar: two red eyes floating in a sea of black. Not exactly a welcoming graphic to greet visitors. Then again, Derek doubted Grimwell was known for its tourism. Derek spotted the fireplace inscribed with the letter *C* where Eldrid and Belinda had shared a roast hedgehog. On the mantel, which Derek remembered had been carved from the head of an elder tree, there was a small phallic-like vase. If the rules of fiction applied to Grimwell, it had to be a symbol. For what, Derek wasn't sure.

"Hi," Kat began, approaching the bar with her hand out, ready to speak the language of the bartender. "We're not from around here."

The bartender nodded. Hesitantly shook her hand as if unfamiliar with the custom. Which, Derek supposed, was more than possible, considering this was a fantasy village. How did grimkins greet one another? By shaking tails?

"Any sights we should see?"

The bartender, as if finally finding his page in the script, puffed his cheeks into a wide smile, and put the glass down. "Oh sure, we have Bumbling Falls not too far away, a beautiful spot for you two lovebirds." Derek heard "lovebirds," but it might have been his subconscious translating a species of fantasy animal into something more understandable. "We also have the highest tower in a fifty-grimple radius, so you can climb to the top and practically see Grim City."

"Where are all the other grimkins?" Derek blurted out.

"What?"

"We walked through the town. Last time we were here..." *at least as readers...* "the streets were packed."

The bartender's smile faded. He squinted at them through his beady, mouse-like eyes. He stopped polishing the glass and placed it on the bar. He might not have meant it to be aggressive, but it loudly clanged, and Derek couldn't help but jump. "What can I get for you?"

Derek was hungry, but didn't know if it was appropriate to pause his journey to sample the local delicacies. Kat must've had a similar thought, but with a little less reservation, because she immediately ordered two barley creams.

The bartender nodded and unplugged the tap. A foamy amber liquid poured out of the spout into two glass mugs, which immediately began to frost over.

"Anything to eat?" the bartender asked as he placed the mugs on the bar. "The specials are on the board." Derek glanced behind the bartender where he saw, written in an ornate script:

Roast Squirrel and Pillypot in a Creamy Brown Butter
Roast Rabbit and Pillypot in a Creamy Brown Butter
Roast Hedgehog and Pillypot in a Creamy Brown Butter

Derek held up his hand. "No thanks."

"I'll try the hedgehog," Kat ventured, always the intrepid culinary explorer.

"You got it."

"Now?" Derek asked as the bartender disappeared behind a swinging wooden door. "When we have a journey to complete?"

"What? I'm starving. Plus, it's not like I ever get to travel anywhere. Here's my chance to sample some inter"—Kat furrowed her brow, looking for the right word—"dimensional cuisine."

Derek sipped his barley cream and was surprised that it tasted... disgusting. Like a shot of whiskey mixed with whipped cream. Just another case where fiction disappoints. Kat, on the other hand, slurped the liquid down and seemed quite satisfied, burping quietly as she set the empty mug on the bar.

The small talk with Jabble—that was the bartender's name—was excruciating. After Kat peppered him with questions about the hedgehog—spices, how it was prepared, side dishes—he seemed to loosen up, but not enough to give them any useful information about what had been happening in Grimwell for the last seventy years... *if* time in Grimwell was the same as time on Earth. There was no guarantee that a year in Grimwell was the same as a year in Derek's world. After some small talk about the weather and an unnecessarily long soliloquy from Jabble about different types of barley cream, a squat grimkin in a chef's tunic appeared from the back.

He placed a silver platter containing a mountain of food on the bar and mumbled something. It sounded like "Bon Appetit," but then again, Derek's subconscious might've just been translating the unfamiliar idioms of Grimwell into something more palatable.

True to form, the platter contained the entire hedgehog with an array of vegetables surrounding it, carrots, turnips, and a purple vegetable Derek didn't recognize. Probably pillypot.

"Aux Cuisine," Kat said.

Derek had heard the expression before but didn't know the meaning, which made him realize that it wasn't just Grimwell that seemed strange: the entire world lay just beyond the pages of his latest read. Not knowing the proper response, he nodded and smiled.

"You're just going to eat it?" Derek asked.

"When in Rome," Kat said.

"I can understand Rome," Derek said. "But a fantasy world that we thought only existed in a book? You sure it's... you know, clean?"

"Constitution of a bull," Kat said, readying her fork and knife, thick metallic utensils that looked comically large. She cut into the flesh as Derek watched, unable to escape the gaze of the small mammal.

"You sure you're not going to be hungry?" Kat asked as she chewed with her mouth open, looking more and more like Belinda.

Derek hated to admit it, but he wanted to try hedgehog. In that moment, with his stomach gurgling—why had he packed only granola bars?—he wanted it almost as much as he didn't want a tail.

Which was a lot, but also not a lot—his feelings were getting more muddled as the journey continued. He was growing attached to the tail.

"Pass it over," Derek said.

Chapter 27

It turns out that Jabble was actually a pretty nice guy—or grimkin, if you were being technical about it. He had moved from Grim City to Crimpleton as part of the government's reorganization plan, which sounded a lot like something you'd find in a communist dictatorship, but Jabble assured Derek and Kat it wasn't, though Derek didn't think Jabble knew or understood the meaning of communist or dictatorship.

"It's just Lord Grittlebane's way of building up the rural parts and lessening the divide between city and country. Top you off?" Jabble said, motioning to Derek's empty glass. Derek nodded and Jabble poured him another barley cream, which after his third glass, Derek rather enjoyed.

The hedgehog lay like a picked-over carcass on the bar, its eyes gleaming beneath the dim lights of Crimpleton Tavern. At first it disquieted Derek, but after a while, he'd gotten used to the rodent's glare—or was it a marsupial?—and held its gaze as if in a staring contest. Derek and Kat had also sampled a shabberberry cookie, which had the consistency of oatmeal-raisin mixed with the syrupy sweetness of a macaroon.

"Anyway, I like it here," Jabble was saying. "Fresh air. Good food. Nice grimkins." He spoke somewhere between an English and New York accent. Pomp mixed with working-class circumstance. At least that's what Derek heard. There was always the possibility that Jabble's dialect was a rough interdimensional translation.

"About the people," Kat said, staggering her syllables. That barley cream was strong.

"Where'd they all go?" Derek asked.

Jabble shrugged. He wasn't the most curious grimkin. "I just assumed it was always like this. That's just what Lord Grittlebane does. He builds up these towns and then entices grimkins to live in them. I guess I never really thought about who lived here before. Or where they went."

An eerie feeling swept over Derek, removing some of the buzz from the barley cream. He was once again having to reconfigure his reality. First, he had believed that grimkins like Brittlebee, Brattlebee, and Mayor Frumple were characters in a somewhat entertaining book about a land called Grimwell. Then he'd come to learn they were actually real, plucked from reality by Chester Felten and passed as fiction. Now, at least according to Jabble, Derek had to accept that they had all mysteriously vanished, to use the euphemism of communist dictatorships, which really just meant killed. Victims of Lord Grittlebane's cruel regime, the same regime that had cursed Grimwell and plunged Derek into his current predicament, part love story, part fantasy novel, part dystopian wasteland.

Suddenly, Derek needed to be gone. Needed to figure out a way to save this fantasy world and twist the plot. However, before all that, he needed to pay for lunch, which, as he dug through his wallet and pulled out a few twenties, he realized might be his first test as a hero.

"Do you accept cash?" he offered, feeling the alcohol still blunting his speech, making his cadence slow and measured, like he needed to be wound up again.

"What's cash?" Jabble asked.

"It's a form of currency," Derek said.

"What's currency?"

Just like a fictional world, Derek was amazed at what characters knew and didn't know, still struggling to understand the terms of this strange arrangement.

"It's a form of money," Kat said.

"What's money?" Jabble asked, which reminded Derek that they didn't use the word "money" in the fictional world of Grimwell, but grimkies.

"Our grimkies are in our hut," Derek said, shrugging and eyeing Kat.

"Which hut?" Jabble asked, suddenly not as clueless as he previously sounded.

"The hotel," Derek said.

"What's a hotel?"

Derek sighed. Translating English to grimkin was really becoming a chore. "Look, the truth is, where we come from, we use a different type of grimkie. I wasn't thinking when we ordered the barley cream and the hedgehog."

"And the shabberberry cookie," Jabble added.

"You told me it was the Tavern's specialty!" Derek realized he was yelling. He took a deep breath. "I'm sorry, but we really have to get going. Trust me, our mission here is more important than the price of a hedgehog."

"I'm sorry, but I'm going to have to insist you stay."

Jabble, the friendly, clueless, and relatively nice bartender, pulled out a small dagger from beneath the bar.

The survival instinct took over. Kat's stool toppled over as she jumped back. Like an action hero—that's how Derek perceived it, anyway—he rushed toward the fireplace. Something was guiding him, as if a writer was animating his motions, and in that moment, part of him wondered if the world of Grimwell lay somewhere between fiction and real life, a hinterland of imagination and reality where the two somehow collided. But he didn't have time for philosophizing or speculating—he had only just enough time to grab the penis vase from above the mantel. Jabble launched himself over the bar with the surefootedness of a cat and crouched in front of Derek, his long flowing tail swaying angrily in the air. Derek matched his stance, swinging the vase in front of him—not his ideal weapon of choice, but he supposed it only made sense that because he noticed the penis vase, he would have to use the penis vase. Chekhov's Penis or something like that. Jabble lunged forward with the dagger, just barely missing Derek's side, before turning around with a mischievous gleam in his eye, twirling the weapon in his right hand with ominous intent.

Derek found himself moving with more agility and speed than he thought possible, as if the laws of time and space were somehow slightly altered in the world of Grimwell. He also couldn't help but feel Kat's eyes on him as he held his penis in front of him—not his literal penis, but a figurative penis infused with all the phallic symbolism that befitted a hero—and whirled it over his head toward Jabble, not wanting to kill the poor, innocent grimkin, but also not really worrying if he accidentally did kill him. It would read fine either way. Luckily for Derek, who really wasn't a fan of blood or gore, the vase smashed on Jabble's shoulder, and the bartender toppled into the table and chairs where Eldrid had once sat with Belinda. The fight was over just a little too quickly for this hero's story, even though in truth, to any casual reader keen on ethical theory, it would become apparent that Derek and Kat had dined, refused to pay, and then threatened the poor grimkin with an unfortunately-shaped vase.

But stakes.

It all came down to stakes.

"I'm sorry I had to do that," Derek said, as Kat looked on from the corner of the bar. "But we really do have to get going." Kat made her way to the exit and kicked the dagger away from Jabble, who sat stunned on the floor.

Derek and Kat fled the bar, running toward Crimpleton Common. The town square felt more like a distant memory than a place Derek had only read about. *The Strange Life and Times of Eldrid Babble* had wormed its way inside of him, created an internal compass no different than the one he relied on to get to work each day. Which meant he knew exactly where he had to go next.

About a hundred yards away, he saw a row of stone huts with thatched shabberberry roofs—somehow he knew exactly what shabberberry looked like—extending along Crimpleton's main drag. One hut caught his attention: it had a faded purple door, bright blue shutters, and a small patch of dirt in the front, which clearly had once been a garden. The house looked like a relic from another time, as if it had been untouched—not preserved or protected, but neglected. While the other huts looked shiny and new, Eldrid's hut looked beaten down, trampled by time's slow and steady march.

Derek hurried toward the hut with the purple door that weighed heavily in his imagination. He walked faster and faster, Kat jogging to keep up, until he broke into a sprint, hoping the hut would have answers, or who knows, maybe Grandfather Tree had gotten it wrong and Eldrid would be sitting in his rocking chair, older and wiser, still dreaming about the adventure he'd had all those years ago when he battled the evil Lord Grittlebane.

Would Belinda be by his side?

Could such a happy ending actually exist?

The door knob hung askew as if someone had forced themselves inside. The plaque, meant to discourage unwelcome visitors from knocking, lay on the ground, covered in dirt and debris. Derek could only make out one word: *Before*. Derek knocked on the faded purple door, hoping for a twist.

"I don't think he's here," Kat said.

Derek tried the rickety door knob and pushed with all his might. The door creaked open just wide enough for Derek and Kat to glimpse inside. Taking one last look at each other, they stepped over the threshold.

It was exactly the way Eldrid had left it. Derek found himself walking through the pages of a book, looking at the pictures on the hutch in the entryway, including one of Eldrid's grandfather, Briggledorf, dressed in his soldier's uniform. Derek's attention was drawn to a sword hanging by the picture, a detail not included in Felten's original retelling. Perhaps even Felten had realized some things were meant to be private. Stepping delicately across the creaking floorboards, Derek got his first glimpse of Fizzle, sprawled out on a coffee table with over three hundred spaces and various strange creatures dotting the board. An unfinished game. Eldrid's small-scale replicas occupied every available shelf, the wonders of Grimwell in miniature all around the hut, each only a journey of a single step. Eldrid might as well have been a hoarder, a collector of distant wonders and worlds. On a dusty bookcase near the back of the hut, Derek saw the many volumes published by Eldrid's parents about their exploits all across Grimwell. His fingers yearned to riffle through the pages, an entire new library's worth of knowledge to uncover. And then, tucked in between two of Eldrid's small-scale replicas, one shaped like a pyramid, the other resembling a hand clawing its way out of the ground, Derek saw a very rudimentary photo of Eldrid, the grimkin that had played so vividly in his imagination.

He looked slightly different from Chester Felten's description and the drawing on the cover. Although Derek had mostly imagined Eldrid as a smaller version of human with a tail, the grimkin in the picture had a decidedly fish-like mouth, lips puckered as if sucking on a sour candy. His hair was the same golden brown, but it extended long past his ears, and with his thick beard, he looked wilder than the buttoned-up grimkin Felten had carefully whittled into a hero between the pages of *The Strange Life and Times of Eldrid Babble*. He was standing in front of his hut holding a key, a tradition that apparently extended across dimensions. It was as if Derek had seen his favorite fictional character come to life in a movie, only to have the actor clash with the person he'd constructed in his imagination.

Derek could feel the book buzzing in his backpack, beckoning him to open it and continue reading, the authorial voice intruding into the scene, guiding Derek toward a resolution.

But he stopped himself. He knew what would come. How easy it would be to get sucked into the world captured by Felten. Derek needed to be the one to choose his resolution.

"We've got to go," Kat said.

The air felt suffocating. Dust mites twirled in the faint light that leapt through the windows, solemn and surreal, somewhere between a movie set and a memorial.

Derek didn't expect to feel the way he did, but there, in Eldrid's dim and decaying hut, he couldn't help but feel grief for the grimkin who had somehow become a friend over the last couple weeks.

Derek began to leave, then remembered the sword in the entryway. The very same sword Briggledorf Babble had used in the Battle of the Trembling Forest. It had to be. Derek reached out and grabbed it off the wall. He unsheathed it from its scabbard. There was no mysterious gleam. No sense of recognition like a pet greeting its owner. Instead, Derek only felt the weight of the handle and the cool blade as he ran his finger along the edge. He didn't know what he'd expected, but part of him hoped this would be a key moment in the narrative, confirmation that he'd finally become the hero Grimwell needed.

"Well, that was anticlimactic," Derek said. Still, he slipped the sword back in its scabbard and tucked it into his belt. It hung down just past his knee.

"What'd you expect?" Kat asked.

They slunk out of the hut, unsure of their next step. At least now, however, Derek had a sword, and according to many of the tales Derek had read in the Pemberton Library, that was a prerequisite of becoming a hero.

Chapter 28

After walking farther down the road, they saw Mayor Frumple's hut, about twice the size of the others, with a long, flower-lined walkway leading to a large, oval-shaped door. It was exactly as described in the book with one exception: above the door hung a black flag with ominous red eyes; a breeze rippled the flag, making it appear as if the eyes were squinting.

Derek knocked hesitantly, feeling more and more like Eldrid Babble embarking on his journey to Grim City to face Lord Grittlebane.

Mayor Frumple opened the door almost immediately, as if he'd been waiting for Derek and Kat's arrival. He was an imposing figure—at least for a grimkin. He seemed to carry a little extra at every part of his body: his belly pressed against the buttons of his purple shirt, his neck bulged against his collar, and his tail spilled over his juniebee, which made Derek wonder if he should stop at Templeton's to pick one up for his return home—if the journey proved to be a failure. Like a kid dressed up as a superhero for Halloween, he wore a red cape with the insignia of a hammer and sword, symbolizing the two pillars of old Crimpleton: work and war. But the grimkins of Crimpleton hadn't gone to war in ages. Nor had they done all that much work, either, as Derek remembered the utopian vision of the small town described by Chester Felten. There was something about Mayor Frumple's appearance that bothered Derek, but he couldn't quite put his finger on it. That's when it hit him. Mayor Frumple looked the same as his portrayal almost seventy years ago. Either grimkins didn't age at the same pace as humans or Lord Grittlebane's dark magic was keeping him young.

"How do you do?" Mayor Frumple asked as Derek and Kat stood outside his door, peering inside.

"We were hoping to ask you a few questions," Derek said.

"You're not from around here," Mayor Frumple said.

"That's an understatement," Derek said.

"A grimkin never lets a guest linger or loiter," Mayor Frumple said, playing the part of the politician, smiling widely, almost painfully. "Unless of course…" The mayor squinted at them, the wrinkles around his eyes crimpling and folding. "No, it couldn't be," he said, before throwing the door wide open and inviting them into the foyer.

They entered a hallway crowded with pictures showcasing the mayor's various accomplishments. Derek noted the lack of family photos; indeed, each frame featured only one person, Mayor Frumple, in clearly staged photo ops: The mayor holding a shovel near a trench; the mayor cutting a red ribbon with comically large scissors; the mayor eating a piece of pie; the mayor standing in Crimpleton Common, his cape billowing in the wind.

"Have a seat," Mayor Frumple said cheerfully. "Can I take your bag? Or sword?"

On another page, the mayor's overture might have been considered polite. But his words sounded strained, as if they'd come out sharper than he'd intended; as if they, like a sword, had sliced through his vocal cords.

"No, thanks," Derek said, trying to keep his voice equally cheerful. He placed one hand on the hilt of his sword and tucked the backpack by his feet. He sighed with relief, grateful for space from the book; it hadn't stopped buzzing since they'd entered Crimpleton.

Derek and Kat glanced nervously at each other before sitting down on two rocking chairs in a living room decorated with even more campaign kitsch: signs, buttons, photos, and even a life-size painting of Mayor Frumple posed in a long, flowing cape and holding a golden staff crowned with a red amulet. Could it be the same one Eldrid had sought to destroy? The house was cozy and cavernous at the same time. It appeared to be in a state of continued settlement; a creak here, a squeal there. It wasn't exactly run-down, as much as it was haphazardly updated: in perpetual renovation without a plan or purpose. Mayor Frumple took a seat across from them on a plush green sofa. It seemed to collapse in the middle as he sat, like a Venus flytrap closing on unsuspecting prey.

"What can I do for you?" the mayor said felicitously, as if talking to prospective voters. "It's been so long since I've had any visitors."

"But in the book... I mean, in the past, your house was always bustling with visitors, coming to you with all sorts of problems... Squabbles between Brittlebee and Brattlebee... Mr. Templeton talking business—"

"You sure you're not from around here?"

Derek shifted uncomfortably in his seat; the rocking chair tumbled backwards, and Derek had to lurch forward to steady himself.

"We visited," Kat said. "A long time ago."

It was true in the way a book could make a place you read about feel familiar. In the way a book could make you feel nostalgic for people and places you had never actually known or visited.

"Crimpleton is a lovely place to live," Mayor Frumple said. "Renovated huts. Excellent place to raise a family. If you two are starting one that is." He chuckled, flashing a bright, white smile. "Best of all, right now we're running a promotion where you can upgrade to a hut on a hill at no additional charge."

"We're not looking to stay," Derek said.

Mayor Frumple's face darkened, a portrait of a politician in distress. "Then why are you here?"

"Because we're looking to leave," Kat said. "A long time ago a writer visited this place and wrote about what he saw. Ever since then, his book's been cursed."

Mayor Frumple tapped his foot nervously on the floor. Still, he kept a smile on his face, even as his eyes narrowed.

"Lemon cake, lemon cake," Mayor Frumple said. "How could I have been so rude? I bake it every day just in case someone knocks on my door and today was my lucky day. The bell has tolled. Sure, I'm buried in paperwork and the projects keep piling up from the capital—but there's always time to eat cake and have a pot of sweet leaf coffee, am I right?"

Mayor Frumple disappeared into the kitchen. "You know, you picked a funny week to come," he called over the clinking and clanging of plates. "So much of the town on vacation this week. Lord Grittlebane insists on it." He chuckled. "But what matters is you found yourself here," he shouted over the high-pitched shriek of a kettle boiling.

Derek got a funny feeling in his stomach. Something wasn't right. He wished he could be a protagonist like Sergeant James Wilks, who always seemed to know what to do, but he was just Derek, overwhelmed with the many possibilities of a blank page.

Mayor Frumple returned with three plates of lemon cake, three cups stacked on top of one another, and a pot of sweet leaf coffee balanced precariously in his hands. He delicately placed the cake on the table and began pouring the coffee.

"You know, I think we better be going," Derek said.

"Going? Why would you be going, you just arrived, and from my calculation that means you have a whole middle and end before you leave." Although the mayor was smiling, his words sounded flat and monotone. He was stalling.

Kat looked anxiously to Derek.

"You said everyone was on vacation," Derek said.

"Oh, yes. It's a beautiful week for vacation."

"But earlier you said you haven't had any visitors in a long time."

Mayor Frumple's hand started to shake, splashing coffee from the pot onto the table.

"You're not who you were," Derek said, remembering the charming, friendly, albeit slightly power-hungry mayor who, many years and pages ago, had knocked on Eldrid's door warning of a potential sorcerer. Something had corrupted him; spoiled him; like a worm crawling into an apple and then concealing itself. Something had slowly eaten the mayor from the inside.

Mayor Frumple's eyes flashed, a faint spark of the grimkin he once was, before they quickly clouded over once again, snuffing out the brief flicker of light. Whether it was dark magic or greed controlling him, Derek couldn't quite tell, but he did know one thing: he had to leave this place immediately. He had to escape. He had to save Kat.

He stood up and unsheathed his sword, but it was too late: Two guards—the beefiest grimkins Derek had ever seen—cloaked with the eyes of the Grimwell flag on their shields, burst out of the kitchen. Somehow the mayor must've alerted them.

If only Derek could've seen this coming.

Kat wheeled around with Derek's backpack and connected with the guard's head, sending him to the floor, and a small part of Derek resented that he couldn't even play hero on his own magical quest. No matter. No time to fret, because no sooner had Kat smashed Guard 1, had Guard 2 grabbed Kat, leaving Derek free to swing his sword at his helmet. He didn't have the stomach for a full-fledged stabbing—just the thought of the blade going through skin and cartilage was enough to make him squeamish—but the sword against the helmet did the trick, and Guard 2 toppled over.

The mayor huddled in the corner, his arms thrown up in surrender as he flinched away from Derek's sword, peering out of one eye, like an animal caught in a trap.

Derek ran toward him and pointed the sword at his neck, unsure of what he'd say, but confident it had already been written in a version of Eldrid's story.

Kat grabbed a knife from the kitchen, still smeared with lemon cake, which somehow made it look even more menacing. They'd become a real team. Hero and heroine.

"What happened to everyone?" Derek shouted.

"Just kill me," Mayor Frumple said.

Derek jabbed the blade into the mayor's neck. Truthfully, Derek didn't want to kill Mayor Frumple. If he was caught, there'd probably be a trial, and who knew what the judicial system was like in a medieval fantasy world. He didn't want to get bogged down in all that legal red tape.

Still, he pushed the sword deeper, watching a spot of blood pool on the glinting blade.

"Ouch," Mayor Frumple said, apparently not in the mood for torture. "Okay, okay, I'll tell you."

* * *

After Eldrid had been executed, a gloomy pall settled over the village of Crimpleton. The mayor tried to carry on with normalcy, even delivering what he hoped would become a famous speech about the necessity of returning to the Pre-Babble Era, while also promising free bribblebobs to every household (bribblebobs, similar to hula hoops, remain widely popular in Crimpleton, the mayor had explained). But the village was unable to forget Eldrid and his beloved Belinda, who had vanished soon after, never to be heard from again. They held a memorial service for the two fallen heroes, speaking in hushed tones about their bravery, even as Mayor Frumple tried to play intermediary between his constituents and the capital, between his friends and family and what he'd come to realize were his overlords.

First, the requests were small: information on the local baker, Brittlebee, and a leger of his accounts. *Who hasn't been audited?* Mayor Frumple reasoned, and so he supplied the information, asking one of his underlings to break into Brittlebee's shop at night and make a copy of his records. The mayor wasn't taking anything, so it couldn't be called stealing, at least not in the traditional sense of the word, and he had a duty to the capital, especially if Brittlebee was doing something illegal. If he ever wanted to rise through the ranks, he had no choice but to defend the laws of Crimpleton and Grimwell. After all, you can't make an omelet without cracking a few eggs.

A few weeks later, the bakery shuttered, and Brittlebee had gone missing, nothing but a hastily scrawled note left in his store saying he planned to start over in greener pastures. There was a steady buzz about his disappearance, with Brattlebee demanding answers, but Mayor Frumple tried to keep calm, deflecting questions with the poise of a politician, careful not to disclose the midnight audit that had preceded Brittlebee's departure. He was just doing his job. Nothing more.

The requests from the capital became more frequent: an audit of Crimpleton Tavern, information on the comings and goings of Mr. Templeton, and once, a detailed accounting of who had attended the most recent Celebrate the Capital Concert—no one—which featured a flautist—at least the Grimwell equivalent of a flautist—and a spokesperson from Grim City honoring Lord Grittlebane's tenure in office.

The town dwindled in population as Mayor Frumple's power skyrocketed. His intermediary, a goblin named Creteor, even told him they were thinking of appointing him to a prestigious post in the capital; Mayor Frumple had never even been to the capital, let alone left Crimpleton.

Crack a few eggs, the mayor continued to think as he bid goodbye to neighbors, friends, and rivals, though he couldn't help but feel a pang of morality every so often, missing old friends and the bustle of Crimpleton Common, all the while his hut grew more sleek and modern, grimkies flowed in for revitalization projects, and he could finally see his dreams coming to fruition.

But there were other, more troubling signs, that things weren't what they seemed. For one, the forest wasn't itself; every grimkin grows up chasing the tangled tendrils of the Trembling Forest and during his morning walks, Mayor Frumple noticed the vitality draining away from the trees, the grass, and the flowers. Even the sun seemed to have grown dimmer.

Soon, Mayor Frumple could no longer pretend. Not long after, Brattlebee, Mr. Templeton, and Bartle held a protest outside of the mayor's hut demanding answers on the recent spate of disappearances. Mayor Frumple attempted to quell the disturbance, assuring his fellow grimkins that he'd bring the matter up with Lord Grittlebane himself on his upcoming trip to the capital. His assurances did little to calm the group, which by nightfall, had turned into a crowd—or a mob, if you were going by the dictionary definition—of about forty, practically everyone left in the town. By the time the torches were lit, Mayor Frumple knew things had gotten out of control, and despite his misgivings, asked Creteor to call in Lord Grittlebane's guards to enforce order. "Yessss, ssssir," Creteor said, in his serpentine-like voice, flames dancing ominously in his bug-like eyes.

By the time the guards arrived, the crowd was on the verge of storming the mayor's hut.

"Please, please, try to be sensible," Mayor Frumple shouted to the crowd.

"Traitor!" Brattlebee yelled.

Lord Grittlebane's guards formed a line in front of Mayor Frumple's hut, shielding him and Creteor from the onslaught of the crowd. Brattlebee charged, attempting to break through the line of guards—to do what, Mayor Frumple would never know—ultimately stopping short as one of the guards drew his sword. Brattlebee jittered backwards, but the guard had already made up his mind. The sword came down in a long, swooping arc and sliced through Brattlebee's head, which splattered all over the cobblestones, reminding Mayor Frumple of an egg hastily cracked into a frying pan.

He would never eat another omelet again.

"By that point, I was too far in," Mayor Frumple claimed, still with Derek's sword pressed against his neck, which continued to bleed long after Derek had lessened the pressure. He felt bad, but if he apologized, he might look weak. After all, that's what happens when you press a sword against someone's neck.

"Where'd they take the others?" Kat asked.

Mayor Frumple shrugged.

"You mean you didn't ask questions?" Kat said.

"It was easier not to," Mayor Frumple said, a slight tremor in his voice.

"Are they..." But Derek didn't want to say it. Words had power in this mysterious world.

Heat seemed to emanate from Derek's backpack, which now lay in a crumpled pile on the floor: he could read about it. He could find the answer right now. Hear the story from Chester Felten himself—at least the version of him trapped in the tale of Eldrid Babble. But to do that would ensnare Derek even further in a world of fantasy, take away his autonomy and free will, and leave him as nothing more than a character in a book blindly flipping through the pages.

He'd be right back where he started at the beginning of the story.

"You have to understand," Mayor Frumple said. "I had dreams for this town. Big, big, big dreams."

A bugle sounded in the distance, and Derek didn't have to look out the window to know this was the moment where the bad guys closed in. It had to be. Anyone with a working knowledge of story structure would spot a clear tumble into the moment all hope is lost.

"Is there a back door?" Derek asked.

Mayor Frumple shook his head.

Derek pressed the sword deeper into the mayor's neck, seeing the blood pool in thick droplets.

"You're not lying to us, are you?" Derek said. *Am I a hero or a villain?* Derek thought.

Mayor Frumple shook his head again, now beginning to cry. "They're not to be messed with," Mayor Frumple said. "I'm sorry. They have my family."

"What?

"My family lives in the capital," Mayor Frumple said. "That was the part I left out. Things got so lonely. I met my wife at a party in Grim City. I didn't know she'd become a hostage. Or that my daughter would be just a pawn in Lord Grittlebane's game of Fizzle. I'm not even allowed to keep pictures of them, lest I forget where my true loyalties lie. They let me visit every so often, but even then, we're closely watched by Lord Grittlebane's henchmen."

Derek now knew there'd be no grand escape. No twist. No secretly foreshadowed plot point that would only come to light as danger closed in. There'd be no miraculous rescue.

Kat seemed to know it too. She reached for Derek's backpack. "No," he said. "We can't."

"We're already too far in," Kat said.

She unzipped the backpack. The book glowed with the same vaporous hue Chester Felten had described surrounding Eldrid's magic amulet.

Kat opened the book, scanning the pages for answers. Derek could see her draw closer to the pages, sinking into the story until she and Belinda had become one. When she looked up at Derek, he was startled to find barely a vestige of the woman he'd met at McDowell's. Her lips had grown more fish-like and her nose had become less pronounced, as if it had receded into her face. Even though her eyes were now speckled with magenta, Derek recognized the woman he'd fallen in love with staring back, slightly unsure of herself and the character she now inhabited. Triumphantly, a tail rose over her shoulder, light brown, bushy, and dusted with hints of orange and red. A dappled delight. Derek couldn't help but gasp at the beauty of Kat's new appendage.

The guards kicked through the door and Derek dropped the sword and held his arms in the air, not wanting to take a blade to the neck. By the time he turned around with his hands raised above his head—the guards hadn't told him to do that, but he'd watched plenty of movies—Kat was gone.

Chapter 29

Derek woke up in the back of an open wagon that mercilessly jostled and shook along Grimwell's rocky roads. A horse—at least something resembling a horse, with cat-like ears, a long, flowing tail, and gray scales on its back—walked at a casual pace, flanked by two guards.

After the soldiers stormed the mayor's hut, Derek had barely held up his hands in surrender, his sword clattering to the ground, before the blunt end of another sword knocked him out. He had let out a whimper, which he now hoped wouldn't be recorded for posterity in a future book about Grimwell. Whatever Kat had read in her version of *Eldrid Babble*, it had given her a chance to escape, and, Derek couldn't help but notice, leave him behind. Maybe the book had revealed an unseen passage out of Mayor Frumple's hut and she was on her way back to Mac—at least there was that—and maybe it had to be that way. Derek didn't have any family anymore besides Tom (his father barely counted), and Tom was usually filming *Another Planet* in Fiji. Somehow, they'd grown to inhabit different planets themselves. As the wagon bumped along the road, Derek supposed he'd while away the rest of his days in a fantasy prison—unless of course the world of Grimwell believed in execution for non-capital offenses, which, like most quasi-medieval fantasy worlds, it probably did.

Derek had had his adventure. He'd had a chance to finally stick up for himself and become a hero in his own story. Sacrifice was probably the most important part of being a hero, and if he had to die so Kat could return to Mac—as a grimkin or not, who really cared when it came down to it?—then so be it.

Still groggy, suffering from a pounding headache, Derek asked for water, and he felt that same blunt end of a sword crash down on his head, which made the journey much shorter.

He dreamed of his family.

Not the typical dream that might appear in the pages of a fantasy novel packed with portent: no surrealist landscapes with big red suns peering from the edge of the horizon like the squinting eyes of Lord Grittlebane; no cloaked figures in abandoned alleyways offering clues to his predicament. No, this dream was simple. He was sitting in between his mom and dad on the couch watching *Wheel of Fortune*—his mom had loved *Wheel of Fortune*—and eating an ice cream cone. Tom was sandwiched beside him, and even as a child he'd enjoyed the verb, *to be sandwiched* in between his loved ones. Before their own wheels of fortune had started to turn. Before they'd become un-sandwiched. Derek couldn't be sure it had actually happened, or if his subconscious had just manufactured a pleasant flashback, a fantasy about what his family could've been. Should've been. Regardless, he loved inhabiting it, loved being close to his brother, loved seeing his mom alive again, loved having his dad still a part of his story. By the time the dream ended, and Pat Sajak had said goodbye, he was waking up on his back in a dark and dingy cell, barely conscious.

He rubbed his head, feeling the throbbing bump where the sword had made contact. Twice. Unlike other fantasy novels Derek had read where heroes quickly bounce back from serious injury, the preceding pages of his own seemed to weigh down the moment with fatigue and pain, and he felt dazed, possibly brain-damaged.

That's when he felt something scamper up his leg, over his stomach, and onto his chest. He lifted his head and saw a rat the size of a small dog just mere inches from his face.

Derek lay still. There was something human about the rat, something in the black opal eyes perhaps, that made him gulp. Not scream, but gulp.

"At first, the time will go by very slowly," a voice said.

Of course, Grimwell would have talking rats, Derek thought angrily.

"Although, after a few years, time does start to speed up."

The rat continued staring at Derek. It had a withered and raspy voice, almost smoky.

"But that's the thing about time," his cellmate continued. "Fast and slow are relative. What feels like a hundred years might only have been twenty. I have no idea. I've lost track of the marks on the wall. You miss one day, it's hard to begin again."

Derek knew who was speaking: the World War II veteran turned insurance salesman who'd written the book. The writer who'd somehow cursed his readers. The errant adventurer who'd crawled under a tree stump and accidentally stumbled upon a portal to another dimension.

Chester Felten. Now doing time as a rat.

Derek felt the urge to reach out and touch him, just to make sure it wasn't a hallucination, or, who knows, maybe he just wanted to bridge the gap between reader and author—after all, *The Strange Life and Times of Eldrid Babble* had been Derek's book. Was still his book in a twisted, terrible way.

"They carry disease, you know," the voice said. "Which is why I don't eat them anymore. A month of very bloody diarrhea will make you lose your appetite."

That's when Derek realized the voice wasn't coming from the rat, but from a hazy, shadowy figure nearby.

That's when Derek realized he was touching a rat.

That's when Derek screamed.

He shooed the rat off and it scurried away, running straight for the stone wall and disappearing between a small crack.

Derek scrambled to his feet, aware that if there was one rat, chances are there were many rats, not to mention spiders. Derek hated spiders, even though he knew that didn't make him sound very heroic. He also knew that a few spiders, even the giant spiders that might lurk deep within Grim City, were currently the least of his problems.

"Relax," the shadowy figure said. "They don't usually try to eat me. Except during the month's spell I previously mentioned. Do you know what it's like to have fifty tiny mouths gnawing at every part of your body?"

Derek didn't know. His entire life had been spent in relative comfort. Never taking chances. Certainly, never taking a chance that would trap him in a fantasy prison. And now that he was officially—and literally—a prisoner in Grimwell, he didn't know why he'd hated comfort so much. But then he remembered it had been comfort that made him not pursue his dream of becoming something else. Anything else. Stuck reading stories about other times, other people, other places. Comfort had been his motivation, his desire, and his *hamartia*, to use a Greek word he'd picked up during one of his many sojourns in the Mythology and Magic section at the Pemberton Library. But all that changed when he found *The Strange Life and Times of Eldrid Babble* and started reading.

The book had shaken something loose inside of him.

Made him grow increasingly uncomfortable with the comfortable.

And here was the man responsible. He simultaneously wanted to strangle and hug him, which Derek supposed was the mark of a good character.

"You read the book, didn't you?" Felten asked.

"In a way," Derek said. "With some asides."

The author raised his eyebrows. "It's a nasty business stealing an author's voice. Turning my words into a weapon. I take it you identified as Eldrid?"

Derek nodded. His tail curled over his shoulder in agreement.

"I just wanted to be a writer," Felten said. "Don't all authors borrow a little?"

Derek shrugged. Through the dim, he could see Felten, slumped back and sickly, sitting beneath a fragment of light. The sun must've been coming up, which meant he'd been out for at least a day and night; that's what the butt end of a sword will do. Seeing a small sliver of gray sky, Derek realized he wasn't in a dungeon—that was good news—but a tower—that was bad news. With the additional sunlight, Derek took in the true extent of Felten's misery. The author wore a long tunic that at one point must've been white, but now was caked in dirt and grime. His hair hung to his shoulders in thick white clumps, and his beard was greasy and matted. Derek thought he saw two small eyes peering at him from the matted hair—perhaps an unwelcome tenant?

Felten began coughing—more like a bark—as light began to spread in the cell, revealing the miserable quarters Felten had called home for the last seventy years. Small skeletons littered the stone floor: calories. There was a bucket in the corner where Felten must've gone to the bathroom. Good god—Derek had to choke back the vomit—it looked to be nearly full. With his newfound grimkin powers of smell, the scent of excrement and decay hit him like a tsunami. Somewhere between the nauseating smell—Derek didn't know you could smell between smells, but that's exactly what it seemed like—he could also detect a hint of fresh-baked bread on the cool breeze entering the cell. Now that was dissonance. Beneath the barred window, Derek saw someone had etched eight names: *Lucius B. Clay, Sarah Anderson, George Kohn, Jenny Garcia, Frank Grous, James McGovern, Lidia Byberg, Gregory Gagne.*

"I don't remember days," Felten said, catching Derek's gaze. He was fiddling with what looked like a piece of bone, occasionally sharpening

289

it on a jagged shard of rock he must've pried loose from the wall. "But I remember people. Faces. I dream of a blank sheet of paper."

"Those are—"

"My adoring fans," Felten said sadly. "Only three of them tried to kill me. Most of them only shouted at me. A few black eyes. Sarah was actually quite lovely, didn't blame me in the least. I could only learn a little bit about them—call it an author's greed—but that was enough. A name sometimes can be enough. A small echo that I can whisper each day. You're familiar with the saying, 'You die twice. Once on the day you die, the second when someone utters your name for the last time.' I guess that's my mission. To continue saying each name for as long as I can. Maybe that can break these chains. Maybe not."

Derek leaned against the stone wall, staring at the list of Grimwell's other protagonists. What had become of them?

Felten must've anticipated the question, as if he was writing the scene and had slipped in the mystery on purpose. He blew dust off the bone, and Derek saw that it ended in a sharp point. Derek gulped.

"Mostly hanged," Felten said. "Sometimes they get creative. Guillotine. Limbs pulled apart by brimplecorns—kind of like horses, but absolutely vicious. They make me watch, of course. Poor James McGovern was killed by a Boppledoo Monster—you don't want to know what that is—but mostly they stick to the traditional execution. It's no easy task to run a kingdom, and some of the animosity toward me is fading."

"Others have put it together," Derek said, realizing that his journey hadn't been as singular as he'd thought.

"In the early days, when the book was still in circulation, sure. Then, over time, less. You're the first one in…" Felten looked at the faint marks on the wall: thousands of tiny scratches covering every surface. "I have no idea how long."

"I'm sorry." It was all Derek could think to say.

Somewhere, far off, an owl hooted. Probably one of those cool owls Derek had seen earlier, with eyes on its wings. A world away from his old life, Derek thought of his mom, having spent her entire life playing it safe. All she did was calculate odds. Scrimp and save trying to build a retirement fund. Only to have it all disappear when she fell ill, even taking a second mortgage on the house in an effort to carve out a little bit more life, a few more pages, as it were. He thought of Tom and what his character would do in *Another Planet*, the blockbuster series that had catapulted him to fame even as Derek's life had begun to crater, deep, deeper into an abyss. An extinction. That's what it was. He also thought of Kat. How could he not? His fresh start. She had willingly accompanied him on this journey to stop the wave that had begun to crest when an unknown writer penned a secret world. A stolen world. He just wanted her to be safe.

Now, with the sun's faint rays spreading across the cell, Derek collected his thoughts. Which is exactly what a hero would do in one of these books. Derek paced the cell, stepping over Felten's legs, which lay limp in front of him, as if he hadn't moved or even tried to move in years.

Standing on his tippytoes—luckily, Derek was still slightly taller than the average grimkin—he could see over the edge of the cell's small window and glimpse what he assumed to be Grim City below. The scope was breathtaking. Light dappled each of the small huts. Smoke from chimneys billowed into the air. The clatter of carts and voices ricocheted from side streets and alleyways, indeterminable, as if sound was being shoved through a funnel.

If Derek was going to be the hero of his story, then he might as well make an escape. He could stitch together his clothes and Felten's tunic, find a way to slip through the bars, climb down to the next window, kill the guards, grab a key, and then make a break for it. It sounded at least possible. Sure, he'd have to do the entire thing in the nude, but that could all be cleaned up later on when he told the story to Kat—perhaps he could claim to have found a change of clothes in the cell or that he'd had the foresight to steal the guard's key on the way up to the tower (when he was passed out).

While he was debating not just his escape, but the way he'd tell the story about his escape, he heard a clatter from just outside his cell. Metal hitting stone. A muffled groan. Felten must've also heard, because he turned his attention to the cell door. Derek sniffed the air, breathing in a familiar scent, what his newly enhanced olfactory sense inexplicably registered as "dimly-lit tangerine joy." It smelled like Kat.

Derek and Felten craned their neck to the door as footsteps shuffled along the stone hallway.

Moments later, a key turned in the cell and somehow, miraculously, improbably, Derek saw Kat, looking more like Belinda than ever before.

Derek stood dumbfounded as his heart banged against his chest. That's not how this was supposed to happen, but considering he was currently being rescued from a sorcerer's tower, who was he to argue?

"We don't have much time," Kat said.

The light from Kat's torch cast shadows on the stone.

"How'd you find us?" Derek asked.

She held up the book: "Belinda's story. She encountered the very same predicament. Mayor Frumple had called the guards on her too"— she said it excitedly, as if discussing the novel in a book club—"and so I followed her footsteps. Literally. Escaped right through the front door while the other guards were waiting at the back. And then I traced her journey to the capital."

Felten clambered to his feet, as if he'd been saving all his energy for this very moment. "My book!" he wheezed. Then, scanning the list of names on the wall, he whispered: "My book *helped* you?"

"It saved me," Kat said.

Without another word, they ran out of the cell and down a narrow set of stairs, past two guards who'd been knocked unconscious—at least that's what Derek assumed. Death was messy and would overly complicate Kat's heroic rescue. Kat seemed to have an almost preternatural sense of when someone might be coming, which hallways to avoid, and how to find their way out of the winding castle. Once in a while, she'd open the book, scanning the pages, before once again finding her place.

Soon they came to a large room surrounded by stone pillars, empty and abandoned, echoey and cold, with nothing but a pedestal in the middle, on top of which sat a book. Small torches lit the room, their flames scattering shadows on the walls. A few yards away from the book, there was a fireplace, built with the same attention to detail and precision as the one in Crimpleton Tavern, only instead of a hexagonal stone in the center carved with the letter "C," this one featured the letter "G," as if both were purchased and personalized on the internet. The fire crackled, sending small bits of ash into the cavernous room.

"The Master Copy," Kat said.

"My voice," Chester Felten said. The author walked toward it, drawn to the gilded copy like a parent to a child. Derek could see the faded and tattered cover featuring Eldrid holding the glowing amulet in his hand. Derek and Kat crept hesitantly behind. The book seemed to breathe on its own, growing larger with each step they took. A story always in the process of being written.

"I've speculated, sure," Felten said. "But I've never actually seen it."

Derek stopped far short of the book while Felten kept walking toward it. The pages splayed open, riffling forwards and backwards, as if writing and revising the story.

Felten touched the book, fanning through the pages, briefly glimpsing the worlds his story had created. Lives it had ended. The journeys it had started and stopped. The names on his cell wall now characters. The ultimate power: to make your reader truly inhabit your pages.

The three of them stood in the large room, with the faint torch light softening as the sun streamed through the narrow windows.

"What do we do now?" Derek asked Kat as Felten continued reading the book.

"That's the thing," Kat said. "This is where the book ended for Belinda. She tried to rescue Eldrid and break the curse. She snuck into the capital, freed Eldrid from jail, and then they met—"

"Bravo," Lord Grittlebane said, suddenly appearing in the corner of the room, dressed appropriately, as Derek imagined all sorcerers should be, in a black cape and holding a staff. His skin was green and flaky. His serpentine tongue slithered around his thin lips. At one point, he must've been a grimkin, but now he was something else entirely.

Felten's body seemed to stiffen at the appearance of his captor, and he remained in front of the Master Copy, slumped against the stone pedestal. Derek watched as his hands shook. The pages began to turn faster, as if blown by a gust of wind.

"I suppose every artist deserves to see their creation," Lord Grittlebane said.

Felten continued looking down, watching the pages riffle back and forth, as if the book was unsure which direction the story would turn. Still with his back to Lord Grittlebane, Felten's fingers clutched the edges of the pedestal. It seemed to steady him. Give him just enough resolve to deliver a proper hero's speech.

"You're no hero," Felten said, his voice weak but resonant, echoing in the large room.

Lord Grittlebane's thin lips curled into a sadistic smile. "There are two sides to every story, Mr. Felten."

"And you're the villain."

"The winner and the loser," Lord Grittlebane said. He thrust his staff in the air and Felten howled in pain as he clutched even tighter onto the pedestal.

"Why are you doing this?" Derek asked. He doubted Lord Grittlebane would answer, but it was worth a try.

Lord Grittlebane laughed, in that maniacal way evil sorcerers do. He turned his attention away from Felten, who sighed with relief, and then held out his hand like a claw. Derek suddenly felt phantom fingers clenched around his throat. His body stiffened.

"I'll be the one doing the talking," Lord Grittlebane said. His voice was higher than Derek expected, comically so, as if he'd just inhaled helium. Derek fought back the urge to laugh; evil sorcerers generally didn't take kindly to laughter.

Now breathing heavily and clutching his side, Felten turned around to face his captor. "You stole my life. My story."

"Nothing you didn't do yourself," Lord Grittlebane said.

"I made a mistake."

"Writers are vultures," Lord Grittlebane said, now walking toward Felten and the Master Copy. Or maybe floating. He appeared to hover a few inches off the ground. "Just waiting to consume the world. I warned you to keep Grimwell a secret. But I was naive. Foolish. And since then, I've learned my lesson."

Derek and Kat glanced at each other, not the type of glance where the heroes telepathically put together an escape plan, but one of those scared shitless glances, recognition that there was no escape or exit. Simply an acknowledgement that they were, in fact, screwed.

Felten stepped closer to Lord Grittlebane. He was at least a foot taller than the sorcerer, and even though he was wearing a raggedy tunic and his hair hadn't been cut or cleaned in seventy years, he looked positively heroic.

"I've waited a long time for this moment."

"And what is it you'd like to say, Mr. Felten?"

"Nothing," he said, "but there's something I'd like to *do*."

It took Derek a minute to realize what happened next. Felten had reached into his tunic and stabbed Lord Grittlebane with the small piece of sharpened bone he'd been preparing for this very occasion. Lord Grittlebane looked down at his abdomen where green blood

295

began to pool around the wound, staining his cloak and dripping onto the stone floor below.

Derek expected Lord Grittlebane to topple onto the ground and shriek with rage, but instead he began to laugh. "Very heroic," he said in his reedy voice, taking the bone out of his abdomen and chucking it to the side. "*My* turn."

Lord Grittlebane held his staff aloft and pointed it at Felten. What happened next was... not appropriate for a fantasy novel. A horror novel, sure, but Derek had spent most of his life avoiding that section.

Felten's body parts twisted in wrong directions; his left leg exploded, while his right arm pancaked; his right hand froze while the other was lit on fire; a swarm of insects gnawed at his eyeballs. An amalgamation of all the worst ways to die in one brutal curse.

Derek couldn't help but look away. That's not the way Felten's story was supposed to end. That's not the way anyone's story was supposed to end.

Felten screamed in pain until suddenly he stopped. All that was left of the writer was a clump of blood, bone, hair, and a grisly, maroon tunic.

"Like I said," Lord Grittlebane continued, "I learned my lesson about being merciful. Who's next?"

Derek remained quiet. For some reason, the question rattled something loose inside him. *Who's next?* Why should Lord Grittlebane get to decide the next page? Staring at the glowing staff that had cursed Grimwell, Derek felt anger, hatred, and revulsion. Sure, it would've been better to be driven by love or loyalty, but heroes didn't always get to choose their motivation.

Although he was no match for Lord Grittlebane, Derek's time spent reading books in the library had taught him an important lesson: the power of the unpredictable.

Resolved to play the part of the hero—even an insane hero, like the one played by Tom in *Another Planet*—he ran full speed at Lord

Grittlebane. Caught by surprise, Lord Grittlebane tried to hold up his staff, but Derek made impact before he had the chance, and the sorcerer tumbled backwards. Derek fell on top of him. Not having planned that far ahead—Derek's charge was unpredictable even to himself, and therefore what came next, he had no idea—he began punching Lord Grittlebane in the face, just like Tom had done when he confronted the Troglodorf. Even his tail got in on the action, curling around Lord Grittlebane's neck to hold him in place. Although his punches weren't effective, Lord Grittlebane stared at him in disbelief, which gave Kat just enough time to grab his staff. It glowed in her hand. A disloyal servant.

Guards stormed the room, but it was already too late. The pages of the Master Copy were turning, sensing a twist, a brand-new story unfolding.

Derek remained on top of Lord Grittlebane, and even though the sorcerer struggled, he was no match for Derek's newfound strength, which seemed to fill his arms, his legs, even the tip of his tail, until he was just bursting with muscles. Metaphorically, of course; he hadn't lifted a weight since high school.

Lord Grittlebane made one last attempt to free himself from Derek's grip, but Kat bonked him on the head with his staff. Hard. Which seemed anticlimactic, to end an epic journey with a bonk, but considering the alternative, having to duel with a sorcerer trained in the art of dark magic, Derek was happy for the reprieve.

The staff glowed in Kat's hand as she waved it around the room ready to smash the guards now pouring into the chamber, but they seemed almost happy to see Lord Grittlebane on the ground, his green, scaly skin now looking mottled and tinged with gray.

Even as Derek held Lord Grittlebane's arms, he couldn't help but regret not having prepared a tagline for this moment.

With Lord Grittlebane rendered unconscious, Derek got off the dethroned dictator and approached the Master Copy. Kat walked closer too, holding the staff in her hand.

They approached hesitantly as the book abruptly turned to the last page where a curly script appeared, as if long ago branded into the brittle paper, unable to be seen unless under the right light: *THE END.*

"It's over?" Kat said. She held up her copy of *Eldrid Babble*, the very same one Derek had found in the supply closet of the Read and Bean. It no longer seemed to buzz or hum or beckon. It was just a book. An old book. Kat gently handed it to Derek as if returning some important family heirloom.

Derek turned his attention to the fireplace, where the flames now sputtered and sizzled in the quiet room.

"I don't like the idea of ending the journey with a book burning," Derek said.

Kat shook her head. "Me either. Kind of muddles the message."

"Which is?"

"Is that for us to decide?"

Derek shrugged. He ripped a page out of the book. The paper was stiff, but it tore easily, and Derek threw the crumpled piece to the ground. Kat grabbed a piece next and cast another ball of paper to the floor. They took turns ripping out clumps of paper, until the book lay in small piles all around them, and all they were left with was a cover, which featured Eldrid cradling the glowing amulet. A few paces behind Eldrid—how had Derek not noticed this before?—Felten could be seen holding a small journal, just waiting to copy down Eldrid's story for posterity.

Epilogue

Derek sat in between Boris and Gerald, waiting for Kat.

"What if she says no?" Boris asked.

"She isn't gonna say no," Gerald said.

"You can never be sure."

"Take it easy, guys," Julius's voice thundered. "I'm sure Kat will put meatloaf back on the regular menu. Just ask nicely. People forget the power of being polite."

"Do they?" Boris asked, raising his eyebrows.

Julius folded his arms and rippled his pectoral muscles, his own version of sign language.

Gerald clapped Derek on the back. "How about *you*? When are you gonna finally pop the question?"

"Keep it down," Derek said, glancing over his shoulder at the door.

Julius looked around the empty bar. "No one's here. It's three o'clock. On a Tuesday."

Derek had told them of his plans to propose to Kat. Not today, maybe not tomorrow, but when the time was right. First, he had to pass his most important test yet. Meeting Mac.

While Derek hadn't shared the truth about Grimwell with any-one—even his best friends, Boris and Gerald—he couldn't help but stoke the embers of mystery every once in a while. Unable to satisfac-torily answer their questions about his "romantic getaway" with Kat, he'd taken a page out of Boris's playbook and invented tall tales of his own: adventures to save high-level political officials, clandestine spy missions, even alien abductions by a certain species called the Troglodorfs—anything but the actual truth. Sure, no one believed him, but so what? What was life without a little bit of fantasy?

"Let me give you some advice," Gerald said, now looking at Derek seriously. "Always wear clean socks. You never know when you might have to take your shoes off."

"Is that a metaphor?" Derek asked.

"Sure," Gerald said.

Kat and Mac walked in a few minutes later holding hands. They meandered in a spiral around the dining room, as Mac pulled and tugged at his mom like a disgruntled dog on a leash. Derek supposed Kat wouldn't love the comparison.

"Ready?" Kat asked, finally reaching the bar.

Derek nodded. "Just catching up with these two."

Boris and Gerald tousled Mac's hair one after the other.

"High five," Boris said. Mac slapped his hand.

"Pound it," Gerald said, reaching out his fist. They fist-bumped.

"My grandkids taught me that one," Gerald said proudly.

All heads turned to Derek.

"Hiya, buddy," he said in an overly-excited voice. The one he'd been practicing this past week.

"Tone it down, *buddy*," Kat said. "He's a toddler, not a dog."

Derek wisely held his tongue.

After defeating Lord Grittlebane, Derek and Kat had been hailed as heroes in Grim City. Grimkins threw parades. Honored them with feasts and a Prumpton Festival, a type of avant-garde play performed only with feet (it was amazing). Derek and Kat drank copious amounts of barley cream, which Derek had grown to enjoy, and little by little the curse began to fade. Their tails became smaller. Their ears shrank to their original size. The thick layer of hair on Derek's feet retreated, until no vestige of grimkin remained.

Although Derek had returned to his previous physical appearance, the person on the inside would never sweat the small stuff again, at least not for a few weeks until he stubbed his toe or found himself stuck in traffic.

Then again, didn't some journeys last a lifetime?

After leaving Grim City, Derek and Kat trekked across Grimwell, seeing some familiar faces along the way, even Frem the Giant, who claimed to still feel guilty about trying to eat Eldrid and Chester, although he explained they were at fault too because they looked delicious, to which Derek laughed even as Frem began licking his lips. The days seemed to grow longer, the sun brighter; the dull gray sky had turned a vibrant shade of blue. They camped out in the Trembling Forest, and while they heard brimbles howling nearby, they never felt threatened.

Two nights passed, and Derek could tell Kat's need to see Mac had crescendoed into an almost intolerable hum, and so they hurried through the Shrinking City of Bengaloo, accidentally stepping on a hut—thankfully no one was inside—until they finally arrived at the small village of Crimpleton surrounded by mist. Cloaked in it.

"I can't believe we made it," Derek had said.

They squeezed hands.

Following an overly long conversation with Grandfather Tree about the weather, his saplings, and the new book he was working on about the rise and fall of Lord Grittlebane, they made their way through the tree stump and began the last leg of their journey home, their transformation back to their former selves—or characters, so to speak—complete.

They'd continued seeing each other ever since returning from Grimwell, and Kat had finally thought it was the right time to introduce Derek to Mac. A lot had changed since returning from their journey, and truth be told, Derek felt some sort of magic guiding the latest developments, including Dale, the head librarian, abruptly resigning and asking Derek to take over—with the stipulation Derek would go back to school and earn a master's degree in library science. Kat had also stumbled into some unforeseen luck, being hired as the Head Chef at McDowell's and winning an episode of Kitchen Battle on Netflix (Tom had pulled some strings). Maybe it was the magic of Grimwell. Maybe.

Derek edged off the bar stool and crouched down, so he was now face-to-face with Mac.

"Hi there," Derek said, trying out a calmer approach.

"Hi," Mac said, holding his hand up in a perfunctory wave.

"I'm Derek," Derek said. He went for a handshake.

Mac peered at Derek's hand, his big blue eyes shifting from Derek, to the hand, then to Kat. For a moment, it seemed as if everyone was holding their breath, waiting to see what Mac would do. Sure, life could sometimes seem meaningless, without the symbolic glow cast by novels, but occasionally, moments could shine with a resonance brighter than the most carefully written page in a book.

Unfortunately for Derek, the scene didn't pan out the way he expected.

Mac burst into tears.

"It's okay, honey," Kat said, scooping him up.

And so Derek did what all confused adults do when unsure how to interact with a child: he pretended to pull a coin out of Mac's ear, which only seemed to make the crying worse.

"Should I go?"

"He's just being a toddler," Kat said, bouncing him in her arms.

After Mac had calmed down, Derek and Kat said goodbye to the McDowell's cast of characters, and walked out of the dim bar onto Elm Street. A breeze crawled through the air, bringing with it the rich scent of spring—Derek's sense of smell retained some hints of its grimkin powers, and today he smelled something that could only be described as cherry nostalgia. Across the street, the stand of trees that had once beckoned Jackson Wilfred shook in the wind, looking downright human, though missing the one that had previously encased the lapsed librarian. Derek hadn't heard from him, but he hoped he was happily living his sequel. The Read and Bean's windows sparkled in the midafternoon sun, and Derek couldn't help but think of the vaporous hue that surrounded Eldrid's glowing amulet.

"What happens next?" Kat asked.

"I don't know," Derek said, "but I'm excited to find out."

Acknowledgments

While Grimwell is a work of fiction, there are elements of my life strewn throughout, including the reference to the writer slumped on a couch struggling to get in his 5:00 a.m. writing session (I really did find a dead mouse on my kitchen floor one morning). I also occasionally suffer from Derek's inability to make decisions—to bravely climb up Freytag's pyramid and face the unknown—but writing has allowed me to live many lives, embark on adventures, and take risks, all without ever leaving my couch. There are many people who have supported my sedentary journey.

I have Fairfield University to thank for fostering my passion for writing, not only as an MFA student, but many years before when I enrolled in their American Studies graduate program. Thank you to the faculty for providing a creative space for me to develop my voice as a writer, and thank you to the many writerly friends I met along the way.

Thank you to the brilliant team at Woodhall Press, especially Miranda Heyman, Colin Hosten, David LeGere, and Christopher Madden for making the road to publication so smooth. I'm also grateful to Nancy LaFever for her helpful copyediting suggestions on both Chester Felten's writing and my own. And thank you to Dr. Grisel Yolanda Acosta for choosing Grimwell as the winner of the Fairfield Book Prize from a field of worthy manuscripts, and for saying such nice things about the novel when I was lucky enough to meet her in person.

Thank you to Chris Belden for always leading insightful workshops at the Westport Writers' Workshop, and to my fellow workshop members who gave feedback on early drafts of Grimwell. The world of Grimwell, filled with grimkins, talking trees, and evil sorcerers, became more real thanks to each of your incisive suggestions. I'm also indebted to my colleagues at Greenwich High School for their conversation and camaraderie; teaching always finds its way into my writing, and I couldn't imagine my creative process without the punctuation of lesson planning, grading, and of course, discussions about books.

Thank you to my family—Mom, Dad, Megan, Matt, Amanda, and Annie—for their never-ending support of my creative ventures. I'm lucky to have family who have encouraged me along the way, and even luckier to have avoided the fate of Derek and his brother, Tom, by remaining close to each of you long after our journeys splintered across time and space.

And of course, thank you to my wife, Emily, my sons Teddy and Wesley, and our cats, Laura and Louisa, each of whom gives me the courage to be creative, and whose belief in my writing drives me to wake up each day and confront the proverbial blank page. I couldn't be happier that our stories have become one.

About the Author

Michael Belanger is an author, high school history teacher, and ambassador to the world of Grimwell. His debut novel, *The History of Jane Doe*, was a finalist for the Connecticut Book Award and received a *Kirkus* starred review. An avid reader and former barista like his protagonist, he appreciates the occasional foray into fantasy—preferably unaccompanied by trolls or sorcerers. He lives in Connecticut with his wife, sons, and two wonderfully aloof cats.